THE SKELETON UNDER THE STAIRS

BEYOND THE VEIL: BOOK THREE

KM AVERY

Copyright © 2022 by KM Avery

ASIN:

ISBN:

KMA KM AVERY

All rights reserved.

No part of this book may be reproduced in any form or by any electronic or mechanical means, including information storage and retrieval systems, without written permission from the author, except for the use of brief quotations in a book review.

This is a work of fiction. Names, characters, places, and incidents either are the product of the author's imagination or are used fictitiously, and any resemblance to locales, events, business establishments, or actual persons —living or dead—is entirely coincidental.

SPECIAL THANKS

This book is for the one person who puts up with all of my disasters every day and who actually thought it would be a good idea to marry me.

I love you.

1

You would think that seeing dead people would be exciting. And sometimes it is. Sometimes it's amazing and wonderful. Sometimes it's heartbreaking. Sometimes it's downright terrifying. Usually, though, it's just annoying.

Dead people aren't all that different from living people, aside from being mostly insubstantial. You get the nice ones, the smart ones, the dumb ones, and the assholes, exactly the same way you do with the living.

As far as I'm concerned, the only notable benefit to the dead people is that if they *really* piss me off, I can make them go away.

Sadly, this is not something I can do with the still-breathing without breaking several fairly significant laws and my own moral code.

My name is Ward Campion, and I'm a medium, courtesy of a fairly lengthy bout with the magical-ability-granting Arcanavirus about seven years ago. I'm also the co-owner of Beyond the Veil Investigations. My other half—in every sense of the phrase—is Mason Manning, ex-professor, historian, witch, and orc.

Last spring, we'd partnered our tiny little company with the Lost Lineage Foundation, which specializes in helping people find their deceased family—maybe parents, maybe grandparents, maybe ancestors several times removed.

Poor Mason has been up to his eyeballs in archives ever since.

He loves it, the great big nerd.

At the moment, he was off nosing around in some county courthouse going through records dating back a couple centuries, which is why I was having to deal with the irritation that was a living, breathing human being.

The woman in front of me was wearing enough perfume that she was probably violating an EPA regulation, and I was trying my best not to cough or let my eyes water, even through a mask. Admittedly, I am more sensitive than most people to things like scents, but I've been around plenty of people with the capacity to keep their personal *eau de toilette* at less than chemical warfare levels.

She had a short-ish asymmetrical bob that had been liberally streaked by blond highlights, although the base color underneath was a medium brown. Her eyes were also fully made up with what looked, to my admittedly inexperienced eye, like false lashes in addition to at least two shades of pink shadow. Her mask, sliding precariously close to the end of her nose, was covered in tiny, glittery pink flowers.

She had yet to tell me who the fuck she was or what she wanted.

"I want to speak with the *own-er*," she repeated for what must have been the third time, slowly enunciating each syllable.

I sighed—also for the third time—and repeated myself.

"I *am* the owner."

"The real owner."

I was so done with this.

"Ma'am, I started this business, personally, six years ago."

She blinked at me, and I tried to decide whether or not her pupils were actually that color, or whether the intense green was the result of colored contacts. "You're... Edward Campion?"

"I am." I tried not to sound as annoyed as I actually was. My headshot is on the website. It looks exactly like me. I have no idea what she was expecting, if not me. I mean, okay, masks sometimes make it harder to recognize someone, but if the owner is a pale, skinny guy with messy black curls, just how many people who look like that do you think work for his company?

I guess the problem was that headshots don't include the wheelchair. And once she saw the chair, then she made all sorts of judgments about the person in it. It wasn't—annoyingly—uncommon.

Her look of incredulity was evident. "I don't believe you."

"Well, I'm afraid I don't keep a birth certificate at the office," I snapped back. "If you aren't going to talk to me, then you might as well leave, because no one with any more authority is ever going to show up."

She stared at me, her eyes wide. I would have bet significant money that, under her mask, her mouth was hanging open.

I deliberately turned myself around to head back into my office.

"No, wait!"

I didn't bother suppressing the smirk that slid over my face. I had a mask on, after all. Mine was an understated black with dark grey swirls.

I turned myself around again. "Is there something I can help you with, after all?"

The woman drew herself up to her full-but-unimpressive height and looked down her nose at me. It's not hard—in my chair, I come up to the middle of most people's chests. It's still annoying as fuck.

"I need you conduct a séance."

I was going to really hate this woman. "We can discuss your situation to see if conducting a séance is going to be helpful."

She narrowed those green eyes at me. "I *know* I need a séance."

I suppressed a sigh. "That may well be the case. But sometimes there are other, more appropriate alternatives." Like a banisher or exorcist, if the spirit in question was being violent or destructive.

She huffed at me, the sides of her mask puffing out at the exhalation of air. "There is a spirit in my house," she proclaimed.

I nodded. "Did you wish to communicate with them? Or are they making noises or breaking things?"

"I don't think they've broken anything. But there are definitely noises."

"Okay." I didn't point out that houses make settling noises all the time. "Are they posing a problem?"

"I... I don't know."

I felt my eyebrows go up. "You... don't know if they're a problem?"

"Well, I don't know anything about them, now do I? There are.. noises."

I frowned. "What kinds of noises?"

"Just... noises."

I counted quickly to five in my head to avoid saying

something obscenely rude. "What is it that makes you think there's a spirit in your home causing the sounds?"

"I *know.*"

"How do you know?" I pressed.

She sniffed. "Because I do."

Oh, for fuck's sake. "So the spirit does not move objects, write on mirrors, interfere with electronics, or do anything else to indicate their presence? You don't hear words, for instance, or crying?"

"N-no." She sounded a little hesitant, but she didn't elaborate.

"Are the noises loud?"

"No. Just...sounds."

I let the silence stretch for a few minutes before replying. "And what, exactly, makes this spirit a problem, then?"

"You know."

I clenched my jaw. "I'm afraid I don't."

"Well, what if they're... *unsavory.*"

"You're concerned about a criminal spirit?"

"It could corrupt my children."

"Are your children mediums?"

She huffed again. "Of course not."

"Then how, exactly, would they be corrupted by a spirit?"

"Undue influence," she proclaimed.

I was fairly certain she had no idea what that phrase even meant. I tried to steer things back to somewhere less stupid. "So you would like to have a séance to determine whether or not the spirit in your home is some sort of... bad influence?"

"Finally! Yes."

The request was idiotic. I was probably still going to do it anyway. I was bad at saying no to people. And money.

"All right, ma'am. If you'll come into my office, I can pull up our calendar and we can find a time that's available."

We settled on the following Tuesday, although the woman—Paula Kurstis—had objected repeatedly that I wasn't going to help her immediately, or at least not this week. I politely informed her that we typically booked our clients multiple weeks out, and she was lucky to get a time that was only a week away.

After huffing and sighing a good deal more about how put out she was with me and how much of a burden her life was, I finally managed to escort her out of the building.

"She seems... fun," Mason's resonant voice remarked from behind me.

I pulled a face as I unhooked my mask from my ears, turning so that I could see all six-foot-seven of his green muscle and exposed lower canines. Orcs, like all Arcanids, could no longer contract Arcanavirus, so he didn't need to wear a mask.

"I am *not* looking forward to that one," I told him.

"You could have said no," he pointed out, always practical.

I grimaced. "She's paying for it," I answered.

"I'm sure. You do remember that we can actually afford to be picky now, right?"

I sighed. "Yeah, I know. I'm just... used to it, I guess."

"Putting up with bullshit?"

I barked a laugh. "Yeah, apparently."

He stepped out in the hallway to meet me as I rolled toward him. Mason stopped when I reached him, then bent down and pressed a kiss to my lips. His were warm and tasted like chocolate.

"You have candy?"

He laughed. "Yours is on my desk. I didn't want to, ah,

interrupt." In other words, he didn't want to make himself visible to a client who would probably take umbrage at the fact that he was an orc. Sadly, he was probably right, given how much of an issue she had with me.

But chocolate was chocolate, and I reached out and wiggled my fingers, palms up. Still laughing, Mason went into his office, returning with a bar of toffee chocolate.

"Ooh, you got the good stuff."

"I had to bribe Fiona," he replied.

"For what?" Fiona, the librarian in charge of special arcane collections at the Library of Virginia, was a friend and a huge fan of Mason's. She'd probably have done whatever it was without a bribe, although I wasn't judging. I always brought her coffee when I went in. Apparently, Mason had taken to bringing her fancy chocolate.

I wasn't jealous. Fiona isn't into either men or orcs, and Mason doesn't like women. And he always brought me chocolate, too.

"Access to something I probably shouldn't have access to," came the response.

I opened the wrapper on my chocolate and broke off a piece, sticking it in my mouth. "What's that?"

"The diary of Hannah Neale, which isn't in Richmond. I need help getting into to the special collections in the Northumberland County historical society. Rumors about Hannah's abilities suggest that she could not only make contact with the dead, but also command them."

I swallowed my chocolate. "You're trying to figure out if I have some sort of blood magic." The term was used for someone born with magical abilities not tied to Arcanavirus—as far as I knew, I hadn't been born with any such abilities, but what I was capable of doing as a medium went beyond what was typical.

Most mediums could summon and talk to the dead. Some—usually known as banishers or exorcists—could push them forcibly across the Veil. I could do both... which wasn't unheard of. Probably a third to half of all mediums could, to one degree or another.

What I could do was physically make contact with the dead, giving them quasi-tangible—if slightly goopy—form. Nobody Mason or I had talked to had ever heard of a medium being able to do *that*. And to top it all off, I could also temporarily give them the ability to touch other people, although I'd only done that once and I'd been in a state of complete panic at the time.

Mason was trying to figure out if there was historical precedent for what I could do, since he was working on the theory that I had some sort of latent magical ability that had been triggered either by the Arcanavirus or by our run-in with the long-dead magus who was the reason I was in the wheelchair.

The past couple of years had been rather eventful.

I'd met Mason a few months before that—a year and ten months ago, to be specific. The day I'd met him changed my life completely, although it had taken me a few weeks before I'd started to realize just how much.

A couple months later, I'd ended up in a fight with the dead magus, Preston Fitzwilliam, who literally clawed out part of my sacral spine and put me in this chair. And not long after *that*, we'd shut down an institution ironically named Tranquil Brook designed to drain magic from its unwitting patients under the guise of providing them with long-term mental health care. Most of them were doing much better these days.

While investigating *that*, we'd also learned about the existence of a shadowy magical organization known as the

The Skeleton Under the Stairs

Antiquus Ordo Arcanum. And then promptly hit a dead fucking end.

One of the doctors at Tranquil Brook had been a member of the Ordo, but aside from the names of its leaders, he hadn't provided much more information. He was low-ranking, and was only occasionally permitted to attend rituals, at which most members were masked and hooded. And the Ordo had murdered him and two nurses because they were a risk to the operation at Tranquil Brook.

I've yet to hear about a secret society that *doesn't* do some nefarious shit, but this one was a party to at least three—and probably more—murders, the torture of quite a few children and adults, and who knew what else.

I was firmly of the opinion that people who were part of secret societies probably should think very carefully about why, exactly, it was that the people around them hid their faces. Because if the organization is legit, they would have no reason to keep themselves or it secret.

Mason was working on it, as was Detective Hart, who had been the lead investigator on the murder cases. Neither of them had come up with much of anything, though. At least not yet.

And if all that weren't exciting enough, we'd also officially launched Beyond the Veil's office with an open house for both us and Lost Lineage last August. Mason and I had been shocked at how busy we'd been since. The founder of Lost Lineage, Elsbeth LeFavre, had been very, very good at drumming up business—particularly from wealthy clients. After only a few weeks, she'd brought in a handful of people who clearly needed to find more ways to spend their money. And it wasn't long before we'd started getting occasional pro bono cases funded by Lost Lineage—most of them through the Elegba Society's connections throughout the American South.

We were now three months from our one-year business anniversary... And I still had to pinch myself sometimes to make sure the whole thing wasn't a dream or hallucination.

Oh, and Mason and I were seven months from our wedding.

And really, really behind on planning.

In theory, I understood that things like flowers and cakes and food and clothing were required, but fuck all if I could find either the willpower or the time to actually sit down and plan any of it. I was half hoping that Mason was doing it, but I also knew that he was just as busy as I was, if not more so.

We really needed to get on that.

2

"The fucknut shitbag took a deal," said the elegant tones of the extremely foul-mouthed elf on the other end of the phone.

"Why, hello, Detective Hart. How are you?" I replied, forcing myself to sound chipper. "I take it you have news?" Even though I was teasing him, my blood pressure had immediately skyrocketed at what he'd said. Because I could only think of one person that Hart would call that and expect me to know who it was.

From across the kitchen, Mason's eyebrows went up, and he turned to partially face me as he stirred a bechamel sauce on the stove.

I heard Hart sigh. "Ward," he replied by way of a half-assed greeting. "Yeah, Lessing took a plea deal."

"Which means what, exactly?" I asked. I knew I must have sounded stressed because Mason shut off the burner and came over to put his hands on my shoulders. I didn't bother hitting the speaker button on my phone because Mason's orc hearing was sensitive enough that he could understand Hart either way.

"It means he's admitting guilt, probably in exchange for a reduced sentence and being put somewhere that isn't going to get him immediately shanked in the shower, more's the fucking pity."

"Okay, so... that means there's no trial?" This was the biggest source of my anxiety these days—the idea that I would have to get on a witness stand and testify in front of a whole fucking court that probably included my Auntie Pearl about exactly what Tyler-fucking-Lessing had done to me when he'd broken into the house and attacked me.

And then on top of that, I'd have to somehow explain how I'd managed to enable a dozen ghosts to throw him across a room and cause what they were calling a mini-seizure.

Both of those things had been literally keeping me—and therefore Mason—up at night since they'd scheduled the trial the better part of two months ago.

"No trial," Hart confirmed, and I let out a long, relieved breath.

"Thank fucking God."

Mason's fingers squeezed my shoulders.

"You still bring Doc with you to every scene I'm not at, you hear me?"

I sighed again. Hart had insisted, as everything unfolded, that I always bring Mason with me when I was called in by the police to consult, just in case some of Tyler's buddies decided to try for payback. The idea had made me jumpy as shit at the next five crime scenes, but so far I'd gotten nothing worse than some funny looks, and I might very well have gotten those anyway, since I am the weird guy who talks to dead people.

"I will, Hart, but—"

"No buts, Ward," he interrupted. "I know these assholes.

About half of them are decent, and the rest are varying degrees of shitbags and worse."

"Okay. I'll bring Mason with me. I promise."

"I wanna hear him say it," Hart insisted.

Mason took my phone away. "I'll be there, Hart."

I didn't hear what Hart said in response, because I do not have orc hearing.

"Take care, Hart," Mason said, then hung up and handed my phone back. One big hand ran over my curls. "You okay?"

I leaned my head back into his body. "Yeah. I just get jumpy every time it comes up. But not having to go to trial is fan-fucking-tastic."

Mason let out a short hum.

"What?" I asked him, turning to look up at the uneasy set of his jaw.

"I am glad you don't have to go through that," he replied. "But I can't help but wish worse on that asshole than I imagine he got."

I sighed. "I mean, yeah. But I really just want it over with."

"I know," came Mason's response, his fingers combing gently through my hair.

After everything, Hart and Mason had both insisted I get a restraining order against Tyler—even though he'd been arrested and charged, they wanted him legally barred from getting anywhere near me. I was pretty sure that Tyler wouldn't let a restraining order stop him, but I wasn't about to say so out loud... and I figured Mason and Hart both probably knew that.

At the very least, if he did violate it, it would be worse for him than if I hadn't gotten one.

Assuming I'd live through the next time. Which, if Tyler had half a brain, I probably wouldn't.

What a lovely thought.

I reached up and pulled one of Mason's hands down so that I could kiss his fingers. "Maybe he'll still get shanked in the shower," I said, not really meaning it.

Mason huffed, but didn't respond. He ran his hand over my hair one more time, then went back to the stove and his abandoned bechamel. "Jamie is coming over to talk about the new bedroom tomorrow," he said, changing the subject.

Jamie Reyes was Mason's cousin and a construction contractor. We were renovating several parts of the house, and Jamie was able to offer us a family discount.

We were adding on to the house—expanding the master bedroom to make room for Mason's weights, expanding the master bath, adding on a new office space, and putting in a full bath and bedroom upstairs. Jamie and his team had already redone the kitchen to make it more accessible—there were now multiple counters and a sink I could use without having to twist my whole body, and we'd added more hooks and cabinets within my reach. Mason had gotten us an accessibility grant that would cover both the kitchen and bathroom renovations, but the rest he'd taken out a home loan to cover.

Which just added to the stress I was feeling about debt.

Although I'd finally managed to pay back the money I owed from having contracted Arcana years ago, I'd recently racked up more medical bills in pretty rapid succession—first Preston Fitzwilliam, and then Tyler-fucking-Lessing—and we were borrowing against future contracts with Lost Lineage for a bunch of stuff in the new office, although at least those were rapidly getting repaid.

We were doing well enough at Beyond the Veil that the

debt was shrinking. It was just still going to take a little while.

I went back to slicing mushrooms, which is what I'd been doing when Hart called. Cutting things is not really the best occupation when your brain is distracted by thinking about the fact that unless he died, I was afraid that I wasn't ever going to be able to fully purge Tyler Lessing out of my life.

"Shit!" I stuck my now-bleeding finger in my mouth.

"You okay?" Mason asked, looking over at me.

I took out my finger, which I'd nicked just enough to draw blood. "Yeah," I answered. "It's fine."

We kept a kitchen first aid basket so I wouldn't have to roll myself all the way to the bathroom if I was the victim of accidental self-inflicted chopping wounds.

Mason brought over the basket, and I stuck a bandaid on my finger, holding it up. "See? All good."

He kissed it in response, then went back to the stove.

"You don't mind a little blood in the mushrooms, do you?"

"Extra protein."

"Some vegetarian you are."

"I'll make an exception for you."

I laughed. "Will you?"

The look he shot me was amused and a little flirty. "You know I will."

I rolled myself and the mushrooms over to him and was rewarded with a lingering kiss that I eagerly returned, one hand making sure the cutting board didn't fall off my lap. Then Mason pulled back and took the mushrooms from me.

"Thank you."

"Seriously? I get a kiss like that and you just take the mushrooms?"

His gold-flecked eyes sparkled as he set the cutting board on the counter, then bent down and, one big hand cradling the back of my skull, kissed me again, deeply.

"Better?" he asked when he drew back again.

"Mmhmm." I let go of where I'd clenched a hand in his t-shirt, and he kissed my forehead.

"Good. Because now I need to finish dinner."

———

Over plates of roasted mushroom and tomato alfredo, which was, as Mason's cooking always was, fucking amazing, Mason started telling me about the diary of Hannah Neale.

"She was accused of witchcraft, specifically what looks like necromancy, although the term in the records I was able to find was 'negromancy,' which could be interpreted either as *necromancy* or, possibly, as what it literally translates to, which would be *black magic*."

I watched him, smiling as I chewed, enjoying the gleam in his sunburst eyes, the animation in his face as he waved one hand, currently holding a partially-eaten piece of garlic bread. I nodded my head, indicating I was listening.

"But whether it was necromancy or black magic, one of her daughters, also named Hannah, kept a diary of her own, talking about how her mother taught her to speak with her sisters."

"Her mother had to teach her how to talk to her sisters? Was she deaf or something?"

Mason smiled, taking a bite of his bread. He explained around the mouthful. "No—both of them died as children."

"Ooh." Now I got it.

"Exactly," Mason confirmed. "Which means that our

Hannahs, both mother and daughter, were capable of communicating with the dead—and I would guess that we're talking about more than just Alice and Elizabeth."

"The sisters?"

Mason nodded, popping the rest of the bread into his mouth. "Mmhmm." He swallowed. "Now what's even more interesting is that the younger Hannah mentions that her sisters will move things around the house—leave her shiny stones or flowers or other trinkets on shelves or windowsills."

I chewed my pasta thoughtfully. "There are strong enough spirits to move objects—"

"Move, yes. Pick up and deliberately place? That's pretty rare."

"But not unheard-of."

"True enough. And yet, Hannah talks about needing to perform particular rituals that her mother taught her in order to help her sisters to 'stay hale.'"

I thought about that. "You mean that her mother—and she—were doing some sort of magic to give her dead sisters the ability to move objects?"

"That's what it sounds like to me."

It sounded that way to me, too. "And you don't know of any such rituals or spells?"

"No," Mason replied. He twirled pasta around his fork, then put it in his mouth. "And I asked Gran, and she hasn't heard of any such spell, either." Mason's grandmother, Mariana, was a *bruja* from the Dominican Republic. She had trained him from the time he was eight.

I tapped my fork against the edge of my plate before loading it up again. "So you think that she might have had whatever I have."

Mason nodded. "I think she did, and, as much as I know

you don't want to hear it, I think it's the same thing Preston Fitzwilliam had, too."

I made a face. He was right that I didn't want to hear that. I didn't want to share *anything* with Preston Fitzwilliam.

"If this is a born ability, then at least you know that it's less likely that it's something you... borrowed from him," Mason pointed out.

One of our possible theories about my ability to make physical contact with spirits—something that most mediums definitely could *not* do—was that it was something I had stolen or that had been left behind when Preston Fitzwilliam attempted to take control of me or when I'd destroyed him. Mason had also suggested that it was possible that I had already had a latent ability that had just been dormant—which was a much more palatable option, since it meant I didn't have to have any bits of Preston Fitzwilliam inside of me.

If Hannah Neale and her daughter both had the ability... well, that made the possibility that I'd been born with it a lot more likely.

I gave Mason a weak-ish smile. "I'm not going to complain about not being connected to Preston Fitzwilliam," I said.

Mason's lips twisted around his protruding lower canines in an answering smile. "I thought you might appreciate that." He took another bite. "However, what I have access to doesn't actually give me any of the details—but I think they *might* be in Hannah Neale's diary."

"The mother's?"

He nodded. "Yes."

"And that's the thing you need Fee to help you get?"

Another nod. "She's going to call in a few favors."

The Skeleton Under the Stairs

I grinned. "She'll get it for you."

"Oh, I think it's more likely that I'll have to go to *it*, but I'm very willing to drive out to Northampton for this." He sounded excited. The way most people got about expensive vacations or new TVs.

Not Mason. The chance to play in an archival basement somewhere with dusty or moldy manuscripts was far, far more interesting to him than electronics or palm-shaded beaches.

"You're adorable, you know that?" I observed, spearing a mushroom.

Mason looked startled. "Me?"

I grinned at him, eating my mushroom. "Yeah, you."

3

The Kurstis house was on the edge of one of the wealthier suburbs, and it was a modern monstrosity well-deserving of the title 'McMansion.' Someone had painted it a pale salmon color with yellow trim and carefully planned landscaping that hadn't yet grown into its design. There was a heart-shaped wreath on the door with a 'Live, Laugh, Love' sign hanging in its center.

In the driver's seat of the Tacoma, Mason's expression grew sour, his eyebrows drawing together over the tops of his purple-tinted mirrored sunglasses.

I agreed completely. But the paycheck was going to make it worth it.

At least that's what I told myself.

I should have guessed from my encounter with Paula Kurstis at the office that the whole thing was going to be a fiasco, but I'd thought that as long as I convinced the spirit haunting the house to leave, things would be fine.

That assumed one thing I hadn't actually taken into consideration.

There wasn't a spirit.

The Skeleton Under the Stairs

Just in case it was weak, I opened my Third Eye and reached out. Nothing. Not even the slightest hint of anything that suggested spiritual activity.

Mason got me out of the truck, and I rolled myself—wearing black pants and a black silk button down as well as my favorite moon-and-stars gaiter—up to the front door. Mason, in dark grey slacks and a blue oxford shirt, followed behind me, but he still heard my sigh when I realized how deep the bullshit was in this case.

"What's wrong?" Mason asked, hefting me and my chair up the single step to the stoop.

"There's nothing here," I answered.

"Nothing?"

"No spirits," I clarified. "I've been hired to make sure the spirit in this house isn't corrupting her children, and there's no fucking spirit."

"So..." I knew how Mason felt about the fact that occasionally things like empathy and survival skills led me to lie to clients.

I ran a hand over my curls. "Here's the problem. She... 'knows' there's a spirit here. If I tell her there isn't, she's going to pitch a fit, she'll hire someone else, and probably leave some idiotic Yelp review about how Beyond the Veil is fraudulent."

Mason sighed. "Ward..."

The front door opened, and I heard Paula Kurstis suck in a horrified breath.

But what I saw was Mason's face shut down completely, a muscle ticking in his jaw.

Then Paula managed to drag her eyes from Mason to me.

"Oh! Mr. Campion. I did not—" She swallowed convulsively, her breath rippling a pale yellow mask with tiny beadwork flowers. "I did not realize you employed…"

I felt my eye twitch and opened my mouth to tell her to go fuck herself and her non-existent spirit.

"I help Mr. Campion get around, ma'am," Mason murmured, dropping his head, his voice low and oddly soft.

Fortunately, Paula was so busy staring at Mason that she didn't notice *me* staring at Mason.

"Oh. Oh! Of course. Of course, you must have help." Her eyes were wide, and she slowed down her speech a little. Because clearly she'd forgotten that I could both speak and understand complete sentences despite the fact that I was in a wheelchair.

At least I recovered enough that I was no longer making a giant fish face at my fiancé by the time Paula turned her gaze back at me. I'd plastered on a moderately pleasant expression, at least above the wry twist of my lips that she couldn't see behind my mask.

If Mason was going to play along with this shitshow, I certainly wasn't going to be the one to wreck it.

"Mrs. Kurstis," I said, attempting to salvage some semblance of professionalism. "I'm sure you'd like us to get started?" I'd managed a homicidal dead magus and an institution full of spirits who'd had their magic stripped from them. I could handle one overly-entitled bougie mom and a spirit that didn't exist.

Even if I did also want to throttle her.

Paula led us into the house, which was just as ostentatious and tasteless on the inside as it was on the outside. Pink marble, gilt trim up by the ceilings, large vases that looked like they'd been painted by a drunken artist at a paint night filled with dried cattails dusted with gold glitter.

The Skeleton Under the Stairs

I wanted to see Mason's expression, but he was behind me pushing my chair.

Paula turned, then looked at me expectantly.

This one was going to require theatrics.

"Mason, could you fetch the oak chest, please?" It felt weird ordering him around, even if I was being polite and he'd started the charade.

"Of course," came the smooth reply from behind me. At least he didn't call me 'Mr. Campion' again. I don't think I could have handled that.

I offered Paula what I hoped was smooth confidence. "Once Mason comes back, we'll set up the ritual space and get started. Is there somewhere you have… felt is particularly spiritually active?"

Paula beamed back at me. "Oh, yes," she assured me, nodding furiously. "The spirit is particularly interested in the children's playroom."

I eyed the sweeping curved staircase leading up to the second floor, suspecting that anything known as a 'playroom' was likely to be up there. "And, ah, will I be needing Mason's assistance to get to the playroom?" I asked.

Paula blinked rapidly, and I was a little afraid her overly-long fake lashes were going to get stuck to each other. "Oh! Um. Yes."

I nodded once. "Very well."

Paula kept blinking, then shifted from one foot to the other. I took a bit of perverse pleasure in making her feel uncomfortable simply by existing. Then it occurred to me that if I wanted drama, *real* drama, I could probably get a real spirit to concoct it. And then I wouldn't entirely be lying to Paula about there being a spirit in her house.

Keeping my smile to myself, I drew in a slow breath and

concentrated on the distinctive sensation of lavender, rosewater, and sarcasm that was Lady Sylvia Randolph.

Well, this is a pile of gauche, ostentatious trash and no mistake, the Victorian ghost remarked, slowly spinning in a circle as she took in the foyer.

Paula made absolutely no indication that she had any awareness of Sylvia's presence, which confirmed my assumption that she had as much magical as she did decorative sense.

How do you feel about providing a little drama? I asked Sylvia.

The ghost rubbed her ethereal hands together. **Drama? What sort of mischief are we up to, Nancy?**

Did I mention that Sylvia likes to call me Nancy? What started off as an anachronistic off-color comment about my cowardliness had become a term of endearment... for Sylvia. Anybody else calls me Nancy and we are going to have strong words.

I let Sylvia get away with it because she meant it in a teasingly fond sort of way—her favorite brother had been gay, and they used to watch the college men rowing down the James River together. That, and half the reason she still used it was because she just enjoyed getting a rise out of people, me especially.

Well, our lovely friend here thinks there's a spirit in this house corrupting her precious children.

Sylvia blinked. **And so we're going to give her a spirit because no one wants to be caught dead in this display of nouveaux riche garishness?**

I adore Sylvia. *We are,* I agreed.

Splendid. She looked around. **Where's your larger half?**

Fetching the oak trunk, I replied. *And trying to suppress the urge to strangle Paula over there.*

Oh, so she's a bitch as well as a classless plebian?

It was very, very hard not to laugh at that.

Behind us, Mason returned with the heavy oak chest that held the trappings I used to impress the ignorant: crystals, chalk, charcoal, salt, sage, candles, incense, as well as pendulums and a quartz sphere shot through with fluorite that I used as my crystal ball.

I turned to look at him, and saw his eyebrows rise, probably wondering why Sylvia was here if there wasn't a spirit to communicate with—and then his lips twitched just the slightest bit, and I was pretty sure he'd figured it out.

"Mrs. Kurstis has informed me that the spirit's presence is most powerful upstairs in the children's playroom," I told him.

"Shall I bring you up first?" he asked, still adopting that smooth, servile tone. It was effective, I'll give him that, but I hated it.

"Please," I replied, trying to sound vaguely imperious.

Please tell me you want me to wreak absolute havoc, Sylvia put in, her expression disgusted as she stared at Mason. I couldn't say that I disagreed. I was not a fan of subservient Mason.

Try not to cause too much actual damage, I replied. *I can't afford to pay to fix a place like this.*

Oh, you're no fun, she complained. **But I shall behave. For you.**

I bit back a snarky retort.

Mason set the trunk at the base of the stairs, then turned to Paula. "Could you show me where to go, ma'am?"

"Oh. Yes. Of course." She turned and headed up the

stairs, pausing only long enough for Mason to scoop me out of my chair and follow.

Paula led us to a surprisingly large open room, the rug on the hardwood floor decorated with a pattern that resembled children's alphabet blocks. Shelves and bins around the room appeared to hold toys and art supplies, and there were three easels at different heights on the far side, as well as a corner with a tv and gaming consoles surrounded by beanbag chairs.

It could have been a small school classroom. I briefly entertained the idea of asking her if her children had a governess, but decided that would be both rude and probably over her head.

"The center of the room on the floor should work," I told Mason, who let out a small huff that was audible only to me. He gently lowered me to the floor, where I arranged myself roughly cross-legged as Mason went to get the chest. I turned my attention up to Paula. "Thank you. I believe we can proceed from here. It will take a bit of setup, but if you want to watch, I'd be happy to send Mason to get you, if you wish." I looked at her expectantly.

She blinked a couple times. "Oh. Um. I—I think I would. Like to watch the séance, yes."

I nodded. "Very well. Where should I have him come to find you?" The polite way of asking her to get out—at least for now.

"I'll be—in the media room. Downstairs."

"Great, thank you." I turned away from her.

She took the hint and left.

The cackling isn't helping, Sylvia, I told the ghost, who had, in fact, been snickering through pretty much my entire exchange with Paula Kurstis.

She is so very ridiculous, I can't help myself.

Well, I would appreciate a little effort, at least. I'm trying to convince her this is serious business, and you are not helping.

I'll try, but only for your sake, she promised, although I wasn't about to place bets that she'd actually stop laughing at our client.

Mason sidled through the doorway carrying the oak chest with an absolutely epic eyeroll.

I looked up at him, knowing guilt was written clearly across the visible upper half of my face. "Mace, I'm *so* sorry."

He shrugged, then set it down beside me. "Not your fault," he replied, his tone mild, although I could hear the undercurrent of irritation beneath it.

"I mean, it kind of is? I took the damn client." The longer we were here, the worse I felt about it.

"You are not responsible for other people's idiotic behavior, Ward," he replied calmly.

"I know but—"

"Let's just do this so we can go home."

I was definitely going to have to make this up to him. "Okay," I agreed, although it really wasn't. But I couldn't imagine anything we could do to fix the situation that wouldn't also get us thrown out of the house and possibly sued, and if we were going to go to all the trouble of *doing* this fucking gig, we should at least get paid for it.

Mason handed me the chalk to trace a summoning circle, since chalk would come out of the carpet far more readily than charcoal. He set out crystals and candles, then lit a stick of incense that he placed directly in front of me. I took a deep breath and prepared to start drawing. It was going to be... an approximation of an actual summoning ritual. A real practitioner would immediately think we were either frauds or idiots, and I suppose technically we were—frauds, anyway. Our power was real enough, but we were absolutely making this up for Paula Kurstis's benefit.

And, okay, the nice paycheck that came with it.

Maybe I'm a bit of a dick for conning her out of her money, but the materials that comprised her completely overwrought house told me that she could more than afford it.

And if Paula Kurstis paid our bills, that meant we could keep helping people who couldn't afford the fees to say goodbye to their loved ones, trace their ancestry, find a much-needed inheritance, or even dispel an actually malicious real ghost.

That's how I justified it in my head, of course. While also feeling a bit guilty about the lying I was doing for money.

But I couldn't make myself set chalk to floor.

Sylvia and Mason were both looking at me, the former as though she could tell what I was thinking—which she probably could, since I wasn't actively trying to block her—and the latter with a vaguely unhappy expression that I absolutely hated.

I sighed heavily, then put the chalk back in the box and set my hands on my mostly useless thighs. "I can't do this."

Mason's eyebrows went up, although I thought I saw one corner of his lips quirk for a second. "Do what?" he asked, anyway.

"This," I repeated, waving a hand.

So I don't get to trash her downstairs?

I rolled my eyes. "No, Sylvia, you don't get to trash the downstairs. Or the upstairs."

If I did, then she would have a real ghost problem, Sylvia helpfully pointed out.

I sighed again. "Sylvia, I don't want to solve her problem by *creating* the problem."

The Skeleton Under the Stairs

Mason's lips twitched. I could practically *hear* him asking me about the shitty Yelp reviews Paula was going to give us in the kind of way your parents probably did when they were teaching you a very specific lesson. Or, in my case, your Auntie Pearl.

Sylvia looked at me.

Mason looked at me.

I closed my eyes and drew in a deep breath.

And then I heard a thump and a faint giggle coming from somewhere down the hall, and my eyes flew open.

Mason was looking in the direction of the sound, his lips pressed together and an expression of concentration on his face. Then his focus shifted to me, and I watched him smile.

"Do you think I should go suggest to them that they stop imitating ghosts to scare their mother?" he asked mildly.

I thought about it.

"Sylvia...?"

Her expression was mischievous, then thoughtful. **Can you make me visible?**

I blinked. "I—don't know? I can try."

"Try what?" Mason asked.

Instead of answering with words, I reached out a hand, and Sylvia put hers in mine. I focused on the feeling of her skin, slick and slightly squishy, and imagined the sensation spreading out along her arm, across her torso, down her legs, over her head with its perfectly twisted Victorian updo.

And then I concentrated drawing together the threads of her existence, making her solid enough that light wouldn't completely pass through her.

"Holy fucking shit," Mason breathed.

I was guessing that meant it worked.

I opened my eyes to find Mason staring at Sylvia, his sunburst eyes wide with the dark pupils blown open.

Sylvia turned to him, smiled, and waved.

Mason lifted one hand a little and gave a weak wave back.

I grinned. I couldn't help it. This was quite possibly the single coolest thing I'd ever done, and I didn't really care that my back was killing me and I was suddenly exhausted like I'd run five miles... not that I'd ever run five miles in my life, even before the major spinal injury. Which should tell you just how tired I was.

Can he hear me? she asked, looking back at me.

Mason didn't respond.

"I don't think so," I replied.

"Don't... think what?" Mason asked, his words a little unsteady.

"You can't hear her."

He shook his head.

Do you think—

"Don't you ask him right now," Mason said, for all the world as though he *had* heard her. "This already took a hell of a lot out of him."

Sylvia blinked, then looked back at me. **Oh. I'm sorry, Ward, I just thought...**

No, I reassured her. *It was a good idea. And I'm probably going to practice more with you so that it gets easier. Maybe someday we'll tackle talking.* But Mason was right, and I was getting more and more tired the longer she was visible. "You should probably take her down there," I suggested.

"Shit. Right. Lady Randolph, shall we?" Mason recovered himself, then gallantly gestured toward the playroom door for Sylvia to go ahead of him.

Left alone on the floor, I drew in a deep breath, carefully metering out my energy, spinning it into a thread that

The Skeleton Under the Stairs

connected to Sylvia as she and Mason moved down the hallway.

I heard a couple of faint shrieks, followed by the low echoes of Mason's voice, then some louder shrieks, which I could only assume were attached to Sylvia's grand entrance into the situation. I really wished I'd been able to follow them, if only to see the expressions on the kids' faces.

The sound of many feet indicated the arrival of all three kids along with Mason and Sylvia in the doorway.

"You know what you're going to say to your mother?" Mason asked the oldest of the three children, a girl who looked to be maybe twelve years old, her dark hair half held back with a sparky clip that matched the mask she'd put on.

She nodded, looking suitably contrite. The other two children—a boy around nine and a girl of maybe five or six—nodded along with her.

"Good," Mason replied. "I'm going to go fetch her."

The three children stood absolutely silently, looking between me and Sylvia, trying to decide if they were more frightened of the embodied ghost or the man who had brought her into the house. The middle child, a boy with messy blond hair, had on a superhero mask that was a little lopsided, and the youngest, a girl with her hair in pigtails, had one with kittens that was too big for her and had fallen under her nose.

All three started at me, but none of them said a thing.

Full-on fatigue had set in, and I was pretty much running on willpower and coffee, so I didn't particularly care if the children had nothing to say to me. I wasn't all that keen on talking back, either.

By the time Mason returned, with Paula in tow, the youngest was squirming, although her older sister kept shooting her dirty looks.

Paula let out a yelp when she saw Sylvia. Then she turned wide eyes on me. "Is that the spirit?" she asked, her voice breathy.

I shook my head. "No. Sylvia works with us." I deliberately used the plural to include Mason.

"Why are the children here?" she asked, then.

"I think perhaps they can explain that," Mason murmured from near the door.

Paula looked deeply confused.

The oldest girl poked her brother, who stepped forward.

"We made it up, Mom," he said, half-mumbling down at his shoes.

"What?" Paula seemed confused.

The boy looked up, his eyes starting to grow wet. "We made it up. The stuff. The noises were us."

"I told them not to," put in the oldest girl. "But then we thought it was a fun game. And..." She swallowed. "It got out of control."

Paula gaped at her children. "But... why?"

They looked at each other. The boy's ears turned pink, but it was the older girl who spoke.

"During the dinner party you hosted for Dad's work," she said softly. "We didn't stay in bed, and Dad joked about how he could hear ghostly footsteps, and we thought it might be funny to pretend it really *was* ghosts. So when you asked us if we were up, we pretended we weren't. And then it just... was easy to blame the ghosts for stuff." She hung her head.

Paula just stared at them. "I can't—you *lied* to me? You've been lying to me for months?"

The kids exchanged looks.

"We're sorry, Mom," the older girl said softly. The boy and younger girl both nodded.

The Skeleton Under the Stairs

Paula looked stricken.

"Go to your rooms," she said softly.

The children left, shuffling their feet against the carpet.

Once they'd gone, Paula barely looked at me. "I—"

"Aside from Lady Randolph here, there aren't any ghosts on your property, Mrs. Kurstis," I said softly. "Your children were responsible for the noises and for introducing the idea. Kids often think it would be fun to live in a haunted house. And sometimes it is." I took in a breath, surprised at how hard it was to talk that much. I usually talked a lot, but holding Sylvia visible like this was making me out of breath after only a few sentences.

I think you can let me fade, now, Sylvia suggested gently.

Thanks. I let out a heavy breath and let her fade.

Paula's eyes widened. "She's gone?"

"She's still here, but making her visible is... draining," I replied.

"Oh." Paula's eyes skimmed around the room as though she would be able to see some hint of Sylvia's presence in the room.

Sylvia hadn't actually moved and was watching Paula attempt to find her with some amusement, although I was too exhausted now to find it as entertaining as it had been downstairs.

"I—I don't know what to say," Paula admitted, the visible tops of her cheekbones startlingly pink in contrast to the yellow of her mask. "I'm so embarrassed."

I smiled. "There's no need," I replied. "It wouldn't be the first time I'd been called to a house to determine whether or not there *was* a spirit."

"Oh. Well." She cleared her throat a little. "I'll of course still pay your fee."

As though not paying was an option?

I agreed with Sylvia's comment, but I didn't say so.

"I appreciate that," I replied diplomatically, although I could see Mason's lips twitch over her shoulder. "We will pack up and then be on our way."

Mason moved quickly, and it was barely fifteen minutes after that incident that he had me bundled back in the truck, a check from Paula Kurstis in my pocket.

Sylvia had hung around until we left the house, then disappeared after telling me to take a nap.

I forced myself to stay awake for the drive, not falling asleep until after we were home and I'd gotten myself onto the bed. I don't even remember closing my eyes.

―――

I OPENED them when something cold and wet and fluffy shoved itself into my face with a loud, demanding *meow!* I twitched, jerking my head back, then I smiled in spite of myself as I rolled onto my side, pulling Peveril, my fluffy black and tan cat, with me so that I could cuddle him to my chest like a stuffed animal.

Pevs, enormously tolerant for a creature of his species, started purring happily.

I stayed like that, lying on my side with Peveril snuggled up against me warm and vibrating for several minutes, enjoying the feeling of being warm and sleepy, but no longer exhausted. I could tell that the sun was still out, but since we'd gone over to the Kurstis residence at ten in the morning, that didn't actually tell me much.

I felt the bed dip and turned to find Mason sitting on the far side.

I smiled at him. "Hey."

"Welcome back, Sleeping Beauty."

I snorted. "How long was I out?"

"Three hours. Hungry?"

I was. "Of course."

Mason produced a sandwich and two cookies on a plate from where he'd been hiding them behind one thigh. "Ta da!"

I turned so that I could push myself up against the headboard. Pevs, determining that cuddle-time was over, jumped down and sauntered off, presumably in search of kibble or a sunny spot. Mason handed me the plate, and I took a bite of the sandwich, which Mason had thoughtfully cut in half— diagonally, because he insisted that was the only appropriate way to cut a sandwich. I didn't actually care how my sandwiches were cut, something he found vaguely sacrilegious. Apparently, some people cut their sandwiches horizontally or vertically, and that was somehow horrifying.

As far as I'm concerned, a sandwich is a sandwich. I usually didn't bother cutting mine at all. I did not tell Mason this, and whenever I made the sandwiches, I dutifully cut them diagonally. Relationships are about compromise, after all.

The sandwich I was currently enjoying had cheese, pickled onions, avocado, and vegan mayo. It tasted better than it had any right to, probably because I'd completely drained my energy by making Sylvia visible, and now my body was craving as many calories as I could stuff into it.

Then I noticed that Mason was watching me a lot more closely than he usually did.

I swallowed my bite of sandwich. "What?"

He let out a small sigh. "I can't decide whether I should be worried about you or impressed as hell," he replied.

I frowned. "Because of Sylvia?"

Mason looked exasperated. "Do you know anyone else who can make a ghost *visible*, Ward?"

"No?"

"Well, neither do I. And neither do the four people I asked as soon as we got home, including Fiona, who is now rooting through everything she can find in the library."

"Did you ask Beck?"

"I did," he admitted. "But she hasn't texted me back yet."

Part of me hoped that Beck would have heard of such a thing... if only because it would make Mason stress out less about what the fuck I was.

Who was I kidding? It would make *me* stress out less about what I was.

Unless I was some sort of horrible warlock thing. Then it probably wouldn't make me happier.

"Penny?" Mason asked, probably because I have the world's worst poker face and he'd just read that entire train of thought as it ran through my head.

"You don't think... I'm some sort of..."

His eyebrows went up.

I deliberately did not end my question with *monster*, because Mason really hated it when people used that term. "Evil warlock?"

Mason snorted. "You would have to actually be *evil* to fit that epithet," he replied.

"But I could be a warlock?" That was almost as alarming.

"Is there something wrong with being a warlock?" he asked, sounding amused.

"I don't know," I admitted. "Is there?"

"Not the last time I checked, but I don't believe I've ever met any. Have you?"

"No?" I shrugged. "What's the difference between a witch and a warlock? Or a wizard? Or a sorcerer? When I was a little kid, I always thought witches had to be women, although that's obviously not true." Mason, who I can assure you is very much *not* a woman, is a witch, after all.

Mason shook his head. "It has to do with skillsets. Witches have dichotomies." He'd explained this before. "Our power is rooted in nature and the natural balance. Wizards, warlocks, sorcerers are... different."

"What's the difference between a wizard, a warlock, and a sorcerer?"

"They're actually all the same thing," Mason replied. "Personally, I prefer 'warlock.' 'Sorcerer' reminds me of Mickey Mouse and the 'Sorcerer's Apprentice,' and 'Wizard' just sounds too... silly."

"Okay. So what are they? Wizards or warlocks or whatever?"

Mason settled back on his elbows. "They're practitioners, like witches, and blood-born, also like witches, but their skill comes from study, praxis, and ritual."

"Meaning what, exactly?"

He hummed a little. "Well, that their magic isn't rooted in the natural world and doesn't naturally manifest the way that witches' magic does. Instead, they have *activate* their magic through praxis."

"Praxis?" This sounded to me like one of Mason's academic terms.

"Practice, essentially. Both in the sense of repetition and the sense of ritual. The things one does as well as the frequency with which one does them."

"So warlocks are...?" I still didn't think I got it.

"Warlocks are born with magic, like witches, but their magic is dormant until... Well, to be honest, I'm not sure what brings their magic out. My family is all *brujos*."

I felt a weird tingling in the pit of my stomach that had nothing to do with my sandwich. "So like me," I said softly.

Mason blinked at me. "I—yes. I suppose you could well be a warlock." He tilted his head a little to the side. "I wouldn't necessarily say that definitively, but it would... make sense. At least based on what little I actually know about warlocks."

A warlock.

I hadn't even known that warlocks were real things.

"What would that mean, though?" I asked him. "If I were?"

Mason shrugged. "Not much, honestly. Warlocks control their magic using spells, wards, cantrips, incantations, and focus objects, just like witches. The principal difference is that a warlock's magic isn't tied to nature. It's... more like a field of study."

"Like math?"

Mason smiled. "Probably more like a science, but, sure, like math. Where my natural affinity limits what magics I can perform, a warlock isn't so limited in scope. But, as I understand it, anyway, a witch's magic goes much *deeper* and comes much more easily within their dichotomy." He hummed again, thoughtfully. "Of course, warlocks also don't really perform the same exact magics that witches do. There are *things* that overlap, but the magic itself is different. A warlock would need a lot more than just his hands to heal, for instance. And it probably doesn't work the same way."

I thought about this. "Okay, but when I do... whatever it is I do, I'm not using ritual objects or spells."

"That's true," Mason replied. "But it could be that something different happens when a warlock contracts Arcanavirus and becomes a medium."

"Oh, goodie."

Mason shrugged. "You might not be a warlock, of course."

"But." I knew him too well.

"It's worth looking into," he admitted.

"Because I don't make sense."

He leaned over and kissed my temple. "I wouldn't have you any other way," he replied cheerfully.

I mock glared at him. "I'm not an academic puzzle, Mace."

That got me a toothy grin. "You're the best kind of puzzle," he replied, his gold-flecked eyes sparkling.

"Yeah?"

He nodded, leaning forward to brush another kiss against my hair. "Mine."

4

I HAD no idea what time it was when Mason's phone rang, and I was still trying to figure out why his alarm sounded weird and why it was so dark when I heard him answer it.

"Kei? What's wrong?" His voice was a little slurred, but I could hear the worry in it.

I couldn't hear her response, just the sense of her tone, upset, through the tiny phone speaker.

"Slow down, Kei. Start over. What happened?"

I saw his features ease from deeply worried to thoughtful, although there was definitely still concern there.

"Okay, Kei, what's happening right now? Uh huh. Is he awake? Can he tell you what he sees?"

I mouthed the word 'Jackson' at him through the darkness, and Mason nodded, his features just visible to me from the light on the phone. His orc eyes could see me just fine, even in the dark.

Jackson, Mason's nephew, had turned nine in January, a year older than Mason had been when he'd started having magic-related nightmares. Jackson could see ghosts, and since that had become publicly known—two Thanksgivings ago—everyone had pretty much been waiting for the day he'd start having nightmares, too.

It seemed like today was that day.

The primary problem was that neither Keidra, Mason's twin, nor her husband, Deon, was a witch, and that meant that they couldn't help Jackson learn to harness and use his magic. So when it began to get out of control, he was going to have to stop living with them and start living with someone who *could* help. And since Mariana Reyes, Mason's Gran and the only other witch in the family, was in her late eighties, that someone was Mason.

Which, as long as I lived with him, also meant me.

I was not ready for the responsibilities of surrogate-parenthood, even if Jackson's real parents would still be very much a part of his life. But I also wasn't going to be the asshole who refused to make room for a kid who needed help from his uncle.

Mason was still talking. "Okay, Kei, this is going to be hard, but you need to leave him alone. Don't touch him. I know he's upset, but if you or Deon or Ben try to touch him, one of you could end up seriously hurt."

Keidra said something back.

"I know. I know it's hard. Ward and I are on the way there, just in case there's more to this than just a nightmare, okay?"

I heard her voice go up in pitch.

"No, Kei, I don't know that it's anything more than that, but I can't see dead people. I don't know, Kei. It might be a dream. But it might be a spirit that's scaring him. And if that's the case, I can't help him, but Ward can."

She said something more.

"We're on our way, Kei. Call again if you need to."

I had already started hauling myself out of bed,

swinging my butt into my chair. I was wearing a pair of relatively tame pj pants—dark blue with raindrops—so I figured I could keep them on. I pulled a t-shirt on over my head from the drawer, not bothering to check what it was, as Mason threw on a pair of sweatpants and a t-shirt of his own.

I grabbed a hoodie and stuffed it in my lap as I rolled my way toward the back door, following Mason out to the truck and snagging a pair of clogs on the way.

Mason threw the chair in the back and me in the front of the truck, and then we were on the road, heading to his sister's house. I hadn't been there before—all the family dinners I'd attended had been either at Mason's gran's or his parents', not Keidra and Deon's. Mason had picked up the boys a time or two, but I didn't usually tag along for that. But it wasn't like this was going to be a social call.

They lived in Midlothian, so not too far from Mason's house, and practically no one was on the roads at almost three in the morning, so we got there fairly quickly. As Mason pulled into the driveway, the garage door began to go up, and Deon—also wearing sweats and an old t-shirt—came out barefoot. He looked tired and stressed, which made him seem older than his good humor normally allowed.

"He's upstairs," Jackson's dad told us as Mason got me out of the Tacoma and into my chair. Mason had to lift me up the two steps into the house, but Deon came over to help him do it. "He won't stop screaming," Deon rasped. That particular piece of information wasn't necessary—we could both hear the boy's clearly hysterical cries. "We can't tell what about."

Mason nodded once. "Let me see if I can't get him calmed down," he replied.

The Skeleton Under the Stairs

They left me in the kitchen with a clearly-upset Ben, who was sitting on a stool, sniffling. I heard footsteps going up stairs.

"You okay?" I asked Jackson's brother.

He nodded, his brown eyes wide. Ben was almost eleven —a year and a half older than Jackson—but he hadn't shown any signs of magic.

"You sure?"

He chewed his lower lip. "I'm scared," he admitted in a small voice.

"Because Jackson is so upset?"

He nodded. "Mama said that he can see ghosts." He swallowed. "I'm afraid of ghosts."

I rolled myself a little closer. "You know I can see them, too, right?"

Ben nodded.

"Most ghosts aren't scary, I promise. But the ghosts know Jackson can see them, and they want to talk to him because of that. But he doesn't really know how yet." I thought for a minute. "Do you know how to swim?"

Ben nodded. "Mama said it was important to learn how, because Grandma almost drowned because nobody taught her."

"It is. Do you remember when you first learned, how scary the water was?"

He nodded again.

"Talking to ghosts is kinda like that. It's scary until you get used to how it works. I bet you'd have been really scared if someone had just thrown you in at first, right?"

Ben's eyes were calmer, his pupils less dilated. "And that's what's happening to Jackson?"

"Exactly."

Upstairs, the hysterical sounds had stopped. Ben sat up straighter. "Is he okay now?"

I shrugged. "I bet he's still scared, but your Uncle Mason is pretty good at helping scared people feel safe."

Ben nodded again. "Yeah, he is. Nobody messes with Uncle Mason."

I smiled at that.

Footsteps came back down the stairs, and then Mason—Deon and Keidra trailing behind him—carried a still-crying Jackson into the kitchen. And I immediately knew at least part of why Jackson had been so upset.

Following them was a youngish white man in white robes, discolored spatter that had probably been blood all over the front of his costume. And what he was saying was definitely not to be repeated in polite—or impolite, or any —company.

"Oh, sh—oot." I stopped myself halfway through the curse word, mindful of Ben, since Jackson had clearly already heard far worse from the dead man.

"I take it we have a friend?" Mason asked mildly.

"That is... not the specific term I would use," I replied, trying to not to alarm anyone more than they already were. Somehow I got the impression that telling Keidra and Deon that their son was being tormented by a dead Klansman would *not* be particularly comforting.

Mason's eyebrows went up, but he read something in my expression that told him he should wait to ask.

You can shut the fuck up right now, I told the ghost, who turned to gape at me, then drifted closer, challenging me by getting in my space. It meant he moved away from Jackson, so while I wasn't terribly keen on getting close to this particular spirit, I definitely preferred him closer to me than a nine-year-old boy.

You gonna take *their* side in this? the ghost demanded. Jackson's dark eyes were huge. The boy could undoubtedly hear the dead man, even if he couldn't hear my silent side of the conversation—which was probably good, given the language I was using.

You're fucking right I am. Normally, I attempt to negotiate with spirits, even when they're not particularly pleasant. But I had less than zero patience for the waste of aethereal space in front of me. *And if you don't get the fuck out of here right now, I will fucking make you.*

Then you'd better try, you ni— I was not about to let him use that particular term in front of Jackson, although I wasn't naïve enough to think the poor kid had never heard it. Rage pushed through me, and I shoved my hand directly into the ghost's chest cavity.

I was dimly aware of Mason ordering everyone out of the kitchen, but I was concentrating too much on the metaphysical asswipe in front of me to really pay attention. What I was doing took quite a bit of energy, but this sad excuse for a human spirit wasn't even remotely as strong as Preston Fitzwilliam, and, therefore, was apparently not a match for me. I wasn't even panicked, just angry, and that gave me the time to think about what I was doing.

It was weird. Like when I'd given Sylvia physical form, it was very much like drawing on dispersed matter, pulling it together like sticky, slimy threads until it all congealed into something like a gelatinous body.

One that nobody else could see or touch, unless I wanted them to.

I'd have to explain it to Mason—and probably Beck, and maybe Fiona—later.

Right now, I had a ghost to banish.

Get out.

I could have completely destroyed him. I could feel the power buzzing in the tips of my fingers, and, let me tell you, it was damn tempting. But there was still a voice in the back of my head that whispered that if I became too comfortable with that idea, I wasn't going to end up any better than Preston Fitzwilliam, who had murdered dozens of people, consumed their souls, and had tried to tear my spine out through my stomach.

And I wasn't willing to become that. Even—no, *especially* not for this piece of garbage.

So instead I made the very clear point that I *could* tear this sad excuse for a human soul into pieces, and then let him cross over, feeling him pass through the Veil at what amounted to metaphysical gunpoint.

And then I sat in the Turner-Mannings' kitchen, staring down at my trembling hands, which were slick with a greyish slime. My ears were ringing, and I felt slightly nauseous, but only slightly. I guess I was getting more used to physical contact with ghosts.

"Ward?" Mason's voice was hesitant as he stepped into the entryway to the kitchen, having put Jackson somewhere. I could vaguely make out the boy's voice through the ringing in my ears.

"He's gone," I answered. I could tell I sounded tired. I *was* tired, and not just because it was after three in the morning.

"Gone, gone?"

"Crossed over." Ghosts who crossed had to be brought back, so unless someone had deliberately sent the spirit here, he wouldn't return. Cold rushed through me, and I failed to keep the shudders from rippling through my body.

"Are you okay?"

I shrugged. I'd touched ghosts since Preston Fitzwilliam,

of course, but I hadn't needed much force, and I hadn't had to fully banish any of them. This asshole had required both force and banishment, so it was hitting me a little harder.

Mason came over and crouched next to me, reaching out one hand, although he stopped before touching me when he noticed the slime on my fingers and palms. "Towel?" he asked, standing again.

"Please." I had no idea how the fuck he was so calm. I wasn't that calm.

I heard him tear off some paper toweling and run the sink, although I didn't want to smear ghost-goo all over my wheels in order to turn around.

Then Mason was back beside me, and he took one of my hands and wiped it clean, then did the same with the other using a wet paper towel, then he handed me a couple sheets so I could dry my hands.

"Better?" he asked, gently placing one hand on my shoulder.

I nodded.

"Do I want to know?"

I shook my head. "I'll explain later," I said softly. "You can decide what to tell your sister."

He grunted softly, Mason's noise for grudging assent. He didn't like it, but he wasn't going to argue with me. "We should probably still bring Jackson home with us," he said softy. "Because it isn't going to get better, even if that specific ghost is gone."

I took a deep breath. It was something I'd known was coming ever since Jackson had seen Dom, Mason's grandfather, at my first Thanksgiving with the Reyes-Manning-Turners, sparking a family debate about who should train Jackson, but that didn't mean I felt ready to deal with it, even a year and a half later. I didn't feel prepared to take on the role of step-uncle—or whatever—especially because I still hadn't fully figured out how to take care of myself. I was doing better than last year, sure, but I was still a far cry from being fully self-sufficient.

And that wasn't even considering what this meant for Mason's level of personal responsibility. First me, and now Jackson.

But I didn't want to make it harder on him by complaining. "That's up to you and Keidra," I answered, trying to keep my tone light instead of panicky.

Mason squeezed my hands. "I don't think we're going to have any more issues tonight," he said quietly. "I'll suggest the kids take off school tomorrow, and we can talk it over then. Okay?"

I nodded. It wasn't my place to make this decision, although I guess they were going to rely on me to teach Jackson how to do at least some the things I did. Maybe this was the push I needed to really learn what I *could* do, as anxiety-producing as the thought was. Because I couldn't exactly teach Jackson if I didn't know what I was doing.

Mason stood and left the kitchen again, and I took the opportunity to take a couple more deep breaths. I wasn't ready to be some kind of spiritual guide. It looked like I wasn't going to get a choice, but the idea of being responsible for a kid's mental stability... That was a big ask.

It was one I couldn't really say no to.

5

I don't know if anyone in the Turner-Manning household got any sleep after the incident the night before, but I sure as shit didn't. I told Mason all the gory, racist details once we'd gotten back home, and he'd had a few choice things to say about the ghostly Klansman, but then he'd hugged me and thanked me for taking care of it.

I still felt a little filthy about the whole thing, and not just because I'd had to touch the cretinous spirit, although I did catch myself scrubbing my hands Lady Macbeth-style more than once that morning. The idea that anyone would, at any point in their life or death, target a fucking *kid* was physically revolting.

With the ghost gone, Keidra and Mason had decided that Jackson could have at least another day or two at home —for his sake, but also so that the rest of us could figure out the logistics of things like school and schedules and what we would do with him when we had a gig...

The list of things that had to be figured out was pretty staggering once I'd stared actually thinking about it.

The boys periodically stayed overnight at Mason's, so

they had sleeping bags and stuff upstairs, but that was very different than *living* here, so we'd have to either move furniture from Keidra and Deon's house or get new furniture. Mason had already called Jamie about expediting the upstairs renovations, but Jackson wouldn't be able to sleep up there until those were finished, although now that was going to happen sooner rather than later.

Mason was currently hauling things out of his office and sorting them into piles that would either go to Beyond the Veil or end up in the living room or our bedroom to make space for Jackson to sleep in the office—which then wouldn't be an office, at least temporarily. There was a stack of boxes that held books and papers by the back door, the office chair was currently in the living room, and I could hear Mason muttering to himself as he worked on figuring out the computer.

And that was just the physical logistics.

Mason wouldn't have to take Jackson to school—at least for the rest of this year. Jackson would be doing school remotely. Thankfully, it was May, so there wasn't a lot of school left, but nobody knew what we were going to do next year, since we lived in a totally different district than Keidra and Deon. They'd have to figure that out, too. And then get Mason named as a legal guardian so he could make school-related decisions as needed.

And then there was the basic care and feeding of a nine-year-old. I'd been a nine-year-old boy once, and I knew nine wasn't far from the pre-teen and teenage growth spurts that necessitated absurd amounts of food.

Our grocery bills were already high. Mason's an orc. Six feet, seven inches of heat-producing muscle burns a lot of calories, and he also runs and lifts weights. Add another adult male with weird metabolism issues, and now a growing kid.

To say nothing of entertainment, babysitting, sports, or any other clubs.

Fuck. Parenting is hard.

And Jackson didn't even live with us yet.

I was trying to stay out of Mason's way and also be helpful, which meant I was in the kitchen attempting to cook food because there was no way I could actually move anything heavy or larger than my own lap.

Thank God for prepackaged pesto and dried pasta.

I was competent enough to sauté some vegetables and open a jar of kalamata olives and some feta, so we would at least be having something more complex than sandwiches for lunch.

It was a nice bonus that I got to watch Mason shoving his desk across the house on a rug, the muscles of his arms flexing as he pushed the clearly-still-fully-loaded piece of furniture to the far side of the living room.

That task accomplished, he came back and leaned in the kitchen doorway, watching me push mushrooms and peppers around in a pan, his eyes dancing and a twist shaping his lips.

"I'm not taking specific orders," I told him. "You get what the chef makes."

His smile widened, showing me both sets of canines. "I like it when you cook," he replied.

"Why? When I cook we eat sad bachelor food."

Mason laughed at that, then came into the kitchen and pressed a kiss to my hair. "I don't think technically anything you cook can be properly defined as 'bachelor food,' given that you aren't a bachelor."

"True," I admitted, taking my attention off the sauté pan to look up at him.

He ran one hand over my curls, then bent to kiss me, which I encouraged by sliding my free hand—the one without the spatula—into his braids. His tongue teased at my lips, and I let him deepen the kiss, meeting his tongue with mine.

He hummed softly against my mouth, and the sensation sent tingles through me.

Then he pulled back. "I wouldn't want to ruin your bachelor food…"

I laughed, then kissed him again, although I let him go before the kiss got too heated. "I thought you liked my bachelor food," I teased.

"Hmm. I said I liked it when you cook."

I raised my eyebrows in mock offense. "But you don't actually like my food."

"Your food is fine," he replied, running his hands over my hair again.

"Fine," I repeated, teasing.

"Mmhmm. You're sexy when you cook it, though."

I laughed outright at that. "You're absurd."

"You don't think cooking is sexy?"

"*You* cooking is sexy," I retorted. "Me cooking is an exercise in sad choices and awkward body positions."

"Which is why we redid the kitchen."

"It only helps so much," I replied. "I've always been awkward—now it's just ten times worse."

He bent and kissed the top of my head. "You're not that awkward, Ward," he said gently. "And your cooking is fine."

I went back to stirring the veggies, feeling a little self-conscious, although I knew he wasn't trying to be critical. I

The Skeleton Under the Stairs

was hoping that if I occupied myself with cooking, he wouldn't notice my anxiety.

Obviously, he did anyway, because he's Mason, and he knows me far too well.

"Do you want to talk about it?" he asked.

"If by 'it,' you mean 'Jackson,' then no, not really."

Mason let out a long sigh. "Ward…"

"Look," I said, stirring the innocent vegetables a bit more savagely than was warranted, "I recognize that this is not a great situation for anybody, and it's probably worst for Jackson. I know he doesn't *want* to have this happen to him, but I also know that he *should* be trained, *and* I know that your gran is probably too old to chase around a nine-year-old." I took a deep breath. "So I *know* that this is the best choice for him." I looked up at Mason, expecting to find anger or accusation in his expression.

I saw neither.

What I saw was understanding and love.

One big hand ran over my curls again. "But?" he asked gently.

"I'm scared," I admitted. "I don't know the least thing about kids. I sucked at being a kid when I *was* a kid."

Mason laughed at that. "I don't know if it will make you feel any better," he said. "But me, too."

I shot him a look that said it did *not* make me feel better.

"It'll be okay," he promised.

I nodded. "Yeah, probably," I agreed. "But it's a bit of a steep learning curve."

"Jackson adores you. And he needs your help as much as he needs mine."

"That would be a big part of what terrifies me," I admitted. "I don't even know what the fuck I am, much less if I can teach any of what I do to someone else. Especially a kid."

Mason pressed another kiss to my temple. "You're great with Jax. And you'll be a better teacher about the dead than anyone else I know."

I felt my cheeks coloring.

Then the kitchen timer went off.

"And that is?" Mason asked.

"Pasta," I answered.

He moved around me, fetching the colander, grabbing the pot, then taking both to the sink to drain the noodles.

I transferred the veg and pesto into a bowl, and, when it was drained, Mason poured the pasta on top so I could stir the whole thing together.

We sat at our kitchen counter to eat, since there were still boxes and piles scattered around the living room from our sudden office move.

"Mace?"

"Mmm?"

"Should we..." I wasn't sure how to ask this question without seeming like a selfish jerk.

Mason seemed to recognize the seriousness of the unasked question and set his fork down. "Should we what, Ward?"

I toyed with my food. "Maybe wait on the wedding?" My voice went up at the end, almost ending on a squeak.

Mason looked at me for a long time, and I couldn't read his expression. That scared me a little. "Is that what you want?"

"No?"

Now his expression was exasperated, although he smoothed it away quickly. "Ward. What *do* you want?"

I could feel emotion pushing at the back of my eyelids, and I tried very hard to keep it there. "I *want* to marry you. I want to figure out what the fuck I am. I want to make our business work. I want to renovate the house. And I want to help Jackson." I looked up at him, feeling the tears heavy in my eyes. "I also don't know if I can do all of those things at the same time."

Mason reached out and covered my hand with one of his, running his thumb over my ring finger, where the twisted band wrapped around an amethyst and an aquamarine—my birthstone and Mason's. The ring he'd given me when he'd asked me to marry him.

"So what do you want to do most?" he asked.

"Marry you." I swallowed. "But Jackson can't wait. And the house can't wait. And Beyond the Veil can't wait."

"Okay. What's the most important thing you want at the wedding?" He was so calm. So patient.

"Um. You?"

That earned me a twisted smile. "You have me. Always. Wedding or not. What else?"

I laced my fingers through his, staring at the play of my thin, pale fingers against his bigger, olive green ones. "Family. Friends."

"I agree. And they'll go anywhere we ask them to. Whenever we ask them to show up. What next?"

I thought about this. "That's it, really," I admitted. "I mean. I want people to have fun. I want *us* to have fun. But... I don't really care about all the rest."

Mason's eyebrows went up.

"Okay. I want..." I sighed. "I want it to be perfect. But I have no idea what that *is*."

That made him laugh.

I stabbed irritably at my noodles.

"You know I love you, Ward," he said, tightening his fingers on mine.

"And I love you," I replied, still scowling down at my bowl.

"But you *know* I love you," he repeated.

I felt my cheeks heat. "Yeah," I whispered.

"Then as far as I'm concerned, as long as I end up married to you at the end of it, whatever it is *will* be perfect."

I rolled my eyes. "That's sweet, Mason, but it doesn't help any of the rest of it."

He ran his thumb over the backs of my fingers. "I don't want to wait to marry you," he said, his voice soft. "And if that means it's a bunch of us in a basement wearing sweatpants, then that's fine with me. We'll figure it out." He picked up his fork and put more pasta in his mouth, then spoke around it. "And we'll use Jackson as manual labor."

That made me smile. "I'll put him in charge of the cake."

Mason looked mock-horrified. "Do you want a Lego-themed cake?"

I grinned. "Why not?"

"No."

"So you do have opinions?"

"Yes. Not Legos."

"Star Wars?" Jackson was also a huge Star Wars fan.

"No Star Wars. No Legos. No Batman or Marvel or Disney."

"But I was going to go as Ariel. Get a tail and everything."

Mason rolled his eyes. "Then I'll go as Shrek."

"That's not even Disney," I protested.

"That's my point."

"Okay, fine, no Disney."

The Skeleton Under the Stairs

MASON SPENT most of the afternoon on the phone, first with Keidra, then their mom, then Keidra again, then his gran, and finally Keidra again.

I was sitting on the couch, pretending to get work done. I had been trying to actually *do* work, but the snippets of Mason's conversations with Keidra and his mom—the one with his gran was held entirely in Spanish, which I can't speak—were making me anxious.

Keidra, understandably, didn't want to essentially give up her son. It wasn't like that, exactly, but I'm sure it felt like it to her.

I got the impression that she wanted to keep him at home because this had just been a ghost—and since I'd made the ghost go away, then Jackson wouldn't need to leave. And even though I could tell from Mason's tone that his grandmother thought the boy should already be living with us, Mason wasn't going to push his sister to do something she didn't want to do.

I could also tell Mason wasn't particularly comfortable with it, either, and God knew I was only a few steps south of terrified. But Mason knew what it was like to go through what Jackson was going through. He'd been the kid who had to leave his parents and essentially grow up in some other relative's house.

I mean. So had I, although in my case it was because Arcanavirus had killed my mom and my dad had functionally committed suicide by snowbank. My parents weren't still alive—and I wasn't entirely certain whether that was better or worse.

Which I guess meant that Mason and I were actually both pretty well situated to understand what Jackson was feeling.

I hadn't at all meant to talk myself *into* this, but it did help ease the borderline panic at the thought of becoming a functional step-father to a nine-year-old death witch.

Also, Keidra's resistance was somewhat reassuring, at least to me, since I figured his mom knew him better than I did. And I was a big chicken about this whole thing. On top of that, I couldn't tell if Mason was more anxious about Jackson coming to live with us or Jackson *not* coming to live with us.

Mason finished his conversation with Keidra, then came and flopped down on the empty side of the sectional, his legs hanging over the arm and his head resting against the side of my thigh. I closed the laptop I was only pretending to use and put it to the side, and Mason settled his head in my lap. I put one palm on his chest and ran the fingers of my other hand over his braids as he closed his eyes.

"Kei doesn't want to let Jackson go just yet," he said.

"Can you blame her?"

He grunted. "No. And I'm sure Jackson wants to stay with them, too. I didn't want to go to live with Gran, either. I think it was probably easier for Mom than for Kei because the first time I had a really bad magic-related nightmare, I..." He swallowed. "I hurt Dad. Really hurt him. Mom knew to call Gran right away, but..." He drew in a shaky breath, and I could tell that he still felt guilty about whatever he'd done to Israel, his dad, even though he'd only been eight.

"It still must not have been easy," I replied. "For you or your parents."

"I didn't want to hurt Dad again. Or hurt Mom or Kei. Even that young, I understood that the only way for them to be safe was to go to Gran's."

"Well, Jackson hasn't hurt anyone," I pointed out.

Mason grunted again.

"You think he will?"

The Skeleton Under the Stairs

"Life-death is often close to heal-harm," he answered. "And—" He let out a long breath. "I'm actually worried that he could do worse than hurt one of them."

I sucked in a breath.

"Accidentally, of course," Mason quickly continued. "But if he's really scared and his magic is out of control..."

"Shit," I replied, my fingers stilling on his hair.

"Exactly."

"But *making* Keidra let him go isn't a good option, either."

"No."

"I'm sorry, Mace."

"Not your fault, Ward." He reached over his head to rub a hand against my hip.

"I'm not exactly making it easier, though," I pointed out. "Since you're going to have to drive *two* of us around."

"I could always ask Jackson to wait for his magic to manifest until he's sixteen and can drive..."

I snorted. "Does that work?" I assumed he was being sarcastic, but I had to ask, just in case.

"Sadly, no." He shrugged. "We'll figure it out."

"You always say that," I pointed out.

"We always do," he replied.

So far? Yes. We had always figured it out, whether *it* was dealing with Preston Fitzwilliam or shutting down Tranquil Brook or moving me into Mason's house or figuring out how I could adapt to life in a wheelchair or coping with the trauma of what Tyler had done to me. We'd always figured it out.

It just seemed like there was a lot more to figure out these days.

Most people got a couple years after marriage before they started thinking kids. We were going to end up with a nine-year-old before we even got married. And maybe we'd finish the house at some point in the middle of it, or maybe we wouldn't.

I mean, okay, a medium and an orc witch are hardly 'most people,' but I was starting to wish that I could do even just one thing in my life the normal way.

Auntie Pearl always said normal was boring.

Boring was starting to look pretty good from where I was sitting.

Then again, with boring, I wouldn't have Mason, and I would absolutely trade boring in any day just to have Mason in my life. Which I guess, technically, is kinda what I did.

I went back to stroking his braids. "Yeah," I said finally. "We do."

Mason smiled at that, his eyes still closed, and the twist of his mouth made my chest feel warm. He took the hand resting on his chest and brought it to his lips, pressing a kiss to my fingers. "I love you," he murmured into my skin.

"I love you, too," I answered.

He half rolled off the couch, trailing one hand from my hip to my thigh as he did, ending up on his knees. My breath caught in the back of my throat as he gently tugged my leg off the cushion, lowering my foot to the floor. Then he reached around and shifted me, pulling me closer to him and turning me so that his body was between my knees.

Big green hands ran down the inside of my thighs, and I could feel heat starting to pool in my groin. His hands slid upwards again, then around my hips so that he could pull me even closer. With a soft hum, he bent and nuzzled his cheek against my quickly-hardening cock through my pajama pants. The loose fabric didn't do much to hide my growing erection, and Mason rubbed his face against me, breathing in deeply as he did, a soft growl building in the back of his throat.

I ran my hands over his hair, my fingers sliding through the texture of the braids against his skull as I whimpered.

His hands worked my pants off, and he growled louder when he discovered that I hadn't actually bothered to put on boxers.

And then I clenched my fingers and dropped my head back as he swallowed me, not bothering to ease me into it, the sudden heat and wet of his mouth almost painful it happened so fast.

He sucked and swirled, sliding his mouth along me without ever leaving me fully exposed, the transition between the heat of his mouth and the shock of air hitting wet skin making my balls draw up tight as I gasped and whimpered.

And then he pulled back, his big, warm hands sliding up my body as he pulled my t-shirt over my head. "You are so —" He kissed the side of my neck. "Fucking." The spot behind my ear. "Responsive." My lips, long and deep.

Then he leaned back to strip off his own shirt, then stood and pulled off his pants and boxer briefs. I reached out and wrapped a hand around the thick heat of his erection, and he leaned into my hands, running his fingers through my curls.

I pulled him closer to me with my other hand until I could slowly—very slowly—run my tongue over the head of his cock, feeling his fingers tighten in my hair. I rolled my tongue around him, then deliberately eased him between my lips, drawing him in deeper as he let out a low groan.

I loved the feel of him, the ridges and veins along his shaft, the smooth-yet-textured feel of his skin against my lips and tongue, the heat that radiated off every inch of him, the harsh rasp of his breath, and the faint, breathy growls he made when I sucked him deeper.

I could feel the muscles of his thighs tremble under my hands as I swallowed him as far into my throat as I could, his fingers gripping my curls.

And then he pulled back, and I let out a small whine of protest.

"Impatient," he teased, as he moved just far enough to grab the lube from the side-table drawer and come back, already slicking the fingers of one hand. He settled between my knees again, pushing my thighs apart so he could tease at my body with one finger.

I whimpered, trying to push my hips closer to him, and he chuckled, low and breathy. He slipped one finger past the ridge of muscle, his other hand on my hip as he settled one cheek against my knee, watching his finger working at my body, stretching, loosening.

It was fucking hot.

I whimpered, and he kissed the inside of my knee before easing in a second finger. He pushed my legs wider, starting to kiss his way up the inside of my thigh.

I was very glad I could still feel this, even if it was a little muted and my legs didn't tense or tremble. I still felt the warm press of his lips, the brush of his cheek, the heat of his breath against my skin. Every nerve was alive, made more sensitive by what he was doing to the inside of my body.

"Oh, God, *fuck*, Mason," I rambled, as he ran his tongue up the length of my already-weeping cock at the same time that he worked in a third finger.

He grinned up at me. "Ready?"

"Fuck, yes. *Please.*"

He slid his fingers out of me, slowly, teasingly, and I made a small, involuntary sound in the back of my throat—I didn't want him to stop, but I also very much wanted what came next.

Big hands ran up the outside of my thighs to my hips, then under my ass as he stood, hooking the back of one thigh under one of his knees so that he could half-kneel on the seat of the couch. Then he did the same with the other, using his hands to tilt my hips so that the dripping head of his thick cock was pressed against me.

He paused long enough to slick himself with one hand, his erection jumping against his palm—watching him stroke himself was enough to send a spiral of heat straight to my balls.

"Mace—" I pleaded.

Both hands came back to my hips, and he guided himself just far enough that the head of his cock was pressed into me, my breath fast and my fingers tight on his forearms. Then he paused, his eyes fixed on mine, and placed both my arms around his neck.

And then he pushed his body forward, both hands on the back of the couch, surging into me hard and fast. I cried out, my head dropping back as I felt him fill me, the stretch and fullness of it constricting at the back of my throat.

Mason groaned into the skin of my neck, and I could feel his muscled arms shaking as he waited for my body to adjust to his.

"Mace, please," I begged, the tension too much. I needed him to *move*.

He nuzzled against my hair, drawing in a deep breath as he drew his hips back, his cock sliding almost all the way out of me before he pushed back in again, as sharp and fast as the first time.

I moaned, my fingers falling from his neck to his shoulders, tightening against the muscle as he repeated the movement, first easing his way out, then driving himself back into me, pushing so hard I saw stars.

Trapped in the best possible way between Mason's body and the back of the couch, I let my hands slide down his arms, which were braced against the couch, my body at once wound tight and pliant as he thrust into me.

"Mace—" I gasped out.

He growled low in response, the vibration of his chest sending tingles rolling through me that had no chance to abate before he pushed into me again, the force of it sending my eyes rolling back as I came in electric pulses, milky ropes pulsing out onto my stomach.

"*Fuck*, yes," he snarled into the skin of my neck, thrusting forward only once more before I felt the thick heat of him throbbing out his orgasm inside of me.

His chest still heaving with rapid breaths, he ran both palms down my back, cradling me against his body as he turned and eased us down so that he was lying on his back, holding me on top of him. His fingers traced abstract patterns along the skin of my back.

I turned to rest my cheek against his chest, soaking in the warmth of his body and the feeling of being loved and protected.

Mason's breathing slowed and deepened, his pulse steadying. One hand wandered up the back of my neck and into my hair, toying with my curls and running over the shell of my ear, gently playing with the silver hoop at the top of the curve.

"Penny?" Mason asked.

I turned to rest my chin on my hands on his chest, finding his sunburst eyes looking down at me. "We're going to have to have less sex on the couch when Jackson comes to live with us," I pointed out.

Mason huffed a breath out through his nose. "Remind me to move the lube," he said.

I felt my eyes widen. "Shit. Yes. Move it now."

"And if we want it again?"

"You can run down the hall to get it," I told him. The idea of Jackson rooting through drawers and asking about lube... Nope. Not going to deal with that.

"Or I could just use my tongue," he suggested, the hand on my back smoothing lower to cup one of my ass cheeks.

"Or that," I readily agreed.

"You're okay with it, though?"

"Jackson finding lube? Absolutely not. And there will be no discussions of how much sex we've had on this couch, either."

Mason chuckled, and the vibrations in his chest sent a pleasant shiver through me. He must have assumed I was cold, because he reached overhead with one hand and pulled the blanket from my side of the couch to throw over me. "Better?"

I smiled. "Perfect." I didn't mention that it had been perfect anyway, but he looked so pleased with himself that I didn't want to wreck it. Besides, the blanket was not in any way making cuddling with Mason any less perfect.

"But you're okay with Jackson living here?" he persisted.

I sighed. "I know it's the right thing for him," I answered. "I—I'm nervous that I'll mess something up. That I'm not ready for whatever it means to have him living with us."

Mason took several breaths in silence, but his expression told me that he was thinking about something. Probably about whether or not to be mad at me for being an immature, selfish asshole.

But what he said surprised me.

"Did you ever want kids?"

"I—kind of?"

The hand in my curls went back to playing with them, the other coming to rest on my lower back. "Kind of?"

"I was always... interested in the idea, I guess? But it wasn't exactly something I went out of my way to plan for. It's not like I was going to marry a woman and have them the, uh, traditional way."

He made a small half-hum. "Never interested in women?"

"Ew. No."

He laughed at that. "Ew? That's not very polite. They're generally cleaner than most guys, you know."

I felt my cheeks turning pink. "Okay, maybe that wasn't quite the best word choice, but no. I've never felt even the slightest attraction to women. You?" It had never occurred to me that he might, but there was certainly no reason he couldn't.

"I had a few girlfriends in junior high and high school because it was what I thought I was 'supposed' to do, but I wasn't ever particularly... enthusiastic about it," he replied. "Gran did make it very clear that regardless of my choice of partner, she wanted more great-grandbabies, though."

I smiled. "I do remember you mentioning that before we even started dating," I replied.

I was amused to note that it was Mason's turn to have his cheeks color slightly, shading to a more brownish tint.

"That probably should have been a significant clue that I was interested," he murmured.

"Well, I'm pretty oblivious," I responded, running my fingers over the muscle of his chest. "I had no idea you thought I was anything but a complete fuckup."

He snorted. "You're not a fuckup."

"I almost barfed on your shoes."

"I had that under control."

"I passed out on you."

"In my arms," he retorted. "It was—"

"Sweaty, gross, and a little traumatizing," I interjected.

Mason laughed again. "Okay, yes. But also a little bit cute."

"You have a messed-up idea of cute."

He raised both eyebrows at me. He thought I was insane for thinking he was hot, so I guess I could allow him to think that my sorry ass was cute.

"Did you want kids?" I asked him.

He let out a hum. "I did," he answered, the words slow. "But I'd also given up on the idea."

"Why?" I asked him.

He ran his hand over my curls, brushing them back from my forehead. "I'd given up on finding someone I would want to raise kids with," he said softly.

I frowned at him, unsure what to say. Mason is too good for me on every conceivable level. He's sweet and considerate, gentle, fucking brilliant, witty, and one of the most genuinely selfless people I've ever met. And on top of that, he's tall, strong, with well-defined muscles, a narrow waist, and thick hair he kept tightly braided with black beads on the end of each that sometimes sounded like river-washed pebbles when he moved his head quickly.

I couldn't imagine him having any difficulty either getting a date or maintaining a relationship, orc or not.

Unlike yours truly, who was an emotional hot mess of medical and psychological issues all packed into a skinny, weak body. I hadn't been in a wheelchair yet when Mason met me, of course, and the fact that he was *still* with me should tell you just how amazing he actually is.

But despite all that, Mason had hinted more than once

that he hadn't dated a lot—and Rennie, his mom, had commented at the dinner table after we'd announced our engagement that she'd almost given up on Mason finding someone to spend his life with.

I honestly had no idea why.

And no idea why he'd chosen me.

But, looking at him, I could see him not only as a loving boyfriend and the husband he would be, but as the father he could be. Patient. Kind. Understanding. Always ready to teach instead of command, to explain instead of excuse.

And he deserved that.

"You'd be a great father," is what I said out loud.

His face flashed with surprise.

"You would," I repeated. "You *will*."

And then his arms came around me, crushing me tightly to his chest.

"I love you so much, Ward," he murmured into my hair, and I could hear a catch in his voice that made me wonder what I'd said that was so wrong.

"Mace, I—"

"Marry me, Ward."

I pushed away from his chest so that I could see his face again. "I *am* marrying you," I pointed out.

He smiled, but it was a little melancholy, as he brushed the curls away from my forehead. "Even with Jackson and everything?"

I frowned at him. "With or without," I told him.

"Would you marry me tomorrow?"

"Absolutely, if that's what you want."

His fingers traced over my face, as though he were trying to memorize me by sight and touch. Then he sighed. "My mother would kill me."

"We could just not tell her."

He narrowed his eyes. "Then she would *really* kill me."

"So December, then?"

He pulled me back against his chest. "December."

I made a mental note to call Beck and beg for help. Not that Beck knows anything specifically about weddings, but she is classy as hell and knows just how things are *supposed* to be done. She'd yell at me for an hour because I should already have picked out... well, probably everything, but then she'd help.

And we probably needed it.

"Mace?"

"Hmmm."

"What's bothering you?"

He sighed again, his chest rising and falling under me. "I don't want to lose you," he whispered.

"Not going anywhere," I reassured him, gently stroking his skin with my fingertips. "Not ever."

"I know how much you dislike change, and this—all of this. Beyond the Veil, the Lost Lineage Foundation, the house, the wedding, and now Jackson..."

"But I have you," I said softly, my cheek still resting against the warmth of his skin. "So I can handle all that."

He kissed the top of my head. "I love you," he whispered into my hair.

I kissed his chest. "I love you."

6

We were another three days out from Jackson's visit from the Klan ghost, and so far, the poor kid hadn't had any more encounters with the angry dead or nightmares. Every day that passed, Mason got more edgy, particularly since it seemed like Keidra was acting as though everything was going to be just fine now that I'd banished the spirit who had caused the problem.

Mason thought there was probably more to it than just one ghost. Specifically, he was concerned that Jackson might be hiding smaller nightmares from his parents and Ben because he didn't want to leave home.

I couldn't blame the kid if that was true, but that didn't leave us with a lot of options—and Mason was worried that it was going to build up and do the magical equivalent of explode, which, he assured me, would not involve any literal explosions because Jackson didn't have a fire affinity.

And that made me wonder about things like gas explosions and spontaneous human combustion, although Mason claimed that fire witches apparently couldn't set *themselves* on fire with magic.

But even sans literal explosions, Mason didn't think things were going to be just fine, and as much as I wanted Jackson to be able to stay at home with his parents, I was pretty sure Mason was probably right. One, because Mason is usually right, and, two, because Mason is a witch. He'd been where Jackson was, and he knew full well what it was like.

Regardless, I was busily fussing about what might happen instead of actually checking my email or paying attention to the front door bell of Beyond the Veil's offices, which usually resulted in people shrieking when Mason was the first one to say hello.

I didn't hear any shrieks, so I almost made one myself when Mason poked his head through my office door. "Ward?"

I startled, then, I'm sure, looked guilty. "What?"

"Client. They need a medium. Or possibly Beck."

Oh, goodie.

Beck, aka Rebeckah Kwan, was a banisher, otherwise known as an exorcist, although that usually gave people the idea that she was banishing demons, not spirits, and, as far as we knew, demons did not actually exist. But if Mason thought we were looking at a possible banishment, I probably needed to come out of my office and talk to the client.

"Oh! Um. Coming."

I pulled up my moon-and-stars patterned gaiter mask, then rolled out from behind my desk and followed Mason out to the reception area, reminding myself yet again that we should probably hire an actual person to sit out there so that we didn't have to rely on either Mason or myself to hear people arrive—although with his hearing, Mason always did. But it would probably cut down on the number of yelps from alarmed clients and lower Mason's overall level of irritation.

The people waiting looked up as Mason led me back out. "This is Shoshana Duskevicz and Jacob Miller," he said, gesturing to a woman and man who appeared to be somewhere in their thirties.

The woman had dark brown, wavy hair and eyes that contrasted her fair skin. She was wearing a loose cream-colored blouse and a brown-and-green leaf-patterned mask. Her companion had thick, dark hair and what looked like a beard under his plain blue mask. His skin was a caramel-colored tan that contrasted with the navy blue of his button-down shirt. He kept wiping his palms on his grey chinos.

"Ms. Duskevicz and Mr. Miller, this is Edward Campion, our medium."

The woman stepped forward first. "Please, call me Shoshana. And thank you for speaking with us."

"Edward, please," I replied, shaking her hand.

"Jacob," the man said simply, also shaking my hand.

"What can we do for you?" I asked.

Shoshana and Jacob exchanged a look. "Well," Shoshana began, "We started renovating our house—we bought one of those old Victorians—and we think we might have a poltergeist. Or something."

Properly speaking, a poltergeist was a spirit who caused damage—either to property or people. Usually property, with electronics being the first thing that was likely to go.

Something about spirits and electronics didn't mix—Sylvia had accidentally shorted out one of Mason's monitors and an electric blender, so we were careful to keep her away from our laptops and phones, and Mason had threatened her with banishment if she broke his Kitchenaid. She could sit in cars without causing damage as long as she kept her hands away from automatic locks and windows and didn't try to go through the dashboard—according to her, anyway. She'd fortunately not destroyed any of those things on either Mason's truck or Beck's car. Yet.

"What exactly is it doing?" I asked them.

"Things keep falling off the walls and sills in the stairwell," Jacob answered. "Pictures. Figurines. A few potted plants."

"Were you always there when it happened?" I asked.

"Not always, but we've both seen it," Shoshana answered.

"But either of you? Not just one?"

"I've seen a few photographs fall," Jacob said. "Shana was there for a plant."

On the one hand, that was probably good. It meant the spirit wasn't fixated on one of them—it was generally really awkward and potentially deeply unpleasant to be the object of a ghost's obsession. On the other, it also meant it might be harder to convince the spirit to leave.

When the dead had a singular focus, removing that focus or dramatically altering it could be enough to break their connection to that thing or place or person. But if the ghost just wanted to wreak havoc, it was generally a lot more difficult to convince them to *stop* doing it. Not impossible, mind you. But harder.

As a medium, attracting spirits was my strong suit. As a whatever-the-fuck-else I was—a warlock, maybe?—I had no idea what I was doing, but spirits did nevertheless seem drawn to me. As a banisher, Beck had the opposite effect: spirits wanted nothing to do with her and were generally happy to agree to either behave or go away if it would make her leave them alone.

Not being dead, I had no idea *why* they were drawn to

me and repulsed by her, but it came with our respective arcane talents. I asked Sylvia once, and she had completely failed to explain it.

"I'd be happy to come out and take a look," I offered to Shoshana and Jacob. "See what it is we're dealing with a little more, well, literally."

They exchanged another glance.

"Is that... I mean... How much will that cost?" Shoshana asked, clearly understanding that this kind of work probably wasn't going to come cheap.

I nodded to show my understanding of her situation. "That depends very much on what we find. A preliminary visit and evaluation will cost a few hundred at most. If we need to hold a séance, that will raise it a little more. And if we're looking at a full-blown banishment, well, that tends to raise the cost again." I held up a hand to stop any protests or further questions. "That said, we also take into consideration what your budget is, and we do have ways of offsetting the expense if it becomes necessary."

"What ways?" Jacob asked, exchanging a glance with Shoshana.

Mason jumped in. "In some cases, we have partner organizations that might cover some of the costs, particularly for cases that take extra time or require additional research." He didn't say that one of those organizations might be the Richmond Police in the event that the ghost was haunting the house because they were a murder victim. Murder victims were a fairly frequent cause of poltergeist activity. Murder, suicide, and jilted lovers, although the last often fell into one of the other two buckets, as well. "And we have some funds we can draw from to defray some expenses for very particular cases." He smiled, his lips twisting around his lower canines.

The Skeleton Under the Stairs

Both Jacob and Shoshana blinked at him.

"We'll figure something out," I said. "So that you get the help you need. For now, let's just start with the first visit?"

Shoshana's eyes crinkled over the top of her mask, suggesting a smile. "That sounds good."

7

I was finishing washing the dishes—something I could do now without giving myself a horrible kink in my spine, thanks to our new kitchen sink setup—after an amazing meal of cheese enchiladas and salsa verde. Mason still did most of the cooking, and the new sink made it so that I could at least feel like I was a contributing member of the household.

It was actually rather surprising how important that was to my mental health. Now that I could *help*, it felt less like Mason did nothing but take care of me.

So even though dishes are nobody's favorite thing to do, I was actually quite happy doing them, humming to myself as I rinsed the suds from a stainless skillet. I was about to dry it when I felt Mason's warm fingers run over my scalp.

"Hey."

He continued to play with my curls, humming softly in response.

I smiled as I took the dishtowel and polished it over the surface of the pan, wiping away the moisture. "Are you trying to tell me I need a haircut?"

Mason hummed again. "No." He also didn't stop running his hands through my hair.

"You just want to mess it up?"

"You're done with the dishes, right?"

"Yes?" The skillet had been the last thing.

"Good."

And then I felt his lips just behind my ear as he pulled my head to the side with his hands. I sucked in a breath as he started to kiss his way past the faint stubble on my jaw, then down the side of my neck to that sensitive spot where it met my shoulder.

Mason hummed softly into my skin as he moved his hands from my hair to my shoulders, running them down my arms.

I reached up and behind me, threading my fingers into his braids so that I could bring his lips to mine. He tasted like spices and malt barley, his tongue warm as it gently teased mine.

I drank him in, loving the feel of his mouth against mine, the scrape of his lower canines, and the gentle vibration as he let out a low half-growl against my lips.

I pulled away from him just far enough to speak against his lips. "Are we going to christen the kitchen, or...?"

"Hold on." His voice was low and deep, and I immediately put my arms around his neck as Mason lifted me out of the chair, leaving the kitchen and carrying me with quick strides down the hall to the bedroom.

My eyes widened as he crossed the threshold. Candles dotted the room, glowing softly, and the bedcovers had been turned down.

I shifted in Mason's arms. "Did I forget something?" I asked, mildly concerned.

His lips twisted in a smile. "No."

"Then...?"

His eyes shimmered like fire in the flickering light. "No reason."

Apparently I just have the most romantic boyfriend—*fiancé*—ever. I wasn't about to complain, although I was now feeling a little guilty about it, since the most romantic thing I'd come up with in the last month was not bothering to put pj pants on when I came to bed.

A candlelit bedroom for no reason was several miles beyond not putting on pants.

He gently set me on the edge of the bed, keeping me caged in by his muscular arms as he leaned forward to kiss me again, sucking on my lower lip a little before stepping back and pulling his black t-shirt off over his head.

I reached for my own shirt, but Mason shook his head. "Let me?"

I let go of the hem and nodded. "Okay." My voice was a little breathy.

Mason undid the button on his jeans, pushing them and his boxer-briefs down off his hips at the same time, his semi-hard erection catching a little on the waistband before freeing itself.

I swallowed, staring, watching as the blood stiffened his cock, shifting its hue more toward a dusky brown. I could feel my own reacting to Mason's arousal, my cargo pants becoming less comfortable by the second.

Mason hooked his fingers in the hem of my slightly-ratty *Star Wars* t-shirt, then pulled it up over my head and tossed it aside, bending to tilt my head back and kiss me again. Then he gently nudged my shoulders until I leaned back, letting him gently push me down.

He ran warm hands down my chest, then quickly undid the button and fly on my cargo pants. I expected him to yank them off, but, instead, he slid his hands inside my boxers at the hip, pushing them slowly down my thighs so that he could stop and take my erection into his mouth.

I groaned at the wet heat of his lips and tongue, shuddering at the smooth scrape of his lower canines against me. I heard him draw in a long breath, then release it on a low growl. His fingers tightened on my thighs, and the vibrations as he hummed around me made me gasp.

And then he went back to stripping off my clothes, and I sucked in a quick breath as the cool of the air hit the sensitized skin of my cock.

My pants went somewhere on the floor, and then Mason was back, one heavy thigh crossed over my hips. "Move back," he growled against my cheek.

I moved, scooting my way up the bed until I hit the stacked pillows against the headboard.

Mason followed, crawling up after me until he straddled my hips, my erection pushing against the inside of his thigh.

He bent and kissed me again, his arousal pushing hot and thick against my stomach. I whimpered into his mouth.

He broke the kiss with a teasing nip at my lower lip, easing himself off me and grabbing a pillow from his side of the bed. "Roll onto your stomach."

I obeyed, and he helped lift my hips to tuck the pillow under me before leaning forward, his chest pressed against my back as he kissed the top of my spine, then slowly began to work his way down, his palms sliding along my sides, down my hips, and along my thighs as he went.

My breath was ragged by the time he kissed my tailbone.

I don't know where he'd stashed the lube, but I heard him open it, my breath catching in anticipation.

He gently nudged my thighs apart with his knees,

making space and giving himself access to my body so that he could slowly ease one slicked finger inside me.

I whined.

Warmth pressed against my back, although he didn't remove his hand, still stroking gently. "Impatient," he whispered.

"Ye—ah," I agreed, the word almost incoherent as he rubbed his finger against my nerve endings.

He hummed, and a second finger joined the first, pulling a groan out of me as he stretched me, teasing. Lips brushed kisses against my shoulder blades, along my ribs, over the knobs of my spine.

My hands tightened in the sheets as he added a third finger, my eyes closing as I reveled in the feel of his fingers inside me, his palm and lips against my skin.

I felt spun tight, my body a taut string, heat coiled heavy in my belly. "Mace, please," I whimpered.

Fingers toyed with me.

"Please what?" His voice was low and gravely.

"P-please fuck me," I begged.

He growled, then withdrew his hand, and I gasped at the sudden emptiness. Then hands were on my hips, his legs easing mine wider, and I felt the slicked heat of him pushing against me. I whined again, trying to push back against him.

The friction of the pillow against my erection was both too much and not enough, and I half-growled myself, drawing a deep chuckle out of Mason.

"So fucking impatient." But he took pity on me, pushing into my body in a single, smooth thrust, and I gasped as he stretched me wide, sparkles flickering behind my eyelids.

He waited, letting my body relax, his big palms smoothing over my hips and lower back, easing, soothing.

I forced myself to stop gripping, to make room for him to

move, because that was what I wanted more than anything else. For Mason to fucking move.

As if sensing my thoughts, he settled his hands around my hips again, easing himself back out, then back in, more slowly than I wanted, but fast enough that I was panting from the motion.

I pushed myself up on my elbows, my fingers still fisted in the sheets, so that I could push back onto him using my arms, and he let out a half-snarl that went straight to my already-aching cock. He increased the pace, and I could feel the impact against my hips and prostate as he moved in and out of me.

It was fucking incredible.

Mason's fingers tightened on my hipbones, and his rhythm faltered a little. Then he drove himself deep and hard, causing me to cry out, one, two, three times before a low moan escaped his lips, and I felt him pulse inside me, bringing me with him as I spent my orgasm into the pillow.

I lay there, my heart still racing as I felt him softening inside me. I groaned a little as he slid out of me, then rolled onto his side and pulled me against him, cradled against him like a little spoon. I could feel his chin on the top of my skull, one arm under my head and the other resting on my thigh.

I pulled the hand from my leg around my chest, then pressed kisses to each finger, feeling the faint vibration against my back as Mason hummed.

In the flickering candlelight, his skin was duskier than usual, mine tinted faintly umber against it. I threaded my fingers through his, enjoying the contrast between his brown-green and my orangey-pink.

"They're hands," he murmured into my hair.

"And I love them," I countered, drawing an amused huff from him.

"I love *you*."

———

"Kei?"

I blinked blearily. The clock read twenty-two minutes past one, and Mason was already out of bed.

"Kei, you have to take a deep breath."

That didn't sound good.

I scooted down to the end of the bed to my chair, heaving myself into it before rolling across the room for a t-shirt as Mason struggled to put one on while still holding the phone to his ear.

"Kei, I'm on the way, but you have to calm down."

Definitely not good.

"Keidra."

Oh, boy. I started down the hall, knowing Mason could get to the truck faster than I could, even barefoot.

I made it out to the passenger side by the time he did. "That's good," he was saying. "Deep breaths. Try to get Ben to take deep breaths."

Ben? I wondered if Ben had magic, too, or if, God forbid, something had happened to him. I really hoped he was just scared, and that he was okay. And that Jackson was okay.

"It'll be okay. I'm at the truck, and we'll be there really soon."

I noticed that he'd found ear buds and put them in, the phone in his pocket. Mason loaded me in the truck and threw my chair in the back, talking to Keidra the whole time.

"What does it look like?" he asked, and I could hear the

The Skeleton Under the Stairs

sharp edge to Keidra's response, even if I couldn't hear the words. "Okay. Get cool water on it, but make sure you use a damp cloth, something not fuzzy, or it will stick to his skin."

Mason drove quickly down the turnpike, probably a good fifteen to twenty miles over the speed limit.

That scared me more than anything else, since Mason was usually really cautious about his driving. Not that he wasn't still being careful, but he generally didn't go much more than ten over, and he only went that high with the speed of traffic. There were very few cars on the road, and he even ran a couple red lights, his voice low and soothing as he talked to Keidra about what she could put on Ben's injury, about making sure that they didn't touch Jackson, even if he seemed calmer, about how important it was that she and Deon stayed calm.

I tried to follow his advice, too, but my heart was in my throat as we zoomed past fast food restaurants and storefronts and a couple abandoned hotels. Even those that weren't permanently closed had their lights off and shutters down, some of them with security gates or those stark white floodlights in the front that just made everything seem darker and more empty.

My anxiety wasn't helping, either.

I drew in a long breath, blowing it out slowly so that Mason wouldn't be disturbed by it as he talked to Keidra, but the hand that briefly patted my thigh told me he heard anyway.

We made it to Keidra and Deon's house in less than fifteen minutes, and I let out a sigh of relief when Mason pulled into the driveway, both because we were there and because we'd arrived in once piece without any incidents and without getting pulled over.

Nobody came outside to meet us, and I could see a

muscle working in Mason's jaw. "We're here, Kei. Yeah, I have one." He hung up, tapping one of his ear buds.

"Just go, Mace. If you need me, I'll be here."

I saw him take a breath.

"*Go*," I repeated.

He went.

There is nothing quite like the feeling of sitting helplessly on your ass waiting to find out if things will be okay or if something has gone horribly, horribly wrong. Okay, to see if something is actually worse than you thought, when you already knew things were bad.

I was deeply, profoundly aware of the *tink* of the truck's engine cooling down, the way the closed doors muted the sounds of wind and the rustle of the leaves on the tree beside the driveway.

At least I wasn't hearing any screaming from inside the house. Although screaming meant people were alive and conscious...

I told myself to stop thinking about it.

It didn't work. I honestly didn't expect it to. But I had to try to keep my own brain from running through every possible worst-case scenario it could think of somehow.

I deliberately didn't pull my phone out to look at the time.

It felt like forever.

It was probably about ten or fifteen minutes.

The garage door opened, and Deon came out, wearing striped pajama pants and a t-shirt with a pair of flip flops.

He half-shuffled out to the truck and came over to the passenger side. I opened the door.

"How are you doing, Deon?" I asked. It was kind of a stupid question, but it was probably better than asking if everything was okay. Because I already knew it wasn't.

He nodded, and I could see the lines of strain around his mouth. "This is it," he said.

I understood. Jackson was coming home with us. My stomach was working its way upward toward my throat. I swallowed, then nodded. "We knew it was coming," came out of my mouth. Also a stupid thing to say, but I wasn't a big fan of bullshit platitudes, which were the only other things I could think of.

A frown furrowed his forehead. "Would it make more sense for me to just carry the chair inside and then put you in it? Or—"

"Yeah, probably," I answered. Moving me *in* the chair was a lot more difficult, although Mason did it fairly often. Deon was in pretty good shape, but he wasn't a six-seven orc.

Keidra's husband nodded once, then went to the back of the truck and took out my chair, dropping it off inside the back door before coming back for me. I put my arm around his shoulder, and he hefted me with a soft grunt and expelled a breath upon putting me in the chair when he got me there.

I felt a little guilty, but I couldn't exactly change my weight or suddenly make my legs work.

Breathing a little hard, Deon gestured for me to proceed him, and I rolled myself ahead of him into the kitchen. I paused, waiting for Deon to give me further directions, although I could hear Mason's low voice from somewhere deeper in the house.

"They're in the family room," Deon supplied, and I rolled my way through the kitchen and across the dining area to a short hallway leading into the family's main gathering space.

I made sure to clear the entryway before stopping again,

taking in the scene as Deon moved past me to rest a hand on Keidra's shoulder. Mason's twin had tears sliding down her cheeks, although she seemed otherwise fairly composed. Impressively so, given the fact that one of her sons was undergoing a magical transformation, while the other...

Mason was tending to Ben, who was lying on the couch, his chest heaving with pain or suppressed sobs. Jackson was curled up in a beanbag chair in the far corner, his arms clutching a stuffed white leopard to his chest, his eyes bloodshot, tears still leaking down his cheeks. I remembered being that kid, scared and alone.

I began to roll toward him, but Mason interrupted me. "Not just yet, Ward, please."

I stopped, offering Jackson a smile I hoped was reassuring, instead. It wasn't the same, and I knew it.

I tried to do the next best thing, drew in a deep breath, and reached out into the aether. *Dom?*

I felt his reassuring presence behind me. **Oh, *mijito*.**

Jackson looked over, his eyes wide and hopeful. I didn't have to say anything more, as Domingo Reyes, Mason's deceased grandfather and Jackson's great-grandfather, moved across the room to kneel beside Jackson. **It will be all right, *mijito*,** he told the boy. **It may not seem so now, but it will work out. Your uncle is a skilled healer. Your *hermano* will be fine.**

Jackson nodded, and Dom ran an insubstantial hand over Jackson's thick hair. The boy shivered slightly, but he didn't seem upset by the ghost's touch.

Thank you, Dom.

He turned to look at me. **Thank you for thinking of me, Ward.**

I nodded once.

I couldn't hear if Jackson was saying anything to his

The Skeleton Under the Stairs

great-grandfather, but Dom was reassuring him that things would be okay, that it wasn't as bad as he feared, and all the usual sorts of things you say to someone to make them feel better about a terrible accident.

I hoped they were true, but I wasn't going to hold my breath.

Mason was still murmuring to Ben, his fingers tracing patterns across the boy's abdomen. I wondered what, exactly, Jackson was capable of doing—and what he would be capable of someday when he had control of his magic.

But I was also worried about Mason. Yeah, he was a witch, and a strong one, if his gran could be believed, but could Jackson hurt him if he wasn't prepared for an accidental attack? Could Jackson still hurt him even if he was? And if Jackson was a death-witch, did that mean he could accidentally *kill* one of us?

Because I totally wanted to worry about *that* on top of worrying about traumatizing the poor kid by being a terrible step-uncle-person, to say nothing about the kind of shit I accidentally brought home with me. Like ghosts and homicidal ex-boyfriends.

I tried to tell myself to stop focusing on all the worst-case scenarios, but I'm not exactly an optimistic person by nature. The best things I could come up with at the moment involved Jackson resenting me for being a terrible step-uncle and Mason dumping me over it.

I really needed to work on my positive attitude, but that was pretty hard when I was watching one kid whimper in pain and the other quietly crying to his dead great-grandfather.

On the couch, Ben let out a gasp, and I watched Deon's fingers tighten on Keidra's shoulder. A quick glance over at Jackson showed that the younger boy's eyes were wide, fresh tears spilling from them, his small hands gripping his leopard.

"That's it," Mason said, soothingly. "Deep breaths, nice and easy."

Ben obeyed, sucking in another lungful of air.

"Better?" Mason asked him, and Ben nodded, spurring sounds of relief from both his parents.

Mason sat back on his heels, looking up at me as Keidra and Deon hugged Ben, running their hands over him gently to reassure themselves that he really was okay.

Mason looked exhausted—not just the kind of tired that happens when you wake up only a few hours into sleep, but the kind of bone-deep fatigue caused by giving all your energy to something. Like healing your nephew.

I knew what that felt like.

Mason looked up and met my eyes. I held his sunburst gaze until he reached out a hand to me, and I wheeled myself over to take it. "You okay?" I whispered.

He nodded, then squeezed my fingers before pushing himself to standing. I watched as my fingers slipped from his as he walked across the room to kneel beside Jackson and his leopard on their beanbag chair. I winced inwardly as I watched Mason steel himself before reaching out to touch Jackson—and then the boy flinched away from him, and I understood that the preparation had been because he didn't want to react to Jackson's fear, not because he was afraid of the boy.

My heart wrenched for both of them.

When Mason was able to pull Jackson gently into his arms, the floodgates opened, and Jackson sobbed into his chest, one arm around Mason's neck, the other still clinging to his leopard like a lifeline.

The Skeleton Under the Stairs

It was almost four in the morning before Deon and Mason had convinced Keidra that Jackson had to come home with us. It was also clear, even to me, that she knew from the beginning of the argument that Jackson couldn't stay at home. But she didn't want to say it, because admitting it somehow meant—even though it really, really didn't—that she'd failed her baby.

I had no idea what to say or do. I was the literal and proverbial extra wheel... well, set of wheels.

I wasn't a member of the family. I had no idea how to cope with kids. I wasn't a witch, even if I was whatever the fuck magical thing I was. Warlock. Wizard. Whatever. The point was, I was in way, way over my head here on every conceivable front.

I also felt really bad about feeling bad—self-pity isn't attractive when it's justified, and right now I was not any of the multiple people in the room who would be justified in feeling self-pity. So, instead, I was firmly mired in self-loathing combined with guilt and swirled with a liberal dash of terror.

Mason and Deon were upstairs helping Jackson to pick out clothes and shoes and put his toothbrush into a bag, and Keidra was sitting with Ben, coaxing him to drink some hot chocolate.

I was in my chair by the front door, waiting for my life to completely change.

My issue, if I thought about it, which I kind of couldn't help because I didn't have anything else to do, was really that I was getting really fucking sick of things happening *to* me. My parents' deaths. Moving halfway across the country to live with my Auntie Pearl, who I loved, but hadn't known much at all when I was six. Getting Arcanavirus. Having a pissed-off ghost try to rip out my spine. Tyler-fucking-Lessing.

And now this.

There was nothing I could do about it. Sure, I could try to help Jackson learn to speak with the dead and try to be the most supportive step-uncle I could, but I also recognized that I was just as much in need of being taken care of as I was able to help take care of a nine-year-old.

All of which made me feel that much worse about myself, because exactly nothing tonight was about me.

I looked up as Mason came down the hall, Jackson riding on his hip, the boy's dark head tucked against Mason's shoulder, his leopard clutched against his chest.

"Hey, Jax. Can you wait with Ward for me?"

Years of working as a medium were the only reason I kept my expression neutral.

Jackson whimpered something into Mason's neck that I couldn't make out.

"Don't you worry about Ward," Mason replied, settling Jackson down, then crouching so he didn't loom over the boy. "He's survived a really mean ghost and an even meaner man. He's totally tough, okay?"

Jackson gave me the kind of doubtful look only a kid can. "Okaaay."

I was equally skeptical, but I offered Jackson a tired smile as Mason turned and headed back into the living room. "You can tell me about your leopard," I suggested. Kids liked that, right?

Jackson looked down at the stuffed toy. "He's a snow leopard," he said softly.

"Yeah? What's his name?"

Jackson sidled closer to me. "Everest."

"After the mountain?"

He nodded. "Snow leopards live in the Himalayas."

"They do?" It was a genuine question. I don't really know shit about biology or zoology or whatever field it is that studies where animals lived.

"Yeah."

"Is that the only place they live?"

He shook his head. "No." He came closer, so that I could have touched him, if I wanted. "They live in Russia and parts of India, too. In the mountains. Where there's snow."

"That's why they're white?"

He nodded, then held out the toy, showing me its tail. "And their tails are long so they can jump from rock to rock."

"Like mountain goats?"

Jackson's lips quirked. "But no hoofs."

"No? You sure?" I took one of the toy's feet and looked at it as though expecting it to be a goat's hoof.

Jackson actually smiled. It was small and quickly gone, but it was there. And it made me think that maybe I wouldn't be completely terrible at this whole step-uncle thing.

And then Deon and Mason came back downstairs, Deon with a duffel and Mason with a backpack, another duffel, and a toy chest.

I watched Jackson's eyes fill with tears.

"Hey," I reached out a hand and put my fingers on his wrist without thinking.

He sucked in a sharp breath, his dark eyes wide as he stared at me. Nothing bad had happened when I touched him, so I went with it.

"It's okay to be sad," I told him. "But it's gonna be okay.

Your mom and dad and Ben still love you, you just have to come and live with us to learn magic, right?"

He nodded, tears tracking down his still-baby-round cheeks.

"And you'll see them at family dinners, and we'll find other stuff to do, okay?"

Another nod.

"Can you help your Uncle Mason with your backpack?"

He nodded again, turning toward Mason and his dad, but then he stopped. "Will you—will you hold Everest?"

"Of course. I'll keep him nice and safe in the chair with me. Deal?"

Jackson handed over his leopard and went to take his backpack from Mason.

"Do you want to give your mom a hug first?" Mason asked him, and Jackson nodded tearfully.

"Kei!" Deon called her.

Keidra, her eyes bloodshot, came into the hallway.

Jackson approached her slowly, and I saw her eyes skip up to Mason, who nodded, and she immediately enfolded a crying Jackson in her arms, murmuring against his hair. It took a few minutes for her to let him go, and Deon ran a hand over Jackson's hair and onto his back, guiding him toward the door. "Come on, Jackson." Deon's voice was a little rough.

The boy took his small backpack from Mason's big hand and walked past me to the front door, his back completely straight. I rolled myself out as far as the stoop, but I knew better than to try to jump down steps in my chair. The one time I'd tried on the curb, I'd ended up with road rash and a sprained wrist, which had made getting around even more impossible than usual.

So I watched as Mason and Deon loaded Jackson and

his meager belongings into the truck, the boy tucked into the back seat with his backpack, his bags and chest in the bed. Deon stayed with Jackson while Mason came and lifted me down the steps.

He walked with me as I rolled my way back to the passenger side of the truck. "Are you okay?" he asked softly.

I looked up at him sharply. "I'm the last person tonight who should be answering that question."

"You didn't ask for this, though." He sounded worried.

I shrugged. "I didn't ask for a lot of things," I replied, even though I'd mentally been down this road only about fifteen minutes earlier. "Doesn't mean I can't figure out how to make the best of them."

The look he shot me said he knew me better than that. But it's true. I'm not an optimistic person, but I think I've actually done pretty well with my sudden career change from IT technician to medium, and I'm learning to cope with being paraplegic. I like to think I bounce back pretty well, even if I do still have nightmares sometimes.

Mason lifted me into the cab, and I settled in as he put the chair in the back. Deon hugged Jackson one more time, then patted my shoulder before closing the rear door. He said something briefly to Mason, then went to stand on the stoop, watching as Mason got in and backed us out of the driveway, Jackson sniffling in the back.

I'd figure out how to be a step-uncle because I didn't have a choice. Because this was something Mason was committed to, and I was committed to Mason and everything that came with loving him.

That didn't mean I wasn't terrified of fucking it up, but I was all in.

I turned to look at the scared little boy in the back seat of the cab and passed Everest the leopard back to him.

"Everest was worried there for a few minutes," I told him. "He wasn't sure if he was going to get to come with you."

Jackson's eyes were big, and his petted the leopard's plush head. "It's okay, Everest," he told the leopard. "We're just—" His voice trembled, and I heard him swallow. "Just going to a new home where we can learn magic."

Even I could hear the fear in the words.

When I glanced over at Mason, I could see a muscle ticking in his jaw, clenched by emotion. I put a hand on his thigh, and he glanced over at me, a slight twist flashing across his mouth in acknowledgement.

"Is Everest excited to learn magic?" I asked Jackson, turning my attention back to him.

Jackson chewed on his lower lip and nodded.

"What is he most excited about?"

Jackson thought about this. "Learning how to keep people safe," he said, then. "From anybody who wants to hurt them. On purpose or—or by accident." He almost swallowed the last word, and my heart ached for him.

In my peripheral vision, I saw Mason rub at one eye.

"I bet you can both learn how to do that," I said. "Although I think you have to be pretty smart. But you're pretty smart. Is Everest as smart as you are?"

"Smarter," Jackson replied proudly.

"Yeah?"

The boy nodded. "He's not scared of the ghosts, and he knows when they're okay to talk to and when they're not."

"He does?"

I was getting a little weirded out having a conversation about Jackson in the third person through the persona of a stuffed snow leopard, but that's a thing kids do, so we were going with it.

The Skeleton Under the Stairs

Jackson was nodding. "He tells me when it's okay to talk to a ghost and when it isn't."

"How does he do that?"

Jackson shrugged. "He just does."

A glance told me that Mason was paying careful attention to our conversation—not that he would have any trouble hearing it—and his expression was thoughtful. I made a mental note to ask him about it later.

"Well, that's pretty cool. Sounds like Everest is a useful buddy to have."

Jackson nodded again. "Do you have someone like Everest?"

I was about to say no, then thought about it. "Kind of. Do you remember Sylvia?" She'd made appearances when the boys had been over before, and I'd introduced her to Jackson.

He nodded.

"Well, Sylvia helps me sometimes when I have problems with mean ghosts. She's not like Everest, of course, but she is pretty helpful."

Jackson thought about this. "Would she help me?"

"I'm sure she would." She'd seemed to like Jackson well enough, although I think he confused her even more than I did, rambling on about videogames and a school system that was centuries later than the one she remembered.

"D'you think I'll make a ghost friend like Sylvia?" Jackson asked.

"Maybe," I replied. "But I wouldn't try to rush it. It takes a very special ghost who likes you and really wants to stay around the living—*and* wants to help. It took me years of working as a medium before I met Sylvia."

"Years?" Jackson sounded suitably impressed.

"Five years," I replied, then had to conceal the smile that

threatened to surface at his wide-eyed expression. That was more than half his life, after all.

"Wow."

"So you might not find a ghost who wants to do that right away," I told him. "But you shouldn't worry about it. There's plenty you can learn to do without help from a ghost."

"Did you have to learn it on your own?"

I nodded. "I did."

"You didn't have a gran to teach you?"

"Nope. Nobody else in my family has magic." That I knew of, anyway.

"Wasn't that hard?" He was looking at me with awe.

"Yeah, it was. I'd have rather learned from your great-gran or from Mason, but I had my Auntie Pearl."

"But she doesn't have magic?"

"No, but she's got something more important."

"What's that?"

This was about to be the cheesiest thing I was pretty sure I'd ever say. "Love."

Mason smothered a snort, mostly successfully. I squeezed his leg.

Jackson made a face. "Love?" he repeated.

"I know it sounds dumb, but if you have family who love you, it can help you to be patient and figure things out. Without people who care about you and bring you cookies and macaroni and cheese, it's a lot harder to learn."

Jackson nodded sagely at that. "And cornbread," he added.

"You like cornbread?"

Another nod. "Yeah. With honey and butter."

I glanced over at Mason.

"We can manage that," he said, a small twisted smile on his lips.

"And chili?" Jackson asked hopefully.

"Not at four-thirty in the morning," Mason replied. "But I bet we can manage chili and cornbread for dinner tomorrow."

MASON HAD JUST GOTTEN Jackson settled, and the sun was coming up. I was sitting in the kitchen glaring out the window at the lightening sky and trying to decide if I wanted to try to go to bed or if I was going to give up and make coffee.

Mason decided for me, coming in getting out the *cafetera* coffee maker and coffee beans. As he pulled the grinder out of one of the long pantry cupboards, I interrupted.

"Won't that wake Jackson?"

Mason shook his head. "The door's pretty solid, and he sleeps like the dead." He grimaced. "You know what I mean."

"Yeah."

I could tell something was bothering him, so I waited, watching him measure out the grounds, put water in the *cafetera*, and set it on to percolate.

Mason drew in a long breath, then let it out again, his unfocused gaze still directed at the coffee pot.

"He could have killed Ben," he whispered.

I swallowed. "Really?"

Mason nodded. "He's strong enough. He had another nightmare, and Ben tried to wake him up." Mason sighed, then pulled two mugs off the set of hooks over the counter. "I guess they've been doing this for a while now, Ben waking him up when he has a nightmare so that their parents didn't find out and Jackson wouldn't have to leave."

"Shit," I breathed.

"I can't say that I blame them. Not really." He sighed again, pulling the small sugar bowl—mine, and shaped like a cat, with the tail as the handle of a spoon—across the counter. "Kei and I did the same thing when we were little." He shook his head. "Which is exactly why she should have known better."

"He's her baby, Mace. She didn't want to lose him."

Another heavy sigh. "I know, but he literally could have *killed* Ben." He sighed again, heavily. "I think he half woke up and realized what he was doing, then tried to take it back —and magic does *not* like it when you do that."

"Can you teach him, if he's a death-witch and you're a healer?"

"Yeees." Mason drew out the word, hesitant, thoughtful, as he measured out two spoons of sugar into each mug. "I have enough of a tie to life-death that I know how to control it. But I'll only be able to take him so far. He's got a lot of power, and I won't be able to teach him everything he'll be capable of."

I arched my eyebrows. "He's stronger than you?" From my understanding, Mason's magic was pretty strong.

That got me a shrug. "My life-death isn't as strong as his —if his secondary affinity is heal-harm, there will be things he won't be able to do that I can because that's where most of my power lies."

"So it isn't just about total magic—it's what bucket the magic falls into."

Mason let out a soft huff. "I suppose so. There are some things we'll both be able to do—and some things he'll have to learn on his own or find another witch to teach him."

"Should we introduce him to Rayn?" Rayn was the only other death-witch I knew.

Mason shot me a look that said I had just made a terrible suggestion. "Maybe in a decade when they're both capable of not setting the house on fire."

I snorted. "Even I know that two death-witches can't set a house on fire," I protested.

"Not with magic, maybe."

"Mace."

He huffed again. "Rayn is barely more under control than Jackson at this point. He's getting better and he's in a good place, but two immature death-witches in one room is asking for trouble."

"You think they'd end up killing someone?"

"I'm honestly more worried they'd end up *resurrecting* something."

I remembered a story Mason had told me once about a family dog that had died when he was little and decided that I didn't really have any interest in meeting the undead neighborhood pets.

"Yeah, okay. Maybe in a few years. Or only for short periods of time under close supervision."

The *cafetera* gurgled, and Mason pulled it off the burner and poured the coffee, then passed me a mug.

I took a sip, then sighed happily as the dark sweetness of the coffee hit my tongue and propelled the caffeine toward my befuddled and sleepy brain. Mason smirked at me over the rim of his coffee.

"What?" I asked.

"I just love watching you love coffee," he replied, and I could hear the smile in his voice.

"You make good coffee," I told him.

"Otherwise this would never work?"

I snorted, taking another sip. "Don't be ridiculous. It helps, but I could love you even if you didn't know what a coffee bean was."

That got him to chuckle. "So you'd take me over coffee?"

I narrowed my eyes at him. "I would—but I would not be happy about it."

"Don't worry, Ward. I know better than to take away your coffee." He reached out a hand. "Or at least I know enough to give it back. Come sit with me."

I handed him my coffee and followed him into the living room, snuggling up against his chest on the couch before retrieving my mug of lifeblood.

The morning light streamed in the window, and Peveril lifted his head from his fluffy bed on the cat tree as though asking why we were awake and what it was we'd had to run off to do in the middle of the night. I thought about calling him over, but then he put his head back down and closed his eyes, basking in the sun, so I didn't bother. He probably wouldn't listen anyway.

Alma's bed was empty.

"Where's Alma?" I asked Mason.

"On our bed."

I nodded. She had taken to imitating Pevs and curling up at the foot of the bed, which made things a little cramped sometimes, since she was a white German Shepherd and therefore not a small dog. Add a decent-sized cat and one six-foot-seven orc, and sometimes I was surprised that I fit in the bed.

I wouldn't change it for the world.

Except now we had.

"Are you sure you're okay with this?" Mason asked, as though reading my thoughts.

My brain went into panic mode. If I said yes, then

Mason would immediately call out the lie. If I said no, then I was the world's biggest dick, and not in a good way.

I wasn't 'okay' with it. But I was committed to doing everything I could to make this work for all three of us.

I felt Mason sigh behind me, and I knew I'd fucked it up.

"No, I mean yes, I mean... I want this to work. You, me, Jackson. I just. I'm scared," I babbled. I was such a mess.

One of Mason's arms—the one not holding a mug of hot coffee—pulled me tighter against his chest.

"You were great with him. Talking to him about his leopard. About magic. Keeping him from freaking out. That was a lot better than anything I was coming up with."

I grimaced. "Because you were exhausted from healing Ben and trying to calm your sister down," I protested. "Mace, you're *still* exhausted."

"Stop redirecting, Ward," he told me, although his tone was gentle.

I made a face, knowing he couldn't see it. "I just..." I trailed off, shrugging.

"You were you." Mason pressed a kiss to my temple. "Which is exactly what Jackson *and* I needed."

That made me feel a little—a very little—bit better. "You're still exhausted," I pointed out.

"I'll be fine."

"You're drinking coffee."

He chuckled, then took a swallow from his mug. "I am," he agreed. "And I may be having more before we're done with today."

"What else do we need to do?" I asked.

"Right now?"

"Yeah."

He pulled me closer. "Right now, I just need to hold you for a little while."

Emotion filled the back of my throat, but I nestled myself into his chest, turning so that I could rest my cheek against his pecs. I lifted my head far enough to take another sip of my coffee, then leaned into his warmth and strength again.

Mason ran his fingers along my bicep, his fingers tracing faint patterns. I couldn't tell at first whether they were just random movements or something more powerful, but then my skin began to tingle faintly.

It wasn't healing—that felt different. Then it hit me.

Protection.

He was casting a protection spell on me.

To protect me from Jackson.

My heart broke a little.

Mason was trying to protect me from a scared little boy who might very well accidentally throw death magic at me.

I rested my hand against his chest, the one on which I wore the bracelet Mason had cast for me, and his fingers paused.

"It's okay," I said, softly. "I don't mind. But may I remind you that I'm pretty hard to kill?"

Mason let out a small grunt.

"You think a nine-year-old has anything on a three-hundred-some-year-old necromancer?"

"The three-hundred-some-year-old necromancer *did* briefly kill you, remember?" His arm tightened around me.

"And you brought me back," I reminded him.

"I don't want to have to do that again."

"I don't want you to have to, either," I agreed. "But you can. If something happens."

I felt him sigh. "Let's hope it doesn't."

"Fair enough." I shifted so that I could drink more coffee. "Please tell me you moved the lube."

That got him to laugh. "Do you really want the answer to be yes?"

I grinned. "Mostly?"

He ran his free hand over my curls. "Just mostly?"

"First, what if Jackson wakes up? Second, I want to finish this coffee."

Mason let out a small hum. "Valid points," he acknowledged, lifting his own mug and taking a mouthful. "And yes, I moved it."

A tiny part of me *was* a little disappointed, I'll admit, but there was a good deal more relief. Not that I wouldn't have enthusiastically gotten on board if Mason had been in the mood, but the combination of anxiety and exhaustion was doing an absolute number on my mental state.

I felt Mason pull me a little tighter, felt the warmth of his breath against my scalp as he drew my scent into his lungs, and felt the tension in my body ease a little.

"Mace?"

He hummed the question into my hair.

"I love you."

Lips pressed against my skull. "I love you."

8

I was on my third mug of *café Dominicano* and it was still barely noon. Once upon a not-so-distant-time, I'd been used to habitual sleep-deprivation, running gigs until three in the morning, then having to be a functional human being by ten or eleven. Living with Mason and working at Beyond the Veil had spoiled me.

One-and-a-half hours of sleep was *not* enough to make me a reasonable human being. Even Mason, who is a far more patient person than I am on an ideal day, was cranky. He was trying to keep it under control, but I'd felt obligated to abandon the kitchen in order to answer work emails on the couch because I kept getting in the way. He hadn't *said* anything, but the pinched lips and flared nostrils every time he had to move around me—and I'm a bit annoying to have to move around—said that it might be a better idea to *not* be underfoot.

So, instead, I'd answered several query emails and was starting to run through the checklist we'd need for the Duskevicz-Miller house. We were supposed to go in two days, and I had yet to talk to Mason about whether or not we'd actually be able to keep that date...

We needed to order more sage and chalk, so I did that while I waited for Mason to finish whatever he was doing in the kitchen. I'd just sent off the order when a cold nose pressed against my thigh.

"Hey, sweetheart. What's up?" I half-signed *outside* with one hand at Alma, who had come over to put her head on my lap.

Her tail thumped repeatedly, which was her way of answering in the affirmative, so I heaved myself off the couch and into my chair, tapping its side to get the big white shepherd to follow me.

Mason was cutting up cucumbers and already had an assembly line of bread, lettuce, and what looked like curried tofu salad going on the counter. He looked up at me, pausing his slicing, eyebrows raised in a silent question.

"I'm going to take Alma for a walk."

He nodded, still silent, and I felt a little bit of worry tighten in my chest. But I knew he was exhausted, so I didn't say anything, moving through the kitchen to the back room to pull on shoes and get Alma's harness on her.

I was sitting back up when I felt Mason's hands on my shoulders and turned. He bent and kissed me. "Make it a short one?"

"Fifteen?"

He nodded.

"Sure." I offered a smile and was happy to see it returned. I didn't ask if he was okay, because I knew he wasn't. I just took Alma's leash and clipped it to my chair and headed out to take her around the block.

Mason had gotten Jackson up by the time I came back, and lunch was set up on the counter. Jackson was looking suspiciously at his sandwich, and I suppose I couldn't blame him. While I thought Mason's curried tofu salad was delicious, a nine-year-old might have other ideas about bean curd, yellowish vegan mayonnaise, celery, green onions, and raisins. Especially a nine-year-old who hadn't been raised in a vegetarian household.

"Just try it, Jackson," Mason told him, and I could hear the slight exasperation in his tone.

"Okaaay." Jackson didn't sound convinced, but he picked up a triangle of his sandwich and put the very tip in his mouth, his nose already wrinkled up.

Mason was already headed for the fridge, presumably preparing to pull out cheese or peanut butter or some other child-approved food.

Jackson, however, was contemplating the sandwich and chewing, the wrinkle having smoothed out a bit from his nose.

"Whadda you think?" I asked him.

"It's... weird," he answered. "But okay."

In my peripheral vision, I saw Mason pause before opening the fridge. Instead of the peanut butter, he pulled out a bottle of ranch dressing and poured some in a small dish, which he set beside the bowl full of carrots, cucumbers, and peppers.

I took a red pepper and dipped it, then popped it into my mouth, chewing as I pulled a sandwich onto my own plate. "What kind of sandwiches do you usually have for lunch?" I asked Jackson.

"Peanut butter and pickles."

"And *pickles*?" I asked, vaguely horrified.

Jackson nodded, taking another small bite of his sandwich. "Yeah. Dad makes them. They're good."

"What kind of pickles?"

"Bread and butter."

I suppressed a shudder at that answer.

"Well, we can do that," Mason remarked, his tone neutral, taking two sandwiches of his own and joining us.

But Jackson shook his head. "Nah. It's okay." He took another bite.

Mason's sunburst eyes found mine over the top of Jackson's small head. I shrugged. Mason let out a breath, then took a bite of his own sandwich.

"So, Jax," Mason began.

Jackson looked up, his eyebrows raised in a manner that was startlingly familiar, and I smiled, hiding the expression behind another bite of sandwich.

"I'm going to need you to make a list of things to get from your mom this weekend."

"Things?" Jackson asked.

"Mmhmm. We brought some of your stuff, but I want you to keep a running list of anything you want or need that we didn't remember."

"Oh. Okay."

"You see that little white board on the fridge?"

Jackson nodded, then dipped and ate a baby carrot.

"Put your list on there. Then we'll call your mom and figure out when we can get it. Okay?"

"Okay."

"And your mom is going to call the school and get the rest of your work for the year." It was late May, so Jackson only had three more weeks of school—but he wasn't going to be able to go back until he got his magic under control.

I'd asked Mason how long that would be, and he'd shrugged, saying it depended on Jackson.

I really hoped it wouldn't take longer than summer—because I didn't think I was up to being a home-school teacher on top of everything else. Not that Mason couldn't do it—he was a former professor, so he probably knew a thing or two about teaching—but he didn't need any more jobs, either.

Jackson had made a face at Mason's announcement of homework, and I didn't blame him. "Do I have to do virtual school?" he asked.

"Not unless your teacher says so," Mason answered. I knew some schools had virtual options for kids who contracted Arcanavirus or in case there were classroom outbreaks, but I didn't know if Jackson's school was one of them. I remembered giant packets and instructions from the first year after Arcana broke out before the schools managed to pivot to remote video learning.

"Ben had to do it last year for a month," he said. "He hated it."

Mason nodded. "I had to do virtual school for two years as a kid."

Jackson's eyes went wide. "Two *whole* years?"

Mason nodded. "When Arcanavirus first appeared, and nobody knew anything about it yet, nobody knew how to keep us from catching it. So we had a year of just homework, then two years of virtual school."

Jackson turned to me. "Did you have to do school that way, too?"

I nodded. "Yeah. But I didn't live here, then."

"Where did you live?"

I dipped a cucumber slice in the dressing, then ate it. "Well, when Arcana first started, I was in Michigan."

"Michigan! It's cold there, right?" Jackson asked.

"In the winter, yeah. It's really cold. But it's nice in the summer."

"When did you move here?"

"I was seventeen. But we lived in Baltimore and Chapel Hill, first."

"Did you like it in Michigan?" Jackson asked.

"Yeah, I think so. But I was younger than you when I moved to Baltimore."

"Why'd you move?"

I saw Mason open his mouth to say something, a slight furrow to his brow, but I answered before he could—presumably—tell Jackson to be less nosy.

"My parents died," I answered him.

Jackson's little face crumpled. "Oh."

I reached out and gently patted his hand. "It sucked, but it's okay. A lot of people got sick back then because we didn't understand the virus. My mom caught it really early, and nobody knew what to do."

"Did your dad get sick, too?" Jackson asked, his dark eyes focused intently on me.

"Yeah, but not with Arcana. Sometimes, people's minds get sick, and that's what happened to him when my mom died."

Jackson's frown was serious. "What made his mind sick?" he asked.

Mason was the one who answered, this time. "Some people have mental illnesses," he said. "A lot of people who have them are born with them—their brains don't make the same chemicals as other people, or they don't have enough of the right ones. And when really big things happen, especially if they're sad things, the sickness they already have gets worse. Sometimes a lot worse."

"And that's what happened to Ward's dad?"

"Mmhmm." Mason nodded.

Jackson looked at me, and I nodded, too.

"Did you go to live with your gran?" he asked me.

"My Auntie Pearl."

"You remember Pearl, Jax," Mason reminded him.

"The lady with all the cats, right?"

"That's her," I confirmed.

Jackson smiled. "I like her. She's funny."

I smiled back at him. "Yeah, she is. And I like her, too. She was pretty great to grow up with." I'd spent a lot of time wishing my parents hadn't died, but Auntie Pearl had been amazing. I was only just starting to appreciate how awesome she was—and I'd been a step-uncle for only a handful of hours.

We finished lunch, and Jackson begged to go outside with Alma, so Mason took them and I cleaned up, honestly a little relieved to have a break. Jackson was a good kid, but he was—like kids were—deeply curious and highly energetic. And I was exhausted.

So was Mason, of course, but we couldn't just leave the poor kid alone. So I was going to wash up, and then take over throwing a ball or something. Whatever it was that kids did in the yard. Sure, I'd been a kid once, but I wasn't the kind of kid who liked outdoorsy things. Or athletic things.

A glance out the window saw Jackson running in circles with Alma. I couldn't see Mason, although I knew he was probably watching both of them like a hawk. If all Jackson wanted to do was play with the dog, I could handle that.

I finished the dishes, dried my hands, and rolled myself out to the back porch. Mason was leaning on the railing, watching Jackson chase the dog, whooping with delight. I put a hand on Mason's back, and he turned to look down at me.

"This, I can handle," I told him. "As long as he doesn't want me to chase the stick, I'm good."

"Are you sure?"

"I can watch a kid play with a dog, Mace."

He let out a long sigh. "I'm sorry, Ward. I'm just—"

"Exhausted? Completely drained? Stressed out?" I rubbed my hand on his hip. "I know."

He offered me the flash of a twisted smile. "I don't want to overwhelm you," he said softly.

"You aren't. I got this. Go... I don't know. Finish setting up your desk. Or nap. Whatever."

He took a breath to say something, and then the phone in his pocket trilled. He pulled it out, then looked up at me for a second.

"Go on," I told him, and he went back inside.

I turned to watch as Jackson, still giggling, tugged at a good-sized stick that either he or Alma had found somewhere, Alma attached by her teeth to the other end, her tail wagging and her ears perked up. To her, this was a fun game. It seemed Jackson agreed.

It was a beautiful day, the sun high, the sky blue, and the humidity not yet at the stifling levels that it soon would reach during a Virginia summer. I pulled out my phone and took a few pictures of Jackson playing with Alma—it was idyllic. You'd never know, just from looking at the images, that the dog was deaf, the boy was a death-witch with the ability to cause considerable harm to someone just with his hand, or that the photographer was in a wheelchair because his spine had been irreparably damaged by a psychotic ghost.

I texted it to both Mason and Keidra.

Keidra sent back a series of little hearts almost immediately.

Mason sent nothing, but he might still be on the phone. I leaned back, enjoying the sun and Jackson's laughter as he talked to Alma, who of course had absolutely no idea what he was saying, but was enjoying the game of alternating fetch and tug-the-stick.

A warm hand settled on the back of my neck.

"Cute picture."

"Thanks."

"That was Fiona. She got me access to the Northampton archives."

I turned to look at him. "That's great."

He was frowning.

"Is that not great?"

"It is," he replied, the words slow and a little hesitant.

"But?"

Mason sighed. "But I can't take a whole day right now to drive out to Northampton with Jackson here."

I reached up and put a hand on his wrist. "I'm sorry, Mace."

"She's going to go for me," he replied.

"Yeah?"

"Can you... talk to her about what you can do?"

Right. Because the point of this trip was to figure out what the fuck I was. I hadn't really been sharing all of the gory details about my weird ghost-related abilities with everybody. Beck, yes. But I hadn't talked about them to Fiona or even Auntie Pearl.

"Yeah, I'll talk to her," I answered Mason. "She won't be much help otherwise."

One arm wrapped around my shoulders, and he kissed my cheek. "Thank you."

I turned my head so that I could kiss his lips. I'd meant it to be quick, but Mason wasn't having that, immediately deepening the kiss. I was more than happy to oblige.

"Eeeeeew. Gross."

I felt Mason smile against my lips before he pulled away and stood up.

"Do you say that to your parents when they kiss?" he asked Jackson, although his tone was teasing.

"Duh." Jackson rolled his eyes. "Kissing is gross."

Well, at least Jackson was an equal-opportunity anti-kisser.

9

We dropped Jackson off with his parents on Sunday morning so that we could head over to the Duskevicz-Miller house to deal with their poltergeist problem. Keidra and Deon would be hosting the family dinner, and we'd take Jackson home with us after that. Mason thought that as long as Jackson was awake, it would probably be fine, but he'd told both Jackson and Keidra that if anything seemed even slightly weird, they were supposed to call him.

I'd asked Dom to keep an eye on him, too, and Mason's grandfather gladly agreed. Not that he could *do* anything if something went wrong, but he absolutely could come and find me.

The house we pulled up to was a sprawling late-Victorian monstrosity that *looked* like it was haunted. This wasn't a painted lady with delicate tracery and pastel colors. This was a massive brick-and-stone Frankenstein's monster of a house that seemed as though it had been designed by at least three different architects all giving directions at the same time. Some of the stones were weathered and aged, their sandy tone blackening along the cracks and edges.

Looks aside, the damn thing *felt* haunted as Mason unloaded me from the truck, depositing me in my chair on the sidewalk. The hair on the back of my neck bristled, and the air around the house felt thick and oily, heavy and humid like an August afternoon without any of the warmth.

Oh, goodie.

"Ward?"

My face was so easy to read. I sighed. "This is not going to be easy," I replied in answer to Mason's question.

"Not easy as in...?"

"As in there's some nasty shit going on here, but I can't quite tell what," I answered.

Mason's brow furrowed over the top of his lavender-tinted sunglasses. "Nasty. Shit," he repeated. The deliberate pause between the words said that he was not pleased about this development.

I wasn't, either. God knew we had enough to deal with without having to cope with some sort of complicated supernatural problem.

Sorry. *Another* complicated supernatural problem.

"Can we call Beck?" Mason asked.

"Let me see what we're dealing with first. Then, yeah, if I need to, I'll call Beck."

Mason hefted me up the three front steps to the porch, then rang the doorbell as I pulled up my gaiter mask, this one black dusted with multihued glitter.

Shoshana answered the door, and I immediately noticed a dark bruise on her forearm. "Mr. Campion, Mr—Dr. Manning," she corrected herself. The corners of her eyes wrinkled as she smiled behind her sunflower mask.

"Edward, please. Can I ask if the spirit caused your bruise, Ms. Duzkevicz?" I inquired.

"Shoshana," she said almost absently. "And yes. It—well,

I suppose *threw* is the word—it threw a metal vase at me off a table on the landing."

"Ouch," I replied sympathetically.

Her eyes crinkled in another smile. "It wasn't the most fun evening," she admitted. "But please, come in."

She led us into the living room, which had probably been a receiving parlor when the house had first been built. The thick, greasy feeling that had hovered around the outside of the house was much stronger here, and I could feel the weight of *something* pushing against my chest.

Whoever—or whatever—was here did not appreciate my presence.

That was just too fucking bad.

I could feel Mason's eyes on me, confirmed when he removed his sunglasses. The lines of his face were serious.

But this is what I did for a living. I preferred it when the dead weren't overtly hostile, of course, but I was rapidly getting used to spirits of the more irascible variety. Apparently including this one.

I took the bag containing sage and candles off my lap and handed it to Mason.

"Would you like me to do something with this?" he asked.

I shook my head. "Let's try being civil first."

His expression said he was dubious about this plan, but he didn't say anything out loud.

I took a deep breath and opened my Third Eye.

And winced at the shriek that spiked through my skull. "Shit!"

I saw Mason shake his head sharply when Shoshana sucked in a breath to, presumably, ask why I'd said what I'd said. I rubbed at my temple with a finger, then followed the

The Skeleton Under the Stairs

source of the sound to the main staircase that led up from the front foyer.

A little girl, maybe five or six years old, wearing a stained sundress that looked like it was probably from a decade or so ago, was sitting on the bottom of the stairs, screaming.

Please stop that, I thought at her.

She did, thank God, but instead leveled a glare filled with absolute hatred at me. The expression was made more disturbing by her rosy cheeks and dark pigtail braids. Even for a ghost, she looked pale, possibly sickly.

Can you tell me why you're upset?

No! It was the petulant refusal of a child.

Why not? It was worth a try.

You're magic. Magic people are bad. Not what I was expecting.

Why are magic people bad?

She glared at me with colorless eyes. **You know why.**

I didn't. *I'm sorry*, I replied, *but I don't know why. I try very hard to be a good person, so can you tell me why magic makes people bad?*

The glare faded a little. **Magic people hurt people.**

Did magic people hurt you? I really didn't need to ask, but I did anyway.

They said they would let me go if I did what they said. That they would hurt me if I was bad, but it would be okay if I did what they asked. The glower returned to her face. **I did what they asked, and they still hurt me. And I'm still here, and they won't let me go home.**

They won't let you? That was slightly alarming and more than a little disturbingly close to what had happened at the Fitzwilliam house.

The little girl shook her head, her braids shifting against

her shoulders. **They made a spell, and I can't get out of it. I tried and tried.**

A containment spell of some sort, maybe on the house, maybe around it. "Mason?"

"Yes?" He was right behind me, but I didn't want to take my eyes of the girl.

"Can you check the house for a containment spell of some sort?"

"A what?" came Shoshana's voice from the doorway.

"A containment spell," Mason repeated for me. "It honestly could be the source of your problem if you have spirits who are trapped in the house and don't want to be. We eliminate the spell, and your spirits are free."

"Don't you need a witch for that?" she asked.

Even though I didn't turn, I could almost see Mason's smile.

"Oh," I heard her say. *Smart lady.*

Why is she smart? The little girl wanted to know.

I smiled at her, even though she couldn't see my lips. Expressions can be communicated mentally if you actually felt them. *Because she realized that Mason—that's my orc friend—can sense the spell because he's a witch.*

The girl's attention moved to Mason, but her expression was far more curious and less disgusted than the one she turned on me. **The magic people wouldn't like that,** she said. **They wouldn't like him.** She turned her pale eyes back on me. **I like him.**

"You've made a friend, Mason," I told him.

"Have I?" He sounded surprised.

"She likes you." *Can you tell me your name?* I asked her.

I'll tell him, she replied, pointing a tiny finger at Mason.

He can't talk to you, I told her. *Only I can.*

The Skeleton Under the Stairs

She frowned. **You aren't like the other magic people,** she said, then.

How am I not like the other magic people?

She studied me, the animosity from before rapidly diminishing. **You feel different. The same, but different.**

That wasn't particularly explanatory. *Can you say more?* I asked.

She frowned again, but it was a thoughtful frown rather than an angry one. **Like they do, only more.** Her expression darkened. **I want to talk to you. But I don't want to because you're like them. Sort of.**

Okay. I could work with that. *Well, I can tell Mason your name, if you'll tell me.*

She studied me.

If you don't want to tell me your whole name, you could just tell me something to call you. My name is Edward. Fair's fair.

She stared at me for a long time, and I saw something resolve on her face. **Jenny.**

It's nice to meet you, Jenny. Out loud, I said, "Mason, Jenny would like to be introduced." I waited until I felt him just behind my shoulder. "Mason, this is Jenny. Jenny, this is Mason."

He's big, the ghost observed.

"He is big," I replied out loud, mostly for Mason's benefit. Mason snorted softly.

"Are you talking to someone?" Shoshana whispered.

"I am," I answered. "Jenny, this is Shoshana. She lives in the house now. Are you the one who has been knocking things off the walls? And threw the vase at her?"

Jenny pouted. **It's my staircase,** she said. **Mine.**

The pieces came together.

"Shoshana? Have you done any work on the staircase? Or under it?"

It's mine! Jenny screamed. A picture fell off the wall, and Shoshana squeaked, alarmed. A big hand settled gently on my shoulder.

"U-under it? No..." Shoshana's voice shook a little.

"I think we may... need to," I replied, ignoring the shrieking ghost who proceeded to knock another photograph off the wall, followed by a small metal dish filled with spare change.

No no no no no!

Jenny. I waited for the child spirit to stop having her tantrum. She kicked the bowl across the carpet, sending it tumbling down the stairs to land near my feet. Then, in a flash, she stood beside it, glaring at me. *Are you ready to listen?* I asked her, as calmly as I could.

It's mine, she repeated, sullenly.

What is yours?

The cubby under the stairs. It's mine. It's all that's mine.

Jenny? Is your body under the stairs?

Insubstantial tears slid down her translucent cheeks. **It's mine.**

I know, I told her. *We'll be gentle. But don't you think that if we find your body, you might be able to leave?*

Her eyes widened. **Leave?**

I nodded. *Find your parents. Your friends.*

My mom?

I bet your mom is waiting for you beyond the Veil. I can help you cross over if you let us help you. Bring your body out of there.

Jenny chewed her lower lip. Maybe a minute passed while I held my breath before she answered me. **Okay.**

"Mason? Can you call Hart, please?" I asked.

"How many?" He inquired, already pulling out his phone.

"Just the one. For now."

"Who's Hart?" Shoshana asked.

"Special homicide detective with Richmond PD," Mason answered. "We work with him."

"Homicide?" Shoshana whispered.

"Your ghost seems to be here because her body is under the stairs," I put in, still not taking my eyes off Jenny, especially not after her little outburst. She watched me back, still and silent.

There's nothing quite like the judgment of the dead to make you edgy.

I could hear the low rumble of Mason's voice as he spoke to Hart. Shoshana drew in a couple deep breaths, trying to calm herself, presumably. I was more worried about Jenny, and didn't take my eyes off her.

It's mine, Jenny repeated, although whether to herself or to me, I wasn't sure. **I want it back.**

What's yours? I asked her. I'd thought she was talking about her body, or possibly the space under the stairs, but if she wanted it *back*, then that didn't make sense.

Someday I will learn not to be surprised by the fucked up shit that happens in my life.

This was not that day.

Tears hanging in her eyes, Jenny held her hands to her chest, and then reached out, something trapped between them. It took me a few seconds, but I realized with horror that she was holding a human heart. Judging by the dark stain that was spreading over the front of her dress, it was probably her own.

"Shit," I whispered.

"Ward?" Mason asked softly.

I shook my head. I'd explain later. I wasn't sure Shoshana would be okay hearing this particular detail.

"Hart will be here in about ten minutes," Mason told me.

I nodded. "Thank you." I couldn't stop watching Jenny's heart dripping its ethereal blood into the carpet.

Mason began speaking to Shoshana, their voices fading as he led her away from the stairs. Probably better that way.

When she was out of earshot, I refocused on Jenny. *They took your heart?* I made my thoughts soft, gentle.

The ghost of the little girl nodded.

Is that how you died?

Tears slid down her cheeks, and she nodded again.

I swallowed around that thought. *I'm sorry, Jenny,* I told her.

I want it back, she whispered.

I had no idea how we were going to do that. *We'll do our best to get it for you*, I promised. I wished I could be more certain, but I knew better than to make promises to the dead that I didn't know if I could keep.

The magic people took it. A frown creased her tiny features again. **They do things to it**, she said.

I blinked. *They do things to it?*

Jenny nodded. **It hurts.** The words felt like a sucker punch to the gut.

Just when I thought things couldn't get worse. Whoever had her heart was using it for some sort of magic that caused the little girl metaphysical pain.

We will help you, Jenny. I promise.

She studied me. **They cut it out with a fancy knife.**

Probably an athame. I nodded. *What else can you tell me?*

Her expression shifted to look thoughtful. **There were candles**, she said. **And there were funny drawings carved in the floor. They added more, with chalk. Like the kind you use in school.** A shadow flickered across her face. **I miss school.**

The Skeleton Under the Stairs

I couldn't think of what to say to that, but then Jenny kept talking.

They brought me here and put me in a room upstairs. At first the lady was nice to me and brought me candy and soft bread and soup. But then they took away Bear-bear and made me wear this dress and covered my head and took me to the room with the chalk and candles. They were wearing robes and hoods, and I was scared.

I still wasn't sure how to respond, but the words were pouring out of her now, and she didn't seem to mind that I stayed silent.

The ones who held me down had rough hands, and they made me hold still while they cut it out with the knife and took it away. Her voice—even though I couldn't actually hear her—hitched, her emotions still very much at the surface, even all these years later.

Jenny, I am so sorry this all happened to you, I told her. *We're going to help you. I promise.*

She studied me for a few moments. **Mom was a little wrong,** she said. **She said all magic people were bad, but you're a magic person and you're nice.**

Thank you, Jenny. I think you're nice, too.

She flashed me a smile that lit up her whole small face. **Most people are scared of me. I'm glad you're not.**

I didn't tell her she was fucking terrifying, because while she was, that wasn't something she needed to hear, and I wanted to help her a lot more than I was afraid of her. She wasn't responsible for the fact that some cult had trapped her here, after all.

The doorbell rang, and I just about jumped out of my skin.

Shoshana hurried out of the former parlor and opened the door. Mason waited behind her in the doorframe as she swung it open. A familiar voice greeted her with a lot more politeness than I usually warranted.

"Ma'am, are you Ms. Duskevicz? Detective Hart."

"Yes, detective. I—I'm afraid I have no idea what to do. It was Edw—Mr. Campion who said you should be called."

"Yes, ma'am, he usually is," came Hart's now more-familiarly sardonic tone.

"Please, come in. Whatever you need to do." Shoshana stepped back, allowing the elf and two CSI team members to enter the foyer.

"Ward." Hart's lips twisted in something that was half a smile and half a grimace.

"Hart," I replied.

"Whaddyou got for me?"

"A little girl, around five or six—"

I'm six! Jenny interrupted.

"Definitely six years old. I think she's under the stairs."

"Does, ah, this Jenny have a last name?"

I looked over at Jenny, who stared back at me blankly. *Can you tell me your full name, Jenny?*

Jennifer Martin.

I relayed this information to Hart, who scribbled it into his phone with a finger.

"Under the stairs?"

"Yeah."

The CSI techs began inspecting the wainscotting along the side of the staircase, and Hart turned to Shoshana. "We, ah, might have to remove some parts of your staircase, ma'am."

Shoshana nodded, a slight crease in her forehead a sign of resignation. "Well, we were hoping to leave that in one piece, but do what you need to do, I guess."

"Appreciated, ma'am." Hart turned back to the two techs. "What're we looking at?"

One of them, a short, pale woman with a long, dark ponytail, looked up, her eyes carefully made up to highlight the blue of her irises. "Actually, I should be able to get in there with a philips."

"I have one in the kitchen, if you want," Shoshana offered, seeming to brighten up a bit at the thought that they weren't going to take a sledgehammer to her stairs.

"Yeah, great! Thanks!"

Shoshana went and fetched the screwdriver, returning to hand it over to the gloved hand of the CSI tech, whose much larger partner held an evidence baggie for the screws as she pulled them out of the paneling.

The wainscotting piece came away easily once the screws were removed, although dust sifted down from the seams as they pulled it off. The smaller tech stuck her head into the opened cavity, then let out a whistle. "You're gonna want to see this, detective."

Hart looked down at me. "Are you ever wrong?"

"Not about dead people," I retorted.

Hart snorted, then eased around a potted palm plant to look in the cavity under the stairs. "Shit. Doc, this is all you."

I turned to look at Mason, who peeled himself away from the doorframe leading into the parlor to swap places with Hart, the CSI techs scooting back to give Mason's bigger body space.

"Well, that's... disturbing," he remarked calmly.

This was definitely not a day when I loved my job.

WE BARELY MADE it back to Keidra and Deon's in time for dinner, which was good old-fashioned grilled cheese sandwiches and tomato soup. Keidra had also made eggless oatmeal raisin cookies, and the boys had helped her turn them into ice cream sandwiches.

There were a few tears when Jackson had to hug his parents goodbye, but he brushed them away quickly, although I did notice that he held Everest the leopard particularly tightly in the truck on the way home. Mason managed to coax Jackson into talking about his day—playing with Ben, doing homework, helping Keidra in the kitchen—helping to ease him back into the generally cheerful little boy he usually was.

I couldn't help but compare Jackson, living and breathing, to Jenny, whose pale, dead eyes had watched as Hart and the CSI team had carefully removed her corpse from under Shoshana Duskevicz's stairs. The chest had been cracked open, which suggested that her heart had, in fact, been removed, although we'd have to wait for confirmation from the ME's office on that.

Jackson was older than Jenny had been—but he was still innocent, young, holding tight to a stuffed animal, although a leopard rather than a bear, in order to make himself feel better.

I didn't really want to think about a little girl locked in a bedroom, a tray with the remaining crumbs of bread and dregs of soup—not so unlike our grilled cheese and tomato soup from tonight—sitting by her doorway, curled in a big bed around a stuffed toy that provided the only source of comfort she had left.

Comfort they'd taken from her before holding her down and cracking her chest open to remove her heart.

The containment spell holding Jenny to the house had

been inscribed on the floor under her body in her blood—Mason had been able to break it once they'd removed Jenny's corpse. When I'd attempted to help her cross over, however, it was clear to both of us that she was still tied to this plane—just not the house.

At that point I'd summoned Sylvia, asking the older ghost if she could help Jenny learn about being dead while we searched for the little girl's missing heart. I hoped that being able to explore a bit would help to compensate for the fact that she was stuck among the living—at least for now.

It also made me wonder if Sylvia ever thought about passing beyond the Veil. The idea gave me a small pit in my stomach—I'd become really fond of Sylvia over the past couple of years, and the idea of not having her there to help with séances and investigations cast a bit of a pall over my already somewhat dark mood.

Jackson cuddled up next to me on the couch and begged to watch *Coco*, which I put on while I answered a few emails and Mason sat on the far end of the sectional, reading, his glasses flickering in the multicolored light of Disney's world of the dead. When I'd finished with the emails, I put aside the laptop, and Peveril replaced the machine on my lap, rubbing his furry head against my palm for petting.

I watched Mason, reading the faint ticks and shifts of muscle in his face as he read, reacting to the action of the plot or the emotions of the characters. I couldn't see the exact title, but Mason was fond of murder mysteries and thrillers, and I was fairly certain this was yet another of those. The bookshelves in our bedroom were filled with them, along with my small collection of fantasy and sci fi. Mason was also working through those—he'd alternate between one of his genres and then one of mine. At this rate, he'd probably be done before the year was out.

While I enjoyed reading, I wasn't nearly as voracious a reader as Mason. I'd also started reading his books, but he was much farther through my collection. The last one I'd read, which had been quite good, actually, was an Agatha Christie named *Sad Cypress*, and Mason had suggested I pick up something called *The Girl with the Dragon Tattoo* next.

But it was so much easier to just snuggle up with Pevs, Jackson, and Everest and watch *Coco* and its happy ending for the dead than to read a psychological thriller that undoubtedly contained trauma or think about the real-world murder and magic that had torn the beating heart out of the chest of a little girl a decade ago.

I wish every murder wrapped up nicely with the happy reunification of the dead with their loving family on both sides of the Veil.

Jackson had just gotten up to go to bed when my phone began to play the theme song of *Hart to Hart*.

I pulled it out with a grimace. "Hart," I greeted the detective on the other end of the line.

"I need you back at the Duskevicz-Miller house," came the response.

I frowned. "Is Jenny throwing things again?"

"Nope. But Jenny has a friend I'd like you to meet."

I looked up at Mason, whose sunburst eyes watched me curiously. "There's *another* body?"

Mason's expression went from inquisitive to resigned.

"No, I'm making things up. Of course there's a second fucking body." Hart was irritated.

I bit back my snarky response, mindful of Jackson.

Mason's eyebrows were arched in question.

I glanced over at Jackson, and I saw understanding cross

Mason's face. "We'll drop you off, but tell the elf he's bringing you home."

I heard Hart sigh, and I knew he'd heard Mason's comment. "Yeah, fine."

———

Mason not only drove me there, but deposited me on the front porch, giving me a quick kiss before heading back to the truck where Jackson waited, studying the outside of the house. I made my way inside, ducking under the police tape that the taller CSI tech, a fair skinned guy with messy blond hair and freckles, lifted to let me through.

"Thanks. Is Hart here?"

The tech pointed at a well-toned backside and legs sticking out from under the stairs. "Over there," he answered in a raspy baritone.

I blinked. "I really hope he doesn't expect me to crawl in there," I remarked, and the tech chuckled.

"He wasn't happy with the pictures I took," he replied. "I don't blame him. I couldn't move in there, so they were pretty bad."

There was a thud, followed by Hart cursing.

"I'll just wait here, then, shall I?" I remarked, and the tech laughed again before wandering off somewhere.

"No goddamn fucking smart-ass comments, Ward," came Hart's elegant baritone, slightly muffled from inside the cavity under the stairs.

I smirked. "I didn't say a word," I called to him. Not that Hart didn't have a great ass—he did, because of course he did, he's an elf—it was more that commenting on it was entirely irrelevant since I wasn't interested in it, *and* Hart would have killed me if I'd even thought about flirting with him. I was pretty sure Hart would kill *anyone* who dared flirt with him.

The legs turned, accompanied by more muffled cursing, this time involving "Christ" and "chicken" and "monkeys," although I didn't quite catch how those three things were supposed to be connected to one another, if at all.

Hart can be a deeply creative curser.

The worst part about Hart is that even crawling ass-backwards out of a cubby-hole cut in a set of Victorian stairs with spiderwebs and fuck-all knows what else in his hair, he still managed to look immeasurably more elegant than I ever had or ever would. He stayed on the floor, resting his elbows on splayed and dirty knees, and looked up at me, his hair pulling loose from his ponytail to somehow look windswept despite the lack of wind indoors.

"Problems?" I asked him.

"I have a second fucking body through a trapdoor *under* the other goddamn body, and we haven't gotten it out yet because we have to document the damn crime scene first and this jerk—" he gestured at the laughing CSI tech "—can't take a fucking picture."

A glance at the tech showed that he wasn't taking any offence at Hart's diatribe. If it didn't bother him, then I wasn't going to let it bother me.

I turned back to Hart. "So you know nothing about them," I guessed.

"Not a fucking thing," came the elf's response. "And without a body, the ME can't tell me anything more than I can already see, which amounts to 'probably an adult.'"

I drew in a long breath, concentrating on the childish rage that had characterized Jenny's essence.

What do you want now? Her voice was unhappy and bitter.

The Skeleton Under the Stairs

I am sorry, Jenny—but we've got a problem, and I was hoping you might be able to help.

She looked at me askance. **And then you'll let me go again? If I help you?**

I'll let you go now, if you don't want to help, I told her.

She looked surprised. **You will?**

Of course. But I'd like it if you would help us.

She looked over at Hart. **Oh.** Like a lot of ghosts, she seemed enraptured by Hart's mere presence. I kind of hoped he wouldn't open his mouth, and not just because Jenny was a little girl. He had the specific impatient kind of expression that he got when he knew I was talking to the dead.

Will you help us, Jenny? I asked her, trying to get her to focus.

She turned to look at me. **Help you how?**

I'd take it. *There's another body under the stairs. Do you know who that is?*

He doesn't like me, she pronounced. **He says I'm rude. I don't want him to come here.**

Can you tell me his name?

Mr. Lagarde.

Do you know his first name?

She shook her head.

Thank you, Jenny. We're grateful for the help.

Can I go now? she asked.

You absolutely can.

She disappeared almost immediately.

I let out a long breath.

"Well?" Hart demanded.

"I've got you a last name—Lagarde. I'm going to see if I can't find him now."

"Who the fuck were you talking to?"

"Jenny."

"The girl?"

I nodded.

"So now we talk to this Lagarde?"

I nodded again. "In theory. If a last name is enough. Jenny didn't know his first name."

Hart waved a hand for me to continue.

I heaved a sigh, then reached out, opening my Third Eye and *pushing* my awareness into the aethereal plane surrounding the house.

It was weird—usually I was more than aware of spiritual activity in a place, but the same thick darkness I'd noticed when we first pulled up was making it difficult, like a metaphysical fog that made it hard to see. Of course, usually I didn't have to bother trying terribly hard—spirits tended to find me without much effort on my part.

Even the Fitzwilliam house, which had been hiding its psychopathic dead patriarch for centuries, hadn't been obscured like this—except when I'd tried to find Preston Fitzwilliam himself.

I very much hoped that Jenny's Mr. Lagarde, whoever he was, wasn't another Preston Fitzwilliam, because I was *not* ready for it, and if attempting to summon him killed me, Mason was going to resurrect me and kill me again.

Hart cleared his throat. "Any fucking time, now, Ward."

I reached out, specifically trying to find Lagarde.

Somehow, I was expecting an older, distinguished gentleman. Maybe from the 1930s or 40s, or possibly even earlier.

What I got was indeed an older man, but 'distinguished' and 'gentle' were not the appropriate adjectives at all.

The hell do you want, sonny? The voice that spoke had clearly spent years smoking, drinking whiskey, and chewing tobacco.

The Skeleton Under the Stairs

I knew my eyes had widened. Mr. Lagarde was a balding, grizzled man, probably in his seventies or possibly his eighties, wearing a wifebeater, suspenders, and elastic-waist jeans paired with fashionable grey Isotoner slippers.

I decided to meet Mr. Lagarde where he was. *My name is Edward Campion. I want to find the assholes who ripped out your heart.*

He let out a wheezing sound that I think was supposed to be a laugh. It was a little creepy, to be honest, but in a dirty-old-man way, not in the suck-out-your-soul way. **Okay, sonny, that I can get behind. Archie Lagarde. Pretty sure it was my goddamn neighbors.**

Your neighbors?

Stuck-up cultish sons of bitches.

It really was too bad I hadn't yet figured out how to make Sylvia audible... Hart would have loved this guy.

You said 'pretty sure'—you didn't see what happened?

'Course I saw what happened. Bastards showed up in robes and hoods like some goddamn Satanist illuminati fuckers, knocked me down, tied me up, and then sliced me open like a goddamn fish!

He was direct and to the point, I'd give him that. *So you didn't actually see if it was your neighbors?*

Lagarde's face scrunched up. It made him look a little bit like a ghostly Popeye. **Naw. But they were the same sort of arrogant fucks. Always complaining about something. Didn't like my garden. Didn't like my dog.** He bared his teeth in a grin. **Liked him less once he was dead, though.**

I blinked. *They liked your dog less once he was... dead?*

You think a mutt's annoying when he's alive? He smells a lot worse dead when he parks his mangy ass on your driveway and don't leave.

I stared at him, struggling to form thoughts. *You. Resurrected your dog. To have him harass your neighbors?*

Lagarde let out another wheezing laugh. **Didn't think white trash like me deserved magic, they didn't. Showed them. When they finally put down Barney, I raised up a flock of birds to sit on their windowsills.**

I swallowed. *You were a necromancer?*

Don't you go using five-dollar words now, sonny.

Sorry. You reanimate the dead? Make... zombies?

Raise up corpses, sure.

Okay. So my dead victim was a necromancer. I wondered if the metaphysical fog around the house was because of that. I didn't think I'd have much enjoyed living next to him, either, if he sicced his dead dog and a flock of undead birds on me, either. I wouldn't have ripped his heart out over it, though.

Can you tell me when this was? When they killed you?

Hottest damn day of the year.

Do you remember which year?

I'm dead, sonny, not stupid. Woulda been thirty-two years ago, middle of June. The twenty-first.

Excuse me a second. "Hart," I said out loud to the impatiently waiting elf. "Mr. Lagarde was killed thirty-two years ago on June 21. He thinks his neighbors may have been responsible."

Hart sighed. "His neighbors got names?"

They let fancy-ass critters in the police, now? He said it 'poh-leece.'

Since their minds work the same as anyone else's, yes.

Touched a nerve, did I, sonny?

I was starting to sympathize with Lagarde's neighbors. I settled for a perturbed glare. Lagarde wheezed his old-man's laugh again.

Old men don't shift their ways easy, sonny. But I'll tell your fancy-boy what he wants to know. I couldn't imagine Hart's reaction to being called a 'fancy-boy.' Actually, yes, I could. I really had to figure out how to make ghosts audible, because I wanted to see that. **You're looking for Oliver Picton and his idiotic secret-magic-society bastard buddies.**

The name Picton was all too familiar. So was Archie's description of a violent secret magical society. Ice slithered through my veins, although it was mixed with a dose of anticipation. Maybe this time we'd get enough to take them down.

Did this Oliver Picton have a son named Victor, by any chance?

Lagrange's eyes narrowed. **He did, indeed, sonny. He pick up where his old man left off?**

I sighed. *I'm afraid so. And was this secret magical society the Antiquus Ordo Arcanum?*

Not so secret anymore, I take it.

We have... encountered them before, I hedged, and Archie snorted.

Nothing good ever came out of that lot.

No, it did not, I agreed. "Hart," I said out loud, "the neighbor was Oliver Picton, and I believe we're looking at the work of the Antiquus Ordo Arcanum. Again."

Hart pushed himself up. "Same Picton family as the Ordo boss named by Greer?" Dr. Frederick Greer, a former psychologist at Tranquil Brook, had been a low-ranking member of the Ordo who was killed for attempting to leave—although none of us were clear on whether leaving Tranquil Brook or the Ordo was the thing that had signed his death warrant.

"Got it in one," I replied grimly.

Hart rose gracefully to his feet. "That's a pretty big fucking coincidence, if you ask me," he remarked. "Anything else your dead friend can tell us?"

Foul-mouthed thing, ain't he? Lagarde commented.

Absolutely, I agreed. *It's part of his charm.*

What else he want to know?

The other people who might have been with him, for starters. I'd been working with Hart long enough now that I knew what he usually wanted to know.

Let's see. The usual cronies were Henry Simmons, Thomas Daggett, Oliver Picton, Fitzhugh Masterson, and Philip Willoughby.

Any guesses which of them were involved?

Lagarde frowned. **Not really. Four of 'em. Could've been any of them.**

So there were four who... participated?

He narrowed his eyes at me. **Fancy way of putting slicing me up like a goddamn turkey.**

I grimaced. He wasn't wrong, if they'd done to him what they'd done to Jenny. *Fair*, I replied. *There were four of them?*

Yep. Chanting like madmen. Downright idiotic, the whole thing.

You don't think it accomplished anything?

Other than getting me stuck on this side of eternity and causing the occasional twinge for no good goddamn reason, it was hogwash. I coulda done it in half the time and without wrecking the bedsheets.

Any idea why they'd want to keep you from crossing the Veil? I asked.

Nope. Far as I can tell, they aren't using me for anything. Just... doing it for the sake of the power. Only reason that lot ever did anything. He seemed to deflate. **Fucking pointless waste.**

Anything else you can tell me?

Not that I can think of, sonny.

Would it be okay if I summon you again if I have more questions?

His eyes seemed to glint, and he gave me a bit of a lopsided smile. **I don't think it much matters what I do and don't want, sonny, does it now?**

I smiled, even though he couldn't actually see it behind my mask. *I prefer not to harass people against their will, alive or dead, if I don't have to.*

Breath of fresh air, aren't you? He let out a chuff that might have been half a laugh. **Summon me all you want, sonny, if it'll let me finally get some goddamn eternal rest.**

Thank you. We will do our best.

He disappeared, and I relayed to Hart what Lagarde had told me.

Hart's response to the news was predictable. "Don't make my fucking day."

10

WE MADE it five whole days before I looked down at my ringing phone to see Shoshana Duskevicz's name. I sighed heavily. "Shit."

Jackson, who was drawing in a corner of my office on the coffee table that Mason had carried in from the reception area, giggled.

I looked up guiltily. "Sorry, Jax."

He grinned at me. "I won't tell Mom."

I winked at him as I swiped across the phone. "Shoshana, what can I do for you?" Given that the poor woman had not one, but *two* ghosts and dead bodies in her house, I was inclined to be accommodating.

Since we were looking at an actual homicide—well, two of them—the RPD would be getting the invoice from Beyond the Veil, which made me feel better about continuing to offer my services to Shoshana and Jacob, who were being more than a bit inconvenienced by the intrusion of the dead into their lives.

Shoshana sounded upset. "It's happening again!" she all-but-wailed. "Except now it's upstairs."

I frowned. "I am so sorry. Are the police still there?"

She sniffled a little. "N-no. But the whole bottom of the stairs is still blocked off."

"Okay. I'm going to get in touch with Detective Hart, because I have the suspicion that if there's still spiritual activity, it's probably because there are other victims still on the premises."

I heard a whimper through the phone that sounded like Shoshana was trying to choke off a sob. Guilt hit me in the stomach.

"I'm so very sorry, Shoshana. I really am. I'm going to also put a call in to another colleague—she's a banisher—and we're going to set up a more formal summoning to make sure we get everyone this time."

"O-okay."

"And don't worry about the cost—homicides get covered by the police by law." They also had to pay a set rate that covered my expenses, thank God. "And this has gotten personal—I'm going to make sure we find everything in that house and get it all sorted out. Especially since your spirits probably don't want to be there."

Shoshana sniffed again, but when she spoke, her voice was a little steadier. "Thanks, Edward. I—we appreciate it."

"I'll give you a call this afternoon when I have a better sense of when I'll be able to come back."

"I'll be here. Well, downstairs so that it doesn't throw things at me again. I think the living room is safe..."

"Be careful, Shoshana. I mean it."

"I will. Thanks." She hung up.

I immediately called Beck. I'd been keeping her updated on the house, and she'd promised to come back with me if necessary. But she didn't answer, so I hung up and sent her a text message trying to succinctly summarize the situation and telling her to call me when she had the chance.

"Jackson, can you go ask Mason to come in here, please?"

He popped up and scooted out of the room. Less than a minute later, Jackson returned, Mason in tow.

"What's going on?" he asked, a slight furrow on his brow.

"Shoshana Duskevicz called again."

"Uh oh."

"Yeah. Apparently now there are things being thrown around upstairs."

Mason's frown grew deeper. "But you didn't sense more than one spirit?"

I shook my head. "I didn't sense much of anything, honestly. It was... foggy. Hard to get anything at all. Jenny screamed, which is how I found her. But I had to search for Archie Lagarde, and it was like trying to look through pea soup."

"Is there a way you can actively search the house without names or possessions or—"

"Body parts?" I grimaced. I really hated it when Hart made me touch the victims because there weren't any other options.

"You touch body parts?" That was Jackson. "Cool!"

"No," I replied, "it's disgusting. And I don't touch them unless I absolutely have to."

"But you *have* touched body parts?" Jackson persisted.

I sighed. "Yeah, I have. But it isn't cool-gross, it's just gross-gross."

Jackson made a face, but didn't press the point.

"Can you search the house?" Mason asked again.

I frowned. "I can... I'll get Sylvia to help, but..." I trailed off.

First of all, I didn't want to scare Jackson. Second, while I was absolutely willing to go back to Shoshana and Jacob's house to bring closure to the house and the dead who were trapped there, it was clearly more complicated than a simple haunting. I wanted to bring Beck with me, and if I couldn't have Beck, I absolutely wanted Mason and his magic. Depending on just how big of a mess we were actually looking at, I maybe wanted both of them.

But Beck hadn't texted me back yet, and we also had Jackson to think about, so I wasn't sure what to say.

I felt Mason's sunburst eyes on me, and I looked into them, trying somehow to convey the fact that I needed his help without scaring Jackson or demanding that Mason choose me over his nephew.

I saw the moment he made a decision, and then he pulled out his phone.

"Hey, Kei. You at home? Can I drop off Jackson for a while? No, he's been doing really well. Work. I'm not sure, honestly. But we'll come get him, even if it's late. No, don't have him share with Ben. We shouldn't be *that* late, but I'll call you. Yes. Yes, okay. See you in twenty, and thanks."

Jackson had started packing up his markers and paper in silence, and my heart ached for him. People often didn't think kids were aware of the nuance of what happened around them, but as a kid who'd been surrounded by tragedy, I can promise that they're painfully aware. And I could see in the set of Jackson's shoulders that he understood that he was essentially being pawned off on his parents because he wasn't old enough and didn't have enough control over his magic to be trusted to come with us or stay at home by himself.

I resolved to be a better step-uncle and spend more time with him working on learning how to keep his Third Eye closed and how to protect himself from spirits—and talk to them, if he wanted to. At least that way he could come along for some of the less volatile séances, which would make everybody's lives easier, including Jackson's.

Mason loaded us all in the truck, Jackson uncharacteristically quiet.

"Hey, Jax," I said, turning to face him.

He looked up from where he'd been toying with one of Everest-the-leopard's ears. "Yeah?"

"We've got to do a grocery run tomorrow... What kinds of stuff do you think we should get?"

The look he gave me said that he knew exactly what I was doing—distracting him from the fact that we were dumping him at his parents' house—and didn't really appreciate it, but he was going to play along not to hurt my feelings.

Nine-year-olds aren't dumb. Thirty-something guys? We totally are.

―――

I WAS STILL FEELING guilty about dropping Jackson off when Mason parked on the street in front of Shoshana and Jacob's sprawling Victorian, and the thick cloud that descended on me from its proximity did nothing for my mood. I made a point of trying to be patient and polite to both Mason—who usually bore the brunt of my crankiness—and Shoshana, who had already opened the door by the time we made it to the porch.

I winced when I saw the bruise that was blooming across her cheek bone, visible over the top edge of her mask.

She made a face that wrinkled the top of her nose, and I imagined a grimace. "I look like I've been abused," she complained, although her tone was more apologetic than malicious—and I wouldn't have blamed her a bit if she had been pissed at me for not having actually solved the house's problems.

"Technically," I pointed out, "you have been."

She huffed a little. "I don't want people to think Jacob hits me," she replied. "It's... super awkward."

I nodded sympathetically as we followed her into the house. "Let's see if we can't fix this for good this time. If you can tell us where upstairs things are happening, we're going to try to do a deeper search to make sure we get everybody. Hopefully, we're looking at the same problem we had with Jenny, and we can release them pretty easily." I couldn't get them to move on just yet, but at least Mason could untether them from the house.

"I hope so," Shoshana agreed, her voice intense. "It's the guest room at the top of the stairs. I was in there sanding to put on a fresh coat of paint, and the spirit or whatever grabbed the paint tray and—" She gestured at her face.

"Let's make sure that doesn't happen again." I turned to look at Mason. "You can probably leave the chair down here," I told him, getting a nod in return as he scooped me out of it, the satchel carrying his casting supplies still over his shoulder.

Mason carried me upstairs in silence, easily finding the room with the painting supplies—several of which were scattered across the floor. He settled me on the edge of the bed, the plastic drop-cloth crinkling under my butt.

"Mace?"

He sighed. "I don't like this," he said, answering my unasked question. "This house feels wrong, even to me. And I'm worried about Jac—"

He stopped abruptly as a paintbrush hurtled toward his

face, although Mason apparently has much better reaction time than Shoshana, or, truth be told, than me, because he got an arm up in the way before it actually hit him.

Even though it was just a paintbrush, it pissed me off.

And you do not want to piss me off if you're a ghost.

That increasingly familiar feeling gathered in my gut, the feeling that sent out electricity through the air, seeking the chill sense of *presence* that characterized the dead.

It took less than a second to find her, and I poured my awareness into her, thickening the already-heavy air into the humanoid form of a woman who appeared to be in her seventies or eighties—marginally older, perhaps, than Sylvia, who suddenly swept into the room on a cold gust of lavender and alarm.

Ward! Sylvia stopped abruptly, staring at the other ghost. **And who might you be?**

The other woman bared her teeth and hissed.

"Holy shit," Mason breathed, which drew my attention to the fact that I'd not only controlled her, but had given her physical form in the process.

She was translucent, but definitely there, the ectoplasmic manifestation of her form oozing slightly, a few drips having already fallen to the drop-cloth covered carpet.

"Can you tell me who you are?" I asked her, speaking out loud for Mason's benefit.

She bared her teeth at me.

How rude, Sylvia remarked, sounding offended.

The dead woman turned her attention back to Mason, and I realized that she'd been fixated on him the whole time. She'd thrown the brush at him, hissed at him—

And then she lunged, one hand extended out, her fingers hooked like claws, reaching for Mason's chest or throat, I couldn't quite tell.

The Skeleton Under the Stairs

He took a step back, his arm raised again, but she never made it.

The scream she made as I held her in place was high-pitched and horrific, and Sylvia put both metaphysical hands over her ears.

And then the woman turned on me directly.

She had a lot of rage and a lot of hatred, thick and cold and black.

But she wasn't Preston Fitzwilliam, and my arms were longer.

Her hands scrabbled at my arms, clawing at my skin and raising welts and thin lines of beaded blood against my skin. But my fingers tightened around her throat, which was a good deal less fragile and frail than it appeared.

It didn't really matter *what* part of her I took hold of. It wasn't like ghosts could breathe.

She let out a semi-human snarl.

"You can stop that right now," I snapped, tightening my fingers and pushing power into her, finding the strings and shimmers of her essence and tugging at them, presenting the very real evidence that I could end her if I so chose.

She dug her nails into my arm once more, then went limp in my grasp, still glaring hatred.

I didn't bother thanking her.

"Who are you, and what the *hell* is your problem?" I demanded. I was most definitely not in the mood for politeness.

She bared her teeth at me again. **I don't have to answer you.**

"You do, actually," I snapped back.

You're nothing but—

I pushed more force and will into her, and she writhed,

struggling against both my physical and magical grip. "Nothing but *what*, exactly?"

The next word, when she said it, was a hiss across the surface of my brain. *Sorcerer*. It was one of the terms Mason had used to talk about what I was—or might be. I wasn't sure I liked it coming up again in this context.

I bared my teeth back at her. It was childish, but I wasn't feeling very much like being a mature, responsible adult, given the circumstances.

Her features took on a slightly confused cast, although the anger remained. **Why did you bring this *thing* with you?**

Watch your mouth, Sylvia snapped.

The confusion increased, mingled now with disdain. **You can't think it's equal to a human being.**

I would say that he's superior to most, you included, I thought at her. Mason might like it when I get indignant, but he also didn't need to take this shit from a paint-brush-throwing dead waste of space.

The ghost scoffed. **They are magical abominations, created from those who do not possess the talent.**

As though he heard her, even though I knew he couldn't possibly, I felt a faint prickle of something at the base of my skull, and I took a moment to look over, seeing the fingers of one hand twisting their way through sigils in the air.

You see, he is weak.

I sent a silencing thought in Sylvia's direction, and although I could feel her seething, she said nothing.

"Why don't you tell me who you are and why you're terrorizing the people who live here?"

The woman sneered, and I pushed my will onto her, tugging again at the threads that made up her energy. She hissed at me again. **I am more important than you will**

ever be. And the Ordo will remember my name centuries after you turn to dust.

It clicked. "You were sacrificed," I said, a hypothesis that seemed to be confirmed by the grimace that passed over her ghostly features. "A part of the Antiquus Ordo Arcanum until..." I pulled at more threads, sensed a shadow that wrapped around her ribs. "Until you were diagnosed with terminal cancer," I guessed again. "So you let them kill you, the same way they killed the others. How long ago?"

Another angry expression accompanied only by more silence, but those ethereal eyes flickered toward the attached bathroom.

"Sylvia?" I prompted.

The Victorian ghost floated over to the adjoining bathroom, slipping through the wall rather than bothering to use the doorway.

Oh, yes, this is definitely her, came Sylvia's imperious tone, triumphant as the ghost in my hands squirmed a little.

"In the wall?" I inquired.

There is a crawlspace here—what appears to have been an old passageway.

I was about to ask Mason to call Hart, but he already had his phone tucked against his ear. "We have another one. Yes, the Duskevicz house. Yes, *another* one." I couldn't make out the words, but I recognized the tone in the tinny little voice in the phone—Hart was *not* happy.

Of course, Hart was rarely happy when I needed to call him, so that was nothing new.

It was then that I realized I was still holding on to this spirit, my fingers still embedded in her metaphysical flesh, her body still both visible and tangible.

I drew in a long, deep breath, trying not to let the surge of adrenaline—a mix of fear and shock—show on my face.

A few weeks ago, manifesting Sylvia, who wasn't fighting me, had drained me easily in a few dozen minutes.

It had been just as long that I'd been holding this woman, but I felt okay. I had that kind of physical and emotional tiredness that wasn't all that far from exhaustion, but I was okay.

And then I remembered the faint tingle at the back of my skull.

Mason had been casting supportive magic—giving me strength and energy so that I could continue to hold on even though she was fighting me.

Maybe I'd be able to get her name out of her before Hart showed up with the CSI team.

———

It took several more threats, and some considerable magical strong-arming, but she finally informed us that her name was Winifred Vaux, and she had died twenty-two years ago.

If Winifred Vaux had died twenty-two years ago, and Archie Lagarde had died thirty-two years ago, and Jenny Martin twelve years ago...

I would have bet a lot of money that someone else had probably died *two* years ago. And forty-two, and so on.

Sylvia.

More walls to search?

I clenched my jaw. *The whole place. I think there could be a few more in this house.*

Oh, joy. She disappeared through a wall again.

Vaux confirmed my theory by glaring daggers at me.

With Mason out of the room, I was growing tired holding Vaux, and I could almost feel her testing the limits of my strength. Mason had gone downstairs to talk to Shoshana and Jacob about the fact that there was a dead woman in the wall between their guest room and bathroom.

Vaux pushed against my grip, the cold of touching her making my arm ache all the way up to my shoulder, snaking down my spine and into my lumbar vertebrae. The ache settled in the same place Preston Fitzwilliam had clawed through to put me in a wheelchair.

You're wasting your magic, sorcerer. And corrupting it by consorting with that *creature*.

I tried to ignore her, although I could feel my fingers twitch with a combination of anger and fatigue.

With your power, you could have become one of us, but you chose to waste it, instead.

I glared at her. *I would quite literally rather do anything else than join your Ordo,* I snapped back. I could think of several things. Like eating actual shit or getting set on fire. I wasn't going to share those things with Vaux, though. She might get ideas.

Sylvia sailed back into the room, and I could feel her trepidation.

I sighed internally. *How many?* I asked her.

I found two in the basement.

"Oh, for fuck's sake." Exasperation made me say it out loud.

Vaux glared at us.

I ignored her.

Is that everyone? I asked Sylvia.

I hope so, she replied. **Although I'm afraid I couldn't actually check the attic, so I wouldn't necessarily put money on that.**

I sighed. *Do I want to know why you couldn't check the attic?*

Probably not, came the answer. **It felt like slogging through mud. I simply... couldn't.**

Well, that was going to be fun. My money was on there being someone else up there. Probably someone important. From what I understood about magic, they were likely to be either the oldest or the most recent victim.

Footsteps on the stairs alerted me to the arrival of the living, one set heavy enough to be Mason's, and I felt a flood of relief. Even though I had the power to control her, being essentially alone with Vaux was making me agitated.

Hart stomped his way in first, with Mason next. Jacob stayed in the hallway.

I'd forgotten that Vaux was semi-visible. "What the ever-loving fuck?" Hart gasped, taking a step away from me and my squirming aetheric prisoner. "The fuck is going on now, Ward?" Hart demanded, quickly regaining control of himself.

In my grip, Winifred Vaux screeched and struggled. Apparently as much as she didn't like orcs, she hated elves even more. That was interesting.

I pushed even more energy into controlling the thrashing spirit, feeling sweat starting to gather at my temples. Sylvia grabbed the woman's wrists, pulling them away from my increasingly scratched-up arms and trapping them behind her back.

Stop it, you insufferable bitch!

Vaux hissed at her.

A tingle at the back of my neck, accompanied with the faint sensation of spreading warmth, told me that Mason was casting energy in my direction again, and I was deeply grateful for it.

"Ward?" Hart sounded both irritated and slightly concerned.

"Dead woman in the wall," I answered, my focus on Vaux sapping my ability to be more eloquent.

"*In* the fucking wall?" Hart repeated.

I nodded. "Yeah. In the wall."

"And we know this, how?" Hart asked.

"Sylvia says there's a crawlspace. The body's in there."

"You got that on your plans, Mr. Miller?" Hart asked Jacob, who was hovering outside the door, his complexion a little grey and his eyes wide.

"I—we don't have very good plans for this house," Jacob replied. "Someone made up some rough drawings about a decade ago based on floor measurements, but the math doesn't always work out." He paused, then sighed. "Because there are crawlspaces in some of the walls, I guess."

"Is *that* all the dead people, Campion?"

"No. Sylvia says two in the basement and *something* in the attic," I answered.

"Oh, Jesus *fucking* Christ on a cracker," Hart swore. "Why can't things ever be straightforward with you?"

"Not my call here, Hart," I snapped back.

"Fuck," the elf muttered. "Okay, does this dead woman have a name?"

"Winifred Vaux, and she's a bitch," I reported. She hissed at me. I ignored her.

Mason let out a soft snort, but the tingle on my neck remained steady. I couldn't even begin to express how much I loved him—and how much I valued his magic, especially right at that moment.

"Mr. Miller," Hart turned to Jacob, who was staring at me. "I'm going to need your permission to open up this wall."

Jacob turned his attention back to Hart. "I—" He sighed heavily. "Yes, go ahead."

"If I can ask you to go downstairs? If Mr. Campion is right, this room is about to become a crime scene," the elf continued.

Jacob sighed again. "Of course." His shoulders slumped, he headed back out of the room, and I heard his footsteps creaking their way down the stairs.

I felt bad for Shoshana and Jacob. They'd bought this house and planned to renovate it—whether to flip it or live here I hadn't asked—and what they'd gotten were multiple ghosts, a set of deconstructed stairs, and now a hole in their guest bedroom wall.

And whatever we were going to have to do to the basement.

Mason looked at me. "What are you going to do with... her?"

I'd been trying to avoid thinking about it.

"I can't banish her," I replied. "Not if they did the same thing to her that they did to the others."

"Have you tried?" he asked.

I hadn't.

"Hang on a fucking second," Hart interrupted. "What if we need to know what she knows?"

"She's not exactly forthcoming," I grumbled as Vaux attempted to break free of Sylvia's grip.

"Look at his arms, Hart," Mason said, his tone even, but edged with a gentle warning.

"Bloody fucking hell," the elf muttered. "Fine. We've got a name. Get rid of her. I'm going to go get a sledgehammer." He left, his feet light enough on the stairs that I only heard a couple of steps.

I swallowed. "If I can," I answered.

I'll help.

Thanks, Sylvia.

You wouldn't dare. That came from Vaux herself, angry and a little panicked. I wasn't terribly sympathetic. It wasn't like I was destroying her, after all.

I bared my teeth at her, but otherwise didn't answer, instead gathering my will, again grateful that Mason was able to lend me some of his strength. I pulled the power into the center of my body, then wove them through the threads of Winifred Vaux, tightening, threatening.

I braced myself. *Unless you want to cross over, Sylvia, I would recommend letting go.*

She released Vaux's wrists, and Vaux immediately began fighting me for all she was worth. Blood dripped from my arm as she opened wider cuts in the skin, and I gritted my teeth.

I pulled open a gap in the Veil, then gathered together the threads of my power and Vaux's essence and pushed her through, her screams echoing in my ears. Whatever held the others here apparently didn't apply to her.

Not for the first time, I wondered what it was that awaited spirits on the far side—some were happy to move on, some desperate to do so, while others... I couldn't tell whether they were afraid of the afterlife because of what they'd believed in this life, or whether they knew something I didn't. No one had ever been willing to tell me—or they genuinely didn't know.

Sylvia told me that I shouldn't ask questions about the mysteries of the dead, but she was also frequently inclined to both dramatics and pulling my proverbial chain.

I sat on the bed in Shoshana and Jacob's guest room, staring down at my bleeding arms as they dripped on the drop cloth on the floor, the weight of my efforts settling heavy on my shoulders. My arms hurt, my back ached, and my head felt a bit funny.

Mason made an upset sound, coming over to kneel in front of me, gently taking my hands in his own, turning my wrists so that he could inspect the wounds. "These need tending," he said softly.

"No hospital," I said immediately, a knee-jerk reaction. I hated hospitals and all of the horrific memories that came along with them.

"No hospital," Mason agreed. "But you need to let me clean and bandage these."

I nodded.

"Hold on." He slid an arm around my back as though preparing to pick me up.

"Mace, I'll get blood all over you," I objected.

He shook his head, picking me up anyway. "That doesn't matter."

I tried to keep my arms tucked against my chest so that I didn't smear it all over him, but I knew I'd almost certainly failed to keep him completely clean.

He returned me to my chair downstairs, then ran out to grab the EMT kit he kept in the truck—he'd worked as an EMT during grad school and keeps up his certification just in case.

"Edward?" Shoshana had come around the corner.

I smiled at her, hoping the expression was visible above my mask, and tried to keep my voice light and unworried. "We were actually able to banish this one," I told her. "But I'm afraid your ghost wasn't terribly happy about it." I tried to give her a smile that would reach my eyes over the top of my mask. "Mason just stepped out to get our first aid supplies."

Shoshana's eyes got wide. "Oh, my goodness. Come into the kitchen. We'll get you cleaned up."

I tried to figure out how to politely point out that I could only move if I used the arms that were rather battered and bloody, but she realized it before my brain could put the words together in a sentence.

"I—you probably shouldn't use them, should you? I can —I can push you? If that's okay?" Pink rose on her cheekbones around the bruise caused by Winifred Vaux.

I smiled again, trying to push the expression into my eyes. "Please," I answered her.

Mason came back as she pushed me out of the hallway and followed us into the kitchen, where he washed my arms and carefully patted them dry with some paper towels supplied by Shoshana.

Four butterfly bandages and a bunch of gauze and tape later, and Mason pronounced me suitably tended-to.

By then, Hart had already called the CSI team and had gotten a sledgehammer out of his car—because apparently he travels with all sorts of exciting things in his trunk—although he'd waited for the team to troop upstairs before he'd started swinging at the walls.

The sound of thudding had lasted about fifteen minutes before it stopped, and Sylvia came downstairs to inform me that they'd found Winifred Vaux's body, not that we'd expected any different.

Mason was finishing packing his supplies back up when Hart stuck his head in the kitchen. "Doc, can I get your eyes on this?"

Mason grunted. "I'll be up in a minute."

"Great. Campion—any more about the folks in the basement?"

Sylvia? Can you tell me anything more about them?

She shook her head. **The bodies are old—older than Winnifred. If their spirits are here, I haven't seen them.**

I drew in a long breath. *Let's see what I can find, shall I?*

"Don't even think about it, Ward," Mason interrupted.

"The fu—" Hart cleared his throat, cutting the curse word off when he realized that Shoshana was still in the kitchen. "Why not?" he finished, still brusque, but a bit less rude.

"Because he's already drained," Mason snapped back. "And if the other ghosts here are any indication, we should probably reschedule when we can bring in a second banisher. For safety reasons that include both Ward *and* your team."

The orc and the elf glared at each other, and I wasn't sure who was going to win until Hart's lavender gaze dropped, taking my jaw with it.

I mean, don't get me wrong, I would *not* want to face down a pissed-off Mason, either, but I hadn't expected that he'd glare down Hart. I honestly hadn't been sure *anyone* could glare down Hart.

"Tomorrow," Hart grudgingly allowed.

"If we can get Beck by then, that's fine," Mason replied, his tone perfectly reasonable as he leaned back, crossing his arms over his chest. "Now, what did you want me to look at upstairs?"

11

BECK WAS in fact available to help with the Duskevicz house, and she'd arranged to meet me, Hart, and a CSI team at Shoshana and Jacob's house the next morning.

I'd brought coffee for everybody. I'd been spending way too much time with these people, and they deserved an apology by way of caffeine.

Since it was the middle of the week, Keidra couldn't take Jackson, so Mason was staying with him. All three of us had grabbed breakfast, and then Mason brought me—and my trays of coffee—inside, kissed my forehead, and disappeared again with Jax, leaving me to hand out caffeine to grateful hands. Beck hadn't arrived yet, and Hart waited for the CSI team to claim their prizes before retrieving his cinnamon latte.

"So what's the plan, then?" the elf asked me, pausing to take a long sip of his coffee.

"You get me into the basement, Beck and I go to work. We wing it from there." I followed up this pronouncement with some of my miel.

"Very technical, Ward. I'm sure that level of fucking detail is what makes you so damn competent at your job."

"It usually works for me," I replied cheerfully, ignoring Hart's irritation.

Hart rolled his eyes. "Tell me this friend of yours is more professional."

I nodded, taking another sip. "Beck is absolutely a professional." Whether or not Hart would like her was a completely different issue. Or, honestly, whether Beck would like Hart.

Well, sonny, have we found the bitch upstairs yet?

I choked on the mouthful of coffee I'd just taken, and Hart turned to look at me.

"Drinking problem, Ward?"

I glared up at him. "No, thank you, Hart. But Mr. Lagarde says hello."

The ghost chortled.

"The fuck does he want?" Hart asked, looking mildly alarmed.

I raised both eyebrows at the ghost, who scratched one armpit. **Well, didja?**

I'm fairly certain you already know the answer to that, Mr. Lagarde, I replied, going for prim. *So would you care to share why you decided to grace us with your presence?*

He chuckled again. **All right, sonny, you got me. But this house is so much more pleasant without that bitch that I just had to stop in to express my gratitude. And call me Archie, sonny.**

I snorted. *She was definitely... something,* I agreed. Although my left arm—the one that hadn't been wrapped around Vaux's throat—was mostly just scratched and grazed, my right arm was still sore and covered in gauze.

The Skeleton Under the Stairs

That said, Mason had been pleased with its condition this morning when he'd changed the dressings. *And it's Ward. Please,* I added the last as an afterthought.

Not gonna miss that woman. Are we finding everyone else now?

I narrowed my eyes at him. *What do you know?* I demanded.

He grinned at me, showing a gap between two of his bottom teeth. **I know dead, sonny. And I know there's a good handful around here, although you're workin' your way through them right quick.**

The two in the basement? And I'm assuming there's at least one in the attic.

Don't forget Eunice.

I sighed. *Eunice?*

Back porch, he replied cheerfully.

"Hart?"

"What?" His arms were crossed over his chest, and he looked deeply put-upon.

"There's another one under the back porch."

"Is he being...?" He left the question hanging.

"Friendly and helpful," I replied.

"So no bleeding all over things today?"

"God, I hope not," I answered.

That the bitch? Archie asked.

Indeed.

Surprised she left, he remarked.

She was... persuaded, I told him, earning a cackle.

Persuaded, he repeated, still laughing. **I like you, sonny.**

I hummed my response to that, not able to think of anything to say.

You know she was one of them, right, sonny?

I did figure that out, yes. Especially since they didn't keep her heart the way they appear to have kept everyone else's.

I wouldn't be surprised if she was one of them watched the bastards butcher me, he put in.

It would have made sense. Vaux had died ten years after Archie—if she had already been a member of the Antiquus Ordo Arcanum at the time of his death, she might well have been a participant in the ritual, even if she hadn't physically held him down.

I thought you said there were four of them, I said to Archie.

Three to hold, one with the knife, he confirmed. **And another half-dozen or so ogling the whole damn thing.**

"Hart?"

The elf, who had been talking to one of the CSI techs, turned back to me and sighed. "What the fuck is it now?"

"How long is the statute of limitations on being an accomplice to murder?"

Hart's perfect brow furrowed. "Whyyy?" he asked, drawing out the word.

"Well, Mr. Lagarde here says that there were some folks who witnessed his murder in addition to the four people who actively killed him. And that's probably also true for Vaux. And for whichever poor person was killed two years ago." I'd already explained to him my theory that this was a ten-year ritual.

"Find me the two-year-old victim, and we're in business," Hart answered. "But I can't touch the rest unless they held the victim or the blade."

I grunted, and Hart went back to his conversation with the CSI tech.

Hart and I had also had a conversation about why it was that I was able to banish Vaux but neither Jenny nor Archie —as I'd said to Archie, I suspected that because Vaux had been a member of the Ordo that they hadn't kept her heart. Or, if they had, that they'd refrained from whatever part of the ritual kept the spirits trapped on this side of the Veil.

Hart had of course wanted to know why it was that she'd still been in the house if that were the case.

I hadn't had a good answer for him, but Mason had suggested that she'd deliberately stayed in the house to either exploit the power held here by the rituals or to protect the house so that the living members of the Ordo could continue to draw on that power. I could only hope that Beck and I weren't going to encounter someone else equally fun today.

As though thinking of her had summoned her, Rebeckah Kwan swept through the front door wearing a flowy skirt in pale pink and a sleeveless blouse in yellow dotted with pink embroidered flowers that perfectly matched her pink mask with yellow embroidered flowers. A long lariat hung down amid the folds of her top, and matching dangling earrings sparkled in her ears.

Hart had turned at the opening of the door, but then stopped dead, gaping at Beck's grand entrance.

I grinned, holding out Beck's cherry mocha. "Hart, may I present banisher Rebeckah Kwan. Beck, this is Detective Hart."

Beck held out one hand, and Hart shook it. "Detective. Do you have a first name?"

Hart scowled. "Detective or Hart is fine," he answered.

I cocked my head to the side, realizing that I genuinely had no idea what Hart's actual first name was. That was kind of weird.

Beck's elegantly groomed eyebrows rose. "Your parents didn't name you Hart Hart, did they?" she asked.

I smothered a grin at the color that suffused his

elegantly pointed ears. "They fucking did not," he snapped. "But they might as well have as far as you're concerned, Ms. Kwan."

Beck shot me a look, her lips quirking in amusement.

"How about we visit the nice dead people in the basement?" I suggested, taking pity on Hart. We'd circle back around to this whole first-name thing at some point in the future. I might be letting it go for now, but I was not going to forget it.

Beck's gaze skimmed over Archie. "Is this a new friend?" she asked mildly.

For you, lovely, I can be, Archie replied, and I didn't bother suppressing my eyeroll.

Beck snorted. "You wish, old man," she replied.

While both Beck and I could speak silently to the dead, we didn't have a telepathic connection to each other, so when we worked together, we spoke out loud.

"I am not fucking asking," Hart announced, then abruptly turned and stalked down the hall to the basement door. Beck and I followed, stopping at the top of the narrow stairs leading down to the basement. "Mays, take the damn chair," Hart said to the big CSI tech. The guy nodded, and Hart bent down. "Hold on, Ward."

I put one arm around his neck, and Hart—disconcertingly strong for his slender frame—picked me up and carried me down the steep stairs into an unfinished basement furnished only with the usual collection of appliances and a utility sink. Beck trailed after, her strappy sandals echoing off the wooden steps.

Archie watched us from the top of the stairs, but didn't follow. I wondered if he could, or if whatever was keeping the two ghosts trapped in the basement kept others out, as well. Mays put my chair down at the bottom of the stairs, and Hart deposited me back in it.

And then the bare bulbs overhead exploded.

"The fuck—" came Hart's voice. I heard fumbling in the dark, then both Mays and Hart pulled their phones out, turning on their flashlights.

Ignoring them, I opened my Third Eye, immediately recognizing that whatever had caused the sudden outage was not a living human being.

It was a dead one.

Ghosts actually glow. If you can see them, anyway. They didn't provide any ambient light to their surroundings, but I —and Beck, of course—could see the boy wearing what looked like a school uniform from sometime in the middle of the twentieth century—I'd have guessed the 1940s or 1950s.

"Hey, there," Beck spoke softly, enticingly. "What's your name?"

The boy made a face at her. **Don' gotta tell you nuffin.**

Apparently being stubborn and irritable was a hallmark of the ghosts in this house. The fact that they'd all had their chests ripped open and their hearts torn out might have had something to do with that.

"No, you don't have to tell me anything," Beck replied to the ghost, and I saw the tension lines at the corners of her eyes that showed she was irritated. "But it would be polite."

Not gon' tell him nuffin, the boy insisted, pointing at me.

I sighed. This, too, was apparently a pattern. "Why not?" I asked.

The boy narrowed his eyes at me, then crossed his arms over his chest.

"I'm not going to hurt you. We want to help you," I said.

He remained stubbornly, sullenly silent.

There was another spirit down here somewhere, and I hoped whoever they were might be more forthcoming. I pushed through the thick air, searching, seeking.

There you are, I thought, finding her tucked in a corner, tucked against the wall beside a utility shelf. She looked to have been in her twenties or thirties, and wore a flapper-style dress, the short skirt edged with fringe. Her hair was in a stylish bob, completing the look.

What do you want? she asked me, sounding about as happy as Jenny had been when I'd first met her, although thankfully with less screaming. Beside me, Beck sucked in a soft breath.

"We're here to help," I answered out loud.

Help? she scoffed. **A warlock?**

Well, this was getting interesting fast. First Jenny had said I felt 'like' the Ordo, then Vaux had called me a sorcerer, and now this woman thought I was a warlock.

"What makes you say that?" I asked, forcing my tone to stay light, although I felt Beck tense beside me.

Beck knew Mason's current working theory that I was, in fact, a warlock mixed with a medium, but how this dead woman from roughly a century ago knew was beyond me.

The ghost's lips twisted. **I can feel you**, she answered. **You reek of the same magic.**

I felt Beck's hand on my shoulder, although I couldn't tell if she was trying to communicate something or just reassure me.

"As the people who murdered you?" I asked. I didn't *want* to feel like that. I didn't want the spirits of sacrificial victims to associate me with their killers.

Yes, of course, came the answer.

Mason had said that warlocks weren't inherently good or bad, but Jenny and this new ghost both immediately linked my magic with that of their killers, which wasn't making me feel better about whatever I was.

The ghost moved across the room to stand in front of me. **Why are you here?**

"We're here to help," Beck repeated. "To find out who you are and to release you from this house."

You won't be able to open the Veil for me, the ghost intoned, her voice hollow and heavy.

"Because the Ordo has your heart," I said.

Her eyes bored into me. **Yes.**

"We can have you released from the house," I replied. "And we will try to find your heart."

Why would you do that? She sounded deeply skeptical.

"Because we're here to help." I didn't know how else to explain it to her.

She stepped closer to me, and Beck sucked in a breath, but I held out a hand. The ghost put her hand in mine, and I pushed energy into her, tying together the threads that made up her existence.

"Holy fucking shit." That was Hart. In the stark light of the flashlights, Mays looked bloodless and terrified.

The ghost lifted her hand, holding it in front of her face, examining it.

That is... smashing.

"Thank you?"

Sharp eyes looked at me. **You aren't a member of the Ordo, are you, warlock?**

"No," I confirmed. "I work with the police. We're trying to undo what the Ordo has done here."

Do you have a name, warlock? she asked.

"Edward."

"And I'm Rebeckah," Beck put in.

Why're you talking t' them? the boy asked her, sounding alarmed.

They aren't like the Ordo, she answered him.

They're magic, he insisted.

"Yes, we are. But we aren't with the Ordo. We're trying to stop them," I explained.

The woman nodded. **Will you release us?**

"If we can, yes."

My name is Andrea Mitchell.

"Can you tell me when you died?"

June 21, 1928.

Beck repeated this softly for Hart, who asked about the location of the bodies. Andrea floated partway across the room and stopped, making eye contact with a somewhat nervous-looking Hart.

I'd start digging here, if I were you.

I grimaced.

"What?" Hart demanded.

"You're going to have to dig up the floor," Beck told him cheerfully.

Hart let out a heavy sigh.

———

Around the middle of the afternoon, Shoshana and Jacob had handed Hart a set of keys and headed to a hotel room. There were enough police in the house that they decided it would be better if they were somewhere out of the way. Hart had a team with heavy equipment working in the basement —where he'd kept us until they'd found the first actual bit of body, which belonged to Tommy Overbury, the boy who had finally been persuaded to share his name.

And then we'd been assigned to help a second team locate the remains of Eunice Talbot under the sweeping back porch. Eunice had been easier to talk to than any of the others, probably because Archie and Eunice seemed to be on friendly terms. She'd immediately provided her date of death—fifty-two years ago—and pointed out her burial site.

Yet despite the uncovering of three more bodies, the house was still mired in its thick pall, the air heavy. I would have bet quite a bit of money that the answers were upstairs. Where Sylvia couldn't go.

Beck was currently standing at the bottom of a set of pull-down stairs leading up into the attic, a deep furrow on her brow.

This was the real reason I'd wanted her here today.

I had the sinking feeling I was very much going to be grateful for her presence before we were done.

I wished Mason were here, too. And not just because he was a witch, although neither Beck nor I possessed the magic to break the containment spells tethering the ghosts' souls to their respective parts of the house. Not because he could bolster my magic, either.

Mason kept me grounded. He was the bedrock that kept me steady—magically, yes, but personally, spiritually. I'd gotten used to having him beside me, calming me, *loving* me. And I missed him, even though I knew he wasn't far away.

Hart had already called Mason to insist that he come over to the house tomorrow to inspect the ritual sigils in the basement and under the porch—and to release the spirits. I could have destroyed the ghosts themselves, of course. As far as the living were concerned, it would be the same outcome as if I banished them or helped them to cross over. But as far as *I* was concerned, it was akin to murder, even if the law didn't exactly see it that way. That, and I was also a little afraid that if I made the offer, some of the dead might take me up on it.

I'd come back to that option if we really couldn't find their hearts—but in the meantime, even if they were stuck on this plane, at least they could get out of the house a bit.

Beck turned to look at me, her hand on the tote bag over her shoulder that contained all the trappings of our trade: chalk, salt, charcoal, sage, crystals, candles, matches. "Are we still doing this?"

"We are," I answered, steeling my spine.

I hope the two of you pack more of a punch than you look, Archie put in encouragingly.

Both of us turned to glare at him.

He grinned. **My money's on you, for what it's worth, sonny.** He put his hand on my chest, just under my sternum. It was cold and tingly and made my stomach feel a little funny.

I sighed. "Thanks so much, Archie." He patted my chest again, then began heading back down the stairs. The tingle, annoyingly, lingered, and I rubbed at it. It didn't help.

Beck sighed. "I take it back about being your friend, Archie," she remarked.

Aw, beautiful, don't toy with a man's heart, he called back as he made his way down the stairs.

I could almost hear her eyes roll.

Hart appeared at the top of the stairs. "We have a problem?" he asked, one eyebrow arched in an expression that very clearly communicated how much he wanted the answer to be *no*.

"I mean, yeah, but that's literally why we're about to go up into the attic," I snarked back at him.

Hart scowled at me, the intensity of it somewhat ruined

by the very large smudge of dirt across one cheek. It was vaguely greyish, so I assumed it was from the dig happening in the basement rather than the one out under the back porch. Then I noticed the reddish smear on the knees of his pants.

"Did they find Eunice?" Beck asked, shooting me a glare that told me to behave myself and be nice to the elf.

Having pulled my gaiter down—since it was just Beck, the dead, Hart, and I up here—I stuck my tongue out at her.

Her mask had been tucked away, too, and her lips quirked at my extremely mature behavior.

Hart grunted. "They found a foot," he answered. "And they're working their way up the rest of her, but it's cramped as fuck under there."

I nodded. None of us had really been in suspense about whether or not we'd find what and who we thought we would. It was just a matter of when.

Hart huffed. "Then let's get this the fuck over with." He bent again to lift me out of my chair, and I held onto him, trying not to sneeze at the combination of dirt, dust, sweat, and—weirdly—eucalyptus that hit my nose.

I failed, although I did my best to turn my head so I didn't sneeze *on* Hart.

"Well, that's some fucking judgment, Ward," he remarked.

"Sorry," I apologized, then sniffed.

Hart sighed. "Not like I can get any fucking grosser," the elf muttered.

I sneezed again.

"Jesus fucking Christ."

Already halfway up the ladder, Beck giggled.

Hart waited for her to clamber to the top before following. I held onto Hart's neck as he awkwardly hauled both of us up the ladder—even Hart couldn't make this graceful.

Hart managed, somehow, to get us both off the ladder in one piece, then stopped, looking around for someplace to put me. Or, at least, I assumed that's what he was doing.

While he did, I studied the attic, trying to see if I could find the source of the oppressive pall that hung over the house. Beside us, Beck was doing the same.

"Box?" Hart asked me, nodding with his head toward a crate up against the wall.

"Sure," I agreed. I was going to get covered in dust, but I didn't think that was something I was going to avoid—and it didn't much matter since I was also now covered in cement dust from the basement and mud from under the porch, thanks to Hart's clothes.

He set me down, and I shifted tentatively, making sure the crate supported my weight. For the time being, anyway, it held.

I frowned anyway, rubbing at the tight cold spot at the base of my sternum.

"Beck?"

"Nothing," she answered, understanding immediately what I was asking. "You?"

"Nope." I took a deep breath, then closed my eyes, reaching deep to send more energy out into the house, pulling it from myself, thread by thread, feeding it out from myself and into the thickness that filled the air around us.

I let out a lungful of air, the long exhalation releasing tension from my back and shoulders. The cold tingle where Archie had touched my chest intensified until it was almost painful, then, suddenly, loosened. The heavy knot of what I'd thought was anxiety at the base of my ribs relaxed, unfolding, unraveling.

The Skeleton Under the Stairs

I gasped as the delicate strings unspooled and energy surged through them, power like electricity that I'd had no idea was inside me. I opened my eyes—both the physical ones and my Third Eye—and looked at the room around me.

The attic was painted in lines varying from off-white to black, shades and coils of magic that wrapped around the boards of the floor, the beams of the roof, down the ladder and into the very bones and bowels of the house.

"Ward?" Beck was the one who asked.

I looked at her and knew my eyes had to have been the size of dinner plates. Beck's body was traced in bands of royal blue that wrapped her fingers, her head, and around her throat.

Awed, I swallowed. I had no idea what this was or how it had been unlocked, and I desperately wanted Mason here to explain to me what was happening.

But he wasn't.

I drew in a shuddering breath. "I, uh." I swallowed again. "I think Archie did something to me."

"Did something?" Beck asked, alarmed, at the same time that Hart demanded to know "What the fuck does *that* mean?"

"I can see... I don't know *what* I can see," I admitted to both of them. "But I think—I think I can trace this."

Among the lines threaded throughout the attic were thick, dark tentacles that seemed to pulse and throb with acrid magic. And I could see exactly where they led.

I pointed a hand at the far wall. "There. Whatever it is that is casting the darkness on this house, it's there."

Hart immediately walked the length of the attic, running a hand over the wall before turning back and sliding his way down the ladder again, already calling for some of the CSI techs to come upstairs with tools.

Against the wall, the dark tendrils writhed, as though alive. I really hoped I would be able to figure out how to turn this off again. It was fascinating, and eerily beautiful, but I didn't think I'd be able to stay sane if I started seeing the entire world overlaid with blazing neon technicolor.

But that was something I would deal with later. Hopefully with Mason's help. Or maybe when we were done up here Archie would be able to turn it off again.

Right now, we had to figure out what was behind the wall.

"Ward?" Beck repeated my name, and I turned to look at her, the blue that surrounded her beautiful and steady. "What's going on?"

"I can see... I'm not sure," I mumbled. "I think it's magic? I—" I stopped, swallowed. Beck waited. "Where Archie touched me, something... opened up. And now I can *see* the threads of magic." I waved a hand. "All around us." I looked into her dark brown eyes, seeing an eerie flicker of blue in them. "Around you. *In* you."

Beck's eyes went wide as she stared at me, one hand hovering in mid-air, stretched out toward me, but stopped by my words.

"Ward, that—" she cut herself off.

"Sounds like warlock magic," I finished. "Archie is a necromancer. I—I never asked Mason specifically, but he's said before that death witches and necromancers are different. I think—I think Archie is a warlock. And he just... I don't know, *unlocked* something?"

My hands were shaking, and I wasn't sure how long they'd been doing it.

Beck did move, then, kneeling on the dusty floor beside

me, taking both my hands in hers. "Okay, so you're a warlock. We can work with that, right?"

I nodded, struggling to swallow the ball of emotions at the back of my throat that couldn't decide if I wanted to scream or cry or laugh hysterically. "And if I'm... a necromancer?"

Beck squeezed my fingers. "Then you're a necromancer. So fucking what? I'll still love you. *Mason* will still love you. Okay?"

I nodded again. "Okay."

The shifting blue bands around her were starting to make me feel vaguely nauseous. *Fuck you, Archie*, I thought.

I swore I could hear him laughing from elsewhere in the house.

I really wanted to go home.

But we had a wall to rip out, and I was absolutely willing to bet every cent I had that there was going to be a body back there. And once we had a body, Hart was going to want to talk to whomever used to own it.

"I can handle this, Ward," Beck told me gently for what must have been the third time as she sat beside me on the crate, shoving against my hip with her butt to scoot me over. I lifted my face out of my hands and pushed myself sideways, giving her room.

"Assuming it's just a run-of-the-mill dead person," I countered. I'd asked her out here because I was fairly certain that this *wasn't* going to be just a body and a ghost, and I hadn't wanted to deal with it alone. Mason hadn't wanted me to deal with it alone. I wasn't about to make Beck do it by herself, either. Especially not when I was perfectly capable of it. My little melt-down about visible magic would just have to wait.

As the rest of the team came upstairs, Beck and I both

put our masks back on, since most of the CSI team were human.

The techs and Hart worked on documenting everything they could about the wall and floor at the far end of the attic. They were trying to make sure they didn't miss any potential evidence that might get destroyed when they started to pull the planking away.

Beck sighed. "It's not going to be just an ordinary dead person, is it?"

It wasn't really a question. "I really hope whatever's in there doesn't go after one of the techs as they pull the wall down," I replied.

"Fuck," she whispered. "Think I should do it?"

I shook my head. "They wouldn't let either of us. We should make Hart do it, though."

Beck raised both eyebrows. "We don't like Hart?"

"We like Hart just fine," I answered. "But Hart is a tough badass and an elf. He can take a bigger magical hit than most normies."

"Shit."

"Yeah." I put my face back in my hands, closing my eyes so I didn't have to keep looking at the undulating ribbons of magic woven through the attic and my friend. I really needed to get this under control—not least because I lived in a house with two witches, and if I had to look at this non-stop for too many more hours, I was totally going to barf.

"Detective Hart." Beck's voice broke through my thoughts.

I lifted my head, finding Hart squatting in front of us, concern furrowing his forehead. "We good?" he asked.

We weren't, but I wasn't going to have him stop now. "We're good," I answered, although his expression suggested that he wasn't entirely convinced.

The Skeleton Under the Stairs

"Anything I should know before we start pulling down boards?" he asked.

Beck and I shared a glance. She nodded once.

"You should do it," I told Hart. "There's some… nasty magic going through that wall."

Hart's eyebrow asked the same question Beck had voiced earlier.

"Better you than the normal humans," I told him.

Hart grunted. "Fuck. Yeah, probably." He heaved out a breath, then stood in a single, graceful motion. "Fuck," he repeated.

"Pretty much," I agreed.

Hart sent the CSI folks back down the stairs, then picked up a crowbar and headed to the far wall.

Beck stood, delicately brushing dust from her skirts. "I'm going to go stand with him," she said, squeezing my hand. I nodded. I couldn't join them, but I'd do what I could from here. Hopefully, it would be enough.

I gripped the edge of the box as they approached the wall, my heartrate rising in anticipation of whatever the fuck was about to happen.

What I really didn't want was a repeat of Preston Fitzwilliam.

I took a couple deep breaths, trying to ground myself, drawing the familiar threads of energy from that now-unfamiliar-feeling place beneath my sternum. It made me anxious having so much power—not because I had it, although that was a bit disturbing, to be honest—but mostly because I wasn't used to it.

You never want to go into a fight, which is what I was anticipating, being uncomfortable with your weapon. My power was my weapon, and it was suddenly unpredictable.

I *hated* unpredictable. Especially when it was me that was being unpredictable.

My heart was pounding in the back of my throat as Hart wedged a crowbar in a gap between two of the wall boards, and I almost threw up as the thick, quivering ropes of magic surged around him.

"Careful, Hart," I called once I managed to swallow down the bile. "It doesn't like that."

"The fuck it doesn't," came Hart's irritable response. "I don't fucking like *it*, then."

"The feeling's mutual," I muttered, wincing as the magic thrashed around the widening crack Hart was making in the wall. He pulled the crowbar out again, then swung it back, setting it more firmly into the splintering wood, then gave a hard push. Rusty nails and old wood protested with a shriek that was partly ordinary house sounds and partly metaphysical as the magic resisted him.

"Fucking hell, this is *stuck*."

"It's not all being caused by the wood," I warned him.

Hart paused, then turned to look back at me. Beck kept her eyes on the crack, her muscles tense as she waited for whatever was on the other side. "What the fuck *is* it, then?"

I swallowed. "Not sure. But it's black and angry and it doesn't want to let go."

Hart snorted. "I'll show it angry," he grumbled, then shoved on the crowbar, pushing his whole weight into it.

As the board screamed its objections, a shimmering gold around Hart flared, its brightness pushing the shadows back as the tendrils retreated slightly. Elves, like all Arcanids, had innate magic. It hadn't been visible before, but apparently when threatened or needed, his magic would push outward.

I let out a breath I didn't realize I'd been holding.

And then I choked on my own spit when I sucked in

The Skeleton Under the Stairs

another one as *something* thick and oily pushed its way out of the gap where the board had been pulled from the wall.

Whatever it was, Beck saw or felt it, too, because she lifted her hands, the brilliant blue of her magic immediately trying to cage in the *thing*.

I followed her lead, casting threads of purplish-blue at it even as I tried to pull darkness out of it.

And that bore further consideration—Beck's magic was *in* her. Hart's was in him. Mine? Yeah, I thought some of it was inside me, but now I was also drawing it *out* of that thing.

Nausea surged in my throat, and I swallowed it down again.

I really, really wanted Mason here.

But the shadowy thing trying to shove its way out of the wall required my immediate attention, and I didn't have time to throw up because it was pushing through Beck's magic. I drew on it harder, pulling, wrapping, and binding it with more and more threads. It screamed, and I saw Beck wince at the same time I did.

As I cast my threads around the creature, Beck's royal blue magic grew stronger, and, together, we were able to hold the thing back.

I say thing... but it was a person. It was vaguely person-shaped and it *felt* like a person—a dead one—but it also didn't. There was no sense of identity or individuality or personality. Just rage and hate.

Sweat ran down my spine, my breath rasped in my lungs as it fought us, and my fingers began to ache from how hard I was gripping the edge of the crate. I watched Beck wrap her own magic around her hand with a gesture, and I wove my threads around hers. Then she drew the spirit toward her—something I'd seen her do before without the glow of her magic—pulling it through the gap in the boards and bringing it close to her.

She called that particular move 'getting in its face.' She meant it literally.

It thrashed against her, but, between us, we held it tight.

Her voice, when she spoke, was a little raspy, betraying her effort. "Who are you?"

It screamed incoherently.

I had never seen a spirit pushed this far from its humanity. Even at Tranquil Brook, the spirits who had been the most damaged by the Ordo's magical torture had been recognizably human with distinct personalities and emotions.

Even though this had *been* human, it wasn't anymore.

"Ward?"

"It's not—"

"I know."

"We have to—"

"Yes."

"We have to fucking *what*?" Hart demanded.

"Destroy it," I panted back.

"The fuck you do," he snapped.

I shook my head, annoyed. "You don't get it. This—We have to." I'd explain it to him later. Right now, we had to save ourselves—and Hart, and possibly everyone else alive and dead in this house—and put this thing out of its clear misery.

"Hart."

"What?" He was pissed. I didn't care.

"I need to get to Beck."

I didn't take my eyes off the spirit and Beck, but I saw Hart move into my field of view, approaching me and muttering under his breath.

The Skeleton Under the Stairs

I ignored him.

He picked me up, and I had to struggle to keep the connection to the spirit as I was moved across the room.

If this was being a warlock, it sucked.

Hart brought me over to Beck, and she immediately grabbed my hand with her free one. Her magic slipped over my wrist, and I watched it thicken and strengthen, wrapped in the fine threads of purplish-blue that were mine. Holding me, Hart gasped, and my eyes widened as I realized my magic was drawing faint, shimmering threads of gold from him, as well.

"Put me... down," I managed.

Hart cleared his throat, but his hands tightened. "Do what you gotta do, Ward," he said, his tone almost reverent. "Take what you need."

I didn't want to do that.

I didn't want to be a fucking magical vampire.

I tried to pull as little from him as I could, but his innate magic apparently found something sympathetic in mine, and there were hints of gold in the threads of my magic as they wrapped around and through the spirit's darkness, each thread pushing, pulling, weaving through until—at a nod from Beck—we used the magic to literally tear the spirit apart.

I slumped in Hart's arms, and he staggered a little, but stayed on his feet, although Beck slid down to sit on the filthy floor, putting her head in her hands.

"Fuck," I whispered against Hart's chest.

"No shit," the elf grunted. "I'm—gonna put you down now."

"Okay," I agreed, even though I was already halfway to the floor.

Hart managed to set me down—if a bit awkwardly—before he joined us.

"Sorry," I murmured, not looking at him.

"Don't apologize," the elf replied. "I told you to do it."

"I didn't want to," I admitted. "I tried not to."

A hand settled on my knee, and I looked over at him. Wherever the gold shimmer had come from, I couldn't see it anymore. He didn't say anything, just squeezed my leg, then pushed himself back to standing. He retrieved the crowbar and carried it back to the hole in the wall.

But before he stuck the crowbar back into the wall, he turned and looked at me. "Anything else going to come out of here?"

I blinked, then looked around the room again. There were a few faint veins of greyish and whitish magic throughout the attic, but the thick, pulsing tentacles of black were gone.

"I don't think so," I answered Hart.

"Good." He put the crowbar back in the hole, then began peeling off boards—which came out much more easily now that the spirit behind them was gone.

I shifted my weight to get a little more comfortable, and Beck came over to sit beside me, resting her head on my shoulder as we watched Hart pull down the wall.

"Okay?" she asked me.

"Honestly? No clue," I told her.

"Mason should've been here." There wasn't malice in it, but the comment made my stomach clench a little.

"Agreed," was all I said.

"The kiddo?"

I nodded.

"I'll have him come in tomorrow, look at the ritual elements," Hart said. He set down the crowbar, then grunted

The Skeleton Under the Stairs

as he ripped out two more boards. "See what he can tell us and release the spirits from the house."

It looked like tomorrow I'd be at home with Jackson and my new magic-neon powers.

Fucking hell.

12

At about four-thirty in the morning a scream ripped me from sleep, gasping.

"I've got it," Mason rumbled, still half-asleep, already dragging himself out of bed, headed for Jackson's room wearing only a pair of green plaid pajama pants.

I sat up, rubbing my eyes, trying to decide if I needed to get out of bed, as well. I'd slept like absolute shit, having finally fallen asleep only a few hours before.

I was still seeing magic.

Mason's was a dark, rich green that looked almost like a vibrant tattoo wrapping around his whole body and gleaming in the depths of his pupils. Jackson's was a deep garnet red, flickering and fitful.

At Mason's request, I'd summoned Archie to our house so that he could interrogate—through me, of course—the ghost about what, exactly, it was that Archie had done to me. His answer was simply that he'd "untied what sonny's got locked up in there."

Which had been absolutely no help to either of us.

Mason added it to the list of things to ask Fiona to look up.

I'd spent the rest of the night freaking out about it while trying to pretend I wasn't freaking out. It hadn't worked, and I was pretty sure that I'd only managed to increase Mason's stress.

And now this.

It was abundantly clear that I wasn't going to get back to sleep, and I would have laid out money that Mason wasn't going to, either, so I heaved myself into my chair, pulled on a t-shirt, and made my way into the kitchen. I could hear Mason's voice and Jackson's sobs from the boy's room as I passed, and my heart clenched.

It had been barely two weeks, and yet Jackson had become precious enough that his heartbreak was already mine.

I busied myself in the kitchen putting a kettle on the stove and getting hot cocoa out of the pantry. I set out three mugs, put the cocoa powder in each, then a few marshmallows on top of the powder, waiting for the hot water.

When I was little and had nightmares—about my mother disappearing, about my father's frozen corpse coming to find me, about my aunt dying in a horrible accident and leaving me alone—Auntie Pearl would bring me to the kitchen in the middle of the night and make hot cocoa and marshmallows.

So that's what I was doing. Because I didn't know what else to do.

I heard Mason's voice approaching, still pitched low and soft.

The kettle whistled, and I poured hot water into each cup, stirring gently to mix the cocoa powder, sugar, and dehydrated milk into the steaming liquid.

Mason stepped into the kitchen, Jackson balanced on his hip, the boy's already gangly legs swinging and his cheek against Mason's collarbone.

I put Jackson's favorite mug, which was shaped like a robot, in front of one of the chairs at the counter, and Mason set him down. The boy slid into the chair, still sniffling, and picked up the mug to take a sip.

I handed Mason the second one, a brown clay-style mug with 'Jamestowne' engraved on it. The last one, in a color-changing mug that went from night sky when cold to daytime when hot, was mine.

"Thanks," Mason said softly, the green of his magic a little muted, but strong and steady nonetheless. I looked over at Jackson, noting that his red was dull and weak, but stable.

I rolled up next to him and leaned my arms on the counter. "You okay, Jax?"

He nodded, taking another sip of his cocoa.

"Nightmares suck," I continued.

"D'you have them?" Jackson asked.

"I do," I replied. I wasn't going to tell him what about, since dead parents, violent ex-boyfriends, and homicidal ghosts weren't going to help the situation.

"What—what happens to your magic when you have them?"

I took a drink, buying myself time to word my answer. "Well, I have a different kind of magic, so mine acts differently."

So very differently, since right now both Mason and Jackson looked like they'd been painted with glowsticks. But I wasn't going to tell the boy that, either.

Jackson sniffed, sinking down in his chair until his eyes were barely visible over the rim of his mug. "I hate magic," he grumbled.

"Sometimes I do, too," I agreed.

A warm palm settled between my shoulder blades, and I felt the soft tingle of Mason's soothing magic. I was half-convinced that he did it unconsciously, not that I minded.

"Me, three," Mason murmured, his voice low and soft, although I could hear the exhaustion hovering under the surface.

Jackson turned in his seat to look up at his uncle. "Really?" he asked.

Mason nodded seriously. "Really."

———

THE COLORFUL MAGIC lines were still there at sunrise.

All three of us were dead tired—Jackson had actually fallen back asleep around five-thirty in the morning on the couch, although neither Mason nor I had been as lucky.

When sun came up, Mason went into the kitchen to make coffee, and I followed. "What, if anything, do I need to know if he's still asleep when you go to meet Hart?" I asked.

Mason turned to look at me, apparently shocked that I thought he was still leaving. "I'm not going, Ward."

"Hart will lose his shit if you don't," I pointed out.

"Hart can go fuck himself." Mason was clearly tired and cranky.

"Mace, he needs a witch to look at these scenes. Besides, there are three more dead people who need to be released from that hell-hole of a house."

"They can wait a little longer," Mason snapped.

"Mason." It really wasn't like him to be unwilling to help people, living or dead.

He sighed, placing his hands on the edge of the counter and leaning into them. "I'm not leaving you."

"Because you think I can't handle myself around Jackson." I was also tired and cranky, and I really wasn't in the mood to talk around the elephant in the room.

"It isn't—"

"Yeah," I interrupted. "It is. You don't think I can deal with it."

He still wouldn't look at me, his sunburst gaze focused on the tile backsplash behind the stove. "I don't want you to get hurt, Ward. You or Jackson."

"But you think that if it comes down to it, I'm the one who's going to lose here." I resented that a bit. Okay, Jackson was a burgeoning death witch, but I'd just dealt with Winifred Vaux and a whatever-the-fuck-was-in-the-attic. I'd destroyed Preston Fitzwilliam and banished an entire asylum of spirits. I wasn't a goddamn fainting violet, even if I did still have bandaging on the arm that had been holding Vaux. The other one mostly just looked like Peveril had gone to town on my arm.

Mason sighed again. "I think your magic is still unstable," he answered.

"Well, I'm the one who can fucking see it now, and it isn't unstable in the least," I snapped back.

He turned to look at me then.

"Jackson's is, by the way. Unstable."

I could see the lines of strain around Mason's mouth and eyes, and he worried at his upper lip with his lower canines. "For fuck's sake, Ward. You just gained this new *ability*, or whatever it is, *yesterday*. And yes, Jackson's magic is unstable. If it weren't, I'd be a hell of a lot less concerned. He can't control himself."

"He's never had two nightmares in a row," I pointed out.

"There's no reason he's going to start suddenly now. And, if you're really all that worried, we can wake him up before you leave."

Mason leaned back against the counter, crossing his arms over his chest. He'd put on a t-shirt at some point, and the grey fabric stretched over his biceps. "It's a bad idea, Ward."

"Everything is a bad idea right now," I countered. "But Hart needs your help, and so do Andrea and Tommy and Eunice."

Mason narrowed his eyes at me. I was absolutely not above guilting him into doing this.

"Mace, Beck and I cleared out whatever the fuck was up in the attic, but behind the wall was a whole ritual setup. Some sort of seal burned into the floorboards and chalk and shit on the walls and candles and crystals and salt and bowls of something that I don't know what the fuck it was. Beck didn't either. The thing that was in there is gone, but there are three ghosts still stuck, and that room is probably the key to figuring out what is going on."

Mason sighed again. "Hart can find another witch."

"First, Hart doesn't *want* another witch. He likes working with *you*. And second, you know this stuff." Because of me, Mason—with help from Fiona—had done a lot of additional research into witchcraft, warlock magic, magical societies, group rituals, and death magic. It was likely also going to benefit Jackson, since he was a death witch, but it also meant that when Hart and I dug up rituals, Mason was one of the best qualified witches in the area to tell him what it all meant.

Mason let out a half-growl.

Okay, he was really annoyed.

"Shoshana and Jacob—"

"I don't live with Shoshana and Jacob," Mason snarled. "I live with *you* and *Jackson*."

"And I'm telling you we'll be fine."

I don't honestly know why this was so important to me. I'd freaked out about Jackson coming to live with us in the first place, and that had been like two weeks ago. Two weeks and I was all ready to spend an afternoon with a magically volatile nine-year-old the day after a ghost who took after Archie Bunker had opened up something in my magic so I now saw neon ribbons around people and objects.

I could see why Mason wasn't super excited about this idea.

And I didn't much care.

Whatever was in that house needed to be dealt with, the sooner the better. And it was important to me that Mason be the one to do it. I wanted him to care as much about resolving this thing as I did, because I was going to need his help.

And because this was a big ask.

We had five hearts to find that had been taken by the Antiquus Ordo Arcanum, and they were clearly still okay with killing people. This wasn't a low-risk thing.

Hart was in.

Beck was in.

I was in.

I needed Mason to be in.

Mason growled again, deeper this time.

We might have moved beyond annoyed.

"Ward, why the fuck is it so important to you that I go and do this?" he demanded.

At least he wasn't the type to beat around the bush and get all passive-aggressive.

The Skeleton Under the Stairs

"Because I want you to care as much about this damn case as I do!" I hissed.

I watched him consider this as he drew in a long breath, then let it out again. "Why?" he asked.

I chewed on my lower lip. I honestly didn't know how to answer that question. "Because..." I trailed off. "I don't know," I admitted. "But there are five dead people who can't move on because the Ordo has their fucking hearts and can still hurt them and use them. Because the Ordo gets power from this, and I *hate* them."

I could feel Mason's eyes on me, even if I couldn't look up to meet them. "Because someone abandoned them," he said, softly. "And you don't want it to happen again."

I felt tears welling in my eyes and tried to blink them away. "Yeah."

I heard him move, but I couldn't look at him without crying, so I kept my head down, staring at the dark blue and stars of my pajama pants where they stretched over my knees.

Mason's hands covered them as he crouched in front of me.

"Ward, look at me."

I was tempted to shake my head, but I did as he asked, instead. His gold-flecked eyes searched mine, worry creasing his brow and pressing his lips together around his canines. The deep green of his magic glimmered faintly—dormant, but strong—in the depths of his pupils and traced vine-like patters across his skin.

"I don't like it," he said, softly. "Either what is happening in that house or what is happening in this one."

I nodded, feeling a tear slide out of one eye. I rubbed at it roughly.

"And I don't like the idea of leaving you with your magic

acting unpredictably at all, much less with Jackson right now."

A few more tears slid their way down my cheeks, but I ignored them, feeling defeated.

"But I also realize that I can't just take over and protect you—both of you—from everything." He sighed, then reached up and brushed a tear away with his thumb. "As much as I want nothing more than to keep both of you safe, I can't always do that. And I shouldn't. I just—Ward, if anything happens to you that I could have prevented—" His voice cracked a little, and I half-leaned, half-fell forward into his arms.

I felt him pull me the rest of the way out of the chair, cradling me against his chest, his cheek resting on the top of my head.

"I love you," he murmured against my curls. "And I don't want you to get hurt when I'm not here."

An unspoken *again* hung in the air around us.

"I know," I whispered into the fabric of his t-shirt. "And I love you. But you can't do everything for me."

I could hear the steady beat of his heart, feel the expansion of his ribs as he breathed and the warmth of his body against mine. I wanted to be able to stay in his arms forever, and it was so tempting to just let him always take care of me.

But that wasn't a partnership.

"I know," he said softly, then pulled back far enough to take my face in his hands and gently kiss me. Then he studied my face, reading whatever he saw there, and sighed. "You're sure you'll be okay?"

I nodded, then turned to press a kiss against his palm.

"I'm going to text you every fifteen minutes."

I laughed a little at that. "Okay."

"And if you don't text me back, I'm going to tell Hart to go to hell and come home."

"Seriously?"

"Maybe only if you don't reply after two messages."

I leaned into his body again, and his strong arms tightened around me. "I'll take my phone everywhere," I promised, letting my hands slide under the hem of his t-shirt against his skin.

He hummed softly as I ran my hands over his bare back. "Then you should shower now so you don't have to take the time later," he murmured into my hair.

"Should I?"

"Mmhmm." He picked me up and carried me down the hall, into our bedroom, then into the bathroom, where he finally set me down on the toilet seat.

I arched my eyebrows at him, and he bared his teeth at me in a grin as he pulled his t-shirt off, then hooked his thumbs in the waist of his green plaid pjs and dropped them to the floor.

I apparently didn't rid myself of my shirt fast enough, because he grabbed it and pulled it over my head, throwing it on the floor on top of his clothes.

Then he knelt and worked my pj pants off as I used his shoulders for balance.

I expected him to pick me up again, but, instead, he tugged me to the edge of the lid, then nuzzled against the inside of one thigh.

"Mace, seriously?"

The toilet was not a place I had ever considered for its erotic potential.

I very quickly reconsidered this as he nipped the inside of my thigh, pulling me closer so that he could draw my half-erect cock into his mouth.

My fingers gripped his braids, and I gasped as I very rapidly grew rock-hard under the ministrations of his tongue and teeth.

He growled against me, sending shudders through my body as his hands ran up the outside of my thighs, gripping my hips. I was balanced on the very edge, and Mason pushed my legs farther apart so he could run his tongue down my length. One hand teased my sac, massaging, and then he pushed me back just far enough that he could slide his tongue into me.

I moaned, one hand holding on to the counter to keep from falling and the other on the back of Mason's skull. His tongue worked me, and he growled a little, the vibrations sending shudders through me.

Then he came back to my cock, already hard and weeping, as he slid two fingers inside me. My body clenched in response, and he groaned around me, earning a whimper in response. I was writhing, dangerously close to falling off the damn seat, when he pushed a third finger inside.

"I thought—" I managed to gasp out. "Shower."

He sucked me once more, hard, then drew back, his hands shifting to lift me so that my hips and cock rubbed against his. "Impatient," he murmured into my ear.

"Yeah," I agreed—like I always did.

But instead of putting me in the shower, he turned and shoved my back against the wall beside the towel bar—the only part of the bathroom that had an open wall. I'd been meaning to put something decorative on it, but was starting to develop an appreciation for the aesthetics of empty wall space.

"I have," he hissed, his voice low and thick, "always wanted to fuck you up against a wall."

I could feel the hard heat of him against me, and I

couldn't think of anything I wanted more right in that moment.

"So fuck me," I told him.

With a growl, he shifted my weight, managing to keep ahold of me as he pushed himself into me. I reached out one hand and grasped the towel bar—which was thankfully anchored securely in case I ever needed to use it to brace myself... although I was pretty sure this wasn't what had been meant by 'brace myself'—holding on as Mason pushed his full length into me, pressing me hard against the wall.

I leaned my head back, sucking in air to stave off the darkness at the edges of my vision from the sudden thickness of him inside my body. He waited, although I could feel the slight trembling of his thighs as he forced himself to hold still.

I squirmed, and he growled, slowly easing himself just far enough that the ridged length of him rubbed deliciously against my nerves and muscles, then pushed me back against the wall, hard.

Mason's hands held up my legs, his hips pinning me as I held on to both the bar and the back of his neck, my cock pushed between us as he fucked me.

His rhythm broke a little, and he ran his teeth over the side of my neck as he pushed into me even harder, driving me ahead of him over the brink of ecstasy as I came between us, my body clenching around him and drawing his orgasm out of him.

His chest was still heaving as he kissed the side of my neck, pulling me away from the wall. I held onto him, and this time he did carry me to the shower seat before gently setting me down and kissing me deeply.

"See? *Now* we need a shower."

13

Mason left around ten for the Duskevicz house following a text from Hart, although not without reminders to both Jackson and me that he wanted us to call him if *anything at all* seemed weird or out of control.

Jackson had promised.

I told him, again, that we'd be fine.

Jackson and I then proceeded to have a Disney movie marathon while making a Lego city that spanned the entire surface of the card table next to the couch.

Mason really did text me every fifteen minutes.

He let me know that he'd arrived at the house. Then he texted asking how we were doing.

Then I started getting pictures of the binding seals from the basement and under the back porch, along with reports when he'd released each of the three spirits. Around lunchtime, he also asked me who I thought was most likely following him around.

I asked Sylvia to check in and report back and was able to text him that it was probably Archie, of whom Sylvia did not seem to be a fan.

The Skeleton Under the Stairs

They'd just gotten started on the attic cavity when I made my way into the kitchen to begin making dinner. Jackson had requested spaghetti, which I could manage well enough. I hadn't lived with Mason for a year and not learned how to make primavera sauce.

My phone buzzed, and I pulled it out to see a picture from Mason. It was of the back of the wall Hart had ripped out, which had been reassembled on the floor, revealing the containment spell on the back side.

I texted him back. *That explains that.*

I'd of course told him everything that had happened in the attic, which had spurred a few hours of research into what kind of magic would cause a spirit to become as feral as the one Beck and I had destroyed.

I couldn't think of a better word for it, and I still felt bad. We hadn't had a choice—there had been no reasoning with the spirit, no possibility that we could convince it to pass beyond or even stop what it was doing to us...

But I still felt awful about it.

I got to work gathering ingredients—peppers, tomatoes, mushrooms, onions, and so on. The pasta itself wouldn't take long, but the sauce had to simmer for at least a couple hours.

My phone buzzed.

This time, Mason had sent me a photograph of a ritual sigil, the burned-out snubs of candles around the edge, dust from decades having settled into the hollowed tops.

What's it for? I sent back.

Later, came the one-word response.

I wondered if that boded better or worse for our attempts to find the hearts of our victims.

I went back to my vegetables.

As I sauteed onions and garlic in olive oil, my phone vibrated again.

This one was a very old book.

Anything good? I sent back.

Hart is losing it, but yes.

More later?

Definitely.

I added in peppers and tomatoes next, then turned the burner down to simmer. I'd turned back to chop mushrooms when a piercing scream ripped through the house.

I would have run if I'd been capable of it.

As it was, I rolled myself as quickly as I could back into the living room.

Jackson was pressed against the back of the couch, panting. The magic around him flared—claret red with sharp and angry edges—striking and sparking, seemingly at random. Tears ran down his face, and he was clearly terrified.

A glance in the opposite corner of the room told me Jenny—who was *also* screaming—was just as frightened of Jackson.

"Jackson." I tried to make my voice low and soothing.

Oh, for f—pete's sake, sonny.

Not now, Archie, I snapped mentally.

Jackson screamed again and threw a hand up in the air as though he could push the ghosts away.

I watched the crimson of Jackson's magic lash out in a wave from his body, shoving a lamp from the side table beside him. It bounced off the rug and rolled away.

Perhaps the two of you could go somewhere Jackson isn't and come back tomorrow? I suggested to Archie and Jenny.

Right-o. Archie's eyes were wide as he grabbed the girl, and they disappeared.

I took a deep breath, trying to convince the adrenaline rushing through my veins that I wasn't, in fact, about to die, and it could calm down now.

"Jackson? It's okay. They weren't here to hurt you. And they're gone now."

His brown eyes, crimson magic burning in their centers, were wide and frightened, his back and arms pressed against the far wall.

"No," he whispered.

I reached out to him, and his magic lashed out again. The world slowed as I watched ribbons of carnelian magic wind their way around my wrist and the back of my hand, the pain of Jackson's power against my skin a strange abstraction.

Don't get me wrong, it hurt like fuck, and I immediately understood the angry burns on Ben's chest.

I also suddenly understood death magic a whole lot more personally.

Because it wasn't just the burn where it made contact with my skin. There was that, but I could also feel it pulling at me, both burning and chilling the blood in my veins, somehow stealing the air from my lungs and pressing my heart in a vice inside my chest.

But the weird part was that even before I even had time to think about it, I could see my own magic reacting to it, the thin threads of purple-blue wrapping the red, bleeding into it. Sucking in a breath against the crushing press of magic, I focused on thickening those threads, intensifying them until they almost completely enveloped Jackson's magic.

And then I tugged, the same way Beck and I had pulled at the spirit's magic, the threads cutting through the red, shredding and pulling it apart. As it did, air returned to my lungs, my heart began to pound, and the blood returned to normal inside my body. I let out a heavy breath as the magic dissipated, leaving nothing more than an angry, oozing burn snaking its way around my arm and hand.

Jackson let out a sobbing shriek and ran, knocking over the card table and its Lego city, scattering small plastic pieces everywhere. He pressed himself into the corner of the room, tucked behind the entertainment center and a potted cactus.

"Jax, it's okay." I tried to sound calm and soothing, although my heart was hammering inside my chest like mad, and I could feel every single beat in the burns on my hand and arm.

His sobs were hysterical, and he covered his face with his hands, although it was hard to tell if he was trying not to see me or whether he didn't want me to see him.

"Jackson, please look at me."

He shook his head, still crying.

I wholeheartedly wished I could somehow make the marks on my arm go away. Not because they were painful—although they were—but because Jackson was so obviously heartbroken.

"Jax, come here, please." I kept my voice smooth and even, calm. His flaring magic was already dying down, reality and guilt pushing the energy back where it had come from.

The boy shook his head again.

Fuck it.

I ignored the pain that sliced through my hand as I pushed my way across the room, ignored the crunch of a few Legos that met their plastic ends under the wheels of my chair, ignored everything but the little boy who needed my comfort.

I knew what it was like to feel that way. To wonder if you

were a monster. I still wondered that, sometimes. Like when I had to rip apart a spirit. I'd only done it twice, but that was two times more than I'd have liked.

I didn't stop until I was close enough to reach out and touch Jackson's arm, which I did with the hand that wasn't wrapped in magical burns.

At first, he tried to jerk away, but then, when it became clear that me touching him hadn't caused any sort of catastrophe, he threw himself onto my lap, sobbing. He was half-curled, his knees in my stomach and his arms around my neck. I held him close, running my good hand over the rough texture of his close-cut hair.

"It's okay, Jax," I murmured. "It's okay. We're okay."

Mason wasn't ever going to leave me alone with Jackson again.

MASON TEXTED AGAIN, like clockwork, while Jackson was still cradled on my lap. I'd ignored it. The second one that came about five minutes later I knew I couldn't ignore.

With a grimace, I'd pulled it out of my pocket, fumbling awkwardly while trying to hold Jackson and not use my burned hand. I managed it, then unlocked the screen.

We still good? read the first text. Followed by *Ward, I need you to respond, please.*

I carefully texted back.

Okay. Small scare due to ghost surprise. But okay.

It was about two more minutes before the phone buzzed again.

Are you sure you're okay?

"Is Uncle Mason mad?" Jackson asked in a tiny voice.

"Not at you, Jax," I replied softly. I was fairly certain

Mason was going to be furious with me, though.

"Are you sure?"

"I'm sure," I told him.

Yeah, I texted back to Mason, then took the time to compose a whole, if short, sentence. *We're both okay. Promise.*

It wasn't a lie, exactly. I was okay. Injured, maybe, but okay. I'd been through far worse and come out far more battered. This was practically a papercut in the grand scheme of the shit I had gotten myself into. Hell, I was pretty sure Winifred Vaux had done worse to my other arm only a few days ago. And while Jackson was upset, he was physically perfectly fine.

I let Jackson stay in my lap for a while longer, texting Mason back quickly the next several times he messaged me.

After a while, Jackson sat up and sniffed. "Is the spaghetti going to be ready soon?" he asked. "It smells good."

I smiled at him, brushing a last tear off his still-round cheek. "In a bit," I answered. "It tastes better if you let it simmer longer."

I needed to clean up my arm—wash and bandage it—before Mason got home and completely freaked out. Even though that was inevitable.

My phone buzzed. Jackson looked nervously at it.

Don't wait for dinner. This will be a while.

Okay, I texted back. *Should I save you some?*

Hart's ordering.

Okay. I paused a moment, then sent another. *Love you.*

Love you, came back.

I slid the phone under my thigh. "Okay, Jax. Your uncle is going to be late getting back, so it's you and me. Garlic bread?"

Jackson looked hopeful. "Cheesy bread?"

"I think we can manage that if you help."

"I can help!"

I'D CLEANED and dressed the wound while Jackson picked up the wreckage of the Lego city, even picking the tiny little broken bits out of the rug. We finished dinner, spaghetti and cheesy bread, as requested, and I put Jackson to bed—with an extra pat for Everest the stuffed leopard, a nightlight, soothing music, and his door left open.

I finished up a few work-related emails, replying to Mason's texts that Jackson seemed to be asleep before going to bed myself, although I had no intention of sleeping until Mason actually got home.

I was sitting in bed, reading one of Mason's murder mysteries, or trying to, anyway. I think I reread each page three times. Wondering just how angry he was going to be. Wondering if I'd pushed too far.

Peveril was sitting on the end of the bed, and he lifted his head to look at the doorway—telling me that Mason had probably come in the back door. I didn't have a cat's hearing... or an orc's.

I did hear when he gently shut Jackson's bedroom door. I closed the book and set it on the nightstand.

Mason stepped through the doorway, tall, muscular, graceful. Exhausted, the lines of his magic dulled. And angry. I didn't need magical vision to see that.

He closed the door behind him, softly. Mason wasn't the type to rage or throw things or even stomp his way through the house. If you didn't know him, you might not even know. But I could see the set of his shoulders, the tension in his broad jaw, the thinness of his lips around his lower canines.

"We're both okay, Mace," I said softly.

He paused, standing by the closet. "I can see the bandage," he replied, and his voice was tight, the strings one crank away from snapping.

I swallowed. I'd been trying to figure out what to say all night. I still didn't know. I'd come up with a thousand different things and discarded them all.

"I know," is what I said. "But I'm okay. And so is Jackson."

I didn't wait for him to ask what had happened. I just told him, not leaving anything out. I told him about Archie and Jenny, about Jackson's reaction, and about his magic and my own.

As I talked, Mason came over and sat on the side of the bed, his back to me. When I stopped talking, he turned and held out his hand, palm up.

"You're exhausted," I pointed out. "And it doesn't need healing right this minute."

He left his hand out. "Maybe I do," he replied, and I couldn't quite read the cadence of emotion in his voice.

I put my bandaged arm in his big, open hand, and he slowly began to undo the dressing. I forced myself not to wince, even when the gauze stuck to parts of the burn as he peeled it off.

He didn't say anything, but his breath quickened.

"See? Not so bad."

Gently, he turned my arm over, inspecting the whole of the injury. "This is worse than what he did to Ben," he whispered. "The burn, anyway."

"Mace—"

"This isn't okay, Ward."

"It's—"

"If you say 'better than what Preston Fitzwilliam did,' I

really will get angry," he rasped.

I opened my mouth.

"Or, God for-fucking-bid, Tyler Lessing."

I shut my mouth again. I hadn't been about to say either of those things, but I didn't think he'd appreciate what I *had* been going to say, which was that it didn't even hurt all that much.

Mason drew in a shuddering breath, then slowly began tracing his fingertips against the sensitive skin on my arm. It burned, but I stayed silent.

Mason's breath didn't even out, although the green of his magic played over my skin. I watched as my own purple-blue found his and drank it in, drawing it inward instead of strangling it or pulling it apart.

I almost said something, but decided that my pseudo-scientific observations on thaumaturgy could probably wait.

Mason didn't have a lot of strength left, and while the roughest edge of the pain was now dulled, the deepest of the reds less crimson and more cherry, the burns were still severe. I knew that. Mason obviously knew that.

Then he let go of me and, without a word, went into the bathroom for his EMT's first aid bag.

I focused on not crying. Not from the pain, but because I knew how very badly I'd probably fucked things up. I'd managed to show, yet again, just how little I was capable of handling. That I wasn't ready for this. That, when it came down to it, I couldn't be trusted to handle myself or to take care of Jackson.

I didn't have any excuses, so I just waited.

Mason came back, drawing salve and bandaging from the bag, then carefully tending to the burns, his hands shaking a little, although whether from rage or exhaustion, I couldn't tell. It was probably both.

He finished wrapping my arm in gauze and an ace bandage, the wounds throbbing from new contact with the burn cream and the bandaging, and let go. I gingerly let it rest against my thigh, my eyes focused down at the dark blue of the blanket over my legs.

Mason stood up, taking the bag back to the bathroom, and a few tears slipped out. I roughly brushed them away.

Then he came back out, not even pausing before walking up to and opening the bedroom door—his hand on the doorknob felt like a punch to the stomach.

"I'm going to stay with Jackson tonight," he said, his voice low and tight.

He didn't look back at me, and didn't see my nod, but I didn't trust my voice enough to reply. He didn't wait for one, closing the door behind him.

I closed my eyes and tried to breathe slowly in spite of the tears I could feel falling down my cheeks. I'd fucked up this time, badly, and I knew it.

I curled up on my side, all too aware of the cold, empty bad at my back, and cried myself to sleep.

———

I SLEPT FITFULLY, waking up what felt like every fifteen minutes, until I couldn't stand it anymore. I felt lightheaded and nauseous, and keeping my eyes closed made the room spin. I wasn't in the least prepared to actually get up and face, well, anyone or anything, though, so I stayed in bed.

It was still dark when I gave up and pushed myself back to sitting, turning on the bedside lamp. I picked up my book again, but reading was hard when the words kept swimming and droplets of water kept marring the pages.

I don't know how long I sat there, staring into the white

space between the black smudges of words, when the bedroom door opened again.

Mason walked over to his side of the bed, and I expected him to say something, but he didn't. He climbed on top of the covers and crawled over so that he could lie on his side, knees drawn up, his head on my thigh and one arm around my legs so that his hand rested on my hip.

Now I was confused, but at least it seemed like he was less angry with me. My heart pounded in my chest, and I drew in a shaky breath, uncertain about the right thing to do.

I'd had to move my burned arm to let Mason put his head in my lap, but now I cautiously lowered it again, resting it on his upper arm and using my right hand to gently stroke his braids.

I felt like I had to say something.

"Mace—I'm sorry. You were right, I—"

"No," he murmured into my legs. "I wasn't."

I couldn't possibly have heard him correctly. "W-what?"

I felt him sigh heavily, his arm tightening around my thighs. "I wasn't right." He didn't elaborate.

I swallowed, because I didn't know what the fuck to say to that. I wasn't about to be like *yeah, you were totally wrong*, especially since he hadn't been, but it also felt weird to ask him to explain what he meant, since clearly Jackson had lost control of his magic again, and I'd been hurt as a result.

"You were, though," I said, finally.

Mason's fingers tightened against my leg. "No," he half-whispered. "You were right. I—I was afraid you wouldn't be able to handle Jackson. Not because I don't think you're capable, but because I don't understand your magic." He turned his face a little more into my thigh, his voice muffled, although I could still understand him. "I don't know what I'd do if he—" He didn't finish the sentence.

I wasn't going to finish it for him.

I sniffled, then rubbed away the new tears that had tracked their way down my cheeks as he spoke.

"I can't lose you." His words were rough, raw.

"I'm not going anywhere," I answered, trying to keep my voice steady. I still didn't understand why he wasn't absolutely furious with me. Why he wasn't yelling at me or even speaking sternly.

He didn't say anything, although his arm tightened again.

I kept stroking his hair, not sure what I could say to make things better. I went with the one thing I knew he'd never get mad at me for. "I love you."

The sound he made wasn't one I'd heard him make before, a kind of strangled sound in the back of his throat that made my stomach clench. "Can you forgive me?" he whispered.

"For—for what?" I asked, still not understanding what was going on. "I'm the one who fucked up."

"No," Mason repeated. "You didn't."

I frowned. "I did, though. You said—"

"Don't tell me what I said." I couldn't figure out what emotion colored his words, but I didn't think it was anger.

"But you were right," I said softly. "I couldn't handle it."

He made another strangled sound. "You could," he said. "You *did*."

"But—"

"No buts, Ward." His voice was soft and sad, and I hated it. "You handled it. You made Jackson feel safe and loved and protected. You didn't blame him or make him feel guilty or like he's a bad person." Against my hip, Mason's fingers clenched in the blanket. "He woke up when I went in," he said, his voice ragged. "And the first fucking thing he said was 'Don't be mad at Ward.'"

I swallowed, my heart in the back of my throat. "You have every right to be mad at me," I said, even though I didn't *want* him to be mad at me. "Because I talked you into leaving and promised we'd be fine. Because I didn't think anything would happen. I didn't think... I just didn't *think*," I finished lamely.

Mason let go of the blanket and pulled my hand from his hair down to his lips, gently kissing the back of my fingers. When he spoke again, his lips were still on my skin, and I could feel his breath against my knuckles. "Jackson has been terrified of his own magic for years. It's barely any better than what the kids at Tranquil Brook were put through."

I made a noise of protest at that, but Mason ignored me.

"He thinks I'm mad at *him*. He thinks it's his fault that he can't sleep in a room with his brother and that his parents hesitate before they hug him goodbye." I could hear the cracks in Mason's voice, and I knew he was talking as much about himself as he was about Jackson. "I talk to him about control, about discipline, about deep breathing and staying calm, and he thinks that if he can't do that at nine fucking years old, he's a failure."

His back heaved as he sucked in a breath around his emotions.

"I'm the failure," he rasped out.

I scowled, tightening my fingers around his. "Mason Manning, you are not a fucking failure," I snapped, a lot more harshly than I'd intended.

"I failed Jackson," he insisted. "And I failed you."

"The fuck you did," I retorted. "Failed me how?"

He pulled my hand away from his lips, tight against his chest, and I could feel the rapid beat of his heart. "Whatever you did, Ward, is *exactly* what Jackson needs. He doesn't need someone telling him how to breathe or to count to fucking ten or any of the other things I make him do. He just... needs someone who loves him no matter what."

"You *do* love him no matter what," I pointed out.

"But he doesn't know that," Mason whispered, and I could hear the anguish in each syllable.

"Yes, he does," I told him. "He knows you love him. He knows Ben and his parents love him."

Mason was silent for a few breaths. Then, "He asked if the next time he has a nightmare, if you can be the one to come check on him," he said, all but choking on the words.

I had to swallow hard around the tears balled in the back of my throat. My heart broke for both of them. For Jackson, because all I did was hug him—and all a scared little boy wants is someone to hug him and tell him it's okay... but everybody was afraid to even touch him. Everybody but me, because I was too stupid to realize just how dangerous he was.

And my heart broke for Mason because I know the reason he *didn't* hug Jackson was because he'd been where Jackson was—and I was pretty sure no one had hugged him. I'd watched for the better part of two years just how often people didn't want to touch Mason because they were afraid or repulsed.

And I knew he wanted to do what was best for Jackson—to teach him how to control his magic so that he didn't have to be afraid of hurting other people. And I also knew that Mason spent his life, whether magical or mundane, worrying that he was going to hurt other people.

It wasn't a feeling I could relate to. I was short, weak, and timid. The very notion that I could hurt someone else was utterly alien to me.

I was the person who *got* hurt.

And, okay, yeah, I was the guy with the nasty magic burn on one arm and ghost-claw-marks on the other, but I was pretty sure that of the three people living under this roof, I was probably the one in the least amount of pain.

"Mason, look at me, please."

I lifted my arm to let him roll into his back, his head still on my thigh.

I had to blink back tears again when I saw his bloodshot eyes rimmed by dark, swollen circles. I pulled my fingers out of his so that I could place my palm against his face, swallowing the sob that wanted to escape when a tear slid from his eye to wet the side of my thumb.

"Mason, you are the most gentle, generous, *loving* man I've ever met. Jackson and I are so very lucky to have you. There is literally no one else I would rather spend my life with."

He stared at me for a moment, then turned, this time toward me, putting his arms around me and burying his face in my stomach as sobs heaved his shoulders.

I had no idea what to do. Mason was the most steady thing in my life. Even-tempered. Always sure of himself.

Even when he was upset with me, it was because I'd done something stupid, put myself in danger by taking on a spirit that was too strong or pushing myself too far to channel his grandfather... Even then, he was steady and reliable. Calm, even when he was angry.

I rubbed slow circles on his shoulders with my good hand as tears slid down my cheeks, not really knowing what else to do or how to fix whatever I'd broken.

14

I wasn't sure when—or how—I'd fallen asleep, but when I woke up, Mason was gone, and I had one hell of a crick in my spine. I blinked blearily up at the ceiling, full of pain and regret, trying to orient myself.

Then I recognized the sound of Mason's electric toothbrush and decided that whatever horrible rift I'd caused between us probably hadn't made him actually leave me.

I should really know better than to let myself fall asleep sitting up, and I groaned as I tried to use muscle to pull myself out of the half-slumped, arched-spine, head-back position I'd assumed when unconsciousness took me at whatever-the-fuck o'clock when I'd drifted off with Mason's head still cradled in my lap.

The sound made Mason appear in the bathroom doorway, his magic a little dim and a look of concern on his face made slightly comical by the buzzing toothbrush sticking out of his mouth.

I tried to smile in his direction, but I'm pretty sure my facial expression was more of a grimace.

His toothbrush went off, and he disappeared again. I heard him running the sink and spitting.

By the time he came back into the bedroom, a frown marring his forehead, I'd managed to swing my legs off the side, although I was rubbing my neck and waiting for the muscles in my back to stop spasming.

"I'm sorry," he said, coming over to stand in front of me.

I winced up at him. "What for?"

"I shouldn't have let you fall asleep like that. I just..." he trailed off, and it was clear that the raw vulnerability from last night was still there. He swallowed. "I didn't want to move," he finished.

"I'm a big kid," I replied, trying to lighten the mood. "I could have made a different choice."

I watched him deflate and swore internally, because I'd apparently gone and stuck my foot in my mouth again.

"I know," he said, the words so quiet that I barely heard them. "I'm sorry."

"Mason..." But I didn't know what to actually say. So I just held out my hands.

He took the few steps into the room necessary to take them, then came and gently sat beside me, my hands gently cradled in his. His thumb stroked over my ring finger and the twisted bicolored band with its twin birthstones, his and mine.

He took a deep breath, then let it out again, before he spoke. "I need to let you make those choices," he said softly, his eyes focused on our hands. "To let you decide to do things, even if they might end up hurting you." He sighed again. "I just—I hate seeing you in pain. But it isn't my decision to tell you what you can't do."

"It's *our* decision," I said, squeezing his fingers. "Both of ours."

He looked up at me at that, his expression uncertain.

"I'm going to do some stupid shit sometimes," I continued. "And I don't want you to just let me because... I don't know. It might be important to do anyway, even if it's a risk, but we should at least talk about it first, because whatever happens to one of us, happens to both of us." He kept staring at me, and I started to wonder if I'd gone totally off the rails. "Right?"

One big hand reached out and cupped the side of my face. "Forgive me?" he asked, instead of answering me.

I turned to press my lips against his palm. "There's nothing to forgive," I told him.

"Forgive me anyway?"

"Anything. Do you forgive *me*?"

The frown returned. "Ward, I'm the one—"

"Who wants me to be safe? Who takes care of me? Who makes sure that I don't get my neck broken by crazed spirits?"

His features relaxed a little. "Who gets over-protective and tries to wrap you in metaphysical cotton?"

I offered him a tentative smile. "I might need more than cotton. Like, I dunno, a big inflatable crash pad."

His lips twitched.

"A parachute?" I suggested.

"Ward."

"Mason."

And then he did the one thing I'd been really wanting him to do all along and pulled me into his arms. I closed my eyes as I leaned into his warm strength, breathing in his pine and citrus smell, my unburned arm wrapping around his waist.

I tightened my grip and whispered the question I'd been afraid to ask all night. "Are we okay?"

The Skeleton Under the Stairs

His arms squeezed me. "Always."

And then we heard a crash and a small, extremely nervous, voice from called down the hallway, "Uncle Ward? There's... a ghost here? To see you? I think?"

I sat up, pulling away from Mason. "Well, fuck."

"Get dressed, I'll go... deal with it."

"No, I got it," I told him. "It's probably Archie. Take your shower."

I saw the question—*Are you sure?*—hovering behind his eyes, but he didn't ask it. Instead, he nodded once, then stood and moved my chair closer.

I groaned a little as I put myself in it, then, wincing as my burns protested my use of my arm to wheel myself toward the door, headed out to see who or what was pestering Jackson. I could feel Mason's eyes on me as I did, the worry he held back, and just before I opened the door, I looked back at him.

"There's no screaming this time, so I think we're good."

The smile he gave me was brief and a bit sickly.

"I love you, Mason."

The smile I got in response to that was a little healthier. "I love you."

Archie had wisely decided to show up sans Jenny and was being extremely polite. For Archie, anyway.

When I arrived in the kitchen, I discovered that Jackson had been making himself breakfast—a bowl of cereal without milk sat on the counter, and Jackson was mopping up the milk that he'd dropped over by the fridge, presumably when Archie had startled him. The crimson of his magic was very slight, but steady.

"You okay, Jax?" I asked, keeping my tone light.

"Yeah. I dropped the milk, though."

"So I see. That's why they put it in plastic bottles."

He offered a small, scared smile. "Yeah. I guess."

Mornin', sonny.

Thank you for not terrifying the shit out of him this time, I replied, a little salty about yesterday.

Archie at least had the grace to look properly chagrined. **That was the little missy. She's somethin', she is.**

Given Jenny's treatment of Shoshana and her screaming fits on the stairs, I did not find Archie's assessment at all surprising.

"Is the girl coming back?" Jackson asked, and he sounded nervous again.

I looked over at him, his eyes wide and the hands holding milk-soaked paper towels trembling a little. "Not at the moment," I answered. "What about her bothers you?"

He swallowed. "She did this zoomy thing," he said. "She was over by the door and then she was like, right *there*."

I nodded. "Spirits do that sometimes. They aren't constrained by, well, matter like we are."

"Matter?"

"Stuff." I poked my leg. "Like having bodies or not being able to just float through doors and things."

"Oh." Jackson thought about that. "That's why they just... appear?"

"Exactly," I confirmed.

I bet your orc has some fancy term for it, Archie said.

I raised my eyebrows at him. *My orc?*

He's yours, ain't he?

Mason is an independent person, I told him, bristling. *I don't own him.*

Archie rolled his eyes. **Not what I meant, sonny. He's your... fella.**

Oh.

Jackson giggled.

Well, now I felt stupid.

Yeah, he is, I replied, feeling my cheeks turning red. Archie cackled.

Knows his magic, that one, Archie continued when he'd gotten control over his laughter. **Clever bugger.**

I chose not to comment on his choice of words. *He's a witch,* I informed the ghost.

No shit, sonny.

Jackson snickered again, and Archie flinched a little.

Sorry. I'll try not to curse around the kid.

I waved a hand. "He's heard worse," I said out loud for Jackson's benefit.

Jackson grinned at me.

"Not that you should take that as a free license to swear constantly," I amended, not wanting Archie to get too colorful.

The ghost snorted.

"So why are you here, Archie?" I figured it was polite to at least speak out loud for Jackson's benefit if I wasn't going to be saying anything potentially sensitive. He was going to hear Archie's side of things either way.

Your fella let everyone out, he told me, and I nodded. Mason had said as much in his texts yesterday. **The house is... empty.**

I frowned. "Is that... bad?"

It's right weird is what it is, the ghost replied.

"So you're here because... you're bored?"

Archie snorted. **No, sonny. I can entertain m'self. I'm here because those bas—Ordo folks are up to somethin'.**

I raised my eyebrows. "What do you mean?"

They're... fiddlin'.

"Fiddling?"

He tapped his chest with a sidelong glance at Jackson, who looked confused.

Oh. You mean they're doing something with your hearts? I switched to a mental conversation, not really wanting to explain to a nine-year-old about how Archie and Jenny had been brutally murdered and had their hearts stolen.

Archie nodded.

Can you... I wasn't actually sure what to ask him. I wanted to know who had their hearts, where, and what they were doing, but I was fairly confident that if Archie or any of the other ghosts knew how that worked...

Fuck.

You're going to summon her again, aren't you, sonny?

Winifred Vaux would probably know exactly what they were doing. And possibly where.

Yeah, I answered Archie. *We're going to have to.* I was also going to get Beck to do it with me. *Want to help?* I asked him. Normally, I'd have asked Sylvia, but Archie knew these people and how they worked.

A huge grin split his face. **You bet your sweet as-cot I do!**

Jackson looked over my shoulder. "Uncle Mason, what's an ascot?"

"It's an old-fashioned necktie," came the deep answer from behind me, and I felt the heat of one of Mason's hands on my upper back. "Who is our... guest?"

"Archie," I replied. I thought briefly about making him visible, but I was already running on two nights of absolute shit sleep and I didn't have a lot of energy. "Archie, you remember Mason?"

'Course. Hard to miss, ain't he?

"Mason, Archie's asked for our help to find the Ordo's... ritual site."

Mason grunted, the fingers on my back twitching slightly. "I take it they... haven't stopped with their rituals?"

Nothin' gets past him, do it?

Not usually, I answered. "Yeah, that seems to be the case," I said out loud.

He sighed. "Am I calling Hart?"

I shook my head. "Not yet. I've got to call Beck first."

"Ask her to meet us at the office," Mason told me, moving into the kitchen to start making coffee, carefully skirting around the space occupied by Archie, then noticing Jackson's pile of soggy paper towels that the boy had forgotten when he'd been distracted by our conversation with Archie.

"I dropped the milk," Jackson said, apologetically.

"So I see," Mason replied mildly. "I think you might need a few more towels, Jax."

Jackson went to get more as Mason gathered up the wet ones to throw away.

Ain't that domestic? Archie observed.

I shot him a look, and the ghost chuckled.

Didn't ever have a missus, he remarked. **Just me and Barney. Butch before that.**

Another dog?

Yep. I like dogs.

As though summoned by a conversation she couldn't possibly have heard, Alma trotted into the kitchen to find out why everyone was in there and whether she could beg scraps from someone.

I stifled a laugh as Archie immediately began cooing over her, instinctively trying to pet her and only managing to put a hand through her butt, which made her move, confused about the cold that had just touched her without touching her.

Jackson tried to smother his giggle behind a handful of paper towels and failed.

Mason raised his eyebrows at me.

I shrugged. "Archie likes dogs," I explained.

Mason watched Alma squirming. "He tried to pet her?"

I nodded.

"You could..." He trailed off, looking a little guilty, but I smiled. It was totally going to be worth it.

"Archie." I held out my right hand.

The ghost looked over at me. I wiggled my fingers, and he, confused, floated over to put his hand in mine.

I watched as my blue-purple threads of magic began to wrap around him, essentially covering him in a skin of magic. *So that's how that works. Huh.*

"Whoa," I heard Jackson breathe, but I didn't turn, instead concentrating on trying to solidify Archie's hands. The ghost was staring at them, turning them this way and that, his eyes wide.

Holy shit, sonny. That's some magic you got.

Thanks. I think. Now try petting her.

You... did this so I could pet the dog?

I shrugged. "Mason's idea. Her name's Alma."

The ghost looked over at him. **Tell him thanks. I—I've missed it.**

"Archie says thanks," I told Mason.

Mason nodded at the ghost. "You're welcome."

Alma was staring curiously at Archie, seemingly unconcerned by him, although confused. Probably because he didn't smell like anything. He held out one slightly slick hand—I'd tried to not make him too gloopy, because I didn't want to have to clean up a slimed dog if I could help it—for her to sniff.

She can't hear me, can she? Archie asked.

"She's deaf, so she couldn't hear you anyway," I told him.

Alma sniffed at his fingers, then looked at him, really confused now, but she didn't seem agitated or scared.

"Go ahead," Mason told him, one hand signing to Alma to stay.

Archie ran a hand over Alma's head, and when her tail started to wag happily, let out a ghostly sigh of absolute joy.

This is the best present you could've ever given me, sonny, he said, his voice reverent as he continued petting Alma, who had decided that this weird person who didn't smell like anything was okay because he was giving her attention, her tail thumping against the floor and her tongue sliding out the side of her mouth.

"She likes him," Jackson said to Mason, who smiled down at him.

"Yes, she does."

"She likes you," Jackson repeated to Archie.

She's a good girl, the ghost replied, happily ruffling her fur.

We were definitely going to have to give her a bath.

15

I'D CALLED Beck as soon as we'd gotten Alma scrubbed free of Archie's ghostly goo, which wasn't actually too bad in the grand scheme of things that had to be cleaned off a dog. Mason had ended up doing most of the work, of course, although Jackson and I had done our best to not get in the way more than we were able to help.

Beck was going to meet us at the office in the afternoon to figure out what we'd need to safely summon Vaux again, but we had—all three of us—driven over as soon as I changed and put coffee in travel mugs because Mason was meeting Fiona, who had *stuff* to show him, which meant he needed table space, and that was something we didn't really have in the house.

That, and we were *trying* to be physically present in the office most weekdays, cases permitting. There was a reason we didn't have official business hours and our website told clients to call or email rather than just show up.

Elsbeth had suggested we could have regular office hours once we'd expanded a bit, which I suppose made sense, although I didn't know how many people we'd need before that became a viable possibility. And then we'd probably need some sort of front desk person, too.

At least we had a front desk.

Jackson was currently sitting at it, coloring, while I did some work on my laptop from the reception area's couch, which made my back feel better than sitting in my chair. Mason, a guilty expression on his face, had promised to work on it when we got home.

I was trying to pretend it wasn't so bad. I don't know how well I was succeeding.

Mason and Fiona were currently in our conference room, which now had an actual conference table and a bunch of chairs—this was its inaugural meeting. Fiona had managed to take photos and scans of the diary Mason had located in Northampton, and they were now attempting to figure out if it could confirm that my magic was warlock magic—and maybe help me figure out how to control it better.

So of course I kept glancing up to see if either one of them was leaving the conference room because I was nervous about what they would—or wouldn't—learn.

I'd dragged Archie to the office to ask him more about seeing magic, since it was his fault I could do it. Turns out, he could see magic, too.

He explained that supernatural beings—Arcanids—didn't have magic that was visible most of the time, except in very specific circumstances, like I'd seen with Hart. But those of us with *abilities*, which applied to the blood magic of witches and warlocks as well as the abilities acquired by Arc-humans, had visible magic. Magic was visible when it was concentrated—in spells, like sigils or seals, or when it was being used by a practitioner or an Arc-human.

Mason's twisting vines were because he was a witch, and

his magic had pathways—pathways that seemed to mimic the veins in his body, tied to life and healing. Jackson's had a similar pattern, but the red was the opposition to Mason's green life—death magic, still tied to life and death, but focused on the other side of it.

I was actually a little excited to compare mine to Beck's again, now that we weren't actively trying to drag feral spirits out of holes in the wall and then banish them. Or when I was half cross-eyed with exhaustion after having done so.

Archie had disappeared a few hours ago, and I mustered up Jackson's help to go grab subs for lunch, since there was a place only a few blocks away. He'd talked me into getting cookies with our subs and chips in exchange for being willing to carry two of the bags of food back to the office.

We set everything out on the reception area coffee table, since I was pretty sure the conference table was buried under copies and scans and piles of notes. As I pulled out the sandwiches, I told Jackson to go get Mason and Fee. I heard the uneven thump of his feet as he half-skipped his way down the hallway.

"Lunch!"

I heard Mason's reply. "Thanks, Jax. We'll be there in a minute."

A tap on the glass behind me had me turning around, and I saw Beck waving at me through the window, stylish as usual, this time in a long teal knit dress with a heavy enameled belt. The lenses of her sunglasses matched the dress.

I opened the front door to let her in. "How many sunglasses do you own?" I asked her as she came inside.

"As many as I need," she said with a grin, taking them off and tucking them into a pocket somewhere in her bulging purse. Mason had five, which I already thought was excessive, but Beck had to have at least ten. "Oooh, food."

"Beck!" Fiona emerged from the office and trotted—literally—over to give Beck kisses on her cheeks. It was their thing.

Fiona then plopped down on the couch and leaned over to survey the food, grabbing her sandwich. Jackson claimed a sandwich and a bag of chips and took them over to the desk to eat while he drew. I noticed he'd already claimed a bottle of soda and a cookie—important things first. A warm hand settled on the back of my neck, and I looked up at Mason with a smile.

"Progress?" I asked him.

I was relieved to see his familiar twisted smile as he looked down at me. "Yes. Quite a bit—and we can confirm you are, in fact, a warlock."

"Ooh, fun!" Beck looked up from where she'd sat next to Fiona, licking a finger after getting sauce on it from her sub.

"I'm not sure 'fun' is the term I'd use," I objected.

"It is, though!" Fiona interrupted, talking around a mouthful of food. She swallowed. "It means there's a whole new area of magic for you to explore!"

I sighed. "And by 'explore,' you mean 'learn to control.'"

"It can be both," she said, sounding a little disappointed that I wasn't more enthusiastic. I shouldn't really be such a downer.

I smiled at her. "I'm just glad to have an answer. I don't suppose being a warlock connects to seeing magical lines around people?"

"Oh, I've got this one!"

We all turned to look at Beck.

She shrugged. "I decided to do some digging, ask a few

questions. This woman I worked with a while back in Florida knows a vodun who she asked about it, and he said that it's a highly sought-out ability among high priests."

"I don't think I want to be a voodoo priest," I said.

Mason snorted, then went to get himself a chair, since Fee and Beck had claimed the couch. He brought it over and set it beside me, then picked up a sandwich off the table.

"I can just see you strangling chickens," Beck snarked. "Seriously, though. It's really rare, but it does seem to be a skill among warlocks and, well, necromancers."

"I am *not* a necromancer," I insisted. And even if I had the ability, that was not somewhere I wanted to go.

"Nobody said you were," Beck replied calmly. "Although all necromancers *are* apparently warlocks. Unlike resurrectionists, who are all witches."

Mason made a *huh* noise at that.

"What?" I asked him.

He swallowed his mouthful. "Resurrectionists—the magical kind, not the nice-term-for-a-grave-robber kind—are also known as life-casters."

"What you did to Ward," Beck said softly.

Mason's swallow that time had nothing to do with his lunch. "Yes," he answered.

"Does that mean you can do that to someone who is..." Fiona cut herself off, biting her lower lip.

"Deader?" I suggested.

"Yes," Mason replied, although he sounded hesitant. "But... it wouldn't be a good idea."

"That's what my friend's vodun said, too," Beck told us. "You don't do that unless it's within minutes. Because any later than that, and shit gets weird."

"I'm sure he said it just that way," I teased.

The Skeleton Under the Stairs

Beck rolled her eyes, sticking a chip in her mouth. "I didn't ask for specific word choice," she said.

———

ONCE EVERYONE HAD EATEN, Mason and Fiona went back to their pile of copies and Jackson had been given a laptop and permission to stream movies in Mason's office. He'd stolen a couple cushions from the couch and made himself a nest, and I made a note on my phone to do some thrift store shopping for a Jackson corner somewhere in one of the offices.

Beck helped me clean up, following me to the kitchen with a bag of leftover food.

"Ward, this place is *great*," she said, pausing to peer in one of the empty offices we passed. Between our schedule and hers, Back hadn't ever actually managed to get the official office tour. "What are you going to do with all the space?"

I shrugged. "It's for when we figure out what the fuck we're doing and start thinking about growing, apparently."

She laughed. "Apparently?"

I put away the extra drinks and closed the fridge. "So Mason and Elsbeth say. But we've got a lot of shit to get together. I feel like—" I waved my hands vaguely. "I don't know... like I'm on a train with no roof and we're picking up speed?"

"Convertible train bad, huh?"

I made a face. "No, not bad, exactly. It's just... a lot."

"Yeah?"

"I mean. Shit. This whole thing, plus Jackson, plus now I'm seeing everything with extra neon? It's a lot."

"Plus the wedding," she reminded me.

"Ugh."

"Ward, 'ugh' is not an appropriate thing to say about your wedding!" Beck sounded well and truly scandalized at that.

"I'm not ughing *getting* married," I explained. "I'm ughing having to actually *plan* getting married. While also finding some ritually torn-out hearts and solving their murders. And learning what the fuck it means to be a warlock."

Beck studied me for a minute. "I mean, okay, fair. But the wedding is like..." She counted on her fingers. "Seven months away, Ward. You need save-the-dates, invitations, a *place to get married*. You know. That shit."

I made a face at her.

"What does Mason want?" she tried.

"I don't think he actually cares," I admitted, leading the way back to my office.

"Do you?"

"No?"

Beck rolled her eyes again. "You two are impossible. You have to care about *something*," she said, sitting sideways in the chair in front of my desk, one leg hanging over the arm.

"I'm sure Mason will have an opinion about the cake," I offered.

"Mason will probably want to bake it," Beck replied. "And you will not be letting him."

"I won't?"

"No. Wedding cakes are a huge undertaking, and you're going to be busy with everything else. He's not going to be able to disappear for like three days before the wedding to bake a cake."

"Cupcakes?" I suggested, and Beck rolled her eyes again.

The Skeleton Under the Stairs

"You're hopeless."

"Just classless and broke."

"You—" She waved her hands at the office. "—are not broke. Beyond the Veil is doing good, right?"

I nodded.

"Then you aren't broke."

"You haven't seen my medical bills," I told her.

She snorted. "Fine. Hire a banisher next, and you'll be rolling in no time."

I stared at her for a minute. I knew a banisher. A damn good one. With an extensive contact list. "Beck?"

"Reconsidered cupcakes?"

"No. Uh. Would you want to work here?"

She stared at me. "Is that a serious offer? Because I will absolutely say 'yes' in a heartbeat if it is."

I grinned at her. "I mean. I should probably at least *talk* to Mason, but... yeah. Yeah, it's a serious offer."

Beck let out a little squeal and hopped out of her chair to run over and hug me. "Fuck, yeah! If Mason's in, I am *so* in. Although I am going to insist that you hire someone besides Jackson for the front desk."

I grinned at her. "Part-time?"

She narrowed her dark eyes at me. "Fine. To start with. I'm in high demand, though, so you might need more than that."

"We'll deal with that if it becomes an issue." I was getting excited now. Beck knew how to manage a banishing business, which would be damn useful, since it wasn't all that different from what I did. And she could absolutely use Mason—she already did, actually. In fact, now that I thought about it, the only difference between the way we worked now and how we'd work if Beck was officially a part of Beyond the Veil was that she'd physically be in our office and I'd probably have access to her gig calendar.

Which was a lot more convenient if I needed to find her.

I couldn't think of a single downside.

I wondered what Mason would think. I was pretty sure he'd be on board—he's the one who told me to call Beck every time we got a difficult case, anyway.

"You guys have an accountant?" she asked me, interrupting my thoughts.

"Yeah. Eleanor. Pearl's girlfriend."

Beck nodded. "She any good?"

I shrugged. "I think so? Mason deals with most of that side of it."

Beck's eyebrows went up. "You do know how to balance your own books, right?"

I waved a hand. "Yeah, yeah. I used to do them all myself when it was just me, and I didn't fuck up my paperwork too badly. But with Lost Lineage, shit got a lot more complicated."

It was clear from Beck's expression that she hadn't thought about that. I wondered if it would bother her.

"Right. Elsbeth What's-her-name."

"LeFavre."

"That's right. I think my mom knows her."

Beck's mother knew practically *everyone*. And I had no doubt Elsbeth LeFavre was probably among that group, given that they were likely to move in the same society circles.

"Probably," I answered. "Although I can't think of any reason she'd need to hire you, since Lost Lineage is trying to *find* dead people, not get rid of them."

"Fair." She clapped her hands, and I noticed that her

nails had been painted an ombre coral tone that perfectly matched some of the enamelwork in her belt.

"Beck? Did you deliberately match your nails to your *belt*?"

She looked down, then laughed. "I have a lot of things that have this color as an accent. Fun, right?"

It was my turn to roll my eyes. "Sure, Beck."

16

Mason had *loved* the idea of bringing Beck officially into Beyond the Veil, both because she would bring a whole slew of clints and her own amazing reputation, but also because with Beck as a regular, I'd probably get myself into less trouble.

Or at least I'd have help when I got myself into the same amount of trouble, which, honestly, was more likely.

I'd texted Beck immediately, and she'd sent back a whole string of party hats, confetti, and heart emojis.

It also seemed like the idea of having Beck around helped to soothe some of Mason's current anxiety. Maybe just because it meant that there was one more person to pick up the slack, maybe because it meant that he could share the load of keeping me safe, or maybe he was just generally coming to terms with the idea that I was going to keep doing stupid shit.

God knew *I* had come to terms with the fact that I was probably going to keep doing stupid shit.

At the moment, however, we were sitting outside in the shade at Dorey Park, watching some ducks slowly make circuits of the pond, Alma lying beside us chewing a rawhide bone. Jackson and Ben were playing on the extensive play structures, watched by Keidra and Deon. I was enjoying the ability to just sit, not worrying about dead people or death witch magic or the Antiquus Ordo Arcanum.

Mason was sitting in the grass by my feet, using my lower legs as a backrest. I'd set the brakes on the chair so his weight didn't push both of us backwards, and even though it was a pretty typical warm June Sunday, I didn't mind Mason's heat.

I wanted this afternoon to last, wanted to savor long, lazy hours of peace beside the water with our dog and the ducks. I reached out a hand and pulled Mason's head back to rest on my knees, running my fingers over his braids.

As much as I'd come to love Jackson in the weeks he'd been with us, I missed being able to be with Mason, just us, not having to watch out for Legos on the floor or keep quiet so that we didn't wake Jackson or having to steal kisses and caresses in the momentary breaks between one activity and the next.

Even Sundays, which Jackson generally spent with his parents and Ben, were usually crammed with the things that were hard to get done with a young boy underfoot—cleaning, organizing, sometimes a research project that needed several uninterrupted hours.

We were *not* doing those things now, even though the kitchen needed a good clean and there was laundry piling up, and I was grateful to just sit with Mason, to hear the warm tones of his voice as he talked, to be able to take the time to savor the feel of his hair under my fingers and the warm weight of his body leaning against mine.

"Penny?" I asked, borrowing Mason's usual phrase.

He smiled, his lips twisting around his canines. "Not really thinking at the moment," he said, closing his eyes. "You?"

"I'm enjoying not thinking about dead people," I answered, and he chuckled.

"Doesn't that mean you *are* thinking about dead people?" he asked.

"Har har."

He threaded one arm around my lower leg, then pressed a kiss to the inside of my knee that I could only sort of feel between the numbness of my legs and the fabric between his lips and my skin.

"What time are you and Beck going in tomorrow?" he asked, then.

Hart had asked us not-so-politely—this was Hart, after all—to do what he called a "Hostile Dead Witness" interview with Winifred Vaux. Since Beck and I already had a plan figured out, we'd agreed to do it on Hart's timing and turf.

"Ten," I answered.

Mason nodded, his head bobbing against my knees. "Okay."

"You coming?"

"Do you want me to?"

It would mean he'd either have to bring Jackson or find someone to watch him—his gran, probably, since Keidra was going to be working.

"I'm always happy if you want to," I replied, "but Beck and I can handle Winifred Vaux."

Mason made a half-grunt, half-humming sound. He wasn't totally happy about it, but he wasn't upset, either. "Maybe take Archie?" he suggested, then.

"He's already part of the plan," I replied. "You like Archie?"

"He knows something about your magic, at least, which is more than the rest of us do," Mason replied. "And he knows Vaux."

"And doesn't like her," I reminded him.

"Well, she likes me even less," he replied. "So that's a good reason for me not to be there."

I grimaced, although he wasn't looking at me. "Winifred Vaux can go fuck herself," I muttered, earning another laugh from Mason.

"What?" I asked him.

"You know I think it's adorable when you get indignant."

I snorted, but I kept running my fingers over his hair.

"I didn't ever tell you what Hart and I found in the attic, did I?" he asked, then.

"No." I didn't say it was because he was too mad at me to tell me and then too upset. I was pretty sure he didn't need the reminder.

His hand tightened on my calf. "The book I sent you a picture of?"

"Yeah?"

"I think it's a list of Ordo dates and rituals."

"Holy fucking shit, Mason."

"Hart was *ecstatic*."

"That's amazing."

"Too bad we don't know what the names of the rituals actually *mean*."

I felt a surge of disappointment. Of course it wouldn't be that easy. Nobody would ever write *ritual where we cut out a living victim's heart* in a journal. It'd be something in Latin, and would probably be further obscured. "You can't find out?"

"I'll go see Fiona again on Tuesday," he replied. "Hart sent me a copy of some of the pages with the ritual names."

I nodded, even though he couldn't see me. "Let me know if any of them have to do with hearts."

"Of course."

"What else did you find?"

He shifted slightly, moving his legs, but resettled against me. "The sigil was both a spatial anchor, keeping that specific spirit tied to the house, and also a leeching spell."

"A what?" I asked.

"Leeching spell. It was drawing energy from that spirit and putting it into the house itself."

"Why?"

Mason let out a long breath. "From what I could tell, the idea is that the house itself served as a meeting place for the Ordo for some amount of time—probably up to about ten or so years ago. Although they didn't conduct their sacrificial rituals there, they wanted the dead anchored to the house so that they would essentially provide a constant source of energy."

"They were... using the dead people as metaphysical batteries?" That was both horrifying and disgusting.

"More or less," Mason answered.

"And why didn't they do their murdering there?"

"I'm not certain. I think—and this is a *think*, not a *know*—that they need a more ritualized space for that. The house seems to have been more for... casual meetings? Perhaps more like a clubhouse, maybe that included members who weren't part of the inner circle."

"Like Greer, you mean?"

"Exactly," Mason confirmed.

"If there is a second place—"

"Oh, there definitely is. Nobody was ritually murdered

in that house. Hart made me go over the whole damn thing, top to bottom."

"Good to know. But we need to find out *where*, which hopefully we can get Vaux to tell us."

He grunted. "You know she isn't going to just *tell* you, right?"

I sighed. "I know."

"As long as you're ready."

"There will be a full kit." Sage, candles, chalk, charcoal, water, salt, and birch and cedar bundles.

I heard Mason draw in a breath, but he didn't say anything.

"I promise I'll be careful," I assured him, and he blew out the breath.

"Thank you."

I ran my fingers over his braids. "If she gets really nasty, I'll make Hart stand in front of me."

That got him to laugh.

We sat there a little longer, listening to the echoes of playing children and the rasping of Alma's teeth on her rawhide.

"Do you want to hear more about what Fee and I learned from Hannah Neale's diary?" Mason asked, breaking the silence.

"Sure," I agreed.

"It's pretty clear," he said, "that the family had magic—probably warlock magic, since I certainly didn't recognize any of the rituals or spells she listed."

"Are all witch spells pretty similar?" I asked.

He hummed assent. "The terms vary pretty widely, and some of the trappings change depending on era and location and culture, but the core remains fairly consistent. For instance, you might get different colored candles or chalk, or charcoal instead of chalk, or henbane instead of hemlock or witch hazel, but the idea is the same and the root of the magic is the same."

"And Hannah Neale's magic isn't?"

"Correct." He settled a little, getting comfortable. "Because witchcraft relies on dichotomies, it tends to emphasize them. Spells draw on one of the pair, push back against the opposite in some cases—for instance, a healing spell deliberately pushes back against pain. But Hannah isn't doing that at all. There's no balance to her magic."

"No balance?"

"No. It's, well, honestly, it's more like what you talk about with threads. Pulling on ambient energy rather than working within a spectrum or dichotomy."

"Huh." I thought about this. "You don't think about magic like threads?" I asked.

"Not at all," he answered, and I realized we'd never really talked about how either one of us *did* magic. Of course, I hadn't really thought about what I did *as* magic, which probably had a good deal to do with it.

"What is it like?" I asked.

He hummed, thinking, his fingers gently stroking my leg. "Things... feel right or wrong," he said slowly, considering his words as he spoke them. "When you're in pain, for instance, I can feel a kind of shadow or negativity around whatever hurts. And I can... counteract it. Witch magic acts like... an opposing force. Light against darkness, warmth against cold. If pain is dark and cold, I can balance it out by using warmth and light."

I smiled, thinking about the fact that Mason, of course, associated his magic with heat and light.

I'd tried to explain how I saw magic to him, the glowing, vibrant green tendrils that wrapped around him, following the pathways of his body's energy, glowing even in the June sunlight as he sat at my feet.

I was getting used to them, although I still kind of wished I could turn them off. Sometimes I saw someone with particularly strong or unusual magic—like one of the runners who had been doing laps around the pond whose magic was a very, *very* bright pink in a halo around her head—it still threw me off.

Not that it didn't have its uses.

Jackson's magic, for instance, although still dim, had been much steadier over the past several days, less fitful, and that seemed to me—and Mason agreed—to be a good sign.

It was funny, but I couldn't always see mine. If I interacted with someone—Jackson, Archie, Sylvia, Beck—it would spiral down my arms, but for the most part, it seemed to settle somewhere inside me that I couldn't see.

And I couldn't just look in a mirror, either, because magic didn't show up in reflections. So I had no idea where mine lived, if it settled in my chest where I usually felt it come from, or if it was totally dormant when I wasn't actively using it.

"Did Hannah Neale talk about threads of magic?" I asked Mason.

"She did use the word 'ribbons' a few times, and often spoke of 'weaving' spells, which was one of the things that made me think that her magic might be similar to yours."

"Weaving spells?" I could see that. If you took the threads of magic and wound them together, especially if you were drawing from more than one person, that would absolutely seem like weaving.

"Does that make any sense?"

"Yeah, it does, actually," I confirmed.

Mason hummed, then tipped his head back to look at me. "I think we've figured you out, Ward."

I grinned at him. "Never," I countered, and he laughed.

"Maybe a little bit?"

"Maybe."

"Even if I get you butter pecan ice cream on the way home?"

"Maybe a little more."

17

It is amazing what several consecutive nights of actual sleep will do for your sanity and general life outlook. Mason got up early to run—leaving me with a kiss and a very slight look of trepidation, although he didn't actually *say* anything—and I'd gotten up soon after.

By the time Mason came back, I was actually fairly cheerful and making coffee, dressed in jeans and a black t-shirt, labradorite studs and silver hoop in my ears. Jackson was already awake, and we were working on one of his weekly homework packets—math, which he seemed to actually enjoy—over a breakfast of peanut-butter-and-banana toast. His feet kicked absently as he worked, his crimson magic dim, but steady.

Mason gave me a sweaty kiss before heading to the shower, earning us Jackson's usual 'ew face,' which I was pretty sure was more habit than actual disgust. Especially because his eyes sparkled, and I could see a dimple in his left cheek.

We finished up the day's math, and I was putting the dishes in the dishwasher when Mason came back out, dressed for the office in navy blue slacks and matching vest, as well as a cream button-down. His braids had been twisted back, held in place with a single enameled stick, showing off the gold hoops at the points of his ears. I raised my eyebrows.

"Am I forgetting about something important?" I asked, flicking on the burner under the tea kettle for him and wondering if I should have put on fancier clothes.

"Elsbeth is bringing in a possible donor," Mason answered, his voice a little tense. "You and Beck had already planned the summoning with Hart, so I'll handle it."

My eyes flicked over at Jackson.

Mason's lips thinned slightly. "I'm dropping him at Keidra's for Ben's birthday party," he reminded me, running one hand over Jackson's skull. "After which he will absolutely do his reading homework."

Jackson groaned. "Uncle *Mason*."

"We'll do science and art tomorrow," Mason replied. "But you need to get your homework done and submitted before Wednesday. Yes?"

"Yeeeeah." Only kids can make homework sound so horribly torturous. I bit back a smile, remembering how homework as a kid had seemed endless and interminable... and now I regularly lost two or three times the same amount of time just trying to answer the day's emails.

"Good."

"I can ask Hart to wait," I offered, although I didn't particularly have any desire to schmooze with rich donors. Even though I was pretty good at getting people to open their checkbooks because they felt bad for poor me in my wheelchair, Mason knew just how much I hated it.

If people wanted to give money to Lost Lineage because they believed in the work we did, great. I'd happily talk to them all day long about séances and dead people. But there was an annoyingly large number of donors who would pat my shoulder and tell me how *brave* I was for continuing to do my work or who made passing comments to Elsbeth as though I couldn't hear them at how *good* she was to partner with me.

I usually started throwing things after those meetings.

There's a squishy stress ball in my office that I can whip pretty hard against the far wall. If we happened to have taken Alma in with us that day, she'd bring it back to me. Otherwise, the telltale *thump* would usually bring Mason in to talk me down.

"I've got it," he said mildly.

"Someone new?" I asked him.

He gave a small hum in the affirmative.

I looked at him, my eyebrows raised. "Bets?" It was our shorthand for *Do you want to place bets on whether or not they freak out and/or say something bigoted and/or stupid?*

Mason snorted. "You know I don't gamble."

"You're no fun, Mace."

Beside me, the teakettle whistled, and I turned the burner off and poured a mug. Mason pulled down his tea box and rifled through it, pulled out a sachet, and put it into the steaming water. He leaned back against the counter beside me, watching me finish doing the dishes, a small twisted smile on his lips.

I smirked at him, because I knew he liked watching me do domestic shit.

His sunburst eyes sparkled, a core of emerald green magic burning in his pupils. If we'd been alone...

"Why don't you gamble?" Jackson asked without looking up from the picture he was drawing, oblivious as only a kid can be.

Mason rolled his eyes good naturedly. "Because gambling is putting money on an arbitrary outcome over which you have no control."

Jackson looked up at him. "What does *that* mean?"

"That it's stupid," I told him, winking at Mason.

Jackson looked back and forth between us. "Then why didn't he just say that?"

"Because your uncle is a professor, and he likes to use big words to say everything."

The eyeroll I got for that was a little less good natured, but Jackson giggled, so I knew Mason wouldn't hold it against me.

"Don't you have a ghost to summon?" Mason asked me, before taking a sip of his tea.

"Gotta wait for my ride," I replied cheerfully.

"You have everything you need from upstairs?" Our at-home supply of summoning ingredients—sage and salt and so on—was upstairs, so Mason or Jackson would get it for me.

"Beck is bringing her kit," I answered, and Mason nodded, taking another sip of his tea. "What time is your donor?"

"Ten-thirty. So Jackson, go pack up whatever you want to take to your mom's. And then grab your present for Ben."

"Okay." The present—a videogame they could play together through online co-op—was wrapped with a bow on it sitting on the card table in the living room.

Jackson slid off the stool, then trotted down the hall, presumably to stuff Everest and some books and toys into his backpack.

"And pack your homework!" Mason called after him.

"Okaaay," came the grudging response. We both knew

he would, but the show of resistance was a part of the process.

Gold-flecked eyes sparkling, Mason put down his tea, then pushed away from the counter, coming up to me and bending down to rest his hands on the sides of my chair. His face was inches from mine, and I grinned at him.

"Hey."

I was not prepared for the nuzzling kiss on the sensitive spot right behind my ear, and I gasped a little as his lips and canines sent tingles through me.

Then he pulled back, leaving me flushed and a little uncomfortable in my tight jeans. "Hey, yourself."

"Not fair, Mason," I accused.

He chuckled, then pressed his lips to mine, teasing them open and kissing me deeply. I whimpered against his mouth, one hand sliding around the back of his neck, the skin exposed to my fingers.

He drew away, giving one last nip to my lower lip. "Are you still going to respond like that when we're eighty?" he asked, the question half-teasing.

I ran my fingers over his cheek, letting my thumb catch on his lower lip between his canines. "Damn right, I am," I told him.

He caught my hand and put a kiss in the center of my palm. "Do you know how much I love you?"

I laced my fingers with his. "Yeah, I have an idea."

On the counter, my phone buzzed. Releasing my hand, Mason leaned over and grabbed it, passing it to me. "Beck," I told him.

"She here?"

"Yeah."

The kiss he gave me when he bent down again was

much more chaste and controlled. "Be safe, Ward," he said, and I could again hear the thread of tension in his voice.

"I'll do my best," I promised.

He kissed me again, a little more soundly this time. "I love you."

"I love you, too," I told him, then wheeled myself over to the door. "See you tonight, Jax!" I yelled back down the hallway. "Have fun! Say happy birthday to Ben!"

"Bye, Uncle Ward!" he yelled back, drawing a smile from Mason.

As I eased my way out the front door, I heard Mason telling Jackson to hurry up and get his stuff together. I rolled down the walk to Beck's shiny, bright blue Lexus Evo, which, now that I looked at it, glowed the same color as her magic in the sunlight. The best thing about Beck's Evo, though, was that it was low enough to the ground that I could actually get *myself* into and out of it.

I'd teased her when she bought it last year that she'd done that just for me, and she'd grinned and told me that while she hadn't actually included it as a criterion, she had definitely asked about it before signing on the dotted line.

One more reason I love her.

She had already hopped out to grab my chair and throw it in the back—I had a custom lightweight, semi-collapsible chair for just this reason. She was fabulously dressed, as usual, this time in a short pleated grey skirt with yellow ribbon trim and flowing silk sleeveless blouse in a pale pink. Her dark hair had been put into pigtail braids, each with a yellow ribbon on the end. The blue of her magic was loosely looped around her arms and throat, like steadily glowing bangles. The effect was very stylish. It would figure that even Beck's magic would be *haute couture*.

"You look very spring-like," I told her as she got back into the car.

"And you look like your usual I-summon-dead-people self," she teased back.

We stopped on the way for coffee and donuts, bringing a dozen and a box to go for the break room. We also got Hart his very own bag of three donuts and a cinnamon latte, just to make sure he was in a good mood. Even though I'd had coffee already, I couldn't resist getting a salted caramel latte when Beck had ordered her mocha.

The sugar and caffeine somewhat mollified an incredibly cranky Hart, although we were six whole minutes early, so his sourness wasn't our fault.

"Fucking hell," the elf muttered, snatching the bag of donuts—a cruller, a Boston crème, and a chocolate cake—and taking a deep sniff of the latte.

"I can take them back," I told him.

"Do, and I'll rip your fucking balls off," Hart snarled.

I blinked. That seemed excessive, even for Hart. "Bad morning?"

Hart growled, then took a long pull from his latte, closing his lavender eyes.

Beck and I shared an alarmed look. I, at least, was really hoping this wasn't related to our summoning. Whether Beck shared my concerns or whether she was just more generally alarmed by Hart, I couldn't tell and wasn't going to ask in front of the very crabby elf.

Having fortified himself with the latte, Hart re-opened his eyes. "Fuck, yes. I got here yesterday at six and I haven't fucking gone home yet."

"Ouch." I really hoped he meant six at night. I wasn't going to ask, though, just in case.

Beck winced. "Do we want to know why?" she asked.

Hart flopped into his chair, setting his latte on his desk, and opened the bag to peer inside. "Dead orc. Brutal."

I winced. "Thanks for not calling me out on that one."

Hart shrugged. "Looked like a territorial fight. Wouldn't be the first one in that area. Body was dumped, though, so we spent the better part of the night trying to find the goddamn kill spot." I was going to go out on a limb and guess they hadn't succeeded, if Hart's current mood was any indication.

I grimaced, also glad Mason wasn't here. I wanted to ask Hart how they knew it was a territorial fight if they hadn't found the actual murder scene, but I knew there wasn't really a point.

The way the world was, people who lived and died in the poorer neighborhoods didn't get investigated like people who died in the West End, like Frederick Greer, or who were found under the stairwells of old Victorian mansions. But if you were an orc who was beaten to death in Fulton or Mosby Court, well... Even if Hart had wanted to do more investigating, the RPD wouldn't commit the resources to it.

No wonder the elf was pissed off.

Hart pulled the chocolate cake donut out of the bag and bit off a quarter of it. "And now I have to talk to a fucking cunt of a dead woman who likes ripping hearts out of innocent children."

"To be fair," I pointed out, unable to help myself. "She didn't kill Jenny. Or Tommy."

Hart glared at me.

"Just saying," I muttered. Jenny had died ten years *after* Vaux, and Tommy had been dead for fifty—and Vaux herself had been in her 60s, and I very much doubted she'd been a murderer at ten years old.

Okay, I know people *could* kill people at ten—Rayn, for instance, had killed his uncle at six, but that had been an accident, not a brutal cutting open of someone's chest cavity —but I didn't think that was terribly likely in this case.

"Because it's totally fucking fine if she only murders adults," Hart muttered.

"I'm not saying she's a nice person," I pointed out. "Just that she couldn't have killed Jenny and Tommy."

Hart rolled his eyes and stuffed the rest of the chocolate cake donut in his mouth. "What-the-fuck-ever, Ward," he grumbled around a mouth full of donut, which he then washed down with a sip of latte.

Hart sighed, then heaved himself out of his chair, bringing both donuts and coffee cup. "Might as well get this shit over with," he muttered.

Beck gestured for me to go first, and I followed Hart down the hall to one of the extremely clinical and strangely creepy RPD séance rooms.

It had, at one point in its life, probably several decades ago, been an interrogation room. One wall was half mirror, still used as an observation area, since most police séances were conducted as part of ongoing cases—murder victims, deceased perpetrators, and so on. I'd never been behind the mirror, although I'd asked Hart once, and he'd assured me that it was as soulless as the interrogation side.

For the séance rooms, they'd painted the walls and floor black, either out of some misguided idea that they had to be eerily macabre, or maybe because they thought it would make drawing chalk circles easier. But that was it. A bare-ass black room, no table, no chairs, just shitty black paint on cinderblocks and cement.

It honestly always made me feel like I was in a killing room.

That didn't change today.

Beck wrinkled her nose as she walked in, then turned to look at Hart. "Seriously?"

Hart's expression was bland. "What? You think people here have a fucking clue how any of this woowoo shit works?"

Beck rolled her eyes. "I assume you've seen it often enough by this point, detective, that you could enlighten them."

Hart bared his teeth. "You think they listen to a pointy-eared bastard like me? I'm a fucking diversity hire, which is some sad-ass shit, let me tell you."

I controlled the smirk that wanted to cross my lips.

"So you were an elf when you were hired, then?" Beck asked casually.

Hart took a long pull of his latte. "Here, yeah."

"Where were you before?" she asked, sweetly.

"That sugar shit won't work on me," Hart warned her.

Beck blinked innocently, and Hart snorted.

"I believe that like I believe you shit rainbows, missy."

I did laugh at that.

"Seriously, detective, why the big secret?"

Hart shrugged. "No secret. Milwaukee."

"As in... Wisconsin?"

"Yeah, as in Wisconsin. Beer. Brats. Shitty baseball, good football. Snow. It was fucking great."

Beck blinked a couple times.

Hart bared his teeth in a feral grin. "Don't look the type, do I?"

"I suppose that's a good lesson to me to not judge people by appearances," Beck replied, her tone slightly apologetic.

The Skeleton Under the Stairs

Hart snorted. "That's me. Deceptively pretty, complete barbarian on the inside."

I smothered a smile. Hart wasn't a barbarian, of course. Sure, he swore like a sailor and shoved donuts in his mouth one half at a time, but he'd been there for me when nobody else was—or could be. He'd held my hand through some of the most traumatic hours of my life without me even having to ask, and he hadn't complained or thought twice about it.

And he'd probably shoot me if I told anybody that who didn't already know.

Instead of pursuing that line of conversation, I changed the subject. "Are we recording this?"

"Did you want me to?" Hart asked, the question genuine rather than confrontational.

"Not particularly. Beck?"

"Oh, I don't care," she replied, waving a hand.

Hart shrugged. "Then I won't bother traumatizing some rookie by making them watch you talk to dead people."

I nodded once. I didn't know how this was going to go, and didn't see the need for a record if things got particularly weird. I was already enough of a freak in the eyes of most of the department.

Beck slid her satchel around so that she could pull a few candles and a stick of chalk out. "What do you think, Ward? Standard protection or a level up?"

"She's going to be hostile," I said. "She immediately started throwing things at Mason—and she's not going to be happy to see me, since I banished her once already."

"Okay, so let's go a little stronger, then." She pulled out a jar of salt and passed it and the chalk to me. Then she drew out a bundle of sage, which she also handed over, then a silver bowl and a lighter. "Get this smudging?"

"Yeah, sure."

I went to the center of the room and maneuvered myself so that I could draw a circle leaning over the side of my chair. In the middle, I put the bowl. "You have rosemary oil?" I asked.

"Catch." A little plastic bottle—what looked like a repurposed hotel shampoo bottle, specifically—flew from Beck's hand into my lap.

I poured about a tablespoon of oil into the bottom of the bowl, then brushed the end of the sage bundle through it lightly before lighting the dry end, which began to smoke and smolder.

Beck had done a line of salt around the perimeter of the room—a way to make sure that even if we lost control of Vaux that she wouldn't end up finding her way out into the station proper. I'd never had a ghost escape a séance, and I wasn't about to start with this one.

About a foot inside the salt at the narrowest part of the rectangular room, Beck had begun her protective circle.

"Am I staying inside this?" I asked.

"Is that okay?"

"Yeah, of course. I just wanted to make sure I was on the right side before I get trapped in here."

She smiled at me, a little distracted by the careful work of the protective ring.

"Anything I should be doing?" Hart asked.

"Stay in the corner and don't fuck up the salt circle," I replied. I wanted Hart on the outside of the sigils, even if he was going to insist on being inside the room.

"Can I cross it before we get started?" he asked.

"Just don't mess it up on the way in or out. Assuming you're going to stay in here for the summoning?"

He nodded once. "I'll be back." Taking his donuts and coffee, he gracefully—and carefully—stepped over the salt

The Skeleton Under the Stairs

line crossing the doorway, then slowly closed it behind him, making sure that not a single grain was disturbed.

That was one of the many reasons I liked Hart. He might not understand magic, but he listened to the people who did and followed directions—and he respected our work. Sure, he gave me shit, but never about the quality or seriousness of what I did professionally. Only about my tendency to throw up at crime scenes and squeamishness about touching dead people.

At some point, Hart slipped back in, still carrying his latte, down to just his last donut, which he was carrying with three long fingers, the outer two held away from the chocolate frosting with elegant delicacy.

Because of course that's how Hart held a donut.

I shook my head a little, continuing to finish my sigils while ignoring the ache in my back from being folded over so that I could reach the floor.

By the time we were done, Hart had also finished his donut, licking the cream and frosting off his fingers. I noticed that he'd been very careful not to spill any on the floor, although I honestly didn't think it would matter. Donuts are not known for their metaphysical or necromantic properties. The only kind of magic in donuts was good, old-fashioned sugary baked goodness.

Hart remained quietly in his corner, watching us.

Not for the first time, I wondered just how much Hart really did understand about magic. He was keenly observant and had watched more than his fair share of summonings, as well as a few banishings, over the years. He'd seen me work ad hoc, like in the attic, but he'd also seen some of my more formal preparations, like this one. It occurred to me that if we messed something up, Hart might actually notice.

But we didn't—because Beck and I are that good—so when we finished and Beck put away the supplies, after adding a second bundle of sage to the bowl, Hart stood away from the wall.

"Anything else?" he asked.

Beck handed him her bag across the protective circle, and he put it over his shoulder.

"If I ask you for something in there, can you give it to me?" she asked him. We probably wouldn't, but sometimes shit went sideways. It was always good to be prepared.

"As long as I know what it is I'm looking for."

"It should be fairly obvious. Ward?" Beck looked at me.

"I think we're good to go," I replied.

Beck and I took our places opposite one another and reached out to clasp hands over the bowl. Together, we drew in deep breaths, and, together, we reached out, the loops of her magic unwinding as my threads spun out from my arms to meet it. It was kind of neat to see what my magic actually *looked* like—I knew what it *felt* like, but seeing it was pretty cool.

I was the summoner, so I took point, guiding the thick blue ribbons of her magic with the slender threads of my own, sewing them into the fabric of the Veil, giving it first shadow and then substance so that I could push through and find the spirit that was Winifred Vaux.

I felt her, faintly, pushing back, attempting to elude me.
Nice try.

I spun my threads into a net, sticky and strong, that wrapped around the essence of Winifred Vaux, tangling in the aether of her spiritual self, forcing her to cross through the invisible barrier between there and here, drawing her back across the Veil.

She fought me, fought us, but with Beck's strong bands

ов blue, I had no problem bringing Vaux across, despite her attempts to cling to the other side.

Fully in the room, she bared her teeth at me.

Let me go, summoner. She tried to find something to throw at me, but she couldn't touch any of the objects that were part of the circle itself. They were fully anchored into the ritual circle, and that was beyond her.

Not that she was placidly floating there.

Hell, no.

That would have been far too easy, and Winifred Vaux was not in the least about easy.

She was doing the metaphysical equivalent of thrashing like a fish, pulling on her own power, which, although muted by the fact that she was dead, was not insubstantial. I could feel beads of sweat forming on my back, running down my spine. Across from me, Beck's jaw was set, lines of tension visible around her eyes above her mask.

This was hard work.

Vaux attempted to throw a tantrum, lashing out against the threads of magic that bound her to the circle and my will. The magic stretched, but didn't give, and I poured more energy into it until she was forced to hold still.

"What are your questions, detective?" I ground out between my teeth.

"How many of these heart-removing ritual murders did she attend?" Hart asked.

Vaux shrieked, and Beck swayed a little as Vaux started pulling on her own magic, faint grey tentacles that reminded me disturbingly of the blackness that had filled the attic.

Enough, I told her, casting more threads around her, attempting to cut off her access to her magic.

She fought me, hard, and I could feel pressure in my

lungs and against my ribs and spine as she tried to pull at my magic, trying to tear out where it was anchored to my core.

I was tiring fast, that spot under my sternum where Archie had touched me a tight, burning ball. I could feel more magic there... I just couldn't draw on it.

I pushed out a thought, and he was there.

Hello, bitch, he greeted Vaux.

She hissed at him.

Archie, a little help here.

What do you want me to do with her, sonny? he asked.

Not her. Me. I know there's more there, but I can't get at it.

Ah. A slow smile spread over his face. **Deep breath, sonny. This is about to get... interesting.**

I didn't bother point out that things were already interesting.

I also somehow managed not to scream when Archie plunged his hand into my chest. Beck did, but I didn't.

"What is it?" Hart demanded.

"I'm. Fine." I ground out. "Hold on."

That tight, hot ball got tighter and hotter, and then, like a knot of muscle worked at by an insistent thumb, it suddenly gave, and warmth flooded my veins. Every visible thread of magic burned like magnesium, so bright it was painful for a few seconds before settling back into tolerability.

It also opened up the tension in my lungs, and I sucked in a breath of air.

And accidentally let Vaux slip for a second.

She came straight at me, hands transmuted into raking claws. I got my right arm up in front of my face, but I felt her insubstantial talons rake through the skin and muscle of my forearm. Again. Annoyed at both her and myself, I hissed at the pain.

And then I regained control with far less effort than I'd originally been expending to hold it—which was not at all the way this was supposed to work or ever *had* worked before.

The threads were ribbons that wove and unwove at my command, looping around her wrists and throat, binding her legs and feet and twisting around her chest.

I looked quickly at Beck, but she was gaping at me, her eyes wide, so I just kept going.

Answer the detective's questions, I ordered Vaux, tightening the cords of magic around her.

Fuck you, summoner.

Language, you foul harpy, Archie admonished, which I thought was particularly rich coming from him, but I kept my thoughts to myself.

I felt his hand on my shoulder. **You can force her tongue, you know, sonny.**

I was about to ask how, but then felt the information rising in my head. It was disturbing, having Archie share his knowledge with me this way, and I was going to go ahead and have a bit of a breakdown about it later, but right now I had to shove that particular set of emotions into a box and lock it.

Force her tongue.

I took my threads, shaping them and slipping them past her lips, wrapping them around her metaphysical tongue, taking the idea literally.

Curse you, summoner!

Answer the questions.

I felt her resistance, but I could tell it was crumbling, pulled from her by the purplish-blue threads of my magic.

Three rituals, she choked out.
What are they for? I asked her.
The heart holds the key to the power of life. Hold the heart and it becomes possible to draw upon the energy of the spirit.

It sounded to me a lot like what they'd been doing to the patients at Tranquil Brook. That was worth examining later. *You're using them as magical batteries. For what?*

To augment our power.
Why?

The look she leveled at me was filled with hate. **We deserve to control this world, with its pathetic mundanes who cannot even sense the world around them.**

I felt a snarl twist my mouth. It was all fucking classist, bigoted bullshit. They were ambitious and greedy and justified it by stealing magic from the living and the dead.

What about me, bitch? Archie demanded.

She glared at him. **You did not deserve your power.**

According to you, you horrible cunt. God gave me the power, and it ought to be up to God to take it away, not you and your little shit-eating cronies!

I wasn't about to get into a debate about whether or not magic was divine in origin, but I sympathized with the sentiment of Archie's rant.

Why didn't they keep your heart? I asked her. *If that was the point.*

The ritual confers power without it, she answered, still fighting me. But whatever Archie had unlocked this time was like a reservoir somewhere inside my chest that went far deeper than anything I'd ever had access to. And I wasn't going to let it go unused if it could help us.

And it was their gift to you that your life was all you had to pay?

Yes.

She really hated me.

The feeling was mutual.

"Three rituals, detective," I said out loud. "What else?"

"Names," he demanded. "Who else committed them?"

She told me, grinding each name out against her will, and I repeated them. "Henry Simmons. Thomas Daggett. Oliver Picton. Fitzhugh Masterson. Philip Willoughby. Lucretia Moffet. Miranda Vicent."

I knew those sons of bitches were involved! Archie crowed. I ignored him.

"Did they kill anyone else?"

Her expression was vile and hateful. **No other humans.**

I had a sinking feeling in my gut. *Then what else?* I pressed.

Her eyes narrowed. **They are not worthy**, she spat.

Names, I demanded.

I wouldn't know. I really fucking hated her now.

Numbers.

Two elves. Six orcs. Three fauns. Five ghouls. One vampire.

Nausea churned in my stomach, but I repeated the information for Hart, whose long string of vitriolic invectives didn't even come close to encapsulating what I was feeling.

"What else, Hart?" I rasped out.

The well of power was finally starting to run low.

"Where are they? The hearts?" he asked.

The. Underground. Room. She had not wanted to tell me that.

Where is the Underground Room?

She screamed, enraged, and lashed out again, the coils of her magic growing darker.

Sweet Rose.

"What the fuck is 'sweet rose'?" Hart asked, when I repeated her answer.

She screamed again. **Sweet Rose!**

I could feel the blood dripping down my arm, and I was trying to both hold Vaux and make sure I didn't mar the sigils by dripping blood on them.

"Beck," I hissed.

She nodded once, and then I pushed the rest of my rapidly waning energy into her, the blue of her magic flaring brilliantly as she wrapped it around Vaux and used it to pull the still-thrashing spirit back through the gap in the Veil.

And then it was over, and I sagged forward as Beck sank to the floor.

Well done, sonny, Archie praised me, patting my shoulder and making me shiver.

Thanks, Archie.

———

AFTER A BREAK TO eat a granola bar and make sure I didn't need to go to the hospital, Beck had gone home. Hart had offered to drive me back to Beyond the Veil, and since Beck looked dead on her feet, I'd encouraged her to go home and rest.

Someone at the RPD whose name I couldn't remember had cleaned and bound up the claw marks on my right arm, which would now have a set of new scars to complement the pinkish burn that was now mostly healed snaking around my left.

Mason was going to lose it.

Or maybe he'd just sigh audibly, thank Hart for driving, and then suggest that we order lunch because I looked completely drained.

The Skeleton Under the Stairs

His lack of reaction made me anxious, but I also didn't want to start a fight.

I nervously followed Mason back toward his office, glad that at least my hand was unharmed, even if Vaux had sliced up my forearm.

Mason looked up when I rolled into his office behind him. "What did you want to eat?" he asked, his voice still disturbingly calm. He'd picked up his phone and was poking at it.

"Literally anything," I answered truthfully. I was starving.

"Five Guys?"

The prospect of a loaded-up grilled cheese and a giant pile of french fries sounded fucking amazing. "Yeah."

He tapped at his phone, and I realized he was ordering food.

"Malt?"

"Please."

"Regular or spicy fries?"

"Both?"

One corner of his lips twitched, and I entertained the possibility that he actually might not be furious with me. A few more taps, then, "Done. Fifteen minutes, according to this, anyway."

He set his phone down, then, when I didn't say anything, sighed.

"You first, or me?" he asked.

I blinked. "Me or you what?"

He raised both eyebrows. "I had a donor meeting, you had a summoning, I assumed we would be sharing information about those events?"

"You're not mad?"

He sighed again, then came over and crouched beside

me, adjusting his dress pants so that he could bend his knees. He put his hands on my thighs, gently squeezing. "Do I like the fact that you showed up with a new bandage on your arm? Of course not. But we knew summoning Vaux wasn't going not be easy or smooth. So while I'm not *happy*, I'm not mad that you did your job." Then he sighed again, and when he spoke his voice was heavy and sad. "I'm sorry I've made you think I will be."

And now I felt like shit for making him feel bad.

Because, seriously, Mason *not* losing his shit at me for some of the crap I got myself into was a continuous miracle as far as I was concerned.

And, I was beginning to realize, had a lot more to do with *me* than it did with *him*. Because my automatic assumption was that he'd be angry with me. Most of the time it was because he didn't like that I took risks, and I knew that.

It was, it suddenly occurred to me, although I probably should have seen it a long time ago, because he was *scared*. And I was reading his fear as anger.

I reached out and put my palms on either side of his face, leaning forward to press my forehead against his. "No, I'm sorry, Mason." I kept talking over his grunt of protest. "I'm sorry that I keep accusing you of being mad when you're just worried. And I'm sorry I keep making you worry, although I'm probably going to keep doing that part anyway."

He huffed a little, but it wasn't annoyed or upset. His hands tightened on my legs. "Did you at least eat something?" he asked.

"I had a donut on the way. And a granola bar after."

"Ward."

"I am about to eat a shitton of fries, so I don't think it's important that I eat right this second," I pointed out.

He sighed. "I suppose you're right about that." He pushed off my lap, but not before kissing my forehead, then walked around behind his desk and started rifling through some papers.

"What happened with the donor?" I asked. I had the feeling my morning was going to launch a lot more conversation—like how the Antiquus Ordo Arcanum was trying to steal power from the dead just like they'd been doing at Tranquil Brook—and then we'd never talk about Mason's day.

He grunted again, and I got the sense that it hadn't been great.

"I suppose the positive outcome is that we got the donation," he replied.

"But?" I sensed a very large *but* to this.

"But," he repeated, "it was suggested that perhaps it would be better for the foundation if they chose a more... personable representative."

"Personable." I hoped my tone conveyed just how fucking stupid I thought that choice of words was.

Mason's lips quirked. "It may also have been mentioned that this individual of course wasn't bothered by it—"

"It? They actually said *it*?"

"They did," he confirmed.

"Holy shit."

"One could interpret that particular word choice as being referent to the situation rather than, well, me," he pointed out.

"The fuck one could," I argued back.

"Either way, there might have been mention about the necessity for a different *sort of person* standing for the magical side of the foundation's mission."

"Oh, fuck them. And the horse they rode in on," I snapped.

"Elsbeth made it very clear that anyone who had such concerns need not contribute money to Lost Lineage, which was actually quite clever, since it basically forced them into doing it."

"Them?"

"Elwood and Miranda Vincent."

My blood went cold.

"Did you just say Miranda fucking Vincent?"

Mason lifted his head sharply. "Yes?"

"Mace, this is bad."

I had his full attention now. "Why?"

Then his phone buzzed. He ignored it. I didn't.

"Is that food?"

He looked down. "Yes. We aren't done with this, Ward."

"No, we aren't," I agreed. "But I'm really hungry."

He cleared off part of the conference table—the other half still covered with papers from Hannah Neale's diary—while I went and got the bags of food from the delivery guy at the door.

When I brought it back, Mason made a pile of all the fries, then handed me a stack of napkins and my sandwich and malt, and I ravenously took a huge bite.

"I'm going to wait for you to chew that," he remarked, sounding amused, "but then I need to know why it's important that this donor is Miranda Vincent."

I chewed and swallowed, nodding.

"Because if it's the same Miranda Vincent, she helped Vaux cut somebody's fucking heart out."

Mason choked on the fry he'd just stuck in his mouth. *"What?!"*

"Miranda Vincent was one of the names Vaux gave as present for the murders she participated in."

"Fuck."

"How old is yours?"

Mason grimaced. "Sixties, probably."

I did the math. "She could have been in her thirties at the last murder Vaux committed. Forties when Vaux herself was killed."

"*Fuck*," he repeated.

"Vaux didn't mention another Vincent person, though." I grabbed a few more fries.

"Ward."

"I know, Mace."

He leaned back in his chair. "I can't—"

"No, I know. Do you want me to call Elsbeth?"

He shook his head. "No. I'll do it."

"You sure?"

He sighed, then took a sip from his chocolate malt. "I'm sure. Goddammit."

Then he pulled out his phone and leaned back, tapping the screen, then holding it up to his ear.

I ate another bite of grilled cheese, waiting.

"Elsbeth. I just heard some unfortunate news about the Vincents. Well, Mrs. Vincent, specifically."

While he explained the situation—punctuated by periodic tinny yelps from his phone as Elsbeth reacted to whatever he'd just said—I kept eating. Once I'd started, my body had gone into calorie-consumption overdrive, needing to replenish what I'd expended.

By the time Mason got off the phone, I'd probably eaten my half of the fries and then some. My sandwich was long gone.

Mason arched an eyebrow. "You ate breakfast *and* a donut, and you're still this hungry?"

I grimaced. "It was a morning," I admitted. "And Archie may have... kicked me into overdrive?"

Mason sighed, rubbing his temple with two fingers. "Do I want to know what that means?"

"I think... well, it felt like he unlocked something. Again. It was weird, but it was also like all this power just *flooded* me." I went back to the beginning and told him what had happened.

When I finished, he was staring at me.

I almost asked him if he was mad, but I made myself shut up before I said it.

I watched Mason take a few deep breaths and nervously ate another fry. Then two.

"Is there a particular reason you asked him in the middle of the summoning?" he asked.

Okay, he *was* mad. Or at least annoyed.

"I didn't know I needed help until then?"

Another deep breath, then a nod. "Okay."

"Mace—"

He held up a hand. "Ward, I am both incredibly proud of you and utterly terrified that you're going to get yourself killed. Give me a minute."

I shut up again and went back to nervous-eating fries.

Finally, he leaned forward and took a fry himself, speaking around it. "So the thing I'm having the most trouble with," he said, "is what they're using the power for."

"What do you mean?"

"Vaux said they were taking it from the unworthy, right?"

I nodded, eating more fries.

"Well, Tranquil Brook, assuming it is tied to the Ordo, which I still think is a good bet, was taking it from human beings, for the most part. And each of the sacrificial victims is also human."

"But then—"

He held up another hand. "I'm not there yet," he told me. "We'll get to the non-humans in a minute."

I nodded. More fries.

"So we have living victims and dead victims, both of whom are being drained of magic. Vaux claims this is so that they can, what, rule the world? Which, I'm sorry, is an enormous line of bullshit if I've ever heard one."

"She was telling the truth," I told him.

"Then someone else fed her a line of bullshit that she bought into," Mason replied. "You can't just *store* magic like this without putting it into *something*."

"Like what?" I asked.

Mason shrugged. "You can't store *any* amount of magic without objects. Talismans, sigils, idols, *something*. So somewhere there are either a lot of these or one very, very large one."

"But it has to be a thing, not a person?"

Mason looked utterly horrified at that.

"Right?" I pressed when he didn't answer.

"Noooo," he replied, drawing out the answer. "It doesn't have to be an object."

"You don't think..."

"I'm... honestly not sure what to think," he admitted. "But if you were, hypothetically, going to try to keep someone alive for a very long time..."

"You think they're trying to make someone *immortal*?"

He shrugged. "Again, I have no idea. Necromancy would let you keep someone animated for a long time, but their soul would start to... fray."

"Would it make them... feral? Like the spirit in the attic?" I'd told him about that whole thing already.

"It... could."

I ate some more fries.

"Why would you want to keep someone alive like that?" I asked, then.

Mason shuddered. "I wouldn't. But there are any number of stories and legends about rich people doing horrific things to stay alive longer or stay young forever."

"Like the blood bath lady."

"Countess Bathory, yes."

"So this is necromancy?"

"Maybe. Or some other warlock magic I'm not familiar with. Because I'm starting to think that's part of what was going on at Tranquil Brook."

"What do you mean?"

"From what I've gathered from Rayn, nearly all the patients at Tranquil Brook either got their magic from Arcana or were witches. What if the problem is that they're *witches*, specifically, not that they have magic?"

I stared at him, a fry halfway to my mouth. "You're saying that these families are basically committing magical eugenics based on whether their kids are witches or warlocks?"

Mason nodded. "That's a possibility, yes."

"Why do they care?" I asked.

"No idea."

"I mean, our magic is different, but why does it matter?"

Mason just shook his head.

"And what does that have to do with making people live forever?"

"Well, for one thing, no witch worth their salt would *ever* condone that. We operate on balance, and attempting to stave off death for that long breaks pretty much every inherent rule there is about balance."

"You brought me back," I pointed out, shifting uncomfortably.

"I brought you back, I didn't attempt to keep you alive unnaturally or reverse the effects of age so that you live to be two hundred years old."

"Can... is that possible?"

Mason tapped his fingers on the table. "Maybe. Relying on historical legends to provide specific evidence of spells and their outcomes is difficult at best. People several centuries ago weren't always clear on what did what, and a lot of people who kept records of magic were opponents of witchcraft and sorcery, so they weren't exactly concerned with getting the details right."

We sat in silence for a minute. "Preston Fitzwilliam totally would have tried this," I said.

"If he'd known, yes, probably." He huffed a breath. "Maybe he did try it."

"None of these bodies were flayed," I reminded him.

"Again, with the unreliability of magical records," Mason pointed out. "It's entirely possible that you have multiple warlocks or groups trying to sort through old records to find out what works and what doesn't."

"Ugh."

"Agreed."

I ate another handful of fries. "So what now?"

"Not a fucking clue."

18

BEFORE WE'D LEFT the Beyond the Veil offices, Mason had grabbed a bunch of things he thought might be relevant to the Ordo and Tranquil Brook, since we were planning on working from home the next several days.

One of the projects we had to tackle was Jackson's homework—art and science, specifically.

Maybe it was because he was doing school-at-home, but Jackson's science homework was so much cooler than mine had been at his age. They were learning about chemical reactions, so we were going to be playing with vinegar and baking soda. The teacher had given him recipes for two sets of brownies—one that had baking soda and one that didn't.

I was deeply jealous of the fact that the kid had *brownies* for homework.

We were, of course, going to double the recipes, and the brownies were going to be mostly held in reserve for dessert. Mostly.

You can't have a kid bake brownies and *not* let him sample them. For science, of course. But once we made brownies, there was no way Jackson was going to be able to concentrate on anything else, so art was the focus of the morning.

He'd watched a pre-recorded demo from his teacher, and then Mason had set him up on the back deck with some bowls of water and plastic utensils. Jackson was currently making thumb dishes and figurines and coiled bowls with clay, making an absolute mess of the deck and himself.

We'd be baking the clay—which was designed to be hardened in the oven—once he was done, then sending pictures to his teacher.

Before that had gotten started, Mason had called Hart to talk to him about some of our theories about what the Ordo might be up to.

I hadn't heard what the elf said, but it had been loud enough that Mason had moved the phone away from his ear with a wince.

Hart was on his way.

Mason had stacks of books and papers spread out all over the living room, his laptop open on the card table. I was doing my best to avoid getting in the way of... well, all of it.

So I was sitting in the kitchen at the side counter, sipping my coffee and trying not to freak out about the fact that not only did the Ordo use weird creepy magic to snipe people in their homes, cut out their hearts, and turn people into magical batteries, but they *also*—according to Vaux— targeted non-human magic users.

Like my fiancé.

Who was currently sticking his nose very much into their business.

Up until yesterday, I really hadn't fully processed what that might mean, but Vaux's dismissive listing of Arcanids they'd *fucking murdered* had really hammered home the fact that this case was actively putting Mason at risk.

And now I was feeling a lot more sympathetic with his anxiety about me and my uncontrolled warlock magic that kept resulting in butterfly bandages and trips to the hospital. Because now I had to seriously think about the fact that his magic—and the fact that he was an orc—could very well mean that some morning I might roll into the kitchen and find him dead on the fucking floor with a hole in his chest.

And that was fucking terrifying.

I probably shouldn't have been drinking coffee, since it was only going to amp me up even more, but I had to do *something*, and screaming or crying uncontrollably weren't really going to be helpful, and those were the only other things I could think about doing.

Thankfully, Mason was distracted both by Jackson and his art projects and by helping Hart sort through the very same shit that was freaking me out, so he hadn't noticed. Or, if he had, he was too focused on everything else to take the time to grill me about it. Which was perfectly fine by me, since I needed time to process and get my shit under control.

And then think of some way to show Mason just how much I appreciated the fact that he hadn't bundled me in a giant roll of bubble wrap and refused to ever let me leave the house.

So I was sitting in the kitchen, half-watching Jackson through the window as he made a giant mess on the deck while Alma ran around the yard. They both looked like they were having fun, and as long as Alma didn't end up covered in clay, cleanup wouldn't be too difficult.

I jumped when the doorbell rang.

I definitely needed to put down the coffee. But I both wanted my hot morning beverage *and* needed something to do to distract myself, so I dumped the coffee and put the kettle back on. Hot chocolate had always been my comfort drink of choice, so I was going back to it now, even though it was June.

I also got out the marshmallows, because that's where we were.

"I brought presents," Hart announced. "This one's for you, and these are to share."

"Put that... over there," Mason told him, then appeared a few moments later carrying a box from Sugar Shack. He set it on the counter, then noticed me staring at the kettle, the cocoa powder and marshmallows on the counter. "Do you want to talk about it?" he asked me, one big hand running through my curls.

"We're about to," I answered, unsuccessfully trying to keep the strain out of my voice.

Mason gently tilted my head back, then bent to press a lingering kiss to my forehead. "Do you not want to be part of this conversation?" he asked.

"No. I do. I just..." I sighed. "I hate all of it."

He ran his fingers through my hair again. "Me, too," he said. "But donuts?"

I felt a smile tug at the corners of my lips. "Donuts are good."

Hart came in, then, and wiggled his fingers at the box. "Boston crème is mine," he said.

"Did you get maple?" Mason asked him. Maple donuts were his favorite, but they were usually made with bacon, which he didn't eat.

"Maple, check," Hart replied. "And chocolate-filled topped with peanuts. And chocolate with cherry filling and sprinkles." Those were me and Jackson. "And another eight on top of that, because when you buy donuts, you get a dozen."

"Jackson is going to be so high on sugar," I remarked.

"Yes, he is," Mason agreed. "I'll take his out to him so he doesn't notice there are more." He put Jackson's gooey donut on a paper towel and went out the back.

I dug out some small plates and handed one to Hart, who claimed three donuts and put them on his plate.

I picked out my chocolate peanut donut and a chocolate cake with chocolate frosting, graham cracker bits and tiny marshmallows. I put the last three donuts on a plate for Mason, then folded up the box and shoved it in the trash drawer.

"You recovered from yesterday?" Hart asked, and I looked up, surprised.

"Mostly," I answered. "A little tired and a lot freaked out."

Hart's eyes skipped to the door and then back. "Because of the Nids, you mean?"

"Yeah." I couldn't decide if it made me feel better that Hart also got it or whether it made me even more anxious because a homicide detective saw reason to worry.

"We'll get the bastards," he said.

But I knew too much to be reassured. Would Hart try to catch them? Absolutely. My confidence in Hart's intentions was absolute. What I didn't have confidence in was the system—not only did things like bureaucratic red tape, budget cuts, and general incompetence perpetually stall or block justice, but more nefarious things like people with lots of power and money bribing their way out of being punished happened all too often. And the Ordo seemed to be full of people with lots of power and money.

"Did Mason tell you about Vincent?" I asked Hart.

"No? What the fuck about Vincent?" Hart's voice sounded a little tense.

"She and her husband attempted to make a donation to Lost Lineage yesterday," Mason answered, coming back in. "She was... not a fan of my involvement in the company."

"Fucking hell, Doc," Hart muttered. "Vaux named her—"

"Ward mentioned it," Mason remarked, cutting him off.

"Fuck," Hart muttered again, then picked up his strawberry donut and bit off almost a third of it. "Fugh," he repeated, this time around the mouth full of donut.

"We won't be accepting the Vincents' donation," Mason told him.

Hart swallowed his donut. "The fuck you say. You watch your back, Doc. Put up some protection spells or some shit."

I inwardly cursed my failure to think of that as an option, but was distracted by the whistle of the kettle.

"Tea or coffee? Or cocoa?" Mason asked Hart.

"Coffee, if it's not too much trouble." Hart was a giant contradiction—he had the foulest mouth I'd ever encountered, but he could also be extremely polite about the funniest things.

Mason pulled out the French press and the grounds. "Not at all."

I poured water into my cocoa powder and marshmallows, then set it back on the stove for Mason when he finished measuring out coffee grounds. Mason made himself a cup of Earl Grey.

"Let's take this in the other room," Mason suggested, handing Hart a mug of coffee and picking up his tea and donut plate.

I set my plate on my lap and stuck my cocoa in my cupholder, leading the way.

Mason cleared a spot on the card table for plates and mugs, although Hart stayed standing, carrying his mug and the remnant of his donut as he walked through the room, perusing the papers. Mason sat on the couch and immediately picked up the one thing I didn't recognize—a leather-bound book in a plastic evidence baggie. Presumably this was the other 'present' Hart had brought today.

"I'm assuming I can actually look at this?" Mason asked Hart.

"Hang on." Hart shoved the rest of his donut in his mouth, then rooted through a satchel by the door until he came up with a pair of blue latex gloves, which he threw at Mason. "Here. The last fucking thing we need are *your* fingerprints inside that thing."

Mason caught the gloves and pulled them on. "Indeed," he agreed. "I'm allowed to open the bag?"

"Knock yourself the fuck out."

Mason pulled the tab on the baggie, opening it and carefully extracting the book. Then he frowned. "Ward, can you grab some of the acid-free paper in the top drawer of my desk?"

I was happy to be useful, and came back with a few sheets, laying them out so that he would have room to set the open book across them without the cover coming into contact with our table and whatever food or art supplies had been smeared on it.

"The fuck is that for?" Hart asked.

"This is actually quite old," Mason answered. "And I don't want to introduce oils or other contaminants to the leather of the cover or to the pages—they'd deteriorate it further." He grimaced. "I honestly would rather be using cotton gloves, but this is better than my fingers, and I suppose cotton fibers would upset the lab people."

"Yeah, probably," Hart agreed. "Why cotton?"

"Less likely to stick—and the powder coating on gloves isn't the greatest thing for old books and manuscripts."

Hart grunted.

Mason reached out and grabbed his glasses off the side table, perching them on his nose before carefully opening the book.

Hart and I both leaned in, although I was careful not to drop either chocolate frosting or peanut bits anywhere near the book. Hart seemed less concerned, picking up his coconut donut.

"If that dribbles on here, I'm tattling to CSI," Mason warned him without looking up, and Hart backed up a step before taking a bite, shedding quite a few shavings of coconut in the process.

Mason immediately flipped to the end of the pages, then quickly rifled through them until he found what he was looking for. He frowned at the page for a few minutes while Hart fidgeted. "This is still in use," Mason said. "Or it was, anyway. The final pages are blank—but there are a handful of things recorded recently." He stopped on a particular page, then showed it to us. "This one appears to be dated two years ago."

"The last date they would have conducted the ritual," I said.

"Correct."

"The fuck do you see a date, Doc?" Hart asked.

"Here." Mason's blue-gloved finger pointed to a word. "Midsummer."

"There is nothing on that page that says fucking 'midsummer,'" Hart snapped.

Mason smiled. "Litha is midsummer," he replied. "It's one of the powerful points of the year, like Yule or Samhain or Beltane."

Hart looked blank. "Like *what*?"

Mason sighed. "Witch shit, Hart," he said. "Trust me on this one. Litha is midsummer. This ritual was almost certainly conducted on June 21 two years ago."

"And where the fuck does it say the two years ago part?"

"Here."

"Fucking Roman numerals," Hart muttered.

"This is... a strange mix, I'll give you that," Mason acknowledged. "They're blending the pagan cyclical calendar common to witchcraft ritual with Roman numerals and what looks—" he paused, flipping back a few pages, then forward again "—like the Julian calendar."

"The what now?"

"Julian calendar. It's what was used traditionally up until the early seventeenth century when Pope Gregory—"

"Don't care about dead popes, Doc," Hart interrupted, holding up a hand.

Mason snorted. "The year turns over in March," he replied. "And is recorded year, then the three-digit day."

Hart rubbed the bridge of his nose. "Why the fuck would you do that?"

"Because you're a member of a sketchy secret society and you don't want people knowing what date you murdered someone?" I suggested.

Mason chuckled. Hart rolled his lavender eyes.

"Just a thought," I said, leaning back in my chair and popping the last bite of chocolate peanut donut in my mouth.

"Does it list something actually fucking useful in there?" Hart asked. "Names?"

Mason shook his head. "No names. A set of letters that might connect to names... maybe?"

The Skeleton Under the Stairs

"Can you check the one from twenty-two years ago?" I asked, a sudden thought occurring to me.

Mason started flipping backward, his brow furrowed as his eyes skimmed over the pages.

"What else is in there?" Hart asked, then.

"Other rituals, I assume," Mason answered. "Although I'm not sure what. I'd have to spend a bit more time with them. Some are around Samhain, some for Ostara, another set for Yule. I can guess, but I'd want to look more closely."

"I'm going to ask you to do that," Hart said, and Mason nodded.

"Okay, Ward. Twenty-two years ago. Litha. What am I looking for?"

I thought back to the list Vaux had given. "Do you see an MV anywhere?" I asked. "Either by itself or part of another list of letters?"

Mason hummed slightly, then, "Yes." He looked up. "What are you thinking?"

I closed my eyes, thinking back. "The rest are... HS?"

"Yes."

"TD?"

"Yes."

"P... W?"

"Yes. Are these the people Vaux listed off, Ward?" he asked.

"Yeah. LM?"

"Yes."

"And.... OP. And FM."

"Yes. All of them."

"Anyone else?" Hart asked.

"No. Here's the list I have—OPLMHSFMTDMVPW."

"Does it matter?" Hart asked.

"Probably," Mason answered.

"Mace, would they list the leaders first? OP is Oliver Picton, and we know his son is the current whatever—"

"Magus," Mason supplied.

"Yeah, that. And Lucretia Moffet was next, and she could be the other one."

"The Maga. That would make sense."

"Well, she's dead," Hart said. "I looked up the names on the list. The only ones still alive are Miranda Vincent and Philip Willoughby."

"And they're last on the list," Mason said. "If Ward is right about it being in rank order, they would be the youngest members at this point, and therefore the most junior."

"But Oliver Picton had a son, and his son is now the Magus," I pointed out.

"There's no Harrod on that list," Hart said. "And we know there current Maga is Lilian Harrod."

Mason flipped back to the end. "But there *is* LH on the list from two years ago," he said. "Right after VP."

"Victor fucking Picton," Hart muttered. "Fucking hell." He ran a hand over his ponytail. "Can you sub in the names we have and tell me how far back the living Picton and Harrod go?"

"I can," Mason answered. "And can you tell me if Lilian Harrod is her married name?"

"Fuck. Yes. Yes, I can." Hart went back to his bag and pulled out a laptop, then sat on the far end of the sectional. He bit off a huge chunk of his Boston crème, then began typing furiously.

I picked up my s'mores donut and broke off a piece.

"Ward?"

"Notebook?" I asked.

Mason glanced up, the lenses of his reading glasses glinting as he smiled at me. "Please."

I brought it over to him, along with the high-end mechanical pencil Keidra had bought him for his Ph.D. graduation. He always used it to take notes when working on old documents. He said that it was a lot easier to clean possible graphite smudges off old paper than ink.

He hummed his thanks, flipping the notebook open and turning it to an empty sheet before beginning to write, splitting his attention between the Ordo book and his own notes.

"Here," Hart said, holding out his phone. "Lilian Simmons."

I sighed. "Like Henry Simmons."

"Fucking monkey balls," Hart muttered, then began poking at his phone. "Sonofa fucking bitch."

"Her father Henry Simmons?" I asked.

"Of fucking course it is," Hart replied.

Mason started flipping through the pages again.

I finished my donut, trying to decide whether or not I could be at all useful, but was interrupted by Alma trotting into the living room.

Bedroom, I signed at her, and she obediently trotted down the hall. I went to make sure Jackson wasn't covering the whole mud room with, well, mud. I found him standing on the rag rug just inside the back door, smeared pretty much everywhere with wet clay.

I made him stick out his feet so I could wipe them down with a wet washcloth, then snagged the towel Mason had set on a nearby shelf for just this purpose and handed it to Jackson. "Wrap up, go take a shower, get changed, and then we'll get some laundry started. When you're clean and presentable again, we'll bake your pots. Okay?"

"Okay!" He trotted off down the hall barefoot.

I looked out on the deck and found that Jackson had carefully lined up all of his final sculptures and pots along the railing, each on a little piece of wax paper, just like Mason had told him to. When he was clean, I'd have him bring each of them in, and we'd line them up on cookie sheets.

I went back into the kitchen to prep for turning the oven into a makeshift kiln, lining cookie sheets with aluminum foil so we wouldn't be baking clay on the same surface that we put food. Mason had been very specific about this.

In the living room, I could hear Hart and Mason talking about the book, about the Ordo, and about Tranquil Brook.

I could have rejoined them, but... I was done. I'd hit the wall of just how much of this shit I could mentally handle.

I got into mediumship not because I was dedicated to finding justice for the dead or out of a spiritual calling to commune with spirits, but because seeing dead people was my new reality, and I figured I might as well do that as work in IT, which I hated.

The more I learned about what it meant to be a warlock, the more I was learning that I'd probably already had an affinity for this sort of thing, I just... hadn't unlocked it yet. I wondered if that affinity, or whatever you wanted to call it, was *why* I'd ended up as a medium instead of something else.

But if that were the case, it seemed like Mason should've ended up as... I guess an empath. Otherwise known as an emotion-psychic, an empath was probably the closest thing to a healing witch. But he had become an orc, so there went that hypothesis.

I shook my head. We had no idea what made people become Arc-human or Arcanid, although genetics did play some sort of role, since you tended to see patterns in families, if more than one member got sick.

I wondered if that meant that Jackson would become an orc if he ever contracted Arcana. I pushed that thought aside. I hoped Jackson never got sick—not because I didn't want him to be an orc, necessarily, although from what Mason had said, the physical transformation was horrifically painful, but because Arcana was horrible to live through, whether you transformed into something else at the end of it or not. Assuming, of course, that you lived.

I sighed, then turned the kettle on again.

I'd probably have way too much sugar today, between the cocoa and the donuts and the brownies, but I needed something comforting, so I guess I was turning to tea. I wasn't a big tea person, but I liked chai, and it reminded me of Mason, so it worked on both the taste and emotional levels.

I'd only gotten a few sips in when Jackson came padding back into the kitchen, and I sent him to fetch in his creations, which he carefully—one at a time—set on my foil-covered trays. We put them in to bake, and then turned to the next science experiment of the day: lunch.

Jackson helped me to set up a sandwich bar of sorts in the kitchen, washing lettuce, setting out bread, setting out baby carrots and hummus. He wasn't quite at the age where I was ready to hand him a knife, so I did the cutting of the tomato, cheese, onion, and avocado, although he helped mush the avocado so it was spreadable on the sandwiches or available for chip-dipping.

When Hart and Mason came in to get food, Mason paused, setting a hand on my shoulder. "You okay?" he asked softly.

I offered a weak smile. "You'd better be prepared for an

absolute disaster in here after lunch," I told him. "If I'm in charge of the baking soda experiments."

He frowned at me, and I knew he wasn't buying my lighthearted non-answer for a second. "I'm sure we'll manage," he answered, but the fingers on my shoulder tightened.

WE ORDERED Indian food because Mason and Hart hadn't stopped working by dinnertime. Jackson's brownies—minus two squares of each—were sitting on the counter waiting for us to finish dinner. Jackson had very meticulously—hence the need for *two* squares of each type—recorded differences in texture, fluffiness, and flavor in his science worksheet.

We'd also made an enormous mess with baking soda, since both of us had vastly underestimated the amount of frothing that could occur with the amount we'd poured into his makeshift clay volcano—one of the morning's projects.

Jackson had been *thrilled* by its eruption, and had been diligent, if less enthusiastic, about helping me to clean up the foam that had ended up all over the floor and cabinets as well as the counter.

I put Jackson's leftover rice and butter chicken—this was one of his rare opportunities to order meat, and he'd begged for it, although only eaten half—in the fridge alongside my matar paneer and several pieces of leftover naan. Jackson and I had eaten in the kitchen to avoid interrupting the research in the living room, although Mason and Hart were eating in there out of the take-out containers.

Jackson asked about a movie, and I offered my laptop—we could stream it in his room, if he wanted, and he readily agreed. He picked *Encanto*, for probably the seventeenth

The Skeleton Under the Stairs

time, and I wondered if sometimes he didn't wish that he hadn't gotten magic from his family.

But we were what we were. Magic and all.

I tucked him in, nestling Everest in beside him, then made my way back out to the living room, gently closing Jackson's door behind me. I'd managed to avoid the case for most of the day, and it was time to put my big kid pants back on.

I pushed myself back into the living room, both wanting and not wanting to be a part of the discussions I knew were happening.

When I was little, I'd been the kid who hid from the things he couldn't do—the kid who didn't want to play in gym class because he knew he would lose, the kid who avoided doing his homework if he knew he wasn't going to do well at it.

And I didn't want to face the reality that I might not be able to fix whatever was going on. That I might not have the skills or abilities necessary to keep Mason and Jackson safe. I had the terrible feeling that before this whole business with the Ordo was over, it was going to come down to what *I* could do, and I was afraid I didn't have what it was going to take.

But avoiding it wasn't the answer, so I cleared my throat, causing both Mason and Hart to look up.

"Ward, good." I knew Mason was about to ask me to do something. I recognized the tone. "Can you ask Archie to talk to us?"

I nodded once, took a deep breath, and he was there before I barely had time to think.

Hey, sonny. How you feelin' today?

Hi, Archie.

That bad, huh?

I almost laughed. It was either that or cry, and that would be both humiliating and raise a lot of questions I didn't feel prepared to answer right this minute.

I've had better days, I admitted to the ghost. *Mason and Hart have questions.*

I'm sure they do. So we get to play telephone, eh?

I didn't want to play ghost-telephone. To always be speaking for someone else. And if I had more power today than I had yesterday... I held out my hand, and Archie took it.

I exhaled, then sent the purplish threads of my magic out toward Archie, not binding him, as I had Vaux, but strengthening his form, putting my energy into him, using my threads to make his stronger, more visible, more tangible, more *audible*.

Archie's eyes were wide.

Hart's were wider.

Mason took off his glasses, a small smile twisting his lips with something I recognized as pride as he scooped up a forkful of vegetable biryani.

"Well, shit, sonny."

Mason dropped his fork.

"Jesus fucking Christ in a goddamn chicken basket." That was Hart. Obviously.

Archie was staring at his hands, turning them back and forth. **"Son, I was a damn good hand with magic, but this is somethin' fuckin' else."**

I swallowed. "Thanks?"

I could feel the tug of power it took to keep him tangible and audible, but it wasn't half as bad as I'd expected.

Hart made a small, squeaky sound in the back of his throat.

Mason stood up, looking at Archie, his eyes wide. "Mr. Lagarde—"

"It's Archie, son. And I know who you are. One hell of a witch, by the way."

Mason blinked rapidly. "Thank... you."

I couldn't help the flicker of a smile that came to my lips. Archie had that effect on people.

Archie then turned to Hart. **"You're a funny one, you are. I like you."**

Hart swallowed once. "The fuck, Ward?" Although he was clearly talking to me, he didn't take his eyes off Archie.

"Sylvia and I have been... working on it," I said, mostly for Hart's benefit, because Mason knew. "And with the power-boost Archie gave me yesterday, I thought this would be... Easier."

"Fuck," the elf repeated.

"Come on now, pretty-boy. I know you've got other words besides that one."

Hart blinked, then scowled. "How about I ask my warlock friend here to rip you a new asshole?" he asked.

Archie threw his head back and laughed.

At least he thought Hart was funny, rather than horrifically rude. Or maybe rude *was* funny to Archie, given his own propensity for cursing and off-color commentary.

"Hart, please *try* to be civilized," Mason requested.

"I'll be fucking civilized as long as *he*," here Hart inclined his head toward Archie. "Stops calling me that."

I shot Archie a look.

Still chuckling a little, the ghost nodded once. **"All right then, copper. Don't get your knickers in a twist."**

"My knickers are none of your goddamn business, dead man."

Maybe this hadn't been such a great idea.

"Archie, I wanted to be able to give Mason and Detective Hart a chance to ask you some questions directly. That's why I reached out to you."

Archie spread his hands. **"Fire away, kids."**

Hart looked like he wanted very much to say something about being called a kid, but he must have decided that since Archie had been in his seventies when he died and that had been thirty-two years ago, the ghost may in fact be justified in his word choice.

Mason simply nodded, then sat down and put his glasses back on, pulling his laptop toward him. "First, may I ask, Mr... Archie, can you tell us exactly what happened when you were killed?"

"Jump right in, eh?"

"If it bothers you..."

"Death don't bother me, son. Mine or anyone else's." He leaned against the arm of the couch. **"I was at home, about to eat dinner. The doors were locked. Windows closed. They got in anyway. Crafty buggers. I didn't stand a damn chance. Out like a candle in a thunderstorm."**

"They knocked you unconscious?" Hart asked. "With what?"

"Magic, what else?"

Hart looked annoyed, but waved his hand for Archie to continue.

"When I came to, I was tied up like a goddamn hog, wearin' a fuckin' dress."

"A dress?" Hart asked.

"Dress. Stupid ritual gown. Same damn difference," Archie replied. **"White, of course, because of some stupid bullshit idea about what you're supposed to do at a goddamn ritual sacrifice."**

Hart frowned. "You know a lot about ritual sacrifice, do you?"

Archie bared his teeth in a ghostly grin. **"More than you do, I bet."**

Hart shot a look at Mason.

"You, Doc?"

Mason inhaled thoughtfully, then blew the air back out of his lungs. "As I understand it, that sort of ritual dress was traditional when the victims were *willing*, not that anyone has done that sort of things for... well, centuries."

"Someone ever did that sort of thing?" Hart asked.

"Druids," Mason replied. "Some of the ancient pagans in mainland Europe. Central and South America, although they were definitely not wearing white dresses and they were more often prisoners of war than willing sacrifices."

"What kind of fucking idiot would be a *willing* sacrifice?"

"Vaux," I pointed out. "Although she was already dying."

Hart grunted.

"Terrible move, that one," Archie put in. **"Probably put a stain on whatever the fuck they were doing. Sick and dying people don't make for good sacrifices. Somebody messed that one up."**

Hart and I both looked at Mason, who nodded. "That much is true," he confirmed. "The purpose of a sacrifice is to make a *sacrifice*. If the victim is already dying, they really aren't giving much up."

"Well isn't that fucking ducky," Hart muttered, then ran his hand over his face. "Okay, dead man, what happened next?"

"I was alone in the damn room, lying on the cold floor. Stone. Slightly damp."

"So probably underground?" I asked him.

Archie nodded. **"I'd guess so, sonny. Don't rightly**

know how long I was there. Long enough to fuckin' piss myself, which rightly ticked off the head missy."

"The Maga?" Mason asked.

"Don't know and don't care what they call themselves," Archie replied. "When they came in, they processed in little rows, hoods up, shuffling bare feet. Ten, maybe twelve of them total. Three men held me down. The last had the knife." He paused, but none of us knew what to say, so we all just sat in silence, watching Archie wrestling with the cruelty of his brutal death. "The head missy held a silver bowl for when they'd cut out my goddamn heart. I—got lost for a bit, I think. Everything was knives and pain and dark." He shifted in his spot leaning against the couch. "Didn't really come to again until I was under the goddamn stairs. Took a bit to get myself out of that stupid cubby far enough to at least look out a fuckin' window." He shrugged. "And here we are."

"Jesus fucking Christ on a cracker," Hart muttered, running his hand over his ponytail.

"Archie—"

"Don't you apologize to me, son," the ghost told Mason. "You've nothin' to do with it, and yer doin' what you can to help us. Couldn't ask for more than that."

Mason simply nodded.

Archie turned to me. "I think I'd like to go now, sonny." I nodded, then let go of my threads, which fell away from him like leaves or wind-blown petals as he disappeared.

I sagged forward and put my face in my hands.

19

"Ward! I found it!"

I looked up blearily as Beck excitedly waved her hands.

"Found *what*?" I asked, still irritable thanks to yet another night interrupted by one of Jackson's nightmares.

There had been a long moment when Mason and I stared at each other, trying to decide which one of us was going to get up. Mason had told me to go, so I went, although I told him he should come with me. He had hung back in the doorway, although I could feel the prickle of his magic, just in case.

It hadn't taken us long to calm Jackson down, and Mason had come over to sit on the bed with him, letting Jackson snuggle up against him.

Nobody had ended up bleeding or burned, and we'd gotten Jackson back to sleep after only about an hour.

Not that *we* had gotten back to sleep.

Hence my current state of crankiness.

I blinked at Beck, who spun the book she'd been perusing so that I could see what she was pointing at excitedly.

To make the lines of magic visible to the eye, draw upon the centre of power and spin it into the eye beams.

I raised my eyebrows at her. "Into the eye beams?" I read out loud.

"They're from like the eighteenth century, give them a break."

"And this means what, exactly?"

She shrugged.

I sighed. I didn't really want to wrestle with what I was supposed to do with my eye beams. I wasn't even sure what the fuck eye beams even were, although I had the feeling Mason would tell me if I asked him.

I sighed.

What are eye beams? I typed into my phone, then sent it to Mason, who was at the office with Jackson.

Then I looked back at the book.

To again close the eyes to the lines of magic, draw the eye beams inward and choke them off with silence.

I looked up at Beck. "I don't suppose this makes any fucking sense to you?"

She shook her head, her lower lip caught between her teeth. "I thought maybe it would to you."

"Beck, I don't know what the fuck an eye beam even is."

My phone buzzed with Mason's answer.

Until the eighteenth century, people thought that there were invisible beams emitted from the eye that let you see things. And could become tangled in other people's eye beams.

I passed my phone to Beck to share that.

She read it, then looked up at me. "So... does that help?"

I sighed, then rubbed one temple with my fingers. "Maybe? I dunno." I was tired.

"Are you going to try it?"

I nodded, then closed my eyes.

Maybe if I imagined lasers coming out of my eyeballs, it would make more sense. Why the fuck not?

I tried it, imagining I could retract laser beams back into my eyes. At first, I felt stupid, but the more I envisioned spooling threads back through my eyes and into my sinus cavity, then swallowing them until they caught just under my ribs, the more I felt a warmth gathering there at the base of my sternum, tears leaking from the corners of my eyes.

"Ward?"

I held up a hand.

It didn't feel done yet.

And then it did.

I blinked rapidly, clearing the lingering moisture before I focused on Beck.

And then burst into tears when I realized the brilliant blue bands of her magic weren't there. She was just Beck. Lovely and unadorned with metaphysical neon blue bangles.

"Ward..." She came over and sat next to me, putting a hand on my arm.

"It's okay," I managed, wiping away the tears and trying to get control over myself. "I just... *Thank you.*" I put a hand over hers and squeezed.

She got excited again. "It worked?"

I nodded.

Then she hugged me. "I'm so glad!"

Honestly, it felt weirdly anticlimactic. You know, get a magic power when a ghost touches you, and then all you have to do to shut it off—and, in theory anyway, turn it back on again—is to think really hard about it.

I felt like a fucking idiot.

And Beck read me like the fucking open book I am.

"You know you're not dumb for not... thinking of eye beams before, right?" she said.

I just looked at her.

"Ward."

"It basically says to imagine it gone," I pointed out.

"No, it doesn't," she replied. "It says to imagine drawing it back inside you. Those are not the same thing at all, magically speaking."

"Since when are you a witch?" I asked her.

"I'm not," she replied, tossing her ponytail back over her shoulder. "But I have banished my fair share of them and then some, so I've done a lot of reading about what witches and other practitioners—like warlocks—can do. It isn't just *imagining* things, and you know it."

I still felt stupid, although she was right that this was more than just imagining. But it seemed silly that I could have shut it off without a significant expenditure of energy or a ritual or *something*.

That, and I was in a bad mood and wanted to stay cranky.

Beck studied me.

"What's going on, Ward?" she asked.

The woman knew me too well.

I sighed again. "I am glad you aren't all painted in neon anymore," I replied. "But I'm just... done. I know we still have to find their hearts and figure out what the fuck to do with them when we do... And then also figure out how to stop the Ordo from just killing *more* people. And stop them from killing more Nids because they're racist bastards."

Beck grimaced. "Okay, so we might have a lot on our plates," she admitted. "But one step at a time. Now I'm not neon anymore, and that's an improvement, right?"

I sighed yet again. "Yeah."

"Think you can turn it on again?" she asked.

I shot her a sidelong glance. "Why the fuck would I want to do that?"

"To see if you can. Since now you know how to turn it off, right?"

I muttered something under my breath about her spending too much time with Mason, but I knew she was right. I did want to know if I could turn it on again without Archie.

So I closed my eyes again, gathering my threads, pulling them up through my chest, my throat, into my sinuses, then through my eyes—I guess when you thought of your magic as threads, eye beams really weren't that crazy of a concept.

I opened my eyes again and discovered that Beck's bright blue bangles of magic had indeed returned.

"Yep. Can turn it on," I confirmed.

"And now you make sure the last time you turned it off wasn't a fluke."

I scowled. "Thanks for the vote of confidence."

She batted her eyelashes at me. "You know I love you."

"Loving me and believing I'm a drooling idiot aren't mutually exclusive," I pointed out.

"Come on, Ward. You haven't drooled even once today."

I grunted, apparently channeling Mason, and proceeded to once more reverse the process, removing the burning patterns of magic from the world around me.

"So?"

"Yeah, it's off again," I told her.

"Ice cream to celebrate?"

I pursed my lips. "Fine."

Beck made a tsking sound with her tongue. "You really are in a foul mood if even ice cream doesn't perk you up. And I don't think it's just this case, either."

And this is why you have to be careful about having best friends. Because they know you far better than you want them to sometimes.

"That's not enough?" I asked her, pointedly.

"Come on, boo. Ice cream and you tell me everything that's bothering you."

I heaved out another sigh, knowing I wasn't going to win this one.

———

"What the fuck do you *mean* you haven't picked anything out?" Beck asked, her spoon hovering over a bowl with one scoop of strawberry and one of lemon wafer ice cream on the little café patio outside Gelati Celesti.

I glowered down into my scoops of salted caramel and Nutella swirl. "We haven't actually picked anything," I repeated. "Like, I know there are supposed to be flowers and tuxes and stuff, but..." I shrugged.

"Ward!" Beck sounded absolutely scandalized.

"We moved a nine-year-old death witch into the house less than a month ago!" I protested. "It's not like we've been squandering a ton of free time, here!"

"You're getting married in December, still, yes?"

"Yeah."

"Then you at least need a fucking *place to get married*, Ward."

I looked at her helplessly.

"You don't have that either, do you?" she asked, exasperated.

"No?"

"Ugh!" She threw her hands in the air, spoon safely resting in her bowl.

"What?"

"You need to find somewhere."

"Like where?"

"You got engaged at Forest Hill Park, right?"

"Yeah?"

"How about that? Get one of those heated tents and do it outside so people can run around and eat and drink without having to stress about Arcana."

I blinked. "That... is actually a really good idea."

"You should probably text Mason."

"Why?"

"Because he's your fiancé, you idiot, and you can't just pick a wedding venue without him."

I dutifully texted Mason.

When my phone buzzed again a couple minutes later, Beck looked expectantly at me, pausing in the middle of her harangue about generic tuxedo cuts that I didn't even remotely understand.

I showed it to her.

Sure?

Beck rolled her eyes. "You two are the *worst couple ever.*"

"We are not," I objected.

"Okay, fine, you're not. You're fucking adorable. But you're such *guys*."

"I hate to break it to you," I said, starting to be amused in spite of myself. "But we *are* guys."

She frowned at me. "Aren't gay men supposed to care about shit like this?" she asked me.

I raised my eyebrows. "Aren't lesbians *not*?"

She stuck her tongue out at me.

20

"Okay," I said, turning to Jackson, who was sitting expectantly on the couch, bouncing up and down a little. "I'm going to stay right here to make sure everything's okay, but I want you to try to find and call Sylvia."

Hart had dragged Mason off to look at files and photographs; Beck was ordering around moving men at Beyond the Veil, getting all her stuff situated in the office of her choice; and Jackson and I were at home, where I was attempting to teach Jackson how to talk to and summon dead people.

It was going... Well, it was going.

As Mason had reminded me this morning at least five times before he left, witch magic and warlock magic were very much *not* the same. This meant that what I did to talk to and summon ghosts might or might not bear any resemblance whatsoever to what Jackson would have to do.

As usual, Mason had been right, so we'd been doing our best to muddle through. At the moment, Jackson's magic was still fairly steady, although we'd had a small flare earlier that had raised my heartrate for about a half-hour when

The Skeleton Under the Stairs

he'd gotten frustrated that Sylvia couldn't make out his thoughts. In his defense, he'd been trying for almost an hour at that point.

I was also getting a lot faster at pulling on my own magic, although I hadn't actually needed to neutralize Jackson's. Yet.

That doesn't mean I wasn't still a little on edge.

So was Jackson.

I had on a pale pink t-shirt with a little cartoon ghost that Jackson had given me for Christmas last year, and Jackson's eyes kept skipping over the now-shiny scar twisting around my right hand and wrist. The skin was new and pink and still a tiny bit tender, but it was healing fast—mostly thanks to Mason. But healing or not, it was making Jackson nervous, which was a non-ideal situation.

We both had to learn to deal with it.

I was using my newfound ability to see magic in order to keep tabs on how much control Jackson had, and he was periodically counting under his breath and using slow, deep breathing techniques to try to keep that control.

So far, we were doing okay.

And Mason hadn't texted me once.

"What reminds you most of Sylvia?" I asked Jackson, when his screwed-up face and tightly closed eyes had clearly yielded nothing.

He sighed, his shoulders sagging. "She's funny, but also... teacher-y."

I wasn't sure what 'teacher-y' really meant, but that didn't matter because I didn't need to know. "So think about the things that she does that make you think that. Think about what she looks like, but also what she *feels* like."

Jackson's face scrunched up again, and the crimson of his magic intensified under his skin.

Not bad, little witch, Sylvia remarked, her tone showing pleasure as she shimmered into the room. **Not bad at all.**

Jackson's eyes few open.

"I did it!" he yelped. "Uncle Ward, I did it!"

I allowed myself a smile, but I tried not to make it too big in case he thought I was laughing at him. "You did indeed." Honestly, I was a little relieved—for both of us. I'd been starting to wonder if I was just that incompetent a teacher or if there was something impeding Jackson's ability to learn, but clearly we'd just made a breakthrough.

Now try talking to me, Sylvia told him.

His face pinched up again.

At first, Sylvia looked hopeful, but then I saw her features shift into thought.

"Try thinking about the words like pictures," I suggested to Jackson.

He opened his eyes to look at me. "What do you mean?"

"Well, when I think at a ghost, I imagine my own voice inside my head, carefully enunciating the words."

"Enun—?"

"Enunciating," I repeated. "Carefully sounding them out. But you like to draw, so maybe you can think about the words more like pictures than sounds." I was an auditory learner, but Jackson was totally visual.

"Okay," he replied, sucking on his upper lip in a way that was *far* too much like Mason for me not to smile. Fortunately, he'd closed his eyes again and didn't notice.

Sylvia laughed, the sound delighted. **Excellent! Well, done, Jackson.**

"Yes!" he cheered, bouncing on the couch again, although this time with excitement rather than nervousness.

Did that work? I asked her, although I was pretty confident it had.

Sylvia winked at me, turned slightly away from Jackson. **We've got some focusing to do, but I got the general idea,** she replied. **But that's really good progress!**

JACKSON KEPT AT IT—CONTINUING to make tiny improvements—for the better part of two hours before he started to look tired enough that I called an end to it. I released him to go upstairs to play games, reminding him that he had to keep the volume low enough that he could hear me if I called, since I couldn't come up to get him. He'd nodded, then went upstairs.

I turned to Sylvia. *He's really doing okay?*

Quite well, considering the poor thing is barely old enough for school. She shook her head. **He's a good boy.**

I smiled again. *He is. And he's working really hard.*

That much is evident.

The copies of Hannah Neale's diary had contained several spells that Sylvia and I had been working through. The tricky part was that we had no idea what most of them even did. We had thus far found one for chilling things using ghostly energy that I'm sure was a lot more useful in days when things like freezers and refrigerators didn't exist and at least two that we clearly didn't understand because they didn't seem to have done jack shit.

We were turning back to one of those today.

Jackson had helped me roll up the rug in the living room before he went upstairs for easier cleanup if Sylvia dripped on the floor, and now I set out five candles in the pattern prescribed by the copy of the diary entry sitting on the card table.

Sylvia set herself in the center of them, a frown on her elegant features. **Are you sure this is right?** she asked me.

Nope.

She snorted. **I do so love being part of unclear magical experimentation.**

What are you worried about? I asked her. *You're dead.*

Well, I imagine if your fiancé thinks I had anything to do with your death, he'll figure out how to make Jackson summon me back so he can do *something* to me.

Mason wouldn't do that, I told her.

I know, Nancy. But I definitely wouldn't want to be you if you do get yourself killed.

I smirked at her. *I very much doubt this will kill me.*

I would also prefer, for the record, if you don't trap me in another house. She looked around. **Although I do like you better than my idiot descendants.**

I laughed. *Thanks, I think.*

I thought that this particular spell might enable Sylvia to draw from the energy of a place rather than a person—namely, me. But that was a pretty big *might*. Hannah Neale was not terribly helpful, which made sense, since she was taking notes for herself, not some asshole several centuries in the future, and she knew what she meant. I suppose I could have summoned her from beyond the Veil and asked, but that seemed a little selfish, so Sylvia and I were experimenting, instead.

We hadn't managed to get it to do anything yet.

I took a charcoal stick and drew out the lines of the sigil between the candles, then tried to figure out what the hell Hannah's notations meant. She described particular types of patterns and knots, none of which made any sense to me, since I knew shit-all about sewing or lace or any of the needle arts women practiced in the seventeenth century.

I'd asked Fiona for help, and she'd gotten me a book on lace and another on weaving, so I was trying out a new pattern based on something called an 'openwork diamond.' It had looked to me like what Hannah might have called an *open blossom with a tripple starr*. Or maybe I'd just spent too long staring at lace patterns.

But I was going to try it, and I closed my eyes, trying to visualize the magic that, in theory anyway, had seeped into the house itself after years of Mason—and then me—living in it. The room lit up, dimly at first, then more strongly. The threads of magic in the house followed the paths we used and the places where Mason cast his magic—his desk, the living room, the kitchen.

I set about weaving it all together. The house's magic—mostly green and gold with a touch of purple—provided what I thought of as weft, the threads that formed the basis of loom weaving. I worked my purplish threads through it, wrapping and twisting within the five-pointed star created by the candles.

As I worked, the magic brightened.

Ward—

But before I could ask her what she wanted, the magic flared brilliantly, the flames in the candles going from steady to, well... columns of fire. Small ones, admittedly, but still enough to instantly melt the wax into puddles and set off the smoke alarms.

"Shit!"

Jackson came running downstairs, fingers in his ears, as Sylvia very helpfully put out all five small fires by dripping metaphysical goop on them.

"Uncle Ward!"

"It's fine," I yelled over the beeping, glaring up at the plastic device above the kitchen door that I absolutely couldn't reach.

Sylvia followed my gaze. **I'll just kill that, shall I?**

I sighed. *Please.*

She floated up high enough to poke the alarm, which made an odd gurgling sound as it died.

At least it stopped beeping.

Jackson's brown eyes were huge. "Are you okay, Uncle Ward?"

"I'm fine, Jackson," I told him. "I just... made a bit of a mess."

Sylvia cackled at that. **A bit of a mess,** she repeated, still laughing.

Shut up, Sylvia.

You're not going to be able to clean that up easily.

No shit.

She kept laughing.

Jackson was studying the scorch marks on the floor and one wall. "How *do* we clean that up?" he asked.

I sighed as Sylvia's laughter got louder. "We don't, Jax. Instead, we make some very nice dessert for your uncle so that he doesn't spend too long yelling at me for doing something stupid."

Jackson sucked on his lip, looking first at the mess, then back at me. "Did it work?" he asked.

I adore you, little witch, Sylvia told him.

I sighed. "Did it?" I asked her, speaking out loud so Jackson could hear the question.

Sylvia cocked her head to the side, and then I felt the draw on my power dissipate as Sylvia's expression turned shocked.

My God, Nancy. That actually worked. She started laughing again. **Oh, this is fabulous.**

Can you still leave if you want? I asked her, a bit worried that I'd done something rather more permanent than I'd actually intended.

Let's find out.

And then she was gone.

"Is she—"

Did you miss me?

Jackson yelped, but then grinned. "Miss Sylvia, don't scare me!"

"Yes, please, Sylvia, if we could *not* scare people, that would be lovely." I felt tired and drained, but I had just poured a lot of magic into this spell. Probably a good deal more than was strictly necessary, if the aftermath was any indication.

Sylvia spun in a circle, her eyes glittering. **Guess what I can do, Nancy?**

I raised my eyebrows, then felt my jaw drop as she made *herself* solid. "Damn, Sylvia." Maybe it wasn't me doing it at all, if she could do it herself.

This isn't me, Ward. It's your magic mixed with the house, she told me, apparently reading my thoughts without me needing to focus them. I was tired and on edge, so my control was slipping.

A quick glance over at Jackson showed his magic was a little fluttery, but not dangerously so. I'd taken to leaving my magic sight 'on' when it was just the two of us—it at least let me know when things were about to go sideways.

But so far, we were doing fine.

Well, okay. Jackson was doing fine. I'd made a mess of the living room and forced Sylvia to break the smoke detector.

At least none of us were burned or bleeding this time.

"Do I want to know?" was the question Mason asked when he saw the living room. Jackson was upstairs again, having helped me clean up what we could of the mess and then aided in the creation of the lasagna currently in the oven and brownies cooling on the counter—the kind without the baking soda.

"We were... experimenting," I told him. "With one of Hannah Neale's spells."

"We," Mason repeated, not taking his gaze off me.

"Sylvia and I. Jackson was upstairs and uninvolved." Now that Mason was home I felt about five times worse about the whole thing. "I'm so sorry about the floor. And the wall. And the smoke detector."

Mason looked up at it.

He closed his eyes, took a deep breath, then opened them again. "Are you okay?" he asked me, his sunburst eyes intense.

"I'm perfectly fine," I told him. "It's the house that took the beating this time. And the smoke detector."

Mason looked back up at the now-useless device. "I'm going to guess whatever happened to the floor is why it went off?"

"I think I put too much energy into it," I said, softly. "Mason, I'm sorry." I held back the tears, just barely.

Mason ran a hand over my hair, then crouched down so that he was closer to my level. He put both hands on my thighs, studying my face. "Are you sure you're okay?"

"I'm fine. Really."

His expression was skeptical.

The Skeleton Under the Stairs

"I promise."

Mason leaned forward and kissed me softly. "The walls really did need repainting anyway," he murmured against my lips

I felt a smile quirking my mouth, chasing away the tears.

Then he stood and looked down at the floor. "Can I make a request?"

"Yeah?" I asked, nervously.

"If you're going to do it again, please use the same spot so that it's at least covered by the rug."

"Absolutely," I agreed.

"And what were you trying to do?"

"Um. Let Sylvia, or Archie, or anyone I want, really, use the house as a source of power instead of me."

Mason stared at me for a moment. "You tried to turn the house into a power source?"

I nodded. "I mean. It worked, so I kinda *did*."

He sucked in a breath. "Ward. You *turned the house into a power source.*"

"Yeah?" I didn't understand why he repeated it.

"That means you know how to use warlock magic to create a detached power source."

"Ye—oh." It means I understood how warlock magic could put power from a person into an object. Which meant that I might be able to undo whatever it was the Ordo was doing to people. "Holy shit."

Mason bent and kissed me again. "You're amazing, you know that?"

"I'm a hazard," I countered.

Mason snorted. "An amazing hazard," he corrected.

A buzzer sounded in the kitchen, and I jumped.

Mason arched his eyebrows.

"Lasagna," I explained.

"I got it," he told me, running his fingers through my curls again. "Jackson!" he called. "Dinner!"

Jackson was in bed, and Mason pulled me into his lap on the couch, nuzzling against the side of my neck.

I tried—and failed—to turn to look at him. "So you forgive me for the floor? And the wall? And the smoke detector?"

Mason huffed into my hair. "I'm glad you're both okay. And the wall does need repainting."

I grimaced. "At least the rug covers the scorch marks."

Mason's arms tightened around me.

"Thanks for not being mad about the mess." I snuggled back against him.

I felt him chuckle. "You should have seen what I did to my Gran's kitchen when she was trying to teach me how to cast protection spells."

"So house destruction is totally fine?"

He snorted. "Maybe keep it to a minimum?"

I smiled, even though he couldn't see it. "I'll do my best."

"Now tell me what you did."

"And never do it again?"

I felt him shrug. "Not necessarily. But knowing how it works might help me understand some of what the Ordo is doing—or trying to do. And if I can understand it—"

"We might be able to break it."

"Exactly."

I told him what I'd done—how I'd woven together the magic steeped in the house with my own.

"And the house has magic because—"

"Because you live here," I answered.

He frowned.

"I can *see* it, Mace."

He pushed me far enough away that he could look at my face. "See *what*?"

"Your magic," I explained. "It's green."

His expression suddenly looked annoyed.

"It has nothing to do with that, Mason," I told him. "It's life—healing. That magic is green. Jackson's is red—death. Beck's is blue. Mine is… a weird bluish purple. Probably a mix of death and spirit, if Beck's is spirit. But then there's also just—I don't know. Inherent magic? That's gold. At least, that's what Archie thinks."

Mason blinked. "Inherent magic?"

I nodded. "Like Hart's. He doesn't *have* magic, but he *is* magic."

Mason frowned. "But the house—" Then his expression cleared. "The house has ley magic," he breathed.

"Okay, now I'm confused."

"Do you remember us talking about ley lines?"

"Sure." Ley lines were basically habitual pathways of magic caused by people using magic over and over again. "Oh. So because there are patterns of magic here, the house has basically become a ley… line?"

"I would call it a node, not a line, but same idea," Mason confirmed.

"Does that mean…"

"If you can *see* it—"

"I can *find* it," I breathed.

"If we can get you there, yes, I'm pretty sure you would be able to confirm that it was a ritual site." He was watching me with an expression I couldn't quite put together—worry, yes, but maybe also something else. Something like… pride?

Awe? I wasn't sure. And I was pretty sure I didn't deserve it, whatever it was.

I chewed on my lower lip. "And what if I can't? What if it's, I don't know, too faint or something?"

"Then we're no worse off. But it does suggest that perhaps we should run a test—find somewhere we know should have power from ritual and see what it is you see." He smiled, then, a twist of his lips. "Somewhere that isn't this house... or that isn't going to suffer extensive fire damage."

"Speaking of, uh, ritual sites..."

"What now?" he asked, although there was a teasing note in the question.

"Well, we are still planning on getting married, right?"

Mason hummed softly, rubbing his cheek against my curls. "Yes. But I thought you and Beck decided on Forest Hill?"

"Is that okay?" I had a sudden surge of worry that I'd offended him or hurt him by taking Beck's suggestion.

Mason drew in a breath against the side of my neck. "Mmhmm."

"Mace, I'm serious." I was trying to ignore what the feeling of his nose and lips against the skin of my neck was doing to me.

I felt his sigh on my skin. "It's perfect, Ward."

"Mason—"

"I mean it." He placed a gentle kiss behind my ear. "We went on our first date there. You agreed to marry me there. It's perfect." He kissed the curve of my jaw.

"We still have the rest of the wedding, Mace," I pointed out. I wanted him to actually make *some* decisions, even if neither one of us really cared all that much about any of it except the person we were marrying.

The Skeleton Under the Stairs

"Deon will do it," he pointed out. Deon was a judge, so that made sense.

"Okay," I agreed. "What about—"

"Make Beck do it," he suggested, kissing along my jawline, then down my throat.

I made a small, whining sound. "I can't... make her... everything," I pointed out.

"Sure we can," Mason disagreed, one hand sliding under the hem of my t-shirt.

"Mason."

I felt him sigh again, although his hand stayed on the skin of my stomach. "What else do you want to decide?" he asked.

"Flowers."

"Keidra."

"What?"

"I'm going to designate Keidra."

I felt like an idiot for not thinking of that. "Oh. That's. A really good idea."

"Anything else?" he asked, his hand sliding higher on my stomach.

"Um. Clothes?"

"We should probably wear some for the ceremony, anyway." He nuzzled against my neck again. "Although I am just going to take you out of them again."

"So we rent tuxes?"

"No. We *buy* them."

"Mason—"

"I am not *renting* a tux," he informed me. "And neither are you. Beck can help you pick one so it's a surprise."

Well, okay then. I guess I was *buying* a tux. For the first time in my life. I was definitely going to need Beck's help for that.

"How long does it *take* to make a tux?" I asked him.

"You should probably do that in... July or August?"

"Okay then. Um. Okay." I sucked in a sharp breath as he placed a lingering wet kiss against the side of my neck. "Mason!"

He growled softly. "What else, Ward?" One hand pulled me closer, spread against the skin of my chest, until I felt the warmth of his arousal against my backside.

"Cake?"

"Cake," he repeated. "I really don't." His other hand slid under my shirt. "Give a fuck." His fingers undid the fly of my jeans. "About the cake."

"Invi—" His fingers closed around my half-hard erection. "*Fuck.* –tations," I finished.

Mason growled again, his fingers tightening and stroking. "If I promise to sit down and make a list, will you stop talking about this now?"

I let my head fall back on his shoulder. "Shit. Yeah. I'll stop if—" I groaned. "If you promise."

"Then." He stroked me. "I." He scraped his teeth over the spot where my neck met my shoulder. "Promise."

"Okay," I breathed out, reaching behind my head to wrap my fingers in his braids. "Mace?"

"*What*?" He was clearly done talking.

"Bedroom?" I suggested.

Mason picked me up, one arm under my legs, the other around my back. I put my arms around his neck, and he paused on the way down the hall to kiss me, his tongue chasing mine as a low growl rumbled its way through his chest.

I pulled my head back. "Mason."

He growled at me.

"Bedroom," I repeated, a little breathless.

He bit my ear. Gently—not enough to really hurt, but definitely enough to draw a gasp.

I don't think I'd ever been *tossed* onto a bed before, but I definitely was now, and the adrenaline racing through my system heightened the sensitivity of every single nerve in my body. I knew my eyes were wide, but when Mason drew in a deep breath through his nose, I also knew he'd scent lust, not fear.

He stripped off his shirt, then pants and boxer briefs, before crawling up to me. Impatient fingers hooked in the already-undone waist of my jeans. "Off," he ordered.

I let him tug off my jeans and boxers, pulling my t-shirt off myself, barely having time to throw it aside before Mason was all over me, his lips capturing mine as the heat of his body pressed against me. I whimpered a little against his mouth as his erection, hot and heavy, pressed into my hip.

And then his lips came back to my throat, kissing, then nipping, working his way down to my shoulders and chest, where he scraped his canines across one nipple, making me writhe under him. One big hand gripped my hip as he licked, sucked, and bit, my hands tightening on his broad shoulders.

Then he rose back above me, his sunburst eyes burning. "I need you, Ward," he rasped.

I was half-drunk on him. "Anything," I answered, breathless.

He growled again, reaching beside us for the lube.

When he slid a slicked finger inside me, I moaned softly, the adrenaline still in my system tightening my body so that even just one finger rubbed deliciously against my inner muscles.

Mason groaned, then lowered his head to lavish attention

on my other nipple, the heat of his tongue and brush of breath and teeth causing me to make fists in the bedcover. He pushed in a second finger, using his arm to nudge my legs wider and shifting his body so that he settled between my thighs. His other hand ran down my flank, raising goosebumps.

He kissed his way back up the outside of my throat, nuzzling against my shoulder, then gently nipping at the shell of my ear. A third finger pushed inside me, insistent, impatient, riding the edge of stretching me too quicky—and I didn't care.

I wanted more.

His teeth and tongue along and behind my ear, his other hand running up my body to toy with my nipple, his fingers inside me... were making me desperate.

"Mace," I gasped out. "Please."

He growled again, then withdrew his fingers and hooked his arm under my knee so that he could line himself up, pushing into me hard and fast so that the blackness did more than just sparkle at the edges of my vision.

I closed my eyes, hissing through the pressure, riding the burn of stretched-out muscle that was just intense enough to keep me from coming.

And he didn't stop.

Nor did I want him to.

I could feel my breath catching in the back of my throat as I gasped with every thrust, the darkness behind my lids intensifying the feeling of Mason's body inside mine, the slickness of the lube that let him ride me, the heat and hardness of his cock pushing up against nerves and muscle.

I barely felt him bury his face in the side of my throat, barely registered his fingers twining with mine and pressing my arm over my head as he fucked me.

He made a sound that was half-snarl, half-groan, his rhythm faltering as his hand tightened around mine, his thrusts somehow harder, pressing all the way through me and into the back of my throat.

And then I shattered, my orgasm ripping through me so hard I saw stars and felt lightheaded. Mason muffled his cry in my shoulder as he chased me over the edge.

Both of us were breathing hard, and I could feel Mason's breath through the heaving of his ribs under my palm, my other hand still tangled with his. For a moment, he shifted, and I thought he was going to pull away, but then he let himself settle against me, and I couldn't help smiling, running my hand over his back, his body still joined with mine.

I loved the feel of him—the way his weight pressed my body into the mattress, his warmth soothing my aches.

He eased his arm out from under my leg, then ran it up my side, nuzzling closer with a soft hum, shifting his body so that he could rest his cheek against my chest. I ran my free hand over the ridges of his braids, feeling his breath evening out, warm against my skin.

I felt him inhale before he spoke. "Promise me something?"

"What?" I asked, a little apprehensive.

"You won't ever let me hurt you?"

I pulled my fingers from his so that I could turn his face to look at me. He let me, propping himself up on an elbow, worry creasing his brow.

"Mason. You have never hurt me. You never *will* hurt me."

He dropped his eyes, dark lashes standing out even against his dusky olive skin.

"Mason," I repeated, my hands tightening slightly on his cheeks.

He looked back up at me.

"You won't hurt me. Ever. I don't have to *let* you because you won't."

He took one of my hands and pressed a kiss to the center of my palm. "I just—"

"Mason."

He sighed. "Okay."

"What's bothering you? Really?"

He pushed away from me, then, heading to the bathroom. I listened to him run the faucet, and then he came back with a wet washcloth, warm, like it always was, to clean me up.

I took it from him. "Mason, I mean it. What's wrong?"

He sighed again. "I—don't like feeling like I can't protect you," he answered softly. "I know you are perfectly capable of taking care of yourself..."

"But?" I threw the washcloth at the laundry hamper, actually making the shot.

Mason helped me move so that he could ease me under the covers, then joined me, tucking his head against my chest again, one arm across my stomach. "But," he replied, finally, "I feel useless," he admitted.

I snorted as I ran a hand over his hair. "You literally just had to help me get into bed, Mason," I pointed out.

"You and I both know you could have done that yourself."

"But there are a lot of things I can't do," I pointed out. "Like drive, for one. Or reach high things."

"But you can turn the house into a metaphysical battery," he replied.

"And practically set it on fire in the process," I reminded him.

One side of Mason's lips twitched. "I would appreciate at least an attempt at fewer scorch marks," he admitted.

I chewed on my lower lip. "Does it really bother you that I can do stuff like that?"

He sighed again, his arm tightening around me. "No. I would feel better if it were—" He broke off.

"More under control?"

"I mean, yes. But..." Another heavy breath. "I don't like *anything* out of control," he said softly. "You don't like change, and I don't like things I can't understand and predict. And I don't understand your magic, and I can't predict either yours or Jackson's."

And if he couldn't understand it, he couldn't make sure we were safe.

"We'll be okay," I told him. "Both of us."

"I know that, intellectually," he answered. "But I'm still... scared." His arm tightened again. "I really don't know what I would do if I lost you."

"You won't," I told him.

I felt the brush of his lashes as he closed his eyes. "Promise?"

"Always."

21

"Ward, do you have a final summary of the Ashmont séance?" Mason asked, pausing in my office doorway, his eyes focused down on the manilla folder in his hands.

I blinked blearily up at him, trying to reorient my brain. I'd been studying the scans Beck and I had taken of some sorcery manuals at the library, trying to figure out the right pattern for a protection spell. The primary problem was that the author's handwriting was fucking *terrible*, and I had to get through that before I could figure out his obtuse metaphors for everything, so it was slow going.

It also put me in a weird brain space, so it took me far too many seconds to put together the meanings of words like 'summary,' 'Ashmont,' and 'séance.'

"Oh, shit. Yeah. Um. Yeah. Five seconds."

Mason looked up at that, peering at me over his wire-framed glasses. "Not urgent," he replied. "Just running the books for May."

"No, it's here. And done. I just brain farted." I quickly opened an email, then found and attached the file before hitting *Send*. "There. Sent."

The Skeleton Under the Stairs

Mason smiled his twisted smile. "Thanks."

Instead of leaving, he came over and bent to give me a kiss—not long by our usual standards, but probably more lingering than would be considered appropriate for the workplace.

Not like I minded.

"You people here?" came Hart's familiar yell from the front of the office.

Mason grunted. "We really need a front desk person," he muttered, but rolled his eyes and went to go see what Hart wanted.

Beck passed my door as I made my way out from behind the desk, winking at me as she headed toward the reception area.

"Detective!" I heard her exclaim loudly, her tone overly-friendly. "What can we do for you today?"

"You can be less fucking chipper, Ms. Kwan," Hart barked.

In his defense, it was like nine-thirty in the morning, and Hart, despite often working early hours, was not a morning person.

I made my way into the kitchen and turned on the electric kettle so I could make Hart coffee. I'd worked with him often enough now that I could tell by tone when Hart hadn't been sufficiently caffeinated. I was also glad Keidra had taken the day off so that she could take Jackson and Ben to the zoo before Ben's basketball camp started next week. Not that I minded having Jackson at the office, but I felt bad for him being stuck here, *and* now I would have worried about Hart saying something he shouldn't in front of a nine-year-old.

I could hear the low rumble of Mason's voice, Beck's higher tone, and Hart's middle tenor as they discussed something I couldn't make out. I scooped grounds into the single-serve French press that lived in the kitchen. Beck was threatening to buy an espresso machine, and Mason was arguing with her about the relative expense and time required to actually make espresso versus the speed of French press coffee.

I had the feeling Mason was going to lose this fight.

I didn't mind either way. I'm totally a latte guy when given the choice, but I was absolutely happy with French press. Or drip. Or whatever swill I could get at a gas station for ninety-nine cents.

I put the coffee, with creamer, into a travel mug so I didn't spill it, then took it out to the front.

"Nice of you to join us," Hart snarked as soon as he saw me.

I smirked at him. "Be like that, and I won't give you this coffee that I just made you," I retorted, holding out the coffee and wiggling it back and forth.

I saw Hart's lavender eyes widen. "Oh," he mumbled, his pointy ears turning a blushing pink. "Uh. Fuck. Thanks."

I let my expression relax from smirk to smile. "You're quite welcome."

Beck snickered a little.

"Hart wants you to summon Greer," Mason informed me, tension evident in his shoulders. Greer hadn't ever given me any real trouble, and I wasn't sure why Mason seemed uneasy about it. Off to my right, Hart made a small, pleased sound as he sipped the coffee.

"Okay," I replied calmly, ignoring the elf. "Is there something more I should be aware of?"

Mason made a little harumphing noise.

I raised my eyebrows at him.

Mason sighed. "Hart thinks that Greer might know more than he is aware of."

"About the Ordo, you mean?"

"Exactly," Hart put in. He had both hands wrapped around my coffee mug, his face barely inches from the top.

"So you want me to summon him so you can interrogate him?"

"Fucking genius, aren't you?" Hart remarked, his gratitude for the caffeine short-lived.

"If you want me to bring you coffee again, you should really be nicer to me," I pointed out.

Hart took another long dip from the mug. "And I can be even more of a fucking pain in the ass if you don't," he retorted.

"Children," Beck interrupted. "Fighting doesn't raise the dead."

We both glared at her.

"Perhaps you'd care to explain why it is you're in such a foul mood, detective," Mason suggested mildly.

Hart blew out an irritated breath. "It's looking like the victims in the house aren't the only ones," he said, his voice heavy.

I glanced over at Mason. He'd mentioned the fact that there were other rituals in the Ordo book, but he hadn't said there were other ritual *murders*. "More sacrifices?" I asked.

Mason tilted his head. "Not the same kind, no," he replied. "I take it that the 'purgation' spells came back as something... unpleasant?" he asked, this time addressing Hart.

Both Beck and I looked at the elf, who shifted, a frown on his elegant features.

"Bowman thinks..." He sighed again. "Bowman thinks they're specifically targeting Nids. And they think these rituals might be... deliberately targeting them—" he paused, not looking at Mason "—because they fucking have magic."

Dani Bowman was a newly-hired witch at Hart's precinct. I hadn't met them yet, but Mason had, and he'd been happy that there was someone else Hart could drag to ritual homicides. Mason had remarked that Dani seemed to know their stuff. Not like he did, of course, but most people didn't know occult magic like Mason.

Mason's expression darkened. "The Ordo is killing them *because* they have magic."

"That's what Bowman thinks," Hart repeated.

Mason's fingers clenched, then opened again. "That actually... makes sense with the way the ritual was noted."

"What do you mean?" I asked.

Mason grimaced. "It seemed... backwards. I thought the spell was to remove magic from the... subject. But if they're targeting Arcanids, then perhaps they believe they're purifying the magic by purging the... Arcanids."

I blenched. "Fucking hell."

"Damn right," Hart agreed. "So I need to ask Greer about it. Find out what he knows about that."

I glanced over at Mason, then back at Hart. "Greer didn't show any dislike toward Mason," I told them. "Not like Vaux." I thought for a moment. "In fact, Greer seemed surprised that Mason could even *do* magic."

Hart grunted. "Fucking hell."

"It still might be worth asking him," Mason pointed out. "He might not realize what it is he knows—and there were some rituals that had an FG recorded as present."

"These rituals?" I asked.

Mason shook his head. "No. Others. Ones with a lot more people. Some of them seemed to involve... perhaps energy transferal? It's hard to say, precisely, with the way

The Skeleton Under the Stairs

they code things." He turned to Hart. "What did Dani think of the others?"

"More or less the same shit you said," Hart replied, then took another sip of his coffee. "They seemed weird. Like they were making some kind of offering or some fucking shit."

"Offering of what?" Beck asked.

Hart shrugged.

"Best guess?" Mason asked, and the rest of us nodded. "I would say the energy they're drawing from the sacrifice victims."

"What about the Tranquil Brook patients?" I asked.

"Possibly them, as well," Mason replied.

"So then let's raise this bastard," Beck interrupted. "And find out what he knows." She looked at me. "Is he going to be a problem?" she asked.

I shrugged. "He hasn't been thus far." I reached out, finding Greer with almost no difficulty at all. He hadn't crossed over the Veil, nor had he wanted to when I offered, so it was simple enough to draw him to me.

Summoner, he greeted me. **What is it you want from me after all this time?**

I held out my hand. "We have some questions," I told him.

I was surprised when Mason was the one who put his hand in mine. "Detective?" he said mildly, lowering our hands, but keeping mine in his.

Hart blinked a couple times, then cleared his throat. "Right. Dr. Greer." He addressed the air slightly to my left, although Greer was directly in front of me. Greer himself looked mildly amused at this. "We need more details about the rituals you attended for the Antiquus Ordo Arcanum."

Greer was shaking his head. **They aren't particularly**

interesting, he replied. **Ritual cleansings, summoning of deceased former members, gathering of power. Nothing illegal.**

"Other than sucking magic out of innocent mental health patients, you mean?" Beck snarled.

Greer looked at her, a little startled.

"That's right, I can hear you," she hissed.

You are no summoner, Greer said, studying her uncertainly.

She's a banisher, I told him. *An exorcist*, I clarified further, when he looked confused.

Ah. I see. He studied me for a moment. **You have a rather... eclectic collection, summoner.**

I scowled at him. *They're people, not a collection*, I snapped.

Beck's expression suggested she may have thought something similar at him.

"What do you want to know?" I asked Mason, knowing —and not caring—that my irritation at Greer was probably evident in my voice.

Mason's fingers tightened around mine. I'd ask him later why he didn't want me to make Greer visible and audible to everyone—not that I minded holding Mason's hand, instead of the squishy coldness of the dead and disembodied.

"Dr. Greer," he said, knowing better than Hart where Greer was in space, at least. "We know the Ordo conducted a variety of rituals. Would you care to tell us about those you were a part of?"

They were simple things, Greer answered. **Nothing an ordinary practitioner couldn't do.**

Cold ripped through me.

Greer was lying. He hadn't done that to me before—I

The Skeleton Under the Stairs

always knew when spirits were lying—but he was definitely lying now.

Don't make me force you to answer truthfully, I warned him.

He turned to me, stunned.

Try again. I made my tone uncompromising.

Greer stared at me. **I can't.**

Yes, you can. Beck, despite only hearing Greer's side of the conversation, must have understood some of what was happening and cast her magic to join with mine.

They will hurt me, he whispered, his voice barely registering in the back of my mind. I saw Beck's eyes widen.

I unlocked my magic sight and color exploded through the room. Beck's bright blue. Mason's vibrant green. And Greer's, greyish brown, washed out of color the way Vaux's had been, but not so oily or dark.

They can't hurt you across the Veil, I answered him, no longer particularly disposed to be friendly.

They can, Greer replied.

How? He resisted, trying to throw up metaphysical walls, to block me out and push me away, but his magic was as thin and as easily-brushed-aside as spider webs. Annoying, but only for a moment.

His eyes widened as I tore through his defenses, the sharp threads of blue-purple casting aside the flimsy wisps and wrapping around him.

They... can summon me. With the energy... He didn't want to be telling me this.

Energy taken from others, you mean.

Yes. He hung his head.

I'd come back to the idea that someone—or more than one someone—in the Ordo was a summoner capable of reaching across the Veil in a minute. "Greer participated in rituals to transfer stolen energy."

"To whom?" Mason asked.

The... Greer visibly deflated. **Magus and Maga**, he said, then, giving up all attempts to resist my will.

"Picton and Harrod?" I asked out loud.

Yes.

Beck nodded, communicating his answer to Hart, who was swiping furiously across his phone.

"Why?" I asked him.

The Magus and Maga use the power to further the strength of the Ordo.

That sounds like complete bullshit and you know it, I told him, and he grimaced.

That's what they told us, he insisted, and he was telling me the truth, although I could sense that there was more he was holding back.

What else? I pressed him.

His eyes skipped over Mason, lingering a little too long on our joined hands.

My fingers involuntarily tightened, and Mason squeezed back, a question on his face.

You knew about the Arcanid sacrifices, I accused Greer.

Sacrifices? No. No, they wouldn't— Then he bit his lip. **They would, wouldn't they?**

I just stared at him.

They... He sighed. **It was one thing to take magic from the unworthy. That's what we did.**

Beck's expression was furious, and I had the feeling—from Greer's pause—that she was giving him a piece of her mind on that particular subject.

Their magic wasn't clean, he said, although whether he

was explaining this to me or to Beck, I wasn't entirely sure. It didn't really matter.

What do you mean, not clean? I asked.

He looked back at me. **It's... dirty. Earthy. Raw. Our magic is the magic of the intellect, the mind. Of study rather than impulse or disease.**

Warlock magic, not witch magic. My kind of magic, rather than Mason's. Rather than the abilities bestowed by the Arcanavirus infection.

I had all sorts of opinions on Greer's evaluation of the relative merits of different types of magic, but picking a fight with a mediocre dead warlock, whether or not he had been a part of the Antiquus Ordo Arcanum, wasn't going to be terribly productive.

The sacrifices, I reminded him, my tone cold.

I... never participated in any. Never knew... really. I suppose I... I should have suspected.

What can you tell us? I pressed.

Greer sighed. **There was a clearing, on the Harrod property. It's... I know they used it. I was never invited to those rituals. Only the ones in the main house.**

Where?

22

Greer ended up telling us quite a bit. Participants' names, which Mason and Hart were able to match up to the strings of initials in the Ordo book, locations, and some clarification on the types of rituals he'd personally attended.

Mason had grilled me-slash-him pretty extensively on the way that some of the rituals worked, and Beck and I dutifully took turns reporting the answers, even though I could only follow about half the content of the conversation.

It had all resulted in Hart being able to leverage our joint testimony to get a search warrant for the grounds of the Harrod estate, although he hadn't been able to convince the judge to let him into the house, since nothing *in* the house had fallen under the realm of the questionably legal... at least according to the judge.

Whether or not we found actual incriminating evidence at the supposed ritual site on the grounds would determine whether or not Hart was able to continue with this case—he'd grumpily explained in the car that he'd essentially had to bargain with the judge to get the warrant, and that if it yielded nothing, Hart's ass was going

The Skeleton Under the Stairs

to be on the line, raked over the coals, and hung out to dry.

And yes, he did use all three metaphors just to underscore how desperately he needed me—or the CSI team—to find something. He'd also been more than a little pissy about the fact that he got either me or Mason—not both of us. The consensus was that I would be more useful in *finding* something, and Hart could always call Mason out again later if he had to.

The Harrod house was on what Pearl would have referred to, quoting Mrs. Elton from Jane Austen's *Emma*, as "extensive grounds." I took a moment to wonder what the fuck was up with people like the Harrods and Fitzwilliams who couldn't just be happy being filthy rich and also had to fucking *murder* people.

I sat in Hart's car, waiting for everyone to get their shit sorted out. We were parked under a massive magnolia, its broad, dark green leaves at least casting shade over the car and keeping me from roasting alive. We were in a semi-circular drive, the CSI van parked behind us, and people were milling around waiting for orders or directions or for the owners to be informed of the existence of the warrant. Or maybe all three at the same time.

Mays, the big blond CSI guy from the Duskevicz house, was back, and he offered me a friendly wave as Hart got me out of his Charger and into my chair. I waved back, then sighed and waited for Hart to come back over and realize how stupid this whole thing was.

"What the fuck is that face for?" the elf asked, coming up to me.

"There isn't going to be a road or a sidewalk out to this ritual site, Hart," I pointed out.

He stared at me for a second. "Fuck."

I gave him a look that asked if he thought that I found this at all amusing and not humiliating.

He huffed out a breath and repeated himself, only less angry and more resigned. "Fuck."

I guess Hart and I were about to get a lot more comfy with each other. And our respective sweat and body odors, since it was the middle of goddamn June in the South, and 'pleasant and balmy' were not adjectives that one applied to that particular time of year in this climate. 'Muggy' and 'armpit-like' were far more accurate.

Hart stripped off his wrinkled linen jacket, exposing the shoulder holster he wore over his off-white button-down. Then he rolled up his sleeves, exposing both forearms, which were slim, like the rest of him, but still muscular. High on the inside of one forearm was a tattoo I'd never noticed before, since I pretty much never saw Hart in short sleeves.

It was some sort of stylized paw print, oblong in shape with long claws. I was about to ask him about it when his phone rang. "Fuck." He pulled it out and walked a few steps away. "Hart."

He looked thunderous enough when he came back that I decided to leave inquiries about tattoos for another time.

"Something wrong?" I asked him, instead.

"Another fucking body," came the response. "Another orc, same MO as the last one."

I felt my eyebrows go up. "Is that—"

"No. It's not fucking normal. I tried to get you on it, but the chief doesn't want to pay for a goddamn medium for a turf war."

"Is it a turf war?" I asked him.

"Fuck if I know." He ran a hand over his braided ponytail. "I don't like it, Ward," he said, and I started paying extra attention, because it was rare that Hart got confessional. "Two orcs dead in as many weeks, and one ghoul about three weeks before that. It's too many, too close."

"They all died the same way?" I asked. If that was true, it was particularly fucked up that they weren't having Hart look deeper into it.

Hart snorted. "Yeah, but it's not like stabbings aren't common. Nothing else to tie them together. No pattern. No common dump site. Just... dead Nids."

"Dead stabbed Nids," I pointed out.

"Preaching to the fucking choir, Ward," he said, his tone resigned, but no less pissed off.

"I'd do it *pro bono*," I offered.

"The fuck you will. You do one *pro bono*, they'll demand it all for free, and fuck that."

He had a point.

He walked up to me, then looked down and sighed. "I don't suppose you can find anybody dead around here who might be able to tell us where the fuck we're going?"

I looked up at him. "I can try."

I opened my Third Eye—and activated my magic sight, just in case—and looked around. The whole area looked blighted—not nearly as bad as the Duskevicz house, but there were... *smudges* everywhere. Dim patches, like tarnish, on the house, the landscaping, even the grass.

"What?" Hart demanded. I guess he was getting pretty good at reading me.

"It's... dirty. Magically speaking."

"No dead people?"

"Not yet. But I wouldn't be surprised. I also wouldn't be surprised if they're stuck somewhere."

"Like at the fucking house?"

"Exactly."

Hart harumphed at that. I didn't blame him.

A little nervous, now that I knew more about what I might be dealing with, I reached out, trying to find anyone who might be close enough to hear me.

And then she was *right fucking there*, and I sucked in a sharp breath.

"Ward?"

"I'm good," I replied, my eyes still focused on the dead faun standing in front of me. *Hello*, I greeted her. *I'm here to help.*

The fuck you are, sorcerer.

Oh, boy. Here we went again.

I'm not with the Ordo, I told her. *My name is Edward, and I work for the police.*

She bared her very large teeth at me.

We think there might be a ritual site on this property where they're killing Arcanids. Is that what happened to you?

Now she looked skeptical, but that was a step in the right direction from overtly hostile. **Why the fuck do you care, sorcerer?**

I want to stop them, I answered her. *We want to stop them.*

She looked over at Hart, then. **You work with the elf?**

Yes.

Part of me wanted to give her form and sound so that she could talk to Hart directly, but Mason had pointed out after we'd released Greer that it might not be the best idea to flaunt that particular ability too much. First, it would probably scare the living shit out of the rest of the police and the CSI team. Second, if the Ordo knew I could do it, it might make them start viewing me as more of a threat, which had been the reason he stopped me from doing it to Greer.

What do you want from me? she asked, then, hesitant, but opening up.

Can you show us where they killed you? I asked her. *And also,* I added, *where they buried you?*

They don't use this site anymore, she told me. **Haven't for a few years. But yes. I'll show you.**

"Hart."

"Yeah?"

"We've got a victim. She'll take us there."

"Fuck, yeah." He blinked. "Er. Sorry?" he apologized to the air.

The faun looked amused. **Apology accepted,** she replied, then she looked back at me, her eerie horizontal pupils made even stranger by her aethereal appearance. **My name is Thea.**

I'm sorry you were murdered, Thea, I told her. *But it's nice to meet you.*

He have a name? she asked, gesturing to Hart.

Detective Hart.

She nodded once. **Is he going to carry you?**

Yeah. "Hart."

"What?"

"I need a ride."

"Fuck. Right." He came over, then picked me up, strong and steady, although tense. And sweaty, but that was honestly both of us. "Uh..."

I pointed toward Thea, who had started moving through the grass. "That way."

———

HART HAD LEFT me in one of the less-muddy spots under a tree, about twenty or so feet from the ritual site. The magic here wasn't just smudgy. It was old, that much I could tell, and oozed like tar over the surface of the ritual stone, thick and dark and cold. But it wasn't creepily sentient like the magic in the Duskevicz house—just, old and decayed from years of murder and hate.

Thea remained near me, watching as the CSI techs went over the pitted ritual stone, took samples of the dirt, and brushed away leaves looking for anything that might give them a hint about what had happened here.

I could have told them.

I did tell Hart.

They'd brought Thea out here with a bag over her head, her ankles tied together and her wrists bound—but with towels placed between the ties and her body so there wouldn't be obvious marks. And then they'd placed her on the sacrificial stone—a big block of what looked like limestone—and then, chanting, had stabbed her repeatedly with what looked like a kitchen knife.

The murder itself wasn't ritualized. They didn't wear robes—just dark clothes and dark hoods, like ski masks. This wasn't an elaborate attempt to draw out her innate magic.

It was genocide.

They'd killed her because she had magic, and they didn't think she deserved it.

I'd asked her if she'd seen their faces.

No. But I think I must have seen one of them. Not that night, but before.

What do you mean, before?

They must have come into the shop.

What shop?

I worked in a magic shop. Reading tarot sometimes, or tea leaves. Margot is—was? I don't know. She's an empath.

I could always see snatches more. About lovers or impending changes. That's how they knew, right?

They told you they killed you because of your magic?

Thea nodded.

I told all this to Hart, who swore for about twenty straight seconds.

And then he asked her to take us to her body.

They hadn't even buried her—just threw her into what looked like an old cow pond on the edge of the woods. Hart had set me down up against yet another tree and pulled out his phone to call a team that could do shallow dredging. He was currently standing next to the pond with the CSI team, explaining something that required dramatic gesturing.

I'm so sorry, I told the faun as she hovered next to me.

She turned and looked down at me. **You have no need to apologize**, she said simply. **At least you'll be able to let me go home.**

Where's home? I asked her.

I... She sighed. **My parents were in Baltimore. But.**

Not fans of Arcanids? I asked.

No. I had... I had a boyfriend. I don't know... I stayed here, so I don't know if he knows. Or cares.

I can try to find him, I offered.

His name was Greg.

Greg what?

Greg Malineaux.

I pulled out my phone and texted Hart.

We'll see what we can do, I told Thea. *Will you tell me your last name?*

Angevine.

Hart came back over, holding up his phone in a silent question, and I looked up at him.

"Thea Angevine. Boyfriend at the time was Greg Malineaux. He might want to know."

Hart nodded once. "Fucking hell. Thanks."

I wasn't sure if he was thanking me or Thea. Or both of us.

By the time the dredging team got set up, the sun was starting to sink low, the shadows were casting long fingers across the weeds, and I had at least seventeen mosquito bites, two of which were on my legs, which was extra irritating because even though I couldn't move them, they apparently could still itch.

There are others, Thea said suddenly.

I turned to look at her. She was gazing out over the pond, watching as the police dredgers pushed off into the water. *In there?* I asked.

She nodded.

"Hart!" I yelled.

He turned, then jogged toward us.

"The fuck is it?" he asked, clearly fed up.

"There are more of them," I told him.

"Fucking bloody fuckstick. You couldn't have mentioned this before?"

"Sorry. Thea just told me."

Hart ran a hand over his face. "How many?"

I looked at Thea.

Seven. All older than me. One was still here when they killed me. She fell silent for a moment and I passed this on to Hart, who took off back toward the dredging team, swearing.

I agreed to wait for the next, Thea said, then. **So that the woman before me could move on.**

Are they all fauns? I asked her.

She shook her head. **The woman before me was an orc.**

The Skeleton Under the Stairs

She said the man before her had been an elf. She turned back to me. **They hate us,** she whispered.

I know. I'm sorry.

You don't.

No, I agreed. *I don't.*

She settled beside me, sitting with her legs folded under her. The same way Fiona sat. I swallowed around the anxiety that rose in my throat.

Fiona didn't have any magic other than what she was, but she was researching the Ordo. Did that put her at risk? Could she end up in a derelict cow pond somewhere just for helping me? Maybe I needed to stay away from her, and the library, until this was sorted out. To keep her safe.

But staying away from Fiona wasn't going to assuage the worst of the fears sitting like a lead weight in the pit of my stomach.

Mason.

He was an orc and a witch.

Jackson's uncle and guardian. My future husband. My lover.

My heart and my soul.

Losing him would break me.

I'd never understood how my father could leave me and go off to die in a snowbank, but even the thought of losing Mason burned like acid in my chest. If something happened to Mason—

That would mean that Jackson would... what?

He didn't have control of his magic.

I might not be a witch, but I could help him learn to talk to the dead and I could keep him safe.

Around me, the world got a little darker, the shadows stretched deeper into the grasses, the insects buzzed and the summer cicadas screamed in the trees behind me.

No. I wasn't my father.

If anything happened to Mason, I wouldn't do what he'd done when my mother died, even if I wanted to, and I was pretty sure I would.

I wondered if Mason would stay with me, like Dom had stayed with Mariana. If that would be comforting, or just torture because he would feel trapped and unable to move on as long as I wanted him to stay with me. And I would want him forever.

God, I was a fucking mess.

Mason was alive. He was strong. He was careful.

With everything we'd been through, Mason always came through with barely a scratch. I was the idiot who was going to get myself killed. Again.

My self-pep talk didn't help.

If anything, it made it worse, and I was more afraid than I had been before.

Fuck.

23

THEY FOUND ALL seven bodies in the cow pond. One elf. Two fauns. Three orcs. One ghoul. Hart had called me in to get names for all of them.

Thea Angevine. Mayrella Jones. Alexander Chu. Rupert North. Amy Lee Thomas. Javier Salazar. Doreen Swift.

All of them stabbed to death at the stone on the Harrod property. None of them remembered seeing their killers.

I'd helped them all return across the Veil, although Thea gave me a cold and damp hug before she went.

And then I'd spent an entire day curled up in bed because I didn't know how to deal with it. The callousness and fear-turned-hatred that led the Ordo to target Arcanids. The greed that led them to try to strip magic away from anyone who wasn't like them.

The absolute terror that they would try to do the same to Mason. That they would succeed.

Mason did what he always did. He wrapped his arms around me, holding me tightly, coaxing me to come out of the bedroom to watch movies with Jackson on the couch and making me macaroni and cheese.

The terror gave way to a low-grade fear that squatted in the back of my throat like a bitter toad. It was constant, but not crippling, so I dragged myself out of bed and back to work. I wasn't going to physically be able to stop the Ordo if they decided to try to kill Mason, so I'd have to learn to do it with warlock magic.

I asked Mason to give me things to practice with—things he'd used as casting objects, locks and knots he'd made into magical seals, sigils meant to keep me out or deflect my power.

I'd mildly burned three fingers, I'd completely destroyed a piece of wood he'd marked with a sigil (which had *not* been the point), and left two new scorch marks on my desk at Beyond the Veil.

When I got fed up with my inability to work magic to my own satisfaction, I summoned Sylvia or Archie—never both, since they usually spent the whole time yelling at each other—and practiced giving them sound and form. That, at least, I was getting better at. Even after a few hours, they barely left damp spots, and I was no longer nearly as tired. Yes, it was draining, but not so much so that I couldn't get through the rest of the day, even with a séance.

If I'd stopped to actually think about how far I'd come, whether with magic or mediumship—my own special flavor of both mixed together—I might actually have been impressed with myself.

But hitting pause wasn't an option.

We were just about ready to head to the office—Jackson was packing up his backpack and Mason was pulling our already-prepped lunches from the fridge—when my phone rang, playing *Hart to Hart*.

Mason's sigh was audible across the kitchen.

"Yeah?" I answered it.

The Skeleton Under the Stairs

"I'll be there in ten," came Hart's response. "I just got the green light and I need us to do this before they take it back, which they will if they stop to think about it too long, so sorry for the short notice. I need you to crosscheck unsolved crimes... and maybe some that were, uh, misclassified."

I looked up and found Mason watching me, his jaw tight, but his expression resigned.

"You think they're connected to the Ordo?" I asked.

"They go back a ways," he told me. "I've pulled every Nid stabbing for the last thirty years."

I swallowed. If I agreed to this, it was going to be a long fucking day.

"And all the missing Nid cases."

Fuck me.

I saw the flash of something raw that crossed Mason's face and almost told Hart no.

"We'll be okay," Mason said softly before I had the chance, nodding, although I could tell he wasn't happy.

I took almost a full minute before I gave Hart my answer. "Okay," I told the elf.

He hung up on me. I put the phone down, biting my lip as I looked over at Mason.

He crossed the kitchen and walked behind me, bending down to wrap his arms around me and press a kiss to my temple. "You've got this," he whispered into the curls that fell over the side of my forehead.

I turned my head so I could see him. "You sure?"

"Mmhmm." He kissed me gently. "I might worry about you, and I don't like it when you're drained or unhappy, but I'm really proud of you for doing this."

I had to blink back tears. "Mace..."

"Hush." He kissed me again. "Go with Hart. Jackson and I can hold down Beyond the Veil."

"Thank you," I whispered against his lips.

———

FOUR HOURS IN, I really, really wished I'd said no to Hart.

I'd been relegated to a back room—this one a conference room instead of a horrible black-painted hellhole, thank God—with Dani Bowman, the RPD's newest resident witch. Mason had mentioned them before, but I'd not yet had the pleasure. Dani's short hair was neon green, which contrasted really stunningly with their bronze skin and the electric blue of their button-down.

Dani had been obviously terrified of meeting me, and their hand was sweaty when I shook it. We'd gotten past that sometime in the first three hours of me summoning dead Arcanid after dead Arcanid, working through the stack of stabbing victims that *had* names.

About an hour earlier, we'd started the second stack, which was the Jack and Joan Does who were also full of stab wounds. They use different names for unidentified Arcanids than humans, even Arc-humans. Because they somehow need a different categorization.

On the one hand, I get it. It's easier to ID a victim as a Nid at first glance if they're Jack instead of John, Joan instead of Jane. But we don't put in different names for Arcs or other categories of people... It just rubbed me the wrong way.

At least that stack was smaller... barely. The problem, of course, is that they were a lot harder to find when you didn't have a name or a relative or—since these were mostly cold cases—a body.

On the up side, nobody was giving me any trouble, at least not once I found them. There was a lot of confusion—

a *lot*. I couldn't decide if I was happy that most of them weren't Ordo victims, or if I would prefer there to be a singular reason behind so much senseless death.

Out of nearly eighty cases, only seven had been killed by the Ordo. It was a lot of work for not a lot of yield, although Dani had pointed out that at least we had answers for most of the others, even if they didn't fit the profile and the case we were working.

Dani rubbed their hands over their face. "How do you *do* this?" they asked.

I shook my head. "Ask me that again in another..." I eyed the stacks of files Hart had piled up on our table. "Six hours?"

"Ugh." Dani shuddered.

I sighed. "Yeah. What's next?"

Dani passed over the next file. "Jack Doe Seven."

I looked at the photograph in the file, a head-shot only, the pallor of death under his green skin making it painfully obvious that it had been taken postmortem.

It wasn't the first orc file we'd gone through, but something about this orc's features hit me a lot harder than any of the others. I couldn't tell if it was the set of his jaw or the angle of his cheekbones, but all I could see when I looked at him was Mason.

My hands shook as I set down the file, a lot faster than I probably should have.

"Ward?" Dani asked.

"I—I think I just need a break," I said, knowing that my voice was shaking.

"Okay. Um. It's like one anyway, so maybe we stop for lunch?"

I nodded, pushing my trembling hands in my lap. "Yeah. I think—I think that's a good idea."

I had no intention of eating lunch, however, since I was pretty sure I'd just throw it up the minute I had to come back and pick up that file again.

"You want me to bring you something?" Dani asked, pausing on their way out the door.

I shook my head. "No, thanks. Food allergies. I'll sort myself out." Maybe there would be some plain crackers in the vending machine. Or maybe I'd find a banana somewhere. Nice mild foods that I might be able to keep down.

Dani left me at the table, and I tried very hard not to think about the closed file sitting on the table.

I shut my eyes and took several deep breaths.

I knew it wasn't really a good idea to summon spirits alone—particularly when you have my kind of track record for encountering the psychotic dead.

But if I was going to cry like a baby through this whole thing, however short it was, I really preferred not to do it in front of someone I'd just met. Both for their sake and mine.

My heart pounded in my chest as I opened the file folder.

Once I blinked through the tears, I could pick out the individual things that made this poor man not Mason. His nose was narrower. His lower canines were smaller. His jawline softer. He had a mole on one side of his forehead.

I blew out a breath, sniffling. Since I was alone in the room, I pulled it off and roughly wiped the back of my hand under my nose because I didn't have any damn tissues. At least I had sanitizer in the satchel on my chair.

A few more deep breaths, and I held the image of Jack Doe Seven in my head, focusing on the differences between his features and Mason's as I reached out, searching on both sides of the Veil.

The Skeleton Under the Stairs

I was surprised that I found him so very quickly, and on this side.

He started at me, blinking eyes so dark they appeared entirely black. **You were looking for me?**

Yes. I pushed the file forward toward him. *I want to help find your family. Tell them what happened to you.*

He looked down. **Jack Doe, eh?**

My name is Edward Campion, I told him. *I work with the Richmond Police.*

Do you? The words were icy.

I take it you weren't fond of the police?

His black eyes were flat and empty. **Who do you think did this to me?**

Fucking hell.

Can you give me a name? I asked him.

Officer Shelby.

What happened?

He crossed his massive arms over his chest. **Pulled me over. Made me get out of the car, even though I'd done nothing wrong. Hit me with his damn taser. Woke up tied up in the back of a covered pickup getting hauled somewhere with a damn bag over my head. They dragged me through the woods and put me on a slab of stone, then stabbed me to death.**

It was a familiar refrain by now. *They wore dark clothes and hoods?*

You knew.

We didn't, exactly, I explained. *We're looking through old victims with profiles that match, trying to find any who were killed by the Antiquus Ordo Arcanum.*

The what?

Did you have magic? Before your transformation? I asked him.

What? Magic? No.

I frowned. *Are you sure? No... visions or strange senses? Nightmares?*

He shook his head. **Who are these people?**

They're a secret society of warlocks who believe that only... certain people should have magical abilities. They've decided that Arcanids aren't worthy of it.

He blinked at me. **I... used to sometimes know things,** he said, softly. **Like when someone was about to call. Or when my mother died.**

According to Mason, these extra senses were sometimes a sign of latent magic for witches or, possibly, warlocks. *Did anyone else in your family talk about things like that?* Sometimes that was also a clue—an aunt or grandparent who claimed magical talent.

I saw him deflate. **My mother.** But he said nothing else.

I'm so sorry for what happened to you, I began.

But you can't help.

I frowned up at him. *I want to help,* I replied. *And I will do everything I can to help.*

He tilted his head to one side. **You work with the police.**

With them, yes. But I am not one of them. And the detective I work for isn't... part of the club, so to speak.

The look he gave me was deeply skeptical.

He's an elf.

I saw the moment he decided to trust me. **James Harding.**

It fit him. *It's nice to meet you, Mr. Harding.*

James.

I smiled. *James. You can call me Ward.*

He nodded. **Tell me what to do.**

Do you have any family we can contact?

A nod. **My sister. Angelina.**

I wrote it down.

Oh, and some of them didn't have on hoods.

I looked up at him, hardly daring to believe my luck. *Could you describe them?*

He thought about this for a minute. **I don't suppose you can help me hold a pencil?**

James Harding was an incredible artist.

Hart came in before Dani returned from lunch, bringing me a sandwich and a vegan cookie, along with a bottle of unsweetened iced tea. He paused in the door, studying James, who was sitting in a chair at the table, sketching his second portrait. Then the elf wordlessly walked in and handed me the food, then watched, lavender eyes wide, as James's pencil formed the features of a middle-aged woman. I passed the elf the first sketch James had completed, this one of the officer who had kidnapped him.

"Sonofabitch," was Hart's response, causing James to look up from his second piece of paper.

Is he upset? the dead orc asked me.

Probably. But he also just swears a lot. "Hart?" I asked out loud.

Hart waved the paper. "I know this asshole," he said. "Looks about a decade younger, but he's in Fourth Precinct."

Hart pulled out his phone, already dialing as he left the room, James's sketch under his arm.

The ghost started at me.

Best guess? He's calling IAD.

IAD?

Internal Affairs Division. The police you call when the police are the problem.

Does that actually work? James asked, going back to his sketch.

Sometimes. I picked up my sandwich. *Do you mind if I eat?*
Why would I?

I shrugged, then unwrapped my sandwich.

Hart came back again, looking over at James as he drew. "You know how fucking creepy that is, right?"

"Not really," I answered honestly. "It's my every day."

Hart grunted. "Useful," he said. "But fucking creepy."

James snorted a soft laugh through his nose.

"Parikh is going to come and pick up whatever we have for him."

I grimaced. While I was sure that Detective Parikh was a perfectly nice man, I didn't have a lot of positive associations with him—he'd been one of the two IAD officers who had questioned me about the whole Tyler Lessing disaster.

"He's one of the good ones, Ward," Hart said gently, one long-fingered hand resting on my shoulder.

"Yeah. I know." That didn't make me feel much better about it.

The door opened again and Dani let out a squeak.

James ignored them.

"I told you he wasn't a normal fucking medium," was Hart's response.

Dani pointed at James.

"Yeah, that's a dead orc," Hart confirmed.

"What—" Dani seemed to be struggling a bit with words.

"He's drawing his killers," I replied.

Dani's brown eyes got even bigger, and they very carefully inched their way into the room. I suppressed the urge to sigh, feeling very sympathetic toward Mason, and James, since he'd probably experienced something similar when alive.

Is it me or you? the ghost asked me without bothering to raise his head.

Yep. Definitely experienced something similar. *Pretty sure this one's all me*, I replied.

James's strangely dark-yet-aethereal eyes flicked up to meet mine before returning to the pencil and paper in front of him. **This happen a lot?**

I don't tend to show off often enough for it to be a regular thing. Mostly because making ghosts visible and tangible seriously freaks people out.

That got me a soft snort. **Not common, I take it?**

Not even a little.

Dani finally worked up enough courage to pick up the file folder on the top of the stack, then swallowed. "Are... can you..."

"Do more than one at the same time?"

They nodded.

I held out my hand, and they put the next folder—this one a Joan Doe—into it. She was a faun, mid-sixties.

"Let's see who else we've got."

———

HART HAD DRAGGED another three people into our little coterie—Dani, Parikh, me, Hart, a rookie named Ellen Schmidt, and a more seasoned beat cop named Bobby Sanchez who was apparently only two weeks from retirement. Parikh was working with James's sketches, doing whatever it is IAD does, and Dani was writing down accounts of every ritual the dead recounted—through me, since Hart agreed with Mason that I should minimize freaking people out. Schmidt and Sanchez were contacting families.

Once James had finished his drawings, Hart had asked him to write out his statement. I'd been the one to sign it as the witnessing medium, because there wasn't protocol for ghosts writing their own statements. Then, of course, Dani had asked if I could do it for *all* of them, and I told them that if I did that, I'd end up passed out after about six, while we had pulled a hundred and seventy-two cases. Of those, we'd identified a dozen Ordo murders.

A dozen more than we'd known about this morning.

And a hundred and sixty that were either cleared or had new evidence that might eventually lead to them being cleared.

I'd made it through the stack of Jack and Joan Does—none of whom were still Jacks or Joans except for the one elf woman whose name actually *was* Joan. Our new friends were specifically working to track down the next of kin for all of the newly-identified unknowns.

"Shoulda fuckin' done this years ago," Sanchez remarked, coming back into the room to grab another file off the cleared pile. "Clear out the cold Does."

"Except most mediums can't do this," Hart replied. "Campion here is fucking special." Sanchez snorted, then saluted me with the file folder before heading back out the door, presumably to contact another family.

At the moment, as glad as I was that I could help bring closure to these families, I did not feel in the very least special. I was exhausted.

And we still had the final stack to go. Missing persons. It was in theory easier than Jacks and Joans, simply because I had names. But at the same time I had to be certain that when I couldn't find someone it was because they were alive, and not because they were resistant to being summoned.

To be completely honest, it probably wouldn't have been

The Skeleton Under the Stairs

all that difficult if I were fresh—but I'd already worked through a hundred and seventy-two fucking files, and I really didn't have that much left in me.

Dani handed me a file. "Hamish Murray."

Hamish was a ghoul, his grin lopsided in the photo that had been provided by someone who was probably his family.

I was really starting to hate this. I heaved a breath, bracing myself.

Hart rested his hand on my shoulder. "Not going to say it doesn't fucking suck to call a family and tell them their husband or son or brother or whatever is dead, but, believe me, they'd rather have closure than just keep fucking wondering."

I nodded, but was too tired to actually bother using breath to reply.

And then I reached out, searching for Hamish.

It didn't take long.

Hullo?

Mr. Murray. My name is Edward Campion, and I'm working with the police to try to identify cold cases that might be related to a current case. It had become a mantra by now, like the spiel offered by the poor people who had to work at call centers. Hi-my-name-is-Barbara-thank-you-for-calling-the-help-line-how-may-I-help-you.

Oh! You can call me Hamish. He beamed at me. **You're going to catch them?** I assumed 'them' was whoever had taken his life.

We can certainly try. What can you tell me about the people who killed you? I tried not to sound as tired as I was.

They were in some sort of funny cult, Hamish told me.

That got my attention. *What kind of cult?* I asked him.

Well, they wore hoods and took me out to the woods—

Stop there, please, Mr... Hamish. The detective here is going to want to talk to you. Hart was looking at me expectantly. "We've got another one," I told him.

Another what? Hamish asked.

It sounds like you were killed by an organization that calls themselves the Antiquus Ordo Arcanum, I told him. *That's the case we're working on and why we've summoned you.*

Oh. There are others?

I nodded.

Well, I'm happy to help. He looked enormously pleased.

―――

It was almost seven when I closed the last file—a vampire named Carrie Kinesey who had apparently drowned while out for a solo swim in the James River. According to Dani, accidental vampire deaths were surprisingly common because they assumed they couldn't die from accidents. But all it took was a penetrating cardiac wound, and it didn't matter if it came from someone with a stake or, in Carrie Kinsey's case, getting tumbled through the rapids into a submerged tree branch.

It also, for what it's worth, didn't have to be wooden. Anything that went through the heart would do it—wood, metal, you name it. Vampires could and did die in car accidents surprisingly often when a broken rib punctured their cardiac muscle.

I slumped over the table, resting my forehead on my arms. "Fuck me."

Hart's hand patted my back. "C'mon. Let's get your pathetic ass home."

"Fuck *you*, Hart," I replied, teasing him. "This ass just summoned two hundred and three fucking ghosts in one day, you ungrateful loser."

The elf laughed, as intended.

We'd found fourteen total Ordo murders, including Hamish and another orc named Esmerelda. I felt like my whole body was made of Jell-O, and I was starving. I pushed myself off the table and noticed my hands shaking. It was probably a really good thing that I couldn't actually drive, because I was in rough shape.

Pushing my wheels was a lot harder than it had any right to be, but I managed to follow Hart out to his car, forcing a smile at the handful of people who thanked me on the way out. Apparently, I had singlehandedly wiped out more case files in one day than usually got cleared in a decade.

Hart loaded me into his Charger, then got in. As he backed out of the parking spot, he shot a quick look in my direction. "They're all gonna want you to fix their fucking cases now, you know," he remarked.

"Oh, yay." I couldn't really muster much enthusiasm, even though I know the work was important.

"I'd recommend forcing them to go through BTV," Hart continued.

"BTV?"

"You haven't abbreviated your own company before? The fuck is wrong with you?"

Oh. "I'm tired, Hart. I just summoned two hundred spirits. You're lucky I can form words at all."

The elf snorted. "Touché. My point still stands, though. Make them hire you. Make it a fucking selling point. Something you specifically do."

I leaned my head back against the seat. "You think we should advertise clearing cold cases?"

"I think you should advertise finding out if someone's missing relative is dead," Hart answered.

"That's morbid."

"You fucking talk to dead people on a regular basis, and *I'm* morbid?"

He had a point. "Yeah, but—"

"I'm serious, Ward. What you can do is un-fucking-believable. Almost nobody can do that. Maybe actually nobody. You just single-handedly pushed forward like two dozen missing persons cases, either because you know they *aren't* dead or because you just confirmed they are. You got victim statements out of like a hundred and eighty dead people. That's fucking incredible."

"I guess..."

"And that's not something most mediums can *do*, especially not in one fucking day. You damn well better know that."

"Yeah," I conceded.

"So sell it. If they're too goddamn lazy to solve their own fucking cases, make them pay you to do their jobs for them. Force up the damn budget or at least force them to cut the dead weight."

I grimaced. "I can't solve RPD's problems for them," I pointed out.

"Nope, you can't. The RPD's got problems from here to goddamn China and back, following the fucking scenic route. But you can definitely make them pay you, and you might even be able to make a couple people do some reevaluating of priorities."

I had known that Hart had strong thoughts about his job, but I found myself impressed. It wasn't just that Hart wanted to be good at his job—although he did—it was that he wanted to make the job itself better.

I wished him well with that, although I, in my pessimism, would have placed money on it being a losing battle.

"At least talk to Doc about it," Hart suggested.

"Okay. Tomorrow."

He let out a chuffing sound. "Fine. Tomorrow."

"Afternoon. I'm not getting out of bed until at least one."

"Fair enough."

Hart dropped me off, waiting at the curb until I rolled my way up to the door, which Mason opened before I even got there.

I looked up at him. "Hi."

"You look like you had a... very long day."

"You have no fucking idea," I muttered as I rolled past him into the living room. Then I stopped, sniffing appreciatively. "You got me pizza?"

"Yeah!" Jackson crowed. "I told Uncle Mason you would need pizza *and* banana splits."

"Come here." I held my arms out, and Jackson half climbed into my lap to give me a hug. I squeezed him. "You were exactly right," I told him. "Pizza and banana splits is *perfect*."

24

"What now?" I demanded of Hart over the phone, not having bothered to take my face out of the pillow.

"Fibers from Thea Angevine's body have been IDed as a very expensive alpaca wool used in a very particular style of rug that is only sold at one very exclusive shop in Glen Allen. That shop has a lifetime guarantee on their rugs, and they very kindly went through their records and were able to confirm that just such a rug was purchased by one Lilian Harrod about seven years ago."

"Okay..." I wasn't awake enough yet to understand what the fuck the elf wanted me to do with that information.

"It was enough to get me a fucking warrant. I already called the chipper one, and she's in." He thought he was going to need both Beck and me. "Any chance I can get Doc, too?"

I lifted my face out of the pillow and aimed it at the almost-certainly-not-sleeping-but-pretending-to orc next to me. "Mace?"

I got a grunt from the blankets.

"Hart wants both of us," I told him.

The next sound was more of a groan, but he pushed himself up, then padded out into the hallway in only his black pajama pants, taking his phone with him.

"Well?" Hart demanded.

"I think he's checking," I replied, staring the slow process of rolling myself into a sitting position. A glance at the clock showed it was about six-thirty. "Fuck, Hart, it's like the ass-crack of dawn."

"Judge Moreno was up early this morning, what can I say?"

"I hate you."

"Because I'm clearly doing this to you on purpose. What does Doc say?"

"Dunno yet." Mason would go through the rotation, first seeing if Keidra or Deon could take him, then Mariana. I yawned, then, finally, pushed myself up to sitting, my legs hanging off the side of the bed. "Why d'you need both of us?"

"Turns out that the Harrod estate is an old plantation," he said.

"Hart, everything out here is an old plantation."

"Not inaccurate, but is every old plantation historically owned by the Simmons family and named Sweet Rose?"

"Oh, *fuck*."

"That underground ritual space is on this goddamn property somewhere, Ward, and I'm going to fucking find it —and I'm gonna probably need you, Beck, and Doc to deal with whatever the fuck we find there."

"Gran can take him," Mason said from the doorway, his voice still a little scratchy from sleep. "I need to get him up now?"

"Hart thinks they found Vaux's underground ritual chamber."

Mason blew out a breath. "I'll get Jackson up. We should swing by Beyond the Veil and get your chest." I nodded.

"We're going to drop off Jackson," I told Hart, "and then grab some gear from the office." My carved oak chest had most of what we should need—salt, charcoal, sage, oils, crystals, candles, birch bundles, and so on. Beck would probably bring her kit, as well, but I didn't want to be underprepared going into the Ordo's ritual chamber.

"Meet me at the Harrod property," he said. "I'll text Doc the address."

"Okay."

"Sooner rather than later, Ward."

"I'm not doing this without coffee," I told him.

"I won't complain if there's a latte in it for me."

"I'll think about it," I told him, and he hung up.

I ran my hands over my face, then got myself into my chair and went into the bathroom to at least make myself quasi-presentable, even if I wasn't going to have time for an actual full shower.

As I got dressed, having at least shaved and brushed my teeth, I could hear Jackson whining about having to be up. I sympathized. I didn't want to be up and going anywhere, either. I couldn't make out Mason's words, but his tone was low and patient as usual.

My heartrate picked up. If we could figure this out, bring peace to Archie and Jenny and everyone else, and maybe even be able to find enough evidence to bring down the Ordo... then Mason would be safe.

That got me to move a little faster.

An extremely sleepy Jackson was eating a bagel smeared with peanut butter in the kitchen, one hand holding Everest the snow leopard by the paw. His backpack sat on the floor beside his stool.

"You have everything you need, Jax?" Mason asked, sweeping into the kitchen wearing black jeans and a dark blue t-shirt, his braids twisted up.

"Mmhmm."

"Ward?"

"I'm good."

"Bring your bagel, Jax."

I grabbed his backpack as Jackson slid off the stool, putting it in my lap as I followed my fiancé and his nephew out the back door.

We dropped Jackson off at Mariana's, then headed out to the highway after making a brief stop to get coffee and donuts. I'd asked Mason to get enough for the crowd that I assumed Hart would be dragging with him, plus the special orders for Beck, Hart, Mason, and me.

I nursed my caramel latte as I munched my way through a blueberry donut. Mason wasn't eating—although I had a bag for him in my lap—but he did have an actual mocha in one hand, and he sipped it occasionally as he drove.

"Mace?"

"Mmmm?" I felt bad that he was getting dragged into whatever shitshow we were about to walk into.

"You okay?" I asked him.

"Just tired," came the response.

I chewed my lower lip. I wasn't sure that was all that was bothering him, but I also didn't want to start something in the car on the way to a crime scene.

"I slept like shit," Mason offered, then.

"I'm sorry."

He sighed. "I just keep thinking about everything that's happening, and I can't shut it off," he continued. "And then I worry about you and about what would happen if Jackson got pulled into this. We know they've gone after kids before."

I nodded, feeling a bit guilty that I hadn't thought about the risk this posed to Jackson, specifically. I'd been so focused on the fact that the Ordo hated Arcanids that I'd completely missed the part about the Ordo hating witches in general.

"Are you okay?" Mason asked me.

"Ish," I answered honestly.

"Ish?"

"I'm okay. But—"

"But?"

"I'm worried about *you*."

He glanced over at me, and I could tell he was surprised by that. "Me?"

"Mason, you're a witch and an orc. They hate you for both reasons, *and* you're snooping in Ordo business."

He was silent, and a glance over at him told me he was thinking about what to say. That didn't really help me feel any better.

I swallowed.

"We'll stop them," he said softly.

I nodded, not trusting myself to actually speak, and excused myself from the conversation by putting another piece of donut in my mouth. It stuck to my soft palette, and I had to work not to choke on either it or the fear in the back of my throat.

I was still working on it when we pulled into the drive at the Harrod mansion, and Mason leaned out the window to talk to the uniform watching the entrance. He passed me my consultant's badge, which I pulled over my head, then pulled around to the side and parked behind Hart's Charger.

The house, a colonial revival that looked a bit confused about what time period it had actually been built in, squatted at the curve of the drive, glaring at the people milling around on its front lawn and under its mostly unnecessary portico. Paving stones led around to one side of the house where grapevines stretched over an arbor, and two spiral-trimmed cedar bushes flanked the entryway.

The front door was already open, Mays the CSI tech standing in it. He waved when he saw me, and I waved back, then pulled up my plain black mask.

"Donut?" I offered, lifting one of the two boxes in my lap.

"Absolutely," he agreed, then pulled out a jelly donut covered in powdered sugar. "Boss is in the kitchen, which is probably where this should go anyway."

"Thanks, Mays."

"Hey, Mason," he greeted my fiancé.

"Morning," came Mason's reply. "There will be coffee in the kitchen if you want it." Mason had taken charge of the beverages. "Is Beck here yet?"

I hadn't seen her car, so I hadn't bothered asking, but I suppose she could have parked elsewhere or gotten a ride.

"Pulling in now, it looks like," Mays replied, and I looked back over my shoulder to see her bright blue Evo parking behind the Tacoma.

"Perfect timing," I remarked, then continued toward the kitchen. Mason hung back to give Beck her mocha, and they both caught up with me by the time I made it down the hallway and into the kitchen. Hart had set up a kind of headquarters, and people were moving in and out, grabbing equipment, swapping out devices in chargers, and dropping off evidence baggies.

A small cheer went up as Beck helped Mason and I set out coffee and donuts, and then we quickly got out of the way before we got crushed in the press of bodies going after pastry and caffeine.

I handed Hart his bag of personally-selected donuts. "Here. Avoid the mosh pit."

He grunted his thanks, then grunted again as Mason passed him a latte. "About fucking time you three got here. Carpool?"

"We just have excellent timing," Beck told him, tossing her long braid over her shoulder with a flourish and a grin. Today's ensemble included white walking shorts and a brilliantly colored floral sleeveless top with dangling beaded earrings.

Hart snorted, then took a drink of coffee. "Fuck, yeah. Okay, here's the situation. We've got a lawyer incoming, a pissed-off Mr. Charlesworth Harrod who is trying to insist on being present for the search, which we don't have to allow, but we're letting him follow a team around upstairs for the time being. Lillian Harrod isn't here—but she's on her way back from DC and should get here within an hour or so, depending on traffic."

"His name is actually Charlesworth?" I asked, still stuck on that bit of information.

Hart gave me a look. "Seriously, *that's* what you want to fucking know? Not 'where's the murder basement, Hart?'"

"I do want to know where the murder basement is," I replied primly. "But it isn't every day you hear the name Charlesworth being used for an actual living human being."

"He's not wrong," Beck defended me.

"Thank you."

"Shut the fuck up, both of you."

Mason snorted.

"There are two locked doors on this floor, one down the hall that supposedly leads to a basement that Mr. Harrod insists he doesn't have the key to, and this one—" he gestured to a heavy but mostly nondescript door in the back wall of the kitchen that had a rolling counter in front of it "—that he *also* doesn't have the key to that leads to a supposedly unused passageway from the old plantation house that isn't here anymore. He's also insisting that the second one isn't covered by the warrant because it's not part of the main house."

"I smell bullshit," Mason muttered, crossing his arms over his chest.

"Of course you do," Hart replied. "You have an excellent sense of smell. Also, our old warrant covers the grounds, so there shouldn't be anything that *isn't* allowed, but Harrod is making noises that separate structures all need separate warrants, so that should be a fun screaming match."

"Do they?" I asked.

"Un-fucking-fortunately, yes and no," Hart answered. "I'm going to argue that this one *is* covered because it's connected to the house, but I'm also not going to bust the door down until Moreno says I can because you can bet your sweet asscheeks that what we're looking for is behind door number two and I am *not* going to get this search thrown out in court."

I frowned. "So we're waiting?"

"For wherever the fuck that door leads, yes. But Lilian Harrod doesn't keep her formalwear in the basement." Hart grinned, his features arranged into an expression of threat than pleasure. "And blood doesn't come out in the wash very well."

"Did you test it already?" Mason asked, surprised.

"Sure did," Mays answered, coming in with a baggie of what looked like bullets. "Lab will have to confirm type, but preliminary swab indicates the presence of blood." He shrugged. "Could be chicken or human, so it's not conclusive, but..."

"Who keeps bloody chicken-killing clothes in their closet?"

Mays nodded. "Exactly." He handed the bag to Hart.

"The fuck are these?" The elf asked Mays.

"Bullets."

"I can fucking see that."

"Rifle, 308s. Looks like they've got something inscribed on them."

"Doc, come look at this."

Mason took the baggie from Hart, rolling the bullets in his hand as he examined them through the plastic. "This could take a bit of time to figure out," he said.

"What do you want us to do in the meantime?" I asked.

"Any dead people?"

Beck and I exchanged a glance, then we both drew in deep breaths. I closed my eyes, then reached out.

And ran into a goddamn wall.

"Ward?" Beck's voice was concerned.

"Yeah, I sense it."

"Sense what?" That was Mason, although he didn't look up from the bullets. He'd also pulled out his phone and was checking something on it.

"It's like a... wall. A barrier stopping us from sensing much," I replied.

He grunted, and a slight tingle along my skin told me he was investigating it. "Ah."

"Ah? The fuck does *that* mean, Doc?"

"This could... take a moment."

I wanted to watch, so I opened my eyes—all of them. I sucked in a sharp breath at the thick lines of the web blanketing the house, then shuddered.

"Ward?" Beck asked, her voice concerned.

"Careful, Mace," I warned him. "This whole house is..." I wasn't sure how to describe it.

"Give me a hand?" he asked.

Then I noticed he was literally holding one out.

I put my hand in his, then gasped again as his magic pushed through me. "Unravel it, Ward."

I wasn't sure how, but I at least could see the patterns of black, red, and a sickly blue that were woven across the walls, the floor, and the ceiling. I felt along the threads, looking for a weakness that I couldn't find.

"Southwest corner," Mason breathed.

"I don't know which direction that is," I admitted.

He and Hart both pointed.

I traced the lines of magic through the walls—I know it sounds weird, but with my Third Eye and my magic sight both active I could kind of feel-see through the walls—in the direction they'd pointed.

And then I felt it—a fraying at the edge of the house.

All it takes to undo a whole tapestry is just one loose thread.

I found one.

And I started pulling.

"Holy fuck," I heard Hart gasp beside me.

"Easy, Ward," Mason cautioned me. "Don't pull the house down on us, please."

I blinked a couple times, refocusing back on my surroundings.

Multiple people were ducking, a few holding on to tables or doorways.

I shot a slightly panicked look over at Mason and found that he'd stuck a foot under one of my wheels. The twist of lips he offered me was a little sickly. "Lights flickering, a little bit of shaking."

Hart made a strangled sound and even Beck, when I turned to look at her, appeared visibly disturbed.

"Sorry," I whispered.

"Gently," Mason said softly. "Go gently, and I can stabilize it."

Outside the kitchen, I heard shouting.

"Hart," Mason said.

I watched the usually unflappable elf, lavender eyes huge in his fine features, swallow about three times. "Yep. I'll just. Deal with that." He scooted out of the kitchen.

"Gently," Mason said again.

I nodded, then refocused on my threads, slowing down and unweaving, rather than just pulling at the loose ends. I also tried to pay more attention to what was happening around me, noticing the slight flicker of electricity that told me to slow down a bit more. All the while, Mason smoothed out where I unraveled, a faint sheen of green maintaining the integrity of the web even as I weakened its stranglehold on the house.

I paused when I neared the doorway in the back of the kitchen. It was heavily warded, the magic tightly knotted around it. "Do I undo the doorway?" I asked softly.

"Carefully," Mason replied, his fingers tightening on mine. "They won't have left it unprotected."

I nodded. "I know. It's mostly red."

"What does that mean?" Beck asked nervously.

"Death magic," Mason answered her.

"Be careful, Ward," she said softly, putting her hand on my shoulder. I could feel the steady pulse of her magic on offer should I need it.

I covered her hand with mine, my other hand in

Mason's. I had both of them. This would work. Together, we could handle it.

I began carefully untying the knots around the doorway, tugging a thread here, loosening a loop there.

But the door wasn't passive, like the house.

The moment I let go of the threads, they moved, retying, attempting to snare me, to pull me... down.

A tendril whipped out from the doorway, but before it could reach me it flared green and turned to sparks. I stared at Mason, whose free hand had flicked out a finger. He met my gaze steadily.

"Thanks," I whispered.

His features tightened into a hostile smile. "They'll have to do better than that if they want to get around me."

"Maybe don't challenge the sentient evil magic door, Mace."

"It's not sentient. It's a spell like any other. No smarter than the warlock who cast it." Mason's smile spread a little. "And I'm probably smarter than they are."

"Not arguing, Doc, but is this really a good time to get cocky?" Hart asked as he came back into the kitchen.

The door lashed out again, this time going for Hart, and both Mason and I reacted. Emerald sparks flared from the end as he blocked it, and I looped my purple-blue magic around the thread, tying it to me and drawing it toward me.

If I had control of it, it couldn't lash out at me, at Hart, at Beck, or at Mason.

That was my reasoning, anyway.

It might have worked if the door weren't a damn eldritch horror with like twenty tentacles, all of which it decided to throw at me as soon as I caught one of them.

"Did you have to piss it off?" Mason asked me, his voice a little strained as every single tendril sparked green.

"I thought you were shit at protection spells," I muttered, weaving together a mesh of my own magic.

"I've been practicing," he countered. "I've got this. You just pull the damn thing apart."

Beck's fingers tightened on my shoulder, and, out of the corner of my eye, I saw Hart lay a hand on Mason's forearm.

I let go of the thrashing thread of dark magic I'd been holding and went straight for the door itself, trusting Mason to keep all of us from getting flayed by the twists of dark-death-spirit magic.

I had to work fast to counteract the magic's attempts to reknot itself, but after only ten minutes it was clear that I was failing and falling behind, and I didn't know what to do.

I'm not sure if I summoned her or if my desperation was just too much of a siren call, but suddenly Sylvia was there with me.

Help me? I asked her.

I could feel her studying the magic, although I wasn't sure if she saw it somehow on her own or just through me.

Try tatting it, she said, suddenly.

What?

Tatting. Like lace.

I... what?

You're trying to unravel it, correct?

Yeah.

Try... reworking it. Replacing it. Tatting.

Tatting, I repeated. *Fuck.*

That will likely not be as useful, Sylvia remarked, and I felt my lips twitch in spite of the absolutely dire situation. But it helped reduce the tension, ease me away from the edge of panic.

Okay, Sylvia. Speed tatting lesson?

Happy to. She held out her hands in front of mine. **Do what I do, but with the magic threads.**

She could see them. She had to be able to.

I can, thanks to our exciting house-fire experiment.

Um. Sorry?

She smiled. **It's been quite interesting, actually. I'm enjoying it. Do what I do.**

I watched her fingers as they moved through the aether, mimicking them with my own as I knotted, looped, and wove the purplish threads of my magic, tinged bluer by the addition of Beck's power, in amongst the black-red-blue of the doorway's original weaving. And as I wove, the darker threads weakened, their attacks on Mason's protective magic becoming slower, fainter, the gleam fading the more of it I wove through with my own.

And then it flickered, the house groaned, and the threads fell away into ash that slid down the surface of the door and settled on the floor in a small pile.

"The fucking fuck was *that*?" Hart rasped. Beck's hand withdrew from my shoulder as she took a step back to lean heavily against the table.

My own hands were shaking. *Thank you, Sylvia.*

Anytime, Ward.

Stay?

I'd be offended if you wanted me to leave.

I smiled mentally at her, since doing so with my face would be wildly inappropriate.

"Ward? The fucking fuck *was* that?" the elf repeated.

"I'm guessing you can go downstairs now," I answered, my voice a lot rougher than I was expecting.

Then Mason's warm hands were on my shoulders. "Okay?" he asked me, and I could hear the tension and fear in his voice.

"Yeah. That was... That sucked. But I'm good."

Uncaring about anyone else in the room, Mason bent, his arms coming around my chest, and pressed a kiss to my temple. "I love you," he whispered into the curls on the side of my head.

I covered one of his hands with mine. "Love you, too," I whispered back.

Then he straightened, his hands staying heavy and warm on my shoulders. "Tell me we aren't going down there yet," he said, the comment directed at Hart.

"Not yet. Got a call into Moreno, but no." Hart took the lid off his coffee and chugged it. "Fuck."

Beck took a donut out of the box and handed it to me, then took another and passed it over to Mason. She picked up a third and offered it to Hart.

"Fuck, no. I'll be up the damn walls."

She shrugged, then pulled down her mask, broke off a piece of donut, and put it in her mouth.

"You okay?" I asked her.

"Mmhmm. Just need to counteract the adrenaline." She swallowed, then ate another piece. "Cuz this ain't over yet."

I grimaced, but didn't argue, and began eating my donut.

It's nice to see you, too, Rebeckah, Sylvia said politely, presumably responding to something Beck had said to her. **I could teach you, if you wish.**

What are we teaching Beck to do? I asked, curious.

Tatting. Actual tatting, however, not magical tatting.

I looked at Beck. "You want to learn to make lace?"

"I started crocheting a couple months ago because I could make such *cute* sweaters if I get good enough at it."

"Why the fuck are we talking about crocheting?" Hart wanted to know.

"Sylvia is going to teach Beck how to tat."

The Skeleton Under the Stairs

"The fuck does that mean?"

"I believe tatting is a form of textile arts," Mason put in.

"Textile. Fucking. Arts."

"Like knitting. Or crochet," Mason explained patiently.

"Textile arts," Hart muttered under his breath. Fortunately, whatever else he was about to say was interrupted by his phone going off. "Hart. Yes, Judge Moreno."

The rest of us went silent.

"Yes, sir. Yes, sir, that's right. No, sir. No, of course not, sir. Not a foot inside, sir. Haven't even touched the doorknob. Yes, sir, a scan by email will do just fine for now. Yes, sir. Thank you, sir."

It was the most polite I'd ever heard Hart be.

Then he put down the phone. "Fucking *fuck*, yeah!"

"Can I assume we have a warrant for the downstairs passageway and wherever it leads?" Mason asked.

"Fuck yeah. Give it five to come through on email, and we're in."

I quickly ate the rest of the donut Beck had handed me, since apparently we were about to go deal with whatever the fuck the Harrods kept in their creepy under—Underground Room.

"Hart," I said.

"What?"

"Do you remember how Vaux called it the Underground Room?"

"Oh, shit," Beck breathed.

The elf blinked at me. "Do I look like a fucking idiot to you?" he asked. "Of course I fucking remember that. Why do you think I got on this goddamn warrant like white on fucking rice?"

Behind him, Mason rolled his eyes.

Such a charmer, that one, Sylvia remarked, and Beck snorted a little as she tried to suppress her giggle.

Hart shook his head.

Then his phone let out a chime, and he poked at it. "Fuck, yeah. Mays!" he yelled.

"Yeah, boss?" The big CSI tech appeared in the kitchen doorway, looking nervous.

"Sweep up that weird magic dust shit by the door, then we're going in."

"Magic... dust... shit..."

"Sorry," I said. "I kinda... made a mess."

At least you didn't set it on fire, Sylvia very helpfully pointed out.

Beck snorted again.

Mays found a tiny dustpan somewhere and carefully swept up the dust that had fallen away from the door into an evidence baggie.

"Okay, party people," Hart said, rubbing his hands together. "Let's fucking do this."

———

THERE WAS no way I was getting down the absolutely terrifyingly steep set of ancient stairs, so Mason carried me, although he winced a little when the wooden steps groaned loudly under our combined weight. Hart went first, practically skipping, with Beck and then Mason following, Mays coming down last with another three techs I didn't know.

Hart had left another detective—Dan Maza—in charge upstairs to deal with the humans. After Mason had politely pointed out that he might want to have someone with magical ability in case Lillian Harrod became violent, Hart had also called in Dani Bowman, who had arrived just as we'd finished gathering all our gear—because Hart and Mays were insisting that the people walking had to wear booties and that we all had to have gloves to avoid leaving fingerprints.

Beck had her kit, and Hart had grudgingly agreed to carry my oak chest when Mason gave him the choice of the chest or the medium.

The hallway was old—that much was clear—and damp, but it was also very clean, which immediately made it evident that it wasn't, as Charlesworth Harrod had claimed, derelict and unused. It was abundantly clear that it was very much *frequently* used.

And that—along with the thick ropes of black-red-blue magic on the walls—was making me deeply uneasy. I was glad for Mason's steady strength, and I allowed myself to lean into his chest, trying to absorb some of his stoic courage along with his warmth.

"Okay?" he asked softly.

"Yeah."

He left it there. Because we both knew it kinda wasn't okay, but there also wasn't anything we could do about it that we weren't already doing.

I heard Hart's "Oh, fuck this" before I even realized we'd reached the end of the passageway.

When Mason sidled us sideways through the doorway, I completely understood.

This was a Ritual Room with two capital-Rs.

On the center of the floor was a complex binding seal—carved into the stone with the clear outline of a human body in the center.

"Is that..." I didn't finish the question, swallowing down the acid that pushed at the back of my throat.

"It appears to be, yes," Mason answered softly.

Viewed with my magic sight, the lines of the seal pulsed black and red, throbbing like—

"They're here, Mason," I rasped.

"What are?" he asked.

"The hearts."

He was silent for a moment. "Do you know where?"

I forced myself to follow the path of the magic, my eyes skimming over the labyrinthine whorls of the seal until the cut channels disappeared into a step leading to something that looked like an altar. But where the channels stopped, the thick, throbbing lines of magic did not.

I pointed. "In there, I think."

"What?" Hart demanded.

"Ward may have found our missing hearts," Mason answered, his arms tensing around me.

"In that?" Hart asked, having followed the line of my finger.

"You should *not* go break that open, Hart," Mason warned him.

The elf turned to look back at us, one eyebrow up. "You're thinking I just ask nicely and it'll just pop open? Abracadabra? Open sesame?"

"Probably not, no," Mason answered. "Although you're welcome to try."

Let me try.

I turned to look at Sylvia. *I... would rather you didn't,* I told her. The pulsing magic was thick and dark, churning and angry.

Why? It isn't like it can kill me again.

I shook my head. *Sylvia, this is magic designed to drain energy from the dead. We have no idea what it could or couldn't do to you.*

So then let me, sonny.

I felt Mason tense. "It's Archie," I whispered softly, and he relaxed a little.

It's my heart. Or mine's one of 'em, anyway. And I'm no stranger to death magic.

Sylvia scowled. **And you become the hero, is that it?**

Archie scowled right back at her. **Don't need to be a hero, do I? I just want my damn heart back!**

"I think that's enough of that," Beck interrupted out loud.

Hart looked confused for a moment. "There are fucking ghosts in here, too?" The CSI team suddenly looked a lot more nervous.

"Sylvia and Archie, yes," I answered.

"So on our team, then," Hart said, probably for the techs' benefit.

"Yeah," I replied. "Definitely on our team."

Ward—

I sighed. "He's right, Sylvia. If one of you is going to try, it should be Archie." I also wanted it to be Archie because as much as he was growing on me, I liked Sylvia more.

She sniffed, lifting her chin in an aristocratic pose. **If it all backfires, don't complain that I didn't warn you.**

And if it works, don't say you weren't a prissy bitch.

That's enough of that, Archie, I told him. The last thing we needed was for the ghosts to start a fight with each other.

Archie grunted, then pushed his metaphysical sleeves up and began to approach the altar. Mason very deliberately took a few steps away from it, careful not to make contact with the seal in the floor.

"Probably a good idea not to be in contact with the carving," he said.

"You heard him, people. Move your asses away from the creepy shit on the floor!" Hart barked.

Everyone moved, Beck close to us, Sylvia hovering between us and the altar, her back rigid.

Archie cracked his knuckles, then slowly began pushing one hand through the stone of the altar, the magic writhing around him, its tendrils lashing at his insubstantial form. I could see tears in the faintly glowing fabric of his being and cast threads of my own, trying to stich the rents back together.

The Ordo's magic was strong and angry, and it took all my concentration to keep Archie from being essentially pulled apart. I could feel Mason's arms tighten around me, feel the faint tingle as he fed magic into me through his hands.

Archie pushed a second hand into the altar, groaning with the pain of what the Ordo's magic was doing to him. I tried to work faster, but I couldn't keep up.

Archie!

Almost there, sonny.

It wasn't going to work. The angry magic was going to tear him apart and leave us still with no way to figure out what was happening inside the altar.

And then the altar let out a boom like a cannon, the smooth light grey of the stone suddenly split by a crack that seemed to go all the way through, letting out a howling scream as it did. I gasped, covering one ear as I pressed the other into Mason's chest. Beside us, Beck bent over, both her hands over her own ears.

Darkness had all but swallowed Archie, but when Sylvia floated forward, approaching the gaping, shrieking maw in the stone, I didn't have enough awareness to tell her to stop.

Fear—for Sylvia and Archie, for the rest of us—surged through me. I couldn't think, but I could absolutely panic.

And when I panic, dead people show up.

Jenny. Eunice. Tommy. Andrea. Hannah. Sampson. Geun. Erika. Eugene. Dom.

Two ghosts might not be a match for whatever the fuck was inside the altar, but apparently twelve plus a panicked warlock-medium were.

I poured everything I had into all of them, and they took it and... Well, I'm not entirely sure what the fuck they did with it, but there was a scream loud enough that everyone alive in the room heard it, nearly all of them throwing their hands over their ears. Mason hissed and winced, his body flinching at the piercing sound because holding me kept him from being able to do the same.

The really awful part, though, was that *something* crawled out of the altar, black and slick and trailing a viscous liquid that looked like oil mixed with blood.

"The fucking fuck is *that*?!" Hart voiced what everyone was thinking as he recoiled from the thing.

One of the CSI techs fainted, and Mason gasped out, "Get her off the seal!"

But not soon enough.

She screamed, the sound horrible, as her skin began to split, blood beginning to run along the carved seal even as the black liquid from the thing in the altar flowed in the opposite direction.

"*Go*," I hissed, and Mason half-dropped me to the ground, hopping his way through the seal so that his feet didn't hit any of the channels as magic surged through the air.

Mason's fingers were already moving, vibrant green spinning around his hands as he moved, and he snatched the now limp and silent woman, pulling her off the seal. With my magic sight, I could see webbing of black clinging to her even as he lifted, and I flung out threads of my own magic to cut them off.

On the other side of the seal, Mason put her down, then bent, his hands tilting her head back as he began by breathing into her lungs. Hart was beside him barely a second later, his hands coming down on her chest as he began compressions.

Another shriek drew my attention back to the thing, which was holding itself up as though it—like me—couldn't use its legs, parts of itself that must be arms pushing up as it dragged itself toward the center of the seal.

I nearly screamed myself as Beck's hands came down on my shoulders.

"Ward—"

I put a hand over hers, and her fingers tightened, magic pouring into me as she gave me full access to her power.

In turn, I poured it into the dead.

Someone began to mutter a prayer, but I didn't have time to figure out who.

Because all twelve of them were fully visible and tangible, and when Archie began to chat, I realized they were also audible.

I'd given them full form, as though they were still alive. I wove the threads of magic, mine, purplish, and Beck's bright blue, following patterns I'd seen in old tracts, lace patterns from books, anything I could think of to slow down the thing, because despite its inability to walk, it was shockingly fast.

Stop!

I turned my head sharply, seeing the CSI tech outside her body, despite Mason and Hart's efforts to resuscitate her.

No, I echoed her. *Go back.*

She turned to stare at me.

Go back. You still can.

I could see the green of Mason's magic beginning to waver, although he was trying to cast at the same time that he was breathing into her, the emerald of his magic shimmering against her lips when he lifted his head to breathe.

She stared at me. **It hurts.**

Life hurts, I told her.

She shook her head. **No. *It* hurts.** She pointed with a trembling finger at the thing, which seemed to be drawing the blood that had spilled from her and into the channels along the floor into itself.

Sylvia. It needs blood.

I saw her, her hair having come loose—somehow—from the tight bun against her head, floating around her as though she were submerged in water.

And then she was right there beside the thing, and plunged her hands into it.

I think I screamed out loud as the darkness immediately began to crawl up her arms. But then her eyes met mine.

It's okay, Ward.

No. Not like this.

I gave her everything I had left, and then some.

———

"He's not dead." The voice was Beck's, and I could feel cool fingers running over my throat, pressing against my jugular to find my pulse.

"He'd better fucking not be." Hart.

Something icy cold touched my cheek, shocking me out of the foggy haze I'd fallen into and flinging my eyes open.

My head was in Beck's lap, and Sylvia's face hovered over mine, her hair once more in impeccable place.

Hi.

Thank you.

Anytime. Wait, no. I take that back. Please don't do that again. Ever.

She smiled, then patted my cheek again.

"He's awake," Beck reported.

"That's one. This big green asshole isn't yet, though."

That got me to struggle to sit up, and Beck helped. "What happened to Mason?" I asked, fear spiking through me.

Mason was lying half on his side, and I drew a little comfort from the fact that I could at least see his chest rising and falling.

"Whatever the fuck you did," Hart answered from where he was crouched between Mason and the revived CSI tech. She was also unconscious, but I could see her breathing, as well. "Damn near blew up half the fucking room. He put some sort of... barrier around it. Probably kept you from fucking incinerating the rest of us, too."

I knew my eyes had gone wide.

"It wasn't any less than that fucking monstrosity deserved," Archie interrupted, and it took me a few seconds to realize he was speaking out loud. One finger pointed at...

Well, a smoldering pile of charred goo that was at once clearly burnt to a crisp and also still creepily gelatinous.

"What the *fuck* is that?" I asked.

"I was hoping you'd have that answer, because it's fucking disturbing is what it fucking is," Hart snapped.

I shook my head, then looked at Sylvia. *What did you do?*

She smiled. **I turned it into a battery.**

Like we'd done with the house.

And like the candles, when we poured too much power

into it, it had ignited and burned itself down to a gloopy mess.

A gloopy mess that had no magic emanating from it.

"Well, whatever it was, it's dead now," Beck said from behind me.

"We fucking sure about that?" Hart asked.

I nodded.

"Definitely," Beck concurred.

"Yep. That thing is deader than dead."

"Um. Thank you, Mr. Lagarde."

"I've told you to call me Archie, copper."

"Archie," Hart repeated, then ran a hand down his face. "Fuck me."

Beside Hart, Mason let out a cough, then drew in a ragged breath, the muscles of his face tensing as he returned to consciousness.

"How we doing, Doc?"

I watched with relief as his sunburst eyes blinked open. "Is... Are..." He coughed again, then his eyes met mine. "Everybody okay?" he finished, and I knew the question was for me.

I nodded.

"Pretty sure everybody's alive who started off that way," Hart grumbled. "Not sure if everything dead is still dead or not."

"Yep," Archie reported cheerfully. **"That was a fuck of a shield, by the way. Damn good work."**

Mason's eyebrows rose as he pushed himself back up to sitting. "Thank you."

"Sorry," I told him.

Mason pressed his lips together. "If you hadn't done what you did, things would have likely gotten a lot uglier."

"And if you hadn't done what you did, witch, there'd

be at least another half-dozen ghosts in this room. Jury's out on whether sonny would've roasted himself or not."

Thanks for the vote of confidence, Archie.

The ghost grinned at me.

"**It's a him, by the way,**" Archie continued. "**That fucker there? That's Oliver Picton.**"

"He's been dead for twenty-seven years," Beck breathed. "But not... fully dead. What... What is he?"

"A revenant." Mason coughed again, clearing his throat. "That's what they've been using the power for—to keep a revenant... undead."

"Fucking fuck," Hart muttered. "So what do I fucking do with that?"

Mason pushed himself to his feet, letting Hart help, one hand against the wall keeping him steady, although he didn't take his eyes off me. "It's still his body."

The CSI techs all looked horrified at the thought that one of them might have to actually touch it.

"Archie?" I asked, speaking out loud.

"**They're gone,**" he answered. "**The hearts burned up with ol' Ollie there. And everybody but me and Lady Randolph already took off.**"

I nodded.

"They were glad to go," Beck said softly, and I nodded again.

Hart pulled his phone out of his pocket, then scowled furiously at it. "Okay, people. Somebody call another team down here, because you lot aren't touching a goddamn thing, since you're all fucking contaminated, and my fucking phone is dead."

"They all will be," Mason told him. "That was... one hell of a surge."

Hart leveled a glare at me across the room. "You fucking bricked my phone, you are a dead man, Campion."

I smiled at him. "You really want to go a round with me, Hart?"

I saw a mischievous glint in his lavender eyes and knew he wasn't really mad at me. "Not unless I can have your boyfriend on my team."

"Nope," Mason replied. "I'm definitely on his."

You can tell the lovely elf that I'll be on his team.

I burst out laughing, because at that point, what else was I supposed to do?

25

Hart met us at Beyond the Veil four days later with the baggie of bullets, even though he'd already sent a bunch of pictures to Mason for further examination. Mason and Fiona had been working at them for the last two days while Hart had been busy arresting the Harrods, the Vincents, and half of the rest of the Antiquus Ordo Arcanum.

A handful of them had fled not only the state, but the country, and Hart was trying to sort out whether or not he could actually demand extradition for this. I wasn't going to hold my breath.

Three members were still unaccounted for: Roderick Dagget, Alessandra Moffet, and Victor Picton.

Hart showed up with coffee and scones, as well as the baggie of bullets, and I happily accepted the tribute of caffeine, even though I'd already had one cup that morning. Until the rest of the Ordo was accounted for, I wasn't sleeping very well.

With Hart's permission, Mason took out a bullet, then tossed it to me. I caught it, then raised my eyebrows at him. He held out a hand, and I threw it back.

The Skeleton Under the Stairs

"Okay, Hart, go get a piece of paper from Jackson." Jackson was sitting at the reception desk again, drawing. He handed Hart a blank sheet of paper. "Hold it up between Ward and me."

Frowning, the elf did as he was asked.

Mason threw the bullet, and it went *through* the paper—not like you'd expect, punching a hole, but *through* it as though it had rearranged the molecules of the paper and just... passed through them.

"What the *fuck?*" Hart hissed, staring at the paper. I agreed. What the fuck, indeed.

"Well, that answers *that* question," Mason murmured.

"What fucking question?" Hart demanded.

Mason held out his hand, and I nervously threw the bullet back to him. He showed it to Hart. "This series of sigils, which is highly sophisticated and probably developed specifically for *this* ammunition, does a few things. First, this one makes them silent. Second, it lets them pass through anything that isn't their target."

"Fucking hell. That means—"

"In theory, they could shoot through walls, although I'd expect windows are more likely," Mason replied.

"But it's why we didn't see any fucking bullet holes in any of the scenes."

"Exactly."

"But why weren't there any bullets?" I asked.

Mason smiled. "Because of *this* set. This set makes it so that once the bullet has been soaked in the blood of its target, it dissolves."

"*Fuck*," Hart groaned.

"Not terribly helpful in forensic terms," Mason remarked. "But—"

Everything stopped.

Sound. Sunlight. Air.

Everything.

I saw it, shining and silver, glint in the light in the microsecond before the red-purple circle appeared on Mason's chest, knocking him back a step.

I couldn't move my body, but I could throw my magic, the threads wrapping him, binding to his green and gold, weaving around his chest so tightly that had his spirit wanted to escape, it couldn't.

Because I wasn't going to let him die.

I was dimly aware of Hart spinning, searching for the source of the bullet, of Jackson's scream as his power tore across the room, knocking Hart off his feet in a flash of gold as his own magic somehow protected him from Jackson's panic.

And I saw the flicker of black-red-blue across the street.

It wasn't panic, mindless and terrified.

This was rage.

Pure and hot.

Hart had once said I could weaponize the dead.

He wasn't wrong.

I had done it by accident, then.

It was no accident now.

My legs couldn't run, but I didn't need them to.

I had the dead, and the dead don't need to run. But there is no running from the dead.

And these dead were vengeful.

Once, I had stopped them from killing Tyler Lessing.

I didn't stop them from tearing into Victor Picton where he stood in the shadow of a narrow alley between two buildings across the street.

I didn't tell them to leave him alive.

The Skeleton Under the Stairs

I pushed them to do to him what he'd done to them.
I knew the minute they'd stopped his heart.
It was a minute longer than he deserved.
And then everything went black and cold.

26

"He's dead." Hart's voice echoed in my empty brain. "Do you hear me, Ward? He's dead."

I nodded numbly.

"Eye contact, Ward." The elf's tone was firm, but kind.

I looked up at him, blinking blearily. "I heard you, Hart."

Pearl squeezed my hand. Across the hospital waiting room, Jackson leaned into his mother's side, sniffling, Everest the stuffed leopard hugged tightly to his chest. Keidra murmured softly to him. The boy stiffened when the ghost of an old man drifted into the room, a confused expression on his face. Jackson said something to his mom, then came over and climbed into my lap.

I put my arms around him.

"Hospitals have lots of ghosts," I told him.

He nodded, settling his head on my collarbone, and held out Everest. "You can hold him, if it'll make you feel better, Uncle Ward."

I felt tears pushing at the backs of my eyes. "Thanks, Jax." I ran one hand over Everest's soft plush as the boy cuddled closer to me.

The Skeleton Under the Stairs

The old man smiled sadly at us, then drifted on down the hallway.

A nurse came into the room, her mauve scrubs rumpled. "I'm looking for the... Manning family?"

Keidra looked up. "That's us," she said, fear and worry in her voice.

The nurse's eyes flickered around the room, noticing, I'm sure, the fairly wide range of diversity represented in the room—none of which matched her patient. Pearl, Hart, and me, with Jackson on my lap, on one side, Keidra, Deon, and Ben on the other. The nurse opened her mouth, her brow furrowed.

"*All* of us," Keidra interrupted, standing and coming over to place a hand on my shoulder.

The nurse nodded once. "Mr. Manning is out of surgery and should wake up within an hour or two. We've moved him into the ICU. Only one visitor at a time, though."

I looked at Keidra. Mason's twin.

She shook her head. "Go, Ward. We'll be here."

I went.

The nurse let me into the room and closed the door behind me.

I almost burst into tears at the sight of him in the hospital bed, a tube stuck in his nose, heavy bandages wrapped around his torso, an IV in his arm, and a monitor hooked up to him that was softly beeping, measuring out each contraction of his heart.

It all seemed stupid, that a machine could possibly measure out the enormity and warmth of Mason's heart. That a small, round piece of magic-inscribed lead could somehow put a stop to all the generosity and love and brilliance that was Mason Manning.

To make myself feel better, I shifted my sight and was

relieved to see that the gleaming forest green of Mason's magic was steady and strong. He would be okay.

I was half-convinced that the only reason for that was a nine-year-old death witch who hadn't wanted to watch his uncle die. Death magic was the other side of life casting, and Jackson had lashed out with everything he had when Mason had fallen.

Jackson was nine and untrained. He just had that much love and desperation.

I'd done what I could, but my magic didn't control life and death.

I rolled myself up to the side of the bed and reached out, placing one of my pale hands over Mason's big green one, wrapping my fingers around his. The warmth of his skin was somewhat reassuring, although the slightly grey cast of his complexion and all the tubes still had fear running through my veins, despite the steadiness of his magic.

I wanted to be here when he woke up.

Mason hadn't been there when I'd woken up in the hospital nearly two years ago because the Hanover County PD had thrown him in a cell for my attempted murder.

Nobody had arrested me yet.

I wondered when they were going to.

How long it was going to take them to figure out how to charge me with homicide by dead people.

I wasn't sure what I'd plead if they did.

Because I had absolutely killed Victor Picton. And I would do it again in a heartbeat. Fuck. If I'd known he was there, I'd have killed him *before* he shot Mason.

The fact that he *had* shot Mason might be the only thing that would keep me from being thrown in prison right alongside Tyler-fucking-Lessing.

Talk about irony.

The Skeleton Under the Stairs

It had absolutely not escaped me that not only was I a killer, but I'd used the same magic against Picton that I used on Tyler. With help, of course, but dead people couldn't be tried for murder, and they couldn't have done it at all without my magic.

I had no regrets.

Staring down at Mason's nearly-still form swathed in tubes and gauze and antiseptic hospital sheets, I wished a lot of things—that the bullet had missed, that the asshole had aimed it at me, that Mason were somehow indestructible.

I did not in the least wish that I hadn't killed the bastard.

I pulled off my damp mask and set it on the bedside table so I could bend to press my lips to the back of Mason's hand.

"So it turns out I'm not so great a person," I said softly. "I killed him. And I don't care because he tried to take you away from me." Tears started falling, then. I ran my thumb over Mason's hand, enjoying the texture of his skin. Wondering how long it would be before someone came to get me. "I need you, Mace. Jackson needs you." I leaned forward to rest my cheek on his thigh, breathing in the warmth of his body. "I need you to wake up, because I can't do any of this without you."

"Sure, you can." The voice was harsh and ragged, but I recognized it immediately.

I sat up sharply, finding Mason's eyes slitted open, watching me.

"Hi," he rasped.

I burst into tears again, although when I put my face back down, his big hand came to rest heavily on the back of my head.

"You're s'posed to be happy I woke up," he teased, his fingers flexing in my curls.

I turned my face to look at him, my cheek on his hip. "I am," I blubbered.

His eyebrows rose, and I gave him a watery smile.

"I *am*," I repeated. "I'm just... overwrought."

"You've been around Sylvia too long," he told me. The words were getting smoother, less like broken glass and more like Mason usually sounded.

I smiled weakly again. "Maybe," I admitted.

Mason's fingers toyed with my hair. "Ward?"

"Yeah?"

"Did—did you say you *killed* him?"

Fear gripped me. Because of course I had said that, because I had killed him.

"Y-yeah."

Mason's fingers stilled in my hair.

"How?" he asked, and his voice was soft and rough all at the same time.

"The ghosts," I answered, my own voice half-swallowed.

I felt him draw in a deep breath. "What are you afraid of?" he asked, and I could hear the sadness in the words.

Tears fell again. "That y-you'll hate me," I whispered.

Fingers tightened in my hair. "Never."

I toyed with the corner of the sheet.

"Ward."

I looked up at him, expecting disappointment, or anger, or disgust.

I saw none of that.

"Yeah?" I asked, still afraid.

"Good," he said.

I blinked. "Good?"

"He killed at least three people with those bullets. Partic-

The Skeleton Under the Stairs

ipated in the ritual sacrifice of at least a half dozen more. That we know of. He wasn't going to stop with me." Mason ran his hand over my skull. "Are you okay?"

My heart melted, and I started crying again, burying my face in his hip. Fingers ran through my hair, and I felt a faint tingle as he tried to soothe away whatever was bothering me.

Which of course only made me cry harder.

"Ward, you know I love you."

I nodded into his hip.

"Nothing will make me stop loving you. Nothing." His hand came around my face so that he could lift my chin. "Marry me?"

I felt a few tears track their way down my cheeks. "Do you still want to marry *me*?"

Mason's fingers traced over my features. "More every day."

"Even now?"

His face softened. "Especially now."

I caught his hand in mine and pulled his palm to my lips. "I love you so much," I murmured into his skin.

"Then marry me."

"I am marrying you," I reminded him.

"No, today. Here."

I gaped at him.

His fingers tightened on mine. "Marry me, Ward."

I'd lost the ability to speak, but I nodded.

"Say it. Please."

"Yes."

IT TURNS out that nurses will absolutely break the only-one-visitor rule if you get married in the ICU.

It wasn't at all how I'd imagined it.

Keidra, Deon, Jackson, Ben, and Hart were there, and the three nurses and one doctor peeking in the door.

One of the nurses went and got some silicone valve rings from somewhere for us to exchange—I didn't ask what they'd come from. Jackson and Ben took Deon's wallet and bought Little Debbie snack cakes and Sprite from the vending machines. I put Pearl and Eleanor on speaker on my phone, and Keidra called their parents on her phone and put them on speaker, too. Sylvia, Archie, and Dom floated in a corner.

Mason couldn't actually sit up, so I had to do some weird contorting to kiss him when the time came, but I'd never been so happy in my life as the moment his lips brushed mine.

One of the nurses cried.

Keidra cried.

Sylvia cried.

I cried.

Even Mason looked a little teary-eyed, although that might have been the drugs.

Hart just looked alarmed.

After the Little Debbie cakes and tiny dixie cups of Sprite were passed around on pilfered dinner trays, one of the doctors got us moved out of the ICU and into a private room.

I had the feeling this was as much a wedding present as it was an indication of Mason's improving condition.

So we spent our wedding night in a hospital room with me in a lounger one of the nurses had found somewhere, probably a break room, and Mason still hooked up to an IV and an oxygen line.

I lay, semi-reclined, in the dark, listening to Mason's slow breathing, deeply grateful I could still listen to him breathe. Grateful that he was my husband.

We'd taken each other's names: I was now Edward Manning Campion, and he was Mason Campion Manning. Our anniversary was June 30.

He'd already had my mind, body, heart, and soul.

I turned to look at him in the gloom, studying his profile, the soft ridge of his nose, the lines of lips and canines and lower jaw.

I had never loved anyone or anything so much.

Sorry, Pevs.

Not that Mason would ever make me choose. He loves that cat almost as much as I do.

Whatever happened tomorrow, whether they arrested me or not, whether I had to go home and take care of Jackson by myself or ended up in a cell or a padded room at Cyprian's, I had Mason.

And that was more than enough.

THEY DIDN'T ARREST ME.

Hart brought me a report that stated Victor Picton died of a spontaneous myocardial infarction, which Hart explained was a heart attack. Nobody was suggesting it was anything but natural causes.

I'd given Hart a look that asked if he was kidding.

"I'm just passing on the fucking report," the elf told me blandly. I never heard anything else about it.

I had nightmares for six days straight. Not about killing

Picton—about Mason dying in my arms, my hands stained with his blood and his sunburst eyes glassy and empty. Each time, I woke up in a cold sweat, a deep ache in my spine and my breath shallow in my lungs.

The sixth night, Jackson came and crawled into bed with me, handing me Everest the stuffed leopard to hug as he, Alma, and Pevs all snuggled up close. I settled back to sleep, Alma pressed against my legs on one side, Jackson curled up against me on the other, and Peveril on my feet.

I put my arm around Jackson's back so that my hand rested on the back of his skull. He felt small, fragile, this still-growing boy whose life was currently my responsibility. I drew in a long breath, letting it out slowly to avoid disturbing either child or animals.

We'd done okay, Jackson and I, on our own. We'd managed to feed ourselves, keep the animals fed and watered, walk Alma, and even successfully do things like laundry. I'd also somehow been able to keep on top of emails to Beyond the Veil, although I mostly had Beck to thank for keeping the business running.

Mason was due to come home in three days, according to his doctors, and it couldn't be soon enough, as far as I was concerned. Yeah, Jackson and I were doing okay, but we missed him. I missed him. A lot.

Pearl was coming by in the morning to take us to the hospital, as usual. I knew Rennie and Israel, Mason's parents, were planning to be there today, as well.

Jackson had fallen back asleep, his breathing soft, huffing a little as he let out small snores. Pevs slept quietly on my feet, although Alma's paws twitched slightly as she chased squirrels or tennis balls in her dreams.

I was wide awake. I'd once again dreamed of Mason's death, bloodier than the last several nightmares, leaving me covered in it in my mind. I should have been comforted by the pile of sleeping warmth around me, but it wasn't working.

I let out a sigh, and focused.

Well, aren't you just adorable, came Sylvia's sardonic comment, although her expression was softer than her words.

Couldn't sleep, I told her.

She settled herself on the side of the bed, laying an insubstantial hand on my leg and sending a chill through my thigh. **He'll be home soon**, she said.

I know. It would be easier to deal with if I didn't have the nightmares, though.

About?

I felt tears prickling at the corners of my eyes. *Mason dying.*

Oh, Ward. She rubbed my leg, and, oddly, it seemed as though her touch was warmer than it had been. Or maybe I was just getting used to the physical presence of ghosts.

You know, she began, **I didn't marry for love.**

Money? I asked.

What else? She smiled. **I wasn't unhappy**, she continued. **I can't say that I was happy, either, exactly, but I knew what I was getting into. I was never a romantic.** She smiled. **Albert, though. He was terribly romantic. I'm glad he got his romance.**

I covered her hand with my free one, her skin cool and slightly too soft under my palm. I enjoyed the contact, and I was glad she was here. *Me, too.*

27

"Uncle Mason!" Jackson's voice was excited as he bounced up and down on his toes in the kitchen.

"What is it, Jax?" Mason was on the couch, and he called out his question from there.

"I made a pancake!" It was mostly true. I'd used Rennie's recipe, letting Jackson do the mixing, helping him pour into the skillet, and then holding his hands and helping him toss the pancake.

It was a little funny-shaped, but it was cooked and not burnt, so I was taking it as a win. Pancakes were one of the things I was actually pretty good at making, so I'd been fairly confident in helping Jackson make Mason breakfast. There were also vegan sausages on another burner, and I'd pulled the syrup and butter out of the fridge to warm up.

"Okay, Jackson." I drew his attention back to the batter. "Now we just have to do it a whole bunch more times."

Jackson remained enthusiastic for about ten total pancakes, and I released him to take a stack out to Mason on the couch, then follow that with the syrup, butter, and then another plate with sausages. I finished off the rest of the batter, then called Jackson back to bring the remaining serving plate out to the card table beside the couch.

When I joined them, Mason had a plate of pancakes and sausages, both doused in syrup. Jackson was ignoring the sausages, but was happily scarfing down pancakes on the other end of the sectional. I pulled myself up next to the table, serving myself some pancakes and sausages, applying butter and syrup.

Something nudged my foot, and I looked down to find Mason prodding me with one polka-dot clad socked toe. I looked up at him and found him smiling at me, the twist of his lips soft. I grinned back.

Jackson started telling us all about his current videogame, what level he was on, what the characters looked like, how he played it... liberally colored with various sound-effect exclamations and hand-waving. "And Ward played with me," Jackson continued. "And he almost beat me, but I did better."

I smiled again. The game was cooperative, so he didn't really beat me, but there was a leaderboard that listed total points, and Jackson had gotten more than me.

"Did you?" Mason asked. "Do you think you can beat me?"

Jackson gave the question careful thought. "Maybe," he said, his tone optimistic.

After far too many pancakes, Jackson helped me do the dishes. "Can Ben come over to play sometime soon?" he asked.

"Why don't you give your mom a call and ask if they can come over this afternoon?" I handed him my phone. There were still the two skillets to wash, but Jackson had been really great about helping me do everything, so he deserved a little bit of a reprieve.

"Thanks, Ward!" He took the phone and scooted off. I went back into the kitchen to wash the pans.

I'd finished the first and was scrubbing the bits of vegan sausage and oil off the second when I felt a big, warm hand run over my hair.

I looked up at Mason and smiled. "You should be resting."

"I got bored." He ran his fingers through my curls again. "And you know how much I like it when you do domestic things."

I couldn't help my laugh. "Do you?" I reached up and pulled his hand to my lips, my wet fingers sliding against his. I ran my thumb over the thin tungsten band on his left hand—his actual wedding ring. I had a matching one, both of them engraved with one of Mason's charms—these were for long life and happiness.

Mason bent slowly, carefully, and lifted my chin with his fingers for a long, lingering kiss that sent tingles down my spine all the way to my toes.

"Eeeew. Gross!" came Jackson's pronouncement as he came back into the kitchen, his nose wrinkled.

As Mason slowly straightened up, I reached out and grabbed Jackson, pulling him—giggling—into my lap. "Gross? I'll give you gross." I made farting noises as I rubbed my face against his hair, making him shriek with laughter.

I let him go, and he hopped down, handing my phone back. "Mom says in two hours. That's okay, right?"

"Yep," I replied.

Jackson glanced between Mason and me. "Can I go upstairs to play videogames until he gets here? Then you guys can be gross and I don't have to see it."

Mason snorted. "Yes, you can go play videogames," he

answered, and Jackson was off, his feet pounding the stairs leading up to the dormer.

Mason ran a hand over my hair, pulling my head back again. "Where were we?" he asked, right before capturing my lips in another kiss.

"Mace," I murmured against his mouth when he let me go long enough to breathe. "You *just* got home from the hospital four days ago."

He hummed against my lips. "So be gentle with me."

"Mace—"

"We have two hours and Jackson isn't going to resurface until Ben gets here."

I pulled back and looked up at him. "You tell me to stop if anything hurts or pulls, okay?"

He narrowed his eyes at me.

"*Anything*, Mason."

A sigh. "Fine. I promise."

He led the way—slowly—down the hall to the bedroom, where I made sure to close the door behind us.

Mason undid the buttons on his shirt, his sunburst eyes watching me instead of his fingers. I swallowed, already anticipating the feeling of his hands on my body and the texture of his skin under my own hands.

I drew in a shaky breath, then pulled my t-shirt over my head.

Mason stopped halfway down his chest, his eyes on me. Then he kept going.

I rolled up to him to help slide the sleeves off his arms—twisting was something he was not supposed to do with a fairly-fresh bullet hole in his chest—relishing the warm smoothness of his skin. I brought one palm to my lips, pressing a kiss in the center of his hand, and he shuddered.

"Should I stop?" I asked, half teasing.

"Don't you dare."

I smiled into his palm, then placed a kiss on the inside of his wrist before releasing his hand.

He stood, then pushed his hands under the waistband of his sweatpants so that he could slide them over his hips, letting them drop to the floor.

Apparently, he'd gone without underwear this morning.

Heat pooled in my groin as I ran my gaze over the dusky green of his body, the already half-erect cock hanging between his thighs, the muscles of his legs and arms... I frowned a little at the swath of bandage still taped to his chest.

"Stop worrying," he said softly, stepping close enough to run one hand over my hair.

I leaned into him, rubbing my cheek against his hip, my hands following the curve of his hips and butt. I breathed in the pine and citrus scent of his body, enjoying the heat and smoothness of his skin.

I heard him suck in a breath, his fingers tensing in my hair.

I smiled, even though he couldn't see it, knowing where his anticipation was leading. I wasn't about to disappoint him.

I kept one hand on his hip and used the other to bring his heavy cock to my mouth, running my tongue over him, the musky taste making my mouth water. I heard Mason suck in a sharp breath as I drew him between my lips, pulling his thick length over my tongue and into the back of my throat.

Mason groaned softly, the sound drawn out as his hips rocked forward a few centimeters. I relaxed the back of my throat, drawing him in as far as I could, a soft ache at the back of my jaw that was both pleasant and a little painful. It sent tingles through me that went straight to my groin, and I moaned around him.

"Fuck, Ward."

I eased him back out of my mouth, slowly, sucking as I did, drawing a shallow gasp from him.

"Was that a request?" I asked, looking up his body.

I saw his eyes blaze. "It is now."

"Then you'd better get on the bed."

He moved carefully—although faster than I'd have advised, given his injury—settling himself against the pillows, his muscular body laid out on display.

I took my time coming around the side of the bed, letting my eyes drink in every inch of him. Between his thighs, his cock twitched as though responding to my gaze. I hefted myself onto the bed, immediately running one hand up Mason's thigh.

I pulled one of his legs up, bending it at the knee, then used his legs to move myself so that I was straddling his hips, my hands on his knees and his thick erection rubbing against the base of my cock.

I bent forward to kiss the inside of Mason's knee, and he moved his legs down a few inches, dropping my hips and exposing my backside to his questing hands. I rested my cheek on Mason's knee as he massaged my ass.

I heard the sound of the bedside table drawer opening and let out a small whimper, which drew a deep chuckle from Mason that I felt all the way up my spine. And then a slicked finger teased at my body, rubbing over the ring of muscle, just easing the tip inside me.

I gripped Mason's legs, using them to give myself enough leverage to push against his finger. He slid it all the way inside me, his voice a low rumble as he murmured, "Impatient."

"Yeah," I agreed.

By the time Mason worked the third finger into me, I was gasping and whimpering, my cheek pressed to the inside of his knee, my fingers digging into the muscle of his thighs and my cock leaking moisture. Mason pushed his fingers in and out, stretching me so I could take in all of him.

"Mace," I panted. "Please."

I gasped as his hand left me, leaving me feeling a little hollow.

"Up," he rasped, his hands lifting at my hips. Even though my arms felt like jelly, I pushed myself up, allowing him to position himself and me so that he could slowly begin to ease his slicked erection inside me. He lifted his legs to change the angle, letting him sink deep into me.

I moaned as his rigid heat stretched and filled me, my hands over his knees as I slowly eased my body down until my hips met his.

I wanted to move, to feel Mason's raw strength push hard inside me, but I had to take it slow, to be gentle.

It was torture of the best kind.

Mason's hands held my hips, helping to push me up along his length as I used my arms on his knees to press myself away from him. Both because of where I was and because I was being mindful of Mason's injury, I could only lift myself an inch or so before lowering back down, the ridges of his cock massaging the inner nerves and muscles of my body.

Moving smooth and slow was unrelenting, and, before long, I was shaking, my arms beginning to fatigue even as pressure and heat built in my groin, my stomach tight and my cock aching.

Mason's hands were tight on my hips, guiding my body against his. I couldn't see his face, but I could hear the rasp of his breath and feel the thick hardness of his erection inside me.

I could feel the pressure of my orgasm building, and I tightened my body to try to maintain control a little longer, making Mason groan as my muscles clenched around him.

"Fuck, Ward," he growled.

I felt him push his hips up against me, just enough to rub against the sensitized nerves inside me, and I whimpered. I could feel my balls pull up tight against my body, and I gasped out Mason's name as the orgasm poured out of me.

His fingers tightened on my pelvis, the tips digging into my skin hard enough to bruise—not that I minded—as I felt his climax pulsing inside my body, a half-growl, half-groan torn from his throat.

I leaned heavily on his legs, my arms aching as my pulse gradually slowed. Mason's hands gently rubbed over my lower back and the top of my ass, and I shuddered a little, my skin hypersensitive.

His hands stilled. "Ward?"

"Mmmm?" My cheek was still resting on one of his legs.

"Come here?"

My body felt boneless and limp, but he sounded strangely vulnerable, so I pushed myself off to the side, then scooted up beside him, lying on my side against the pillows, letting my hand rest on his shoulder. One of his hands ran through the hair at the back of my head.

"You okay?" For once, I was the one asking.

He turned his head so that his sunburst eyes met mine, a twisted smile on his lips. "Mmhmm."

I traced my fingers across his collar bone, hesitating before I reached the still-discolored bruising on his chest from where they'd had to go in to repair the damage to his heart. There was still a large gauze pad on his torso, medical tape holding it in place, the edges starting to fray. I'd been given careful instructions for how to change the dressings, which I would need to do tomorrow.

"Are you still sore?"

I watched his chest move as he drew in a breath. "Some. Not bad."

Mason's level of pain tolerance was substantially above mine. He'd been taking four Tylenol every five or so hours, but refused anything stronger.

I tamped down my instinctive worry.

Mason took my hand in his, bringing it to his lips, slowly kissing each finger. "I'm okay, Ward," he said softly.

I rested my forehead on his bicep. "You almost weren't," I whispered.

"Almost only counts—"

"In horseshoes and hand grenades," I finished.

"Exactly."

We lay in silence for a little while. "Mace?"

"Mmm?"

"I'm sorry I put you through this. Twice."

He pulled my forehead to his lips. "Not your fault."

"I know, but thinking you might die sucked."

"I didn't, though." Another kiss on my forehead. "And neither did you."

———

MASON FELL ASLEEP, his body still needing rest to heal, and I left him to his nap, taking a quick shower before heading back to the kitchen to throw together the snacks inevitably required by two boys under twelve playing outside in the yard.

The Skeleton Under the Stairs

I'd just finished cleaning up and setting that out when the doorbell rang, immediately followed by the sound of Jackson's feet pounding down the stairs. "I got it!" he yelled, making me glad I'd shut the bedroom door to let Mason sleep.

I rolled myself into the living room, avoiding the two giggling boys immediately headed out into the back yard. "Jackson!" I called.

He skidded to a stop, then came back. "Yeah?"

"Take Alma with you."

"Okay!"

Alma had gotten up at the entrance of these new people, her tail wagging and unhearing ears perked up. I gestured *outside* at her, and she immediately trotted toward the mud room, following Jackson and Ben.

I knew the back gate was closed, so she could run around the yard freely, and I wasn't worried about either her or the boys having to watch her. There was enough area in the back for both a small soccer net and a single cornhole beanbag target that Mason had built and painted with a simple bullseye for Jackson.

As the back door slammed shut, Keidra put a hand on my shoulder.

"Where's Mason?"

"Napping," I answered. "He won't admit it, but I don't think he sleeps particularly well at night."

Keidra frowned. "From pain?"

I nodded. "He says it's not bad. It might be the stiffness from not moving for so long."

"See, Kei?" came Mason's slightly sleepy voice from down the hallway. "You don't need to worry about me—Ward does that plenty."

Keidra snorted. The expression was familiar, which

made my lips twitch in a bit of a smile. "Someone has to," she said.

We brought the snacks and lemonade and followed the boys outside, Mason and Keidra settling in a pair of deck chairs. I rolled up beside Mason's, turning so I could see both of them.

Keidra leaned back, sipping her lemonade, then smiled over the rim. "So you know you're not getting away with that wedding, right?"

I felt my eyebrows go up, but Mason laughed, then winced.

"Mom ask you to make that clear?" he asked.

Keidra hummed her assent.

"I never thought otherwise," he replied, smiling. "But I was done waiting."

Keidra waved a hand. "No judgment from me," she replied. "But Mom wants another wedding, the rest of the family is losing their shit, *Dad's* family is losing their shit, and since you've in theory already paid all the deposits..."

Mason was nodding. "We'll still do the reception as planned."

This was news to me, although now that I actually thought about it, it made sense. We *had* already put down deposits on a few things, and friends and family probably wanted to celebrate with us—which they hadn't been able to do with our last-minute ICU wedding. I'd just been so focused on getting Mason home and healed that I hadn't spent a single second thinking about our now-redundant wedding plans.

Then I noticed that both Keidra and Ward were looking expectantly at me.

"Sorry, I kinda spaced out. What?"

Mason snorted softly, but there was that familiar twisted smile on his lips.

"Wedding reception?" Keidra repeated.

"That we're still doing it? Um. Yeah. Sure." I made a mental note to call Beck and Fiona. We still had a lot of work to do.

EPILOGUE

Mason bent and kissed me, his fingers cupping the back of my head. He teased at my lips with his tongue, and I melted into him, not caring about the hooting and cheering that faded away as I got lost in Mason's kiss.

He broke away, resting his forehead against mine, his hand still holding us close. "I love you," he whispered.

"I love you." I pulled him back for another kiss, this one a little bit less intense.

Then he stepped back and straightened up, the sparkling lights of the Christmas tree behind us casting a warm glow on his olive skin, despite it being the longest night of the year. I grinned up at him.

We were married. Again.

Okay, technically we'd only gotten *actually* married the one time, but Rennie, Mason's mom, had insisted that we essentially go through the whole thing again—complete with vows that I had stressed about for weeks—for Mason's enormous family. Auntie Pearl and Eleanor were there, too, of course, but I had a family of two, and Mason had somewhere north of about fifty cousins, second cousins, aunts, uncles, and so on. About a third of them primarily spoke Spanish, and there was a cheerful mix of languages rippling around under the heated outdoor tent, which we'd spent most of yesterday festooning with pine garland, bunches of holly, and mistletoe—all of which Beck and Fiona had insisted had to be real.

My hands were still slightly sore, both from the prickles of the holly and having to spend far too long scrubbing sap off my hands.

At the moment, I didn't care.

The whole area smelled like fresh pine, greenery, and mulled wine with spices—the beverage Beck had insisted be served from silver samovars positioned around the tent by the hors d'oeuvres and cookie tables. The cake was gingerbread with cream cheese icing.

Most people were sitting around drinking, snacking, or dancing, and Hart was teaching Jackson, Ben, and several other Manning cousins how to fold origami animals out of wrapping paper squares that he'd spent hours cutting just-so with Mason's paper cutter yesterday.

Mason's eyes sparkled in the midwinter lights, his sharp canines—upper and lower—showing as he grinned.

I loved it when he showed his teeth.

I HAD NEVER SPENT SO much time talking to people as I did that night. Beck, Fiona, Hart, Carly, Pearl, Eleanor... and then *all* of Mason's relatives. Elsbeth was there, too, of course, and Jayson and his sister, Nicki. I'd even gotten to meet Mason's childhood friend, Stefan, who was a vet tech out in Albuquerque, although Mason was constantly trying to convince him to come back to Richmond.

And then there were the family friends, Pearl's work friends, Mason's parents' friends, the entire Tuckahoe Knitters' Club—because they were almost as excited about me getting married as I was—and a good dozen or so ghosts, who seemed to be having their own dance in a mostly empty part of the room. Beck had taken Jackson over to talk to them for a while, and I was proud of him for going with her, even though he'd seemed pretty nervous.

Right now, though, I was exhausted. I'd been up since six this morning and it was almost midnight. There were still a good two or three dozen people still dancing and chatting, including Pearl and Eleanor, who were slowly drifting together across the dance floor in each other's arms.

Despite my belief that we wouldn't have a first dance, Mason *had* danced with me, picking me up and carrying me in his arms, moving both of us around the floor to Etta James. I'd nestled my head on his shoulder, breathing in the warmth and pine-and-citrus scent of his body and blinking back emotional tears.

I could not possibly love him more.

I was sitting alone, sipping my mulled wine and enjoying the warm glow of the Christmas lights strung under the tent in probably the only moment of silence I'd had all night.

And then I felt big, warm hands on my shoulders, followed by a kiss to my temple. "Ready?"

I looked up and back over my shoulder at Mason Campion Manning, orc, witch, and my amazing husband.

"Always."

ABOUT THE AUTHOR

KM Avery is an academic who moonlights as an author, and has a husband, cats, and a love for books, movies, videogames, and the outdoors, at least most of the time.

Made in the USA
Middletown, DE
09 November 2024